G000242290

Swept Away

Published in 2009 by Prion
An imprint of the Carlton Publishing Group
20 Mortimer Street
London W1T 3JW

1 3 5 7 9 10 8 6 4 2

A CIP catalogue record for this book is available from the British Library.

ISBN 978-1-85375-734-1

Typeset by Ellipsis, Glasgow

Printed in Dubai

Swept Away

Mills and Boon Classics

CONTENTS

INTRODUCTION

His lips were warm against her throat and she trembled in his arms, feeling she should fight him, yet not wanting to fight him. 'You shouldn't do this – you shouldn't!' was all she found breath to say.

And, in truth, we didn't really want her to say any more. By the time that those lines were written in Violet Winspear's *Lucifer's Angel* in 1961 the breathless passion of the Mills & Boon romance demanded that the heroine should ultimately be 'Swept Away' on a tide of desire in a fantasy world that provided pure escapism for the millions of women who had become dedicated Mills & Boon readers.

In the real world, women were coming of age, asserting their rights, demanding equality through 'Women's Lib' and a conflagration of smouldering underwear. More women than ever before were learning to drive, pursuing meaningful careers and leading independent lives. 'The Pill' delivered a degree of sexual freedom previously unknown and there were fears for the moral integrity of the emerging young generation.

Yet there was still romance – there was still Mills & Boon. Women of all ages were buying the pulse-quickening paperbacks in record numbers, turning the company into the world's leading publisher of romantic fiction. This was not exactly what Mills & Boon had originally set out to do. In 1908, when Gerald Mills and Charles Boon first launched their modest publishing company, neither of them could have foreseen that their very first publication – *Arrows from the Dark* by Sophie Cole – would spawn one of the greatest success stories in the publishing world.

Mills & Boon began as a small, family affair that aimed to publish books on a variety of subjects – everything from travel to crafts – but it was its fiction list that really took off. In its first year of business, Mills & Boon signed up well-known authors such as E. F. Benson and Max Pemberton, and went on to publish novels by Jack London, Hugh Walpole and P. G. Wodehouse.

But it was their romantic fiction that really caught the readers' imaginations, leading to the establishment of the 'June 15' series. This new series, so called because 15 June was the publication date of each title, offered new authors a launch pad and came to signify the arrival of a brand new talent. The first title was *The Veil: A Romance of Tunisia* by E. S. Stevens and it sold 7,000 copies. By 1912, Mills & Boon were receiving 1,000 manuscripts a year from aspiring writers, although only six made it to press that year. But as demand grew for these tales, Mr Mills and Mr Boon came to realize that the genre of romantic fiction would become the lifeblood of the company.

By the 1960s, both Gerald Mills and Charles Boon had passed away but they might have been hard pressed even to recognize as Mills & Boon products the kind of books that were being published by their company. The discreet, brown hardbacks they had known had evolved into colourful paperbacks and the equally discreet, decorous tales, where sex was never mentioned, had given way to an acceptance that married couples did indeed do 'it'. The language used, however, was still oblique and euphemistic rather than explicit.

> *Her mouth was parted on a smile as she looked up at him. But the smile died on a gasp as his mouth descended in hard possession, melting her bones, making her shake with mounting passion.*

Bone-melting clinches like this one from Charlotte Lamb's *Desert Barbarian* are a good indication of how the 'mounting passion' in Mills & Boon romances was starting to heat up in the 1970s.

> *Compelling, ruthless, merciless, he kissed her until she was clinging weakly to him as to a rock in the middle of a flooding river, half drowning, half ecstatic.*
>
> *Behind her closed lids a dazzle of light hypnotised her. She clung to him while he kissed her throat, her ears, pushing aside her blouse to kiss her shoulders and the white softness where her breasts rose, panting from their confinement.*

Clearly there was something special in the kiss of the *Desert Barbarian* that he could manage to reduce the focus of his desire to a half-drowned, hypnotised bundle of ecstasy with breasts that had apparently assumed a life of their own. Set in its proper context within the story, of course, this moment of passion admirably demonstrates how the language of the

Mills & Boon romance had progressed and how scenarios within the books had begun to encompass pre-marital encounters that were steamy and sensual, even if they still remained quite demure.

> *His mouth found hers, kissing her with a fierce hunger that was scarcely controlled and would not long be denied, and for the first time Pandora was able to respond with complete abandon, letting her emotions guide her and moving sensuously against him, longing to be a part of him.*

The 'fierce hunger' in Sally Wentworth's *Summer Fire* in 1981 hints at how Mills & Boon romances were keeping pace with the modern world. Romance and romantic fantasy were still key, but the scenes of passion were now far less restrained.

> *His fingers sought the buttons of her blouse and that, too, fell to the floor, then his hands were cupping her breasts, his thumbs exploring, caressing. Pandora moaned softly, her mouth moving under his.*

Let's leave Pandora some privacy for now, although you can find out how all of these torrid affairs turned out in *Swept Away* because all three novels are reproduced in full, the stories specially chosen for this collection because Violet Winspear, Charlotte Lamb and Sally Wentworth stand tall as three of the most popular Mills & Boon authors from the 1960s, 1970s and 1980s. Sadly, all three have since died, but each author contributed hugely to the development of the romantic fiction genre, pushing the boundaries of Mills & Boon novels. All three were also very prolific: at one point, Charlotte Lamb (a pseudonym for Sheila Holland) was publishing as many as 12 novels a year with Mills & Boon and eventually wrote over 160, more than Violet Winspear and Sally Wentworth combined, though they produced over 70 each.

For today's women, the three tales in *Swept Away* show how the approach to relationships in Mills & Boon romances has changed over the last forty years or so. That they have continued to change with the times, continued to increase in popularity, is reflected in the fact that a Mills & Boon novel is sold every three seconds in the UK and the variety of titles on offer has generated a raft of sub-genres, from 'Historical' to 'Medical' and from 'Blaze' (think 'hot and sexy') to 'Intrigue' (romantic suspense).

At the heart of every book, however, lies romance and, no matter what the scenario, the core of each Mills & Boon novel remains the same: *amor vincit omnia* – love conquers all.

LUCIFER'S ANGEL

Violet Winspear

CHAPTER ONE

FAY SAT gazing at the brand new wedding ring upon her finger – an exquisite ring, fashioned from platinum, with a band of small diamonds encircling it. The autumn sunshine danced in the stones, their glittering beauty filling her with panic rather than pleasure.

The seal that said she was now Lew Marsh's. The band that bound her to him!

She stole a tentative side-glance at him, watched him as he sat at the wheel of the car, weaving the powerful black body of it in and out of the heavy traffic of this Californian highway.

'We're too quiet,' she thought. 'We've just been married – we should at least be smiling.'

'When will we get to the cabin, Lew?' she asked, for he had proposed that they honeymoon in a cabin he owned in the hills of Serena and she had agreed. But as she spoke, her tongue felt wooden. Felt as though it hadn't uttered words for weeks. Not uttered words, when only a little while ago she had said, 'I do!'

She knew sudden dread. It spread over her, touched her body with a paralysing coldness. Why had she married him? It was a mistake. They'd never be happy. Look at him, the way he was so still, so withdrawn into himself. She felt, all at once, desperately, miserably close to tears. Why had he married her, when he plainly felt no joy, no gladness – no anything?

He turned, then, to look at her. 'We'll be there by eight,' he said. 'You do want to go up to the cabin, don't you? I assure you it won't be running alive with spiders and damp rot.' He grinned, that slightly derisive grin, that lifted one corner of his wide, chiselled mouth and sent his left eyebrow in a mocking black peak. 'It's quite a place, as a matter of fact. There's even a bathroom, though I admit the water has to be heated up on an oil-stove.'

'It sounds fine,' she said.

'You said that as though it sounded dreadful,' he reproved. 'What's the matter?'

'Nothing.'

'Oh, come on, something's wrong. You look a regular little ghost. Are you fed up with being married already?'

'Of course not.' She twisted her beautiful ring round and round her finger. It felt heavy and strange on her finger, the diamonds glittered and danced – she wished – oh, she wished she didn't feel like bursting into tears!

'I bet I know what's the matter with you,' Lew said. 'You're hungry. Ten to one all you've had inside you all morning is a cup of coffee.'

'I wasn't very hungry,' she admitted.

'I knew it! First decent restaurant we see, we'll stop and have a meal. You'll feel fine, sweetheart, soon as you've had something to eat.' He smiled at her and returned his attention to his driving.

Fay curled down more comfortably in her seat, forcibly

pushing the thought of tears from her. There was no going back now. She was irrevocably married, and to Lew Marsh.

Lew Marsh – a name to conjure with in the world of film direction, for though only thirty-four he already had several big successes to his credit. Lew Marsh, rapidly climbing the precarious Hollywood ladder of fame, choosing that she should accompany him – yet not from love – not from love.

When he had proposed to her, he had openly told her that he wanted the marriage because he was tired of living alone.

'Will it work out, when you don't love me?' she had asked.

'Love!' He had laughed, contemptuously. 'Shall I tell you about love, baby? It's a pretty-pretty word they put on Valentine cards; an ingredient they stir into popular songs; a puff of air that's here one minute, gone the next. Baby, don't ask me to give you pretty words, I'm not the type. Just take what I can give you, my admiration and my fondness; aren't they good, solid enough emotions for you?'

And because it had seemed a miracle to her that he should want her at all, she had, like a small, wistful bird, snatched at these crumbs of solace he offered. His admiration, which she couldn't quite believe in, for she was not a glamorous person. His fondness, which term, to him, meant that he liked her unobtrusiveness; he could safely forget her whenever he wished, knowing that she wouldn't reproach him, knowing that she would slip quietly away to find some small amusement of her own until he should feel like beckoning her back to him again.

She loved him, of course. She had loved him from the first smile he had given her.

They had met at the house of his grandmother, where Fay had been nursing the irascible and very wealthy Mrs Marsh.

Fay, who was English, had come to America two years before, when her widowed mother had died. She had come under a nursing exchange scheme and she had stayed to become a state registered nurse. This job, which she found far more interesting than hospital work, had taken her into quite a few homes and introduced her to quite a few people, but right from her first day at Laurel Bay she had been charmed and intrigued by the majestic irascibility of old Mrs Marsh, and the rather melancholy beauty of her granddaughter, Della, who lived with her.

These people were different and, though Fay was no snob, she couldn't help appreciating the fact that Mrs Marsh was the wealthiest woman in Casa Roche and that Della's brother was a well-known film director.

Then, one afternoon, he had arrived at the house. Old Mrs.Marsh had been rather sourly flattered that he should have come all the way from Hollywood on account of her gastric ulcer – until he had cynically informed her that he was really in Casa Roche on film business and that he had had no idea that she was laid up with an ulcer. The carelessness with which he said this, actually in front of Fay, informed her that there was very little affection in his attitude towards his grandmother, although she had had the upbringing of himself and Della.

Their father had died when Della was two and Lew twelve. Their mother, an extremely beautiful but very unprincipled Sicilian, had remarried almost immediately. Her new husband had refused to accept the responsibility of her children, so she had callously deposited them on the doorstep of her mother-in-law and carelessly dropped out of their lives for ever.

Fay learned all this from Della, for they had quickly become friends. They were both rather lonely people, linked by the loss of someone they had loved very dearly. Fay's loss was her mother; Della's the young husband who had been killed in a car crash after only three months of marriage.

Fay and Della often talked during those long, warm August days, for Mrs Marsh, despite her rather noisy bursts of temper at times, was a comparatively good patient; she slept a great deal, and it was during these hours that the friendship between Fay and Della warmed and deepened. It was upon Fay's advice, in fact, that Della finally agreed to marry Will Bronson, the engaging and gangling young lawyer, whose family's house adjoined the extensive grounds of Laurel Bay.

He was a persistent visitor at Laurel Bay and Fay was quick to see that he worshipped the tall, melancholy Della. 'The man's crazy,' Della said to Fay one afternoon, as they sat in the old rose arbour that stood in the grounds of Laurel Bay. 'I wish he'd keep away.'

'So that you can go on brooding,' Fay returned, with a flash of temerity that rather astounded her. She wasn't normally a person to interfere in other people's affairs, but she liked both Della and Will and she thought, with Mrs

Marsh, that if Della didn't find something to live for, she would develop into a dour recluse, wanting nothing but her own company and painful memories of a boy who had been wild and reckless, though she had loved him.

'I couldn't ever love Will as I loved Philip,' Della said then. 'I should be cheating him.'

'If you think that, then you're not completely indifferent to him, are you?' Fay said.

Della smiled at that. 'How come you're so wise, you young thing – you look about sixteen, do you know it?'

Old Mrs Marsh was rapidly mending by then, and that Sunday, to celebrate her recovery, the family had tea on the terrace. Fay was invited to the tea-party and joined it rather reluctantly. The sunshine was lush, the afternoon slow and filled with the movement of birds and the lazy fall of leaves from the tall trees in the garden of Laurel Bay. Old Mrs Marsh, regal in black silk, presided over a teapot almost as regal as herself, pleased as Punch that she could drink tea again and as full of pungent quips as her grandson, lounging at the table in grey flannels and a dark blue shirt and looking every bit as dangerous as a corsair in gleaming breastplate and helmet.

This was his tenth day in the house and still Fay was overwhelmingly shy of him. When he spoke to her, she answered him in monosyllables. When he smiled at her, his white teeth clenched on one of the dark cigars he smoked all the time, she thought she saw mockery in his smile and quick colour would mount under the pale skin of her face and her throat. These reactions kept her sleepless at night. Men, until now, had been mere automatons with stethoscopes round their necks; she hadn't known that the world could hold a man like this one. Brazenly handsome as a jungle cat; boldly 'damn your eyes and watch what you value' as any insolent pirate, wearing cynicism, and she suspected callousness, with the same ease with which he wore his expensive suits. He frightened her, yet he fascinated her. He made her want to run to him, yet he made her want to run away. She didn't know, until that afternoon upon the terrace, that she had fallen in love for the first time in her life.

It was as they drank tea, under a sky so blue and speckless it dazzled the eyes, that Della and Will announced their intention of marrying. Della, handsome in cream silk, blushed deeply as she made the announcement. The gangling Will looked like a kid with a dozen toys, while Mrs Marsh nodded with satisfaction.

Fay, sipping her tea, watched Lew. She saw sudden mischief flash in his dark eyes, saw his derisive grin break on his mouth. 'We should be toasting this in champagne, but here goes!' He rose to his great height, towering above the delicate ironwork of the terrace table, lifting his teacup to the blushing Della and the grinning Will. 'Blessings on the union, my children, and don't you forget to call the first little blessing after me – always supposing you get the gender right.' He drank off his tea with a flourish and had the mischievous satisfaction of receiving a scandalized glare from his grandmother.

'You're the limit, Lew Marsh!' she snapped. 'Why don't you go back to Hollywood, where you belong?'

'I am going back, my dear grandmother, just as soon as I've had my honeymoon.'

'Had your what?'

'My honeymoon – those things people have when they get married.' Very deliberately, then, he returned his tea-cup to its saucer, strolled round the table and pulled Fay up out of her seat. 'Come for a walk with me,' he said, and marched her away from the table before she could draw breath to protest.

He walked her under the trees of Laurel Bay, and fear and perplexity were making her heart race and thud in her side so that she had no defence against him when he suddenly stopped walking and pulled her into his hard brown arms. His lips were warm against her throat and she trembled in his arms, feeling she should fight him, yet not wanting to fight him. 'You shouldn't do this – you shouldn't!' was all she found breath to say.

He laughed, softly, deeply. 'I'm doing it, though, baby. Want me to stop?'

'Yes.'

'Little liar!' He took her lips then and Fay was lost. Like a small moth she fluttered in the dark flame of him and it mattered not that destruction might lie beyond the ecstasy he offered now. 'Marry me and come to Hollywood with me,' he said then. 'I'm tired of living alone.' He touched, coaxingly, the delicate fairness of her hair, drew his finger down the delicate curve of her cheek, let it linger at the corner of her mouth. A truly lovely mouth, holding an ardent compassion, and the sensitivity of the born dreamer; her dreams often held, as well, within the vivid blue of her eyes. She wasn't pretty, for her face was too quiet, but an elusive charm lurked about her; an appeal of delicate bones, soft voice and a rather childlike air of loneliness.

'But you don't love me, Lew,' she said.

'Love!' He had laughed, contemptuously ...

They had reached the cabin at eight o'clock, just as Lew had said they would. The sun had died away in a glorious flush of rose and now the sky was shot with lavender. A gentle autumnal breeze moved in the trees and the birds were clamorous at the approach of night.

Lew unlocked the door of the cabin and they carried in the two big bags of groceries they had bought in a town they had passed through that afternoon. Fay stood just inside the door, acutely conscious now that she was very much alone with Lew – Lew, who was her husband, but who was also a tall, dark stranger.

She felt dreamlike. She stood and breathed in a dream. She felt that she would wake in a while and find that all this – Lew, her marriage, this cabin set among tall, aromatic trees and indescribably peaceful – was all just part of a dream.

She watched Lew stride forward into the shuttered gloom of the cabin, watched him put his bag of groceries down on a chair and throw wide the shutters over the two windows. Light shone into the room and Fay blinked, almost crying out in her bewildered delight.

Two big cream couches stood either side of an immense open fireplace of red brick and in between them there gleamed a long, low coffee table. The black parquet floor was strewn with cream rugs and the cream-painted walls were hung with a colourful miscellany of Native American trophies. Against one wall there stood an antique bureau, its wood dark and sheeny, and against another a glass-fronted bookcase, crammed tight with books. It was a high, cool, pleasant room and Fay's eyes shone as she slowly turned to admire everything.

'Like it?' Lew enquired.

'I love it!' she exclaimed.

'No spiders, no damp rot, eh? Come on, I'll show you the kitchen.'

She went with him, carrying her bag of groceries, and when they got into the very neat and compact little kitchen, Lew took the bag from her and put it down on the table. He smiled as she took in, with astonished pleasure, the white cupboards, the white sink, the elaborate little oil-stove.

'How come everything is so nice and clean?' she asked.

'A woman from a farm below comes up to clean and air the place for me,' he told her. 'I like it kept in the pink, because I occasionally drive up through the summer months.'

'I see.' She eyed the cupboards and with a knowing grin he opened one of them, revealing a wholesome supply of canned foods and fruits. 'As you can see, we shan't starve,' he said. 'In this other cupboard,' he showed her, 'I keep oil for the lamps and the stove. In here,' again he showed her, 'linen, cutlery and cooking pots. Now,' he took hold of her hand and drew her from the kitchen, 'now I'll show you the bedroom and the bathroom.'

'The word "cabin" hardly describes this place, Lew,' she protested.

'Oh, I'm well aware of what you expected,' he drawled,

'some broken-down shack with two-tier bunks and a pump outback. Baby, you've got to get used to the idea that you haven't exactly married a penniless piper.'

He squeezed her hand, and as her wedding ring pressed into her finger, she was made acutely conscious of how much the beautiful platinum band, completely encircled with diamonds, must have cost him. Her cheeks reddened and her glance fell away from his.

'Why the blush?' He drew her against his chest. 'What's going on in that funny head of yours now?'

'You shouldn't have spent such a lot of money on my ring!' she blurted out. 'You don't have to buy me, Lew.'

'Buy you?' The smiling indulgence died out of his face. 'That's a hell of a thing to say!' He took hold of her slender left hand and gazed down at the ring. 'I thought the ring a pretty bauble; I thought you'd like it.'

'I – I do – only it's such an expensive ring.' She was acutely embarrassed, wishing she hadn't spoken.

He saw her embarrassment and suddenly he laughed, rather mockingly. 'So I'm buying you, am I? Well, the buying won't end with a wedding ring, I assure you, my dear. Lew Marsh's wife wears silk, not holland aprons!' He swung on his heel with the words and went from the cabin to fetch their suitcases.

As dinner progressed, Lew's slight stiffness of manner wore off. Fay was rather pleased with the dinner she had produced (this was, after all, the first time she had cooked on an oil-stove), and she was gratified to see that Lew ate his dinner with gusto.

'You've a rare hand with a rare steak, my pet,' he complimented her. 'Who taught you to cook like this?'

'My mother. She was a wonderful cook.'

'You were very fond of your mother, weren't you, Fay?' He poured himself a little wine and as he drank it he watched Fay. 'My mother was a bitch!' he said deliberately. 'A beautiful bitch; hard as nails and selfish as hell. Did you know that old Gran thinks I take after my dear mother?'

Fay bit her lip at the sardonic amusement on his face. 'I wish you wouldn't talk like that, Lew,' she said. 'You're always making yourself out as – as perfectly terrible. I think it's half the reason people think you are terrible.'

'Oh, come now, honey,' he raised a mocking black brow at her, 'you don't really think I'm a blue-eyed boy, sadly misunderstood, do you?'

'Well, I certainly don't think you're as bad as you make out.' She rose and collected their plates and took them to the kitchen. She returned with their sweet, a luscious-looking fruit salad topped with whipped cream. Lew eyed it with appreciation.

'You appear to possess all the virtues, my pet,' he said. 'Swell cook! Delicious smile. Optimistic nature!'

'Why have I an optimistic nature?' she enquired, giving him a small piece of the smile he labelled delicious.

'You did say, didn't you, that you don't think I'm quite as bad as I make out?'

'I did. And I believe it,' she replied, biting into a stoned cherry.

'Baby, that's being optimistic.'

'Lew, that's being cynical,' she reproved.

After they'd had their coffee, they washed up the dishes and returned to the sitting-room. Only one of the lamps was aglow and the room looked pleasant and cosy. Lew had lit the fire – for even the summer evenings grew chilly this high in the hills – and the logs crackled and blazed, throwing out a sweet, piney scent.

'I do love this room!' Fay exclaimed, sitting down on one of the big cream couches and clasping her hands about her knees. 'It's the sort of room one dreams about – you know. The sort of room I've always dreamed about, anyway.'

'And what about the husband who goes with the room?' Lew enquired, sitting down on the other couch and taking out his cigar-case. 'Is he the sort of husband you've always dreamed about?'

Fay smiled slightly. As far as looks went, she reflected, he certainly met all the requirements of a dream husband!

'I never thought much about getting married,' she confessed. 'I never thought I would, as a matter of fact.'

'Honey, haven't you ever taken a good look at yourself in a mirror?' he asked lazily.

She coloured, watching him light his cigar. He tossed the match into the fire, lounged back in the couch and comfortably crossed his legs. 'Don't tell me I'm the first guy who's ever told you that you're a rather delectable little dish?' he drawled.

The pink of her cheeks deepened as she nodded her head.

'Incredible!' He smiled across at her. 'And after Olive Hadley's had a go at you, you'll be prettier than ever.'

'Who's Olive Hadley?' she asked.

'Olive, my pet, runs a very exclusive establishment in Hollywood where coltish young starlets go to be turned into elegant young ladies.'

'Is that how you regard me, Lew, as a starlet?' she enquired, looking mischievous.

'You have such charming possibilities, my pet, that I'm naturally eager to see them fully exploited. Olive will style your hair for you, advise you on clothes and make-up. I might add that you certainly appear to need a little advice in that direction. That lipstick you're wearing is much too dark for your mouth.'

'Is it?' She touched her mouth. 'It was very expensive.' She remembered buying the lipstick in a lavender-draped shop in Casa Roche. 'The girl said it suited me.'

'Then she was colour-blind!' He dismissed the girl with a disgusted flick of his wrist, spilling cigar ash on the carpet. 'You've a singularly sweet mouth, Fay, and I don't like to see it daubed with a lipstick that was designed exclusively for brunette business women. It hardens your mouth and detracts from the beauty of your eyes.'

She gazed at him in a kind of stunned wonder. Her mouth sweet! Her eyes beautiful!

He laughed. 'It's easy to see you're not used to receiving compliments. Stop gaping. You've a stunning mouth, you've nice eyes. Why shouldn't I say so?'

'Oh, I don't mind!' she assured him, smiling. She laid her head back against the soft cushioning of the couch, a relaxed happiness coursing its way through her. It was very pleasant, even exciting, to be told that one had a stunning mouth and a nice pair of eyes. Especially by Lew. Most especially by Lew.

'Tell me about yourself, Fay,' he said lazily. 'Where did you live when you were a kid?'

'A rather drab part of London called Holloway.' She wrinkled her nose. 'We lived in a two-roomed flat that always seemed to smell of other people's cooking and to be full of other people's noises. My mother worked in a hot little factory there. It was her idea that I take up nursing, she so dreaded the thought of my working in a factory. When she died and after I finished my training, I went in for private nursing.' She smiled a little. 'I wanted to see other places – see something of the world.'

'Via other people's sickrooms?' Lew drawled. His eyes, in that moment, were curiously gentle, and Fay was confused – startled that he should look like that.

'I suppose that does sound a little silly,' she admitted. 'But private nursing isn't a bad sort of job, not when you've got to earn your own living. And you do move around a bit.'

'D'you think you'll enjoy your new job?' He was smiling as he leant forward to flick cigar ash into the fire, a smile that moved down her slender, relaxed body in the big couch, lingered on her delicate ankles. 'Well?' he insisted.

She turned her face against the soft cushioning of the couch, avoiding his eyes, moved to shyness by his glance. 'I already like my new job,' she murmured. 'Though I must admit my new boss scares me just a little. He will keep looking at my ankles.'

She heard him laugh. 'Baby,' he said, 'the time to get scared is when he stops looking. You bear that in mind.'

The room fell quiet, pleasantly redolent of the piney scent of the purring logs and the aromatic richness of Lew's cigar. The clock ticked softly and there stole in from outside the steady, hypnotic grating of crickets. Fay's eyes drooped and closed contentedly. She could feel the warmth of the fire stealing against her legs, the luxurious softness of the couch like an embrace. She snuggled more closely into that embrace – and drifted into sleep with the ease and naturalness of a child.

She awoke about an hour later – sat up, feeling bemused and rather ashamed of herself. How dreadful, to have fallen asleep like that on Lew! She sat rubbing her eyes, gazing at the opposite couch, no longer occupied by his dark, lounging figure. She rose and wandered out to the kitchen, thinking he might be there, making himself a sandwich, perhaps. But he wasn't. She looked in the bedroom, but it was quite empty, and when she knocked on the door of the bathroom, only silence answered her.

She stood with one hand at her throat, her eyes enormous as alarm darted through her. Where had he gone? Why had he left her?

She hurried back to the sitting-room, crossed to the front door and opened it. A chill night breeze blew in at her, a sombre darkness greeted her. All she could hear at first were the crickets, and then she became aware of other noises. The low, weird hoot of an owl, the rustling of wind-tossed leaves and queer little scuttlings, as of small night creatures scrabbling in the dark.

Fear touched her, moved on her skin like clammy fingers and she drew back into the cabin, slamming the door, shutting out the lonely, crowding darkness. She stood with her back to the door, her heart hammering. Where was Lew? Why had he left her alone? So alone, up here in the hills, with only the darkness and the monster trees to keep her company?

CHAPTER TWO

FAY MOVED woodenly across the room to the dying fire. She crouched down in front of it, encompassed by a quiet so intense that even the rustling of her dress seemed to intrude on it. She stared into the fallen, sombre heart of the fire, one hand clenched hard against her hammering heart.

Panic slowly receded and the return of calmness brought things back into proper perspective. Lew would saunter back from his nocturnal stroll in due course, careless of whether or not it had frightened her to awake to silence and loneliness. A reluctant smile hovered about her mouth. Love for Lew had not blinded her to his failings. She knew him for what he was, an imperious, swaggering pirate of a man, who went his own way; reaching out decisively for what he wanted, rejecting, without a moment's hesitation, that which he didn't want. Superbly, arrogantly free of petty fear or petty disapproval; neither a gentle man nor a patient one, whose temper would create a small hell for her should she ever arouse it.

Yet she loved him – and beneath her fear, in this moment, there suddenly sprang into being, thrilling along her nerves, a primitive gladness that she awaited his coming, that she wore his ring – that she belonged to him.

Then, outside in the night, she suddenly heard twigs break as feet trod them; heard those feet come closer and mount the cabin steps. Very slowly she stood up and the hand that lay over her heart felt its mad racing. She turned towards the door, watching as the latch dipped, watching as the door swung inwards, watching, like a small, ensnared bird, the arrival of Lew. Her pale hair lay ruffled on her forehead, the lemon silk of her dress lay away from the delicate fragility of her throat, and her mouth was very lovely and very vulnerable, offering love, but begging him to understand her slight fear.

He closed the door and came across the room to her, immensely tall in the gloom of the room, and Fay was held motionless, ensnared in his eyes, intent on her as he came for her, reaching out his brown hands and gathering her to him. With a small gasp, she accepted the hard possession of his embrace, pressing her face to him. 'Where did you go?' she whispered. 'Everything was so quiet – so quiet!'

He took her chin in his hand and lifted it, studying her face, a faint smile playing about his mouth. 'I strolled down to see Mrs Pascoe, the woman who comes in to clean this place. She and her husband have a farm about half a mile down. Were you frightened, Fay? I hoped you'd go on sleeping till I got back.'

Her hands gripped his shoulders. 'I didn't know what to think. I didn't know where you'd gone.'

His smile deepened. 'Did you think I'd run out on you? Do I look the sort of guy who'd run out on his bride on his wedding night?' His arms tightened about her and his eyes, gazing down into hers, were very dark, with tiny sparkles caught way down in their depths. Fay was held fascinated by them as Lew lowered his head towards her, then they were lost to her as he pressed his warm cheek to hers. 'Shy of me, Fay?' he whispered.

'A little,' she confessed.

'You don't have to be, y'know, baby.' His lips lightly touched her cheek. Then he swung her up into his arms and as he carried her from the room, Fay laid her face against the hard warmth of his throat, feeling his soft laughter vibrate under her cheek. 'What a feather-weight you are!' he murmured. 'I could wear you in my buttonhole.'

'Like one of Della's carnations?' she enquired, smiling against his throat. Della hadn't liked him wearing her carnations, especially her pale yellow prize-winners, but he had played vandal on more than one occasion, cocking an insolent eyebrow at Della when she flew into a paddy to see one of her 'pets' gaily decorating his buttonhole.

'Ouch!' His laughter deepened. 'Don't scold me on my wedding night, baby.'

For answer, Fay kissed his cheek.

They stayed two weeks at Serena.

They hiked in the hills, fished in the lakes, boated and swam and ate huge farmhouse teas with the friendly Pascoes. And Fay forgot to worry about the future. She dismissed the future. She was too happy with the here and now.

The hills of Serena were peaceful – so peaceful, their sweeping dips and gracefully curving upsweeps dappled with the glorious tints of autumn, and Fay knew that she would remember Serena all her life. And when Lew said to her, at the end of their two weeks, 'Well, we start for home tomorrow, baby, I've got to get back to work,' she murmured a quiet goodbye to those rolling hills beyond the windows of the cabin; said goodbye to the peace and contentment they had brought her. Now tomorrow loomed and though she held her small chin high, she quailed a little at the thought of Hollywood.

Hollywood, with its brazen skies and its stretching, golden beaches. Its sophistication and its glamour. Its black heartbreak for some; its glittering, neon adulation for others.

She must step forth into this glistening whirlpool and accept with equanimity, if she could, the stares and the comments and the amazement. Oh yes, there would be amazement! She didn't doubt it for one moment. But she carried her small chin bravely and smiled when Lew announced their imminent departure from Serena. 'Had fun, my sweet?' he asked.

'I've loved it here,' she said. 'I've loved every second, every hour!'

Three days later, Lew's car drew to a standstill in the smoothly gravelled, circular drive of the exclusive Crystal Court in Hollywood, where Lew had his apartment. Fay gazed at the handsome white building in nervous awe and the feeling did not diminish as she crossed the quiet lobby with Lew, rode with him to the top floor in a lift that moved with the silence and ease of a bird.

They stepped out into a lushly carpeted corridor with wide windows either end, through which the afternoon sun streamed blindingly. While Lew searched his pockets for the key of the apartment, Fay stood at one of the windows gazing down big-eyed upon a vista of wide, clean avenues, where exotic, thick-stemmed palm trees marched like sentinels along the curb edges and big houses stood in secluded gardens of gleaming camellia bushes and lemon trees.

She jumped when Lew spoke to her, whirling from the window and moving tentatively to take the hand he held out to her. The sunshine followed her, turning her hair to a delicate fairness and playing over the blue linen of her dress. She felt Lew's warm fingers close over her cold ones as he drew her into the apartment that was to be her home.

It was large and cool and very, very modern, with a lovely brilliant blue carpet flowing to the soft grey of the walls; with exotic cacti in scarlet pots and a great white couch spread with scarlet cushions. A lush, exciting, film-like place – frightening the life out of Fay. She had never, in all her twenty-three years, known anything like it; alien and elegant and many miles removed from the threadbare little flat she had shared with her mother. How sadly lacking in glamour and luxury that poor little place had been!

'Well, come on,' Lew said suddenly, 'show a little enthusiasm!'

She kept her eyes turned from him, answering with care: 'It's a lovely place, Lew.'

He watched her, saw her hands clench on her white handbag, and his lips twitched with sudden irritation. She looked – why, she looked almost scared! What the devil was there to be scared about?

He stepped across the room to her and took hold of her slim shoulders. 'What are you scared about?' he asked.

'I'm not scared,' she denied.

'You're scared stiff! You're imagining this room filled with my friends and you're trembling in your shoes. What the heck do you think they'll do to you – eat you?'

She ceased pretending. She nodded miserably. 'They'll bite lumps out of me. They'll think me an awful bumpkin.'

'They will if you're going to behave like one,' he agreed. 'If you're going to act like a stranger in your own home, people are going to snigger and talk.'

'But I feel such a stranger!' she burst out. 'I – I —' But she couldn't tell him. She couldn't say, 'I feel so afraid, Lew. All this is so exotic, so unlike anything I've ever known. You've got to give me time to get used to it. Accept my fear, Lew. Accept it and it will soon die.' She couldn't say it, for he wouldn't understand. He was so completely without fear or reserve himself that he had little or no patience with these things in other people.

'I expect I shall soon get used to everything,' she said, her smile careful, her heart apprehensive, the confidence she had known at Serena suddenly stripped from her.

'Let's hope so!' he retorted.

So, with mixed feelings of trepidation and excitement, Fay settled down to married life in Hollywood.

A married life, however, that was filled with a bewildering amount of leisure for a girl who had worked as a nurse since the age of eighteen. Hardly any domesticity was demanded of her, for the cleaning of the apartment was dealt with by the management of Crystal Court; while Lew's only call upon her cooking capabilities was for a breakfast each morning, before he left for the studios. In the evenings they always went out to dine – an arrangement that appealed less and less to Fay as the days passed.

It seemed so silly to her that they should eat dinner in noisy, crowded restaurants each evening when she was a perfectly good cook and the apartment possessed a glittering, gadget-packed kitchen that only got used once a day.

Finally she decided to attack the arrangement and Lew arrived home from work one evening to find her setting out the table in the sitting-room, carefully arranging flowers and table-mats and tall red candles in a pair of pretty holders she had bought that day.

Lew's decisive stride into the sitting-room was checked as he took note of what she was doing. 'What's all this in aid of?' he demanded. 'Are we expecting company?'

Fay turned to smile at him, a smile with just a slight edge of nervousness to it. 'Oh, I thought it would be rather nice if we had dinner at home for once,' she replied. She moved towards him, her fingers caught in the frill edging her apron. 'Do you mind?' she asked.

He didn't answer for a second or two, his eyes flickering up and down her small, aproned figure. His mouth thinned. 'You look like a damned domestic!' he snapped. 'Get that thing off and quit acting the sweet suburban bride – we're going out!'

Fay flinched at the hard edge to his voice, while her eyes travelled warily over his face, which wore bad temper in every chiselled line of it. 'Had a stiff day, Lew?' she asked.

'Yeah!' He swung away from her and poured himself a

drink at the sideboard. 'I've had exactly three blazing rows today, my baby, and I'm feeling as mean as Satan.' He tossed down his drink. 'Those stupid fools in Publicity are kicking up a fuss because I want Connie Carr in *Corn In The City*. They've gone all Puritan Fathers on me because the kid was mixed up in a scandal about three months ago. So what! The kid can act. Who cares about what she likes to do after working hours – I'm sure I don't!'

'What happened, Lew? Did you manage to persuade the people in Publicity to let you have her?' A sudden little smile, that she was quite unable to suppress, played about the curves of Fay's mouth as she pictured the chaos that had probably reigned in the offices of Publicity today. She was learning herself that the curb bit was something this man kicked against with the untamed ferocity of a roped stallion, and like a roped stallion he could be full of damage and danger when the mood was upon him.

He saw her smile and joined it with an irritated laugh.

'I've got her, but I came close to bouncing Belamy Taylor down the garbage shoot. He's the guy who handles most of the stories that are put out about our contract stars; a fat little slug with restless hands! He was grinding his heel down on Connie and I happen to know a couple of kids who've had some sly approaches from the guy; I casually mentioned their names, and that lifted his dirty little heel off Connie!' Lew was looking quizzical as he approached Fay and tipped up her chin. 'Sorry about your dinner arrangements, pet, but I want music and noise tonight.'

'But, Lew, I've got a chicken in the oven!' she protested.

He looked quite unmoved. 'That's your worry, honey, not mine.' He turned from her and made for the bedroom, dragging off his tie as he went.

Fay ran after him, catching at his arm. 'You're being awfully unreasonable, Lew.' Her face, raised to his, was beseeching. 'Is it such a big thing to ask of you, that we stay home this one night and eat in our own home?'

'Look,' his expression became haughty, 'I work damn hard all day long and I happen to appreciate a little gaiety in the evenings. I'm mighty sorry if this doesn't quite meet with your prim approval, Mrs Marsh, but you'll have to get used to pampering my somewhat Bohemian likes and dislikes, or we're going to have these tiresome battles every night of the week. I'm no domestic animal, my baby; I never made out to be one, so quite trying to get the tiger to lie down on the kitchen mat – it won't work!' He shook off her hand and made for the bathroom, tossing his tie and his jacket to the bed as he went.

Fay stood indecisive. He was in a temper and it was probably silly of her to persist in her argument that they stay at home for once, yet she had taken such pains with their dinner. Right now the chicken was turning a beautiful golden brown and the ice-box held peaches in jelly and ice-cream. 'Such a pity – to waste a perfectly good dinner,' she cried out.

Lew glanced back at her as he was disappearing into the bathroom. 'We'll eat cold fowl for breakfast. I'm game,' he drawled.

'And cold baked potatoes and asparagus heads?' she queried.

'Giving in?' He shot a grin at her over his shoulder, that wicked left eyebrow of his a taunting black arch, a deliberate outward sign of the vein of cynical independence that ran in his blood. 'Afraid that I'll dine and dance some cute young blonde if you don't come out with me? You know that I'm perfectly capable of doing just that, don't you, baby?'

And that remark, so carelessly, yet so flagrantly spoken, touched off rebellion in Fay, woke her quiet spirit to a flash of sheer anger. He was so sure of her! So sure that she didn't dare cross him. So sure, and so amused, that she held their marriage like a precariously balanced and extremely delicate glass bowl, a continuous fear in her that she would drop that bowl and their marriage would smash. With passionate dignity, her small frame drawn up tautly as she faced him, she said, 'Get your little bit of gaiety by all means, Lew. Dine and dance half a dozen blondes if you wish. I'll stay at home and eat my very nice dinner, then I'll curl up with a book and not say a word when you come in with blonde hairs on your tuxedo.'

She turned with these words and marched away to the kitchen, feeling rather pleased with herself.

But Fay's pleasure had melted right away by one-thirty, when, for the fourth time, she had switched on the bedside lamp and apprehensively examined the impassive face of the small clock that ticked on the bedside table. She ran restless hands through her hair, then slid down in the big bed, pulling the silk coverlet to her chin.

Lew's independence was so inviolable a thing; a hard glaze about him that couldn't be damaged or softened by love, as hers must inevitably be. She felt shattered now by their fight, feeling it all her fault. It was so much easier, so much less painful in the end to give in to him, for all he really asked of her was that she be his distraction at the end of his long, pressing day at the studios. It was a mistake to play at being the keeper of his home. She was not that. She was just one more ornament he had added to it, something to be picked up and admired at his pleasure – something to be set aside and forgotten. . . .

Then she stiffened in the bed, for there were sudden footsteps in the sitting-room, the careless sound of Lew whistling a certain airy tarantella he was fond of. Fay lay very still. He might think she slept. He must think she slept! She shrank from the thought of him finding her still awake, obviously thinking, worrying – wanting him.

The bedroom door opened and closed and his cheery whistling approached the bed. The lamp clicked on, bathing Fay in its pool of rose-pink light. She knew that Lew was watching her, waiting for her to turn and speak to him. But she wouldn't. He must be the one to capitulate. Her whole body ached for his capitulation.

'Fay?' He spoke softly. 'Fay, are you asleep?'

She didn't move, but he seemed to know instinctively that she was still awake. With a soft little laugh he sat down on the bed and reached for her, pulling her out of the bedcovers and into his arms. His lips quirked as he examined her rebellious face, drawing a teasing finger down her cheek. 'Well,' he drawled, 'aren't you going to ask me where I've been and what I've been doing?'

'I don't know whether I dare.' Her eyes met his with defiance.

'Afraid of a lie or the truth?' He was laughing openly at her, his teasing, travelling finger now at one of the lacy straps of her nightdress.

'Afraid of both, I suppose,' she admitted, shivering slightly at his touch, inwardly contemptuous of her own weak susceptibility to him.

He laughed. 'Don't you want to examine my tuxedo for blonde hairs?'

She shook her head, flinching from the mockery in his eyes – his eyes that openly said that it was entirely immaterial to him whether or not her eyes discovered blonde hairs upon his tuxedo. A sharp little arrow of pain pierced her and as pain spread through her, her face went forward against his warm hard throat. He blew at the soft hair falling childishly on to her forehead, and a tinge of curiosity moved in his eyes as they travelled over her, taking in the delicate modelling of her shoulders, the perfect arching of her small feet, peering out from the hem of her blue nightdress. She seemed good, but was she good, this small thing with her ardent mouth and her heart racing like a mad thing under his hand? Was she good, or was she like all other women, treacherous and shallow beneath the outward softness and sweetness? When those curling lashes hid the blue eyes, as they hid them now, what secret thoughts was she having that he must not read?

'Look at me, Fay,' he suddenly commanded.

But her face pressed closer into his throat and he felt a

little tremor go through her. 'I don't like us to quarrel,' she whispered. 'Let's stop it, Lew – please!'

'It hurts, does it?' He took her chin in his hand, forcing her to look at him, holding her helpless and small across his arm. The gold hair spread against the darkness of his tuxedo and the soft blue of her nightdress threw into relief the soft whiteness of her skin. She looked, Lew thought, his lips curving upon a smile that bordered upon the sadistic in that moment, like a trapped butterfly. 'Listen to me, my baby,' he said. 'When a guy takes as much temperament as I do, taming a bunch of wildcat actors and actresses all day long, he doesn't want it dished up in his own home. So cut out the temperament – I won't have it!' Then, with easy strength, he returned her to her warm little nest in the big bed, drew the coverlet up about her chin. 'How was the chicken?' he asked.

'Horrible.' She tentatively smiled at him, willing him to smile back, without mockery. Willing a show of tenderness from him, even though it was that lazy tenderness for a toy which he sometimes showed her. Even that – even that might banish in some measure the heartache of this evening.

But he didn't smile and her heart jolted at the curious way he was suddenly examining her, his eyes travelling her face with a searching, almost startled intentness. Then, with a peremptory hand, he pushed the tumbled hair back from her forehead, brushed it smooth, bringing the delicate pointed contours of her face into an abrupt definition, which the usual soft waving of her hair about her ears and her forehead was inclined to blur. Lew studied this effect for perhaps a minute, then, with a quiet oath, he swung from the bed and strode to the dressing-table, where he stood removing his cuff-links.

Fay watched him with puzzled eyes, nerves jumping sharply under her skin as he tossed the cuff-links from him and they bounced on the smooth surface of the dressing-table, cutting the silence that lay over the room. 'What's the matter now, Lew?' she asked, quietly.

'Nothing,' he retorted, but Fay, watching his wide shoulders, saw them tauten, as though they braced to take a sudden weight.

'I – I think there is.' She half sat up, the silk coverlet slipping from her shoulders, leaving their young, thin whiteness to pick up delicate fingers of shadow from the rose-pink light of the bedside lamp. Lew could see her through the mirror of the dressing table, and even as the pupils of his eyes expanded, even as her youthful delicacy, still strange and new in his bed, in his home, stirred possession awake in him, he was turning to her with a mouth gone tight and grim. 'All right, if you must know! You're inclined to look like – someone I used to know! Now let's drop the subject, shall we?'

'Someone – someone you used to know?' Her eyes were large and troubled and achingly blue. The tension and the antagonism that lay between herself and Lew was a very real pain at her quickly beating heart. Oh, this tension had to be shattered, had to be broken, or it would break her. With a sudden throwing off of reserve, a sudden abandonment to woman's infinitely greater capacity to forgive, if not to forget, she threw out her arms to Lew. It didn't matter in this moment that he hadn't told her, plainly had no intention of telling her, where and with whom he had spent the long hours of her tormented evening. 'Oh, Lew, a little bit of your past?' she asked, and she even managed to laugh a little.

He stood tall and haughty before her, watching with a cold speculation the play of rose-pink shadow along the white curving of her outstretched arms. Then, with a careless, arrogant laugh, he came to her arms, felt them close softly about his neck. 'Yeah, a little bit of my past,' he rejoined, burying his lips against rose-pink shadow in the hollow of her throat, where nervous little pulses raced under the increasing pressure of his lips.

CHAPTER THREE

'YEAH, A LITTLE bit of my past,' Lew had said, and those words were often with Fay in the days that followed. A persistent undertow, running dangerous and dark beneath the effervescent froth of the Hollywood whirlpool.

She knew that they signified another woman – she also knew that the woman had helped to make Lew the hard, careless person he very often was.

So now she watched when they attended parties, or sat in restaurants and cinemas, watched for a face that might possess something of the look of her own face, but though there were many faces at these parties, in these restaurants, the one she searched for continued to elude her.

In her single days, when she had been neat, sometimes harried, but always efficient Nurse Bryan, she had, along with all the other hundreds of working girls seeking a little colour and escape from the daily rush and routine of earning bread and board, read of Hollywood in the glossy film magazines. Read of its gaiety, its many parties. . . .

The parties did exist – mad whirls, noisy vortexes, where all manner of film people gathered in animated groups and talked nineteen to the dozen about anything and everything connected with films. These parties might, Fay often thought, be the bread of life to anyone connected with the mad, mad business of making films, but she found them bewildering and lonely. She was outside the magic circle, even forgotten by Lew when film cronies carried him off to a far corner, where he would often remain for the rest of the evening, immersed in film talk, lost to her existence.

Yet it was at one of these gatherings that Fay met Cleo Nixon, the girl who was to become the first real friend Fay made in Hollywood.

Cleo, it turned out later, was the wife of a brilliant young cameraman at the same studios where Lew worked, and she and Fay liked one another from the moment Cleo had her elbow jogged and very nearly distributed the entire and rather vegetable contents of a tall cocktail over Fay's dress. With a merry peal of laughter she saved the glass, pulling such a comically malignant face at the man who had so carelessly jogged her elbow that Fay's glance of alarm turned to one of quick amusement.

Cleo, gratified by Fay's amusement, stayed to perch herself on the arm of Fay's chair and within minutes they had got as far as Christian names and were openly confessing to a mutual unappreciation of these smart crushes.

'They're hell, aren't they?' Cleo exclaimed, chasing a piece of cucumber around her drink with a small pointed stick. 'I only come because Ted has to kind of keep up with everything. If you're ambitious, it doesn't do to sit at home and wait for opportunities to come knocking on the door. It's at do's like these that important contacts are made. That's Ted.' She pointed with her little stick at a rather tubby, gesticulating young man in horn-rimmed spectacles, who was in deep and earnest conversation with a long-faced, executive type, whom Fay guessed to be one of the important contacts Cleo spoke about.

'Ted can talk till the cows come home when the mood's on him,' Cleo went on, her glance openly affectionate as it rested on the tubby young man. 'Look at him sounding off there!' She giggled as her glance came again to Fay. 'We're a pair, really, we both like to talk, yet we've a little boy who's as solemn as church bells on Christmas morning.' She eyed Fay with candid, pert interest. 'You seem a little out of all this, if you don't mind my saying so. You're new to Hollywood, aren't you?'

Fay nodded. 'I'm from England.'

'Are you now!' Cleo's brandy-brown eyes expressed an heightened interest. 'Do you like Hollywood?' she asked.

'I – I'm not sure, to tell you the truth.' Fay's smile moved tentatively on her gentle mouth. Could she tell this girl what she couldn't tell Lew, that Hollywood was inclined to frighten the life out of her? That most of the people she met at these parties chilled her to the marrow with their glittering audacity and their determined ambitions? Fears she could not confide to Lew!

Now, watching Cleo, she knew an urge to confide in her, yet loyalty to Lew held her back. All she said was, 'The climate's glorious, isn't it? And I've never eaten so much fruit in my life.'

'So that accounts for your stunning skin,' Cleo returned, pertly grinning at Fay's quick blush. Her eyes moved to the glittering wedding ring on Fay's finger. 'You haven't been married for very long, have you?' she said, spearing a cherry out of her drink and chewing it with dainty pleasure. She smiled at Fay. 'You've got bride written all over you. Who's the lucky guy?'

Fay glanced round the room, searching for Lew's tall figure. She saw him over in a window embrasure, very dark against a background of cream silk curtains, a cigar clamped between his teeth as he frowned and talked to a striking-looking woman of indeterminate age, whom Fay recognized as Claire Remay. It struck her as a trifle awe-inspiring that her husband should be talking to this extremely famous star in such an intent fashion.

'There he is,' she said to Cleo, a twinkle in her eye as she awaited Cleo's reaction. She didn't go unrewarded. Cleo's mouth fell open and she gave a low, startled whistle. 'You're married to Lew Marsh!' she exclaimed. 'Well, button up my high, shiny boots! Who'd have believed it!' She stared at Fay. 'Let me offer you my condolences,' she added cryptically.

Fay laughed. She liked this girl too much to be offended by her impertinence. 'It's the cigar,' she returned lightly. 'He always looks stern and big-business with one of those things between his teeth. You should see him with marmalade on his mouth.'

'He eats marmalade?' Cleo was staring across at Lew. There were many stories about this man and he always, in her opinion, looked every one of them. It struck her as rather grim that this sweet kid, in the peach dress that made her look sixteen, should be tied up to him. He was such a forbidding-looking brute; so darned arrogant – so much the 'monarch of all I survey' type. Not cuddly and easy like Ted.

'He looks like he eats babes like you for breakfast,' she laughed. 'I can almost see him spreading on the jam and munching you up in those fierce white teeth.'

The tentative dimples below the delicate thrusting of Fay's cheekbones came and went. 'You're being most disrespectful about one of Hollywood's most sought-after film directors,' she reproved.

'Does he direct you?' Cleo was watching Fay over the rim of her cocktail glass, and though she smiled, sympathy lurked in her smile. 'No, don't answer that, honey,' she added suddenly. 'You don't have to.'

'Don't I?' Fay touched the shining stones encircling her wedding ring and her somewhat embarrassed glance withdrew from the knowledge upon Cleo's pert face, settling again upon Lew. Now he and Claire Remay had been joined by a tall fair man wearing a rather untidy suit of plum-coloured corduroy. Fay smiled to see him. She liked Bill Symans, with his rather distant blue eyes and the old-fashioned courtliness he showed to all women. He was a writer, and though he and Lew appeared to have very little in common, they were close friends. She said to Cleo, 'Do you know Bill Symans?'

'Who doesn't?' Cleo's exclamation was warm. 'The guy's a saint! I bet if you had a census to find the most popular person in Hollywood, Bill Symans would top the list. He's never too tired or too busy to help someone out of a spot of bother and as fast as he makes money out of those fabulous novels of his, he gives it away.'

'And in the true tradition of a saint, he will die young,' Fay murmured.

Cleo glanced at her sharply. 'What do you mean?' she asked.

'He's a sick man. Lew told me.'

'Oh, no!'

'He has a blood condition, and there's no known cure.'

'Bill Symans, of all people!' Cleo's small suntanned hands folded tight about the tall glass that held her cocktail. 'No wonder his eyes always have that strange faraway look in them – as though he already glimpses heaven, for it's to heaven his sort go.' Then Cleo's shapely little body gave a shake as she threw off gloom. 'Let's talk about my little boy,' she exclaimed. 'We're getting morbid.'

'I'd love to talk about your little boy,' Fay said at once. 'Is he like you?'

'Not in the least. . . . '

Fay began to see a lot of Cleo Nixon after that party. The big apartment was very empty during the day, with Lew gone from it so many hours, and Fay welcomed Cleo's entertaining company.

They toured the exciting Hollywood shops together and Fay, who was provided with an amazingly generous allowance by Lew, found that it was a truly delightful feeling to be able to saunter into one of these fabulous shops and buy herself an extravagantly crazy hat or a bottle of deliciously expensive perfume.

And when Fay didn't want to go shopping, Cleo took her sight-seeing, showing her the elegant, secluded homes of the big stars. One house, the one-time home of the famous screen star, Astra James, and now standing empty and neglected in a garden of tall weeds and brambled hedges, intrigued Fay to such an extent that she and Cleo finally scrambled through an opening in the iron railings surrounding the garden and crept cautiously through the weeds to peer in at the lower windows of the house.

The drawing-room loomed long and lofty and sadly dirty before their eyes, the huge marble fireplace and the painted ceiling, depicting half-clad wood nymphs fleeing before the tempestuous thunder of fierce-looking centaurs, the only reminders left of the past glamour this house had known.

'Can't you just see Astra James draped against that mantelpiece?' Cleo whispered. 'Gold lamé clinging to her from her throat to her heels, her eyes painted up to damnation and a brandy glass held in one hand?'

Fay nodded. 'Whatever became of her? She was awfully famous at one time, wasn't she?'

'She went broke, I think. Anyway, she quit Hollywood years ago. She had too much of everything, I reckon. Too much beauty, too many men; it all probably got the better of her in the end. Perhaps she married some sweet, tame guy and settled down in a quiet backwoods with him.'

'After being so famous! Do you really think she could do that?' Fay looked doubtful. 'Could gold lamé be exchanged for starched gingham, do you think?'

Cleo shrugged and traced a solemn profile in the grime covering the window. 'This is a mighty funny world, honey lamb, and people are mighty funny creatures,' she said, reflectively. 'There's no knowing what we'll do when we're pushed into a corner. We might whimper, we might pass out cold, we might fight like crazy. Then again we might run. There's just no knowing. For my book, Astra James ran off and found herself a little peace, far from the mad noise of Hollywood.'

Fay and Cleo also spent a great deal of time down on the beach, along with Cleo's small son, Eric, running and playing as energetically as he in the glorious sunshine that still persisted, though it was October.

Eric wasn't a bit like his mother. He was a serious-eyed, blond child, whom the other people on the beach were inclined to mistake for Fay's son. Cleo said to her one day, after a woman had pried Eric's blond head out from under his sand bucket and brought him to Fay, telling him to stay by his 'momma' and fill his bucket with sand instead of head, 'You must be the maternal type, Fay, people are always taking you for Eric's mother. You ought to have a baby.'

Fay coloured. She liked children and they liked her, but she didn't think, somehow, that they were included in Lew's plans. But Cleo, taking quick, amused note of her blush, misunderstood. 'Don't tell me you're already having one?' she twinkled.

Fay shook her head.

'Oh, well,' Cleo lounged back on her elbow, watching Fay as she caught Eric into her arms, bending her fair head to his, 'perhaps it's just as well. Your Lew isn't like my Ted. You know where you are with Ted's sort, ordinary down to earth, but Lew Marsh is so darned handsome! Don't you get scared,

Fay? Don't you worry all the time? I know I should, that's why I say thank God for Ted; I know he'll never cause me any sort of – of women worry.'

'I don't – think about what tomorrow might bring,' Fay replied carefully, tickling Eric's ribs and rolling him in the sand, turning her pink face from the friendly curiosity of Cleo's eyes.

'Why did you marry the guy?' Cleo pursued. 'I know he's darned attractive and all the rest, but he looks as though he'd be an arrogant brute to live with. Whereas you're such a gentle, good-hearted kid.' She filtered the glistening sand through her fingers. 'I think you're a whole lot too good for him, if you want my opinion,' she burst out bluntly.

Fay glanced at her, smiling a little. 'Did I come as a very great shock to everybody?' she asked.

Cleo grinned. 'Everybody says he's either nuts or nuts about you. Which is it?'

'Which do you think it is?' Fay countered.

Cleo studied her, her fine-boned face and body, her large eyes that were candid yet shy, her mouth that was ardent and yet gentle. Perhaps, Cleo thought, Fay would appeal to the brute in Lew Marsh – someone soft and innocent for him to hypnotize with his charm and then break. He had, it appeared, grown tired of breaking the more experienced type of female.

'Fay,' she said, with a sudden touch of urgency, 'don't love that guy too much.'

Fay stared at her. 'Why do you say that?' she asked.

Cleo shrugged her shoulders. 'Oh – I just think he's as

hard as nails. I shouldn't like to see him hurt you, he's capable of it. His sort always are. They – use women, but they don't love them. They've a sort of fundamental contempt for women. Haven't you noticed?'

'Perhaps.' Fay turned her eyes towards the sea, gazing fixedly at its blueness, the dazzling shimmer of the sun upon it. Something in Cleo's eyes, something in her voice, had made fingers of apprehension tighten about Fay's heart. What did Cleo know about Lew? What was it brought that alarming expression of – of repugnance into her brown eyes? Fay shivered in the sun, aware of an urgent desire to question Cleo, an urgency that so frightened her that she abruptly leapt to her feet, holding Eric's sticky hand and running him down the beach and into the sea.

She didn't want to know! She ran swiftly from Cleo's knowledge, welcoming the clean rush of the sea. All the yesterdays when she had not known Lew didn't matter – mustn't matter, for in that direction lay heartbreak. Lay the knowledge that yesterdays in his life held the girl who had won his love – and then killed it.

Fay had heard Cleo say, 'Thank God for Ted!' and it was really only a matter of days after she said it that she came to Fay's apartment, breaking into a storm of tears as she threw herself down on the big white couch in the sitting-room.

Fay knelt by her side in alarm. 'What is it, Cleo? Has anything happened to Eric?'

'Ted wants a divorce!' Cleo gasped. 'He asked me – he asked me last night. I can't believe it! I thought he loved me.

We've always – we've always got on so well.' Cleo's sobs tore raggedly out of her throat and her small hands clenched and dragged at the scarlet cushions on the couch.

Fay watched her, aware of profound shock. Cleo had been so sure of Ted's love. She had been so certain that he would never hurt her. 'Oh, Cleo,' she whispered, 'I am so sorry, so sorry!'

'I had no idea!' Cleo gasped. 'I never dreamed he might be seeing somebody else. I thought, when he was late home, that he was working. I believed him when he said he was working. How could he do it? We've been married seven years. Seven years, Fay!' She sat up, pushing the dark hair back from her wet, crumpled face. 'You'd think, wouldn't you, that after seven years you'd know a guy? I thought I knew Ted. I was sure I did. It just goes to show how you can be fooled, just because a guy goes on acting the same – saying the same things, laughing at the old jokes! And kissing!' Cleo's voice rose. 'They're monsters! Men are monsters! They must be, to be able to do it.' Her voice cracked. 'How do we ever fall in love with them? What makes us?'

'Perhaps we're born fools,' Fay said. Her arms encircled Cleo almost fiercely for a moment. 'I don't know what to say, Cleo. Words don't really help, do they? Look, I'm going to the kitchen to make some coffee. Will you be all right?'

Cleo nodded, dabbing at her streaming eyes with a tiny scrap of lace-embroidered handkerchief. 'Yes, make some coffee – I could use some coffee.'

But when Fay returned with the coffee, the room was empty. Cleo had gone. The scarlet cushions on the couch were crumpled where she had lain on them in her torment, and her handkerchief lay crumpled on the floor. Fay set the coffee things on one side and stooped to pick up the handkerchief. The heliotrope scent on it drifted forlornly to her nostrils. Poor Cleo! So happy yesterday, laughing in that gay little restaurant downtown, saying that Ted had been thinking lately of getting a new blue coupé.

Ted Nixon had only been thinking lately of getting a divorce!

A few days later a letter arrived from Cleo; a rather forlorn letter, which Fay read forlornly.

Cleo had left Hollywood. She and Eric had returned to her parents' home in Newport. She wanted no more of Ted, she wrote. 'My love, that was so alive, is now a dead thing, Fay,' she said in that letter. 'But I have my little Eric; I thank God that I have my little boy ... '

Fay's hands clenched on the letter and she stared beyond it to where the sunshine danced gaily in the soft grey walls of the sitting-room, glittered on the pendulums of a little French clock on the bureau. The clock ticked softly and the faint hum of passing traffic came through the open window – and Fay knew that pert, gay Cleo would no longer laugh with that bubbling abandon that had been so infectious, the love she had borne Ted Nixon had been the mainspring of that wonderful laughter – but Ted Nixon had thought fit to kill that love. And Cleo had cried:

'Men are monsters!'

CHAPTER FOUR

BUT CLEO'S departure from Hollywood meant that Fay was left alone again, and Lew, noticing that she seemed depressed, came home in the lunch hour one day and took her back to the studios with him.

He handed her over to a tall, boyish-looking blonde with freckles, whom he introduced as his secretary, Pat Merryweather.

'Show this baby of mine the works, Pat,' he said. 'Let her see the lions. She's a nice quiet kid, so hang on to her, I don't want her lost.' Then he lightly touched Fay's cheek and strode off.

Pat laughed and linked her arm in Fay's. 'You'd better consider yourself highly honoured,' she said. 'Visitors aren't usually allowed. Lew's evidently been turning his celebrated charm on K.C.'

'Who's K.C.?' Fay asked.

'Well, among the Coast elite, of which I'm not a member, he's Karl Christbel. But among the lesser fry, of whom I am definitely numbered, he's King Christmas.' Pat laughed. 'He, honey, is the guy who butters your bread.'

'Lew's boss?'

'Exactly.'

For two hours and more, Fay wandered this fantastic world

of celluloid make-believe with the friendly Pat Merryweather and it had to be admitted that the noise and the excitement effectively stole away her depression.

She saw Shane Ardath, the biggest, latest thing in screen heroes, enact a tragic scene for a new Civil War saga. She heard Silva Copperdene, that beautiful coffee-coloured singer from New Orleans, record a number for a big new musical. And jumping aside to avoid one of the ever-rolling trolleys of heavy scenery, she bumped smack into a stocky young man with a head of rioting black curls and a pair of laughing almond-shaped eyes. He steadied her with quick hands and laughed into her face. 'My, but you're nice!' He made growling noises at her while Pat Merryweather burst into a chuckle to see Fay's eyes fly wide with panic. Then she said to the young man, 'Jerry, this is my guvnor's wife.'

'Lew Marsh!' He withdrew his hands from Fay's slim shoulders in mock horror. 'That guy is seven feet high, I'll depart to find me another piece of sugar.' His almond eyes smiled straight into Fay's. 'You're sweet as a dewdrenched daisy, little one. Tell the big boy I said so – the name's Jerry Kaufmann; he'll hit the ceiling.' He was gone with the words, his hands thrusting into the pockets of a noisy check jacket.

'We-ll!' Fay said.

'Quite!' Pat said. 'Clever as a monkey, that one, but with the morals of an Arabian oil king, I'm afraid. You'll probably see him on the set of *Corn In The City* later; he's in it. Now, how about you and me wending our thirsty way to the canteen for coffee and doughnuts?'

'I'd love to!' Fay said at once.

The canteen was fairly full and Fay gazed with wonder at the multi-costumed, heavily made-up couples and groups sitting at the tables. They didn't look at all glamorous. They looked rather bizarre, Fay thought; like people at a carnival, and she said to Pat, as they sat down with their cups of coffee and their big, puffed-up doughnuts, 'Some of this is rather disillusioning. These people,' she gestured at the nearby tables, 'look like clowns.'

'Well, honey, it's only a factory, more or less,' Pat said. 'Take furniture. If you saw the nails going into it and the glue going on to it, you'd wonder how come it all looked so darned nice in the shop window. Movies are just the same.' She floated her doughnut in her coffee and dipped a hungry head to it, her white but rather widely spaced teeth snapping on the soggy doughnut with frank enjoyment.

Then her eyes, gazing over Fay's shoulder, grew suddenly narrow, and a grotesque look of exaggerated pain spread over her face. 'Fried cat! she growled. 'Here comes that awful Van Deen woman!'

Thalia Van Deen! Fay bit her lip. The woman was a gossip columnist, whom Fay had had the doubtful pleasure of meeting just once, at a party, and whom she had disliked right away. She had read in a book once that the antipathy that exists between some people, and which just can't be overcome, was due very often to their colouring, producing an allergy as strong as that produced by cats, or birds, in some people. Fay believed that red-haired people did this to her, for Thalia was the third red-haired person she had met who immediately made her want to jump to her feet and run out of the room.

She had that feeling now, her hands closing tight around her coffee cup. 'I thought you said visitors weren't allowed?' she said to Pat. 'Isn't she a visitor?'

'She, honey, is Daddy Christmas's little ginger kitten. When Daddy feels smoochy, Thalia, purring, crawls on to his paunch and gets playful.'

Fay looked rather shocked. 'Is that a fact?'

Pat grinned and pressed a hand to her heart. 'Guide's honour!'

Then spiky heels clicked on the floor behind them and an exotic perfume eddied to Fay's nostrils. She tensed as Thalia arrived at the table, clad in a dress that exactly matched the cat-green of her eyes, wearing a smile that was so malicious it was almost an open insult. 'Why, if it isn't Lew Marsh's little bride!' she gushed. 'How nice to see you again!' Then she swung her green glance to Pat, airily dunking a doughnut and calmly meeting Thalia's malicious eyes. 'My, no wonder you're putting on weight, Pat Merryweather,' Thalia said. 'Francy eating those nauseous things, they're just loaded with starch.' She sank down gracefully in a chair facing Fay and took out her cigarette-case. 'I won't offer you one,' she said to Fay. 'They're Egyptian and horribly potent, an acquired taste, in fact.' She smiled, her green eyes glinting as she put one of the slim, yellowish cigarettes into her mouth and lit it. 'How are you liking Hollywood?' she asked.

'All right, thanks,' Fay assured her, recoiling a little from the rank smoke of the cigarette.

'Liking married life?' Thalia pursued.

'Yes, thanks!' Fay quickly lifted her coffee cup and buried her nose in it.

Pat laughed. 'The gal would be a damn fool if she wasn't liking married life with a guy like Lew Marsh,' she remarked.

Thalia's thin lips curled. 'You're always exceedingly coarse, aren't you, Pat? Is it mere affectation, or were you born like it?'

'I'm not coarse, I'm honest,' Pat said, leaning back in her chair and watching Thalia with amused eyes.

Thalia shrugged, delicately, shaking ash off her cigarette. 'I hate coarseness. It's a sign of pioneer blood. Have you pioneer blood, Pat?'

'It's blood, at any rate. It isn't poison,' Pat replied, grinning.

Thalia stared at her, then with a smile of contemptuous dismissal, she turned her green eyes on Fay. 'Do you know,' she said softly, 'you're remarkably like a friend I used to have. Her name was Inez Holden.'

Pat gave a little snort and Fay glanced at her enquiringly. 'Never in your life is Fay like Inez!' Pat exclaimed.

'Oh, come,' Thalia laughed, 'there's a decided resemblance. Fay's just a little more – virginal looking, shall I say?'

'Inez was beautiful!' Pat declared flatly. She grinned at Fay. 'No offence, but Thalia's talking absolute bilge.'

'Oh, I know Inez was beautiful,' Thalia purred, 'but Fay has her colouring. And the shape of her face is the same.'

'Who was Inez Holden?' Fay asked, intrigued by their wrangling and not a bit upset that the unknown Inez should have been beautiful while she was not.

'Oh, don't you know?' Thalia exclaimed, her green eyes widening. 'Hasn't Lew ever mentioned her?'

'Thalia, why don't you shut up about Inez?' Pat growled.

Thalia ignored her. She watched Fay, the rank smoke of her cigarette drifting from her thin, scarlet lips. The expression in her eyes at that moment could have been likened to the hungry, cruel look that comes into a cat's eyes just before it pounces and breaks the back of a mouse. 'Lew was once engaged to Inez,' she said, purringly. 'Didn't you know? She was an actress. Not a very good one, I'll admit, but she was too beautiful for any lack of talent to really matter. She – died, you know.'

'Hell, Thalia, don't go raking all that up!' Pat exploded. 'You're always the same, always wanting to dig up dirt.'

'But, Pat dear, Fay ought to be told about Inez. I'd hate her to hear the story from people less disposed to be friendly.'

'You're not disposed to be friendly,' Pat retorted flatly. 'You're only out to make mischief.'

Fay watched the two of them, beginning to get rather frightened. So that girl had died – that girl she resembled! That girl in Lew's past! 'Look,' she said to Thalia, a small wash of defiant colour coming into her face, 'I don't want to hear anything – anything nasty about Lew, if you don't mind.'

'Nasty or not, it's the truth!' Thalia flashed. 'I know. I was Inez's closest friend.' Suddenly she leant across the table, staring straight into Fay's eyes. 'That girl died – and Lew Marsh was as responsible for her death as if he had held a loaded revolver to her head and pulled the trigger.'

Fay stared back at her, a flinching, frightened mouse before a cat, held as still in her chair as though turned to stone, her heart filled with an aching, inexplicable dread all of a sudden.

When Thalia began to speak again, the purr was gone from her voice and a shimmering spite lay in her eyes, bright green under the mass of blatant red hair. 'Inez was lovely, like a tall golden flower – and then one night she ended up under the wheels of a truck. She walked under them, because Lew Marsh, that high and mighty swine, threw her out of his life. He said she'd played him for a sucker, but I'll never believe it. She loved him; she would have laid down on the ground and let him walk over her. She didn't deserve to be hurt as he hurt her – breaking her contract with Karl Christbel, putting it around that she was pure poison to work with ... ' Thalia gave a thin-lipped smile at Fay's gasp of pain. 'Yes, my dear, that's exactly what he did, so she went out one night and walked under a truck. He brazenly admitted at the inquest that he had "shown her the door", as he so nicely put it. He knew himself responsible for that lovely kid's death, yet he walked from that courtroom with all the urbanity in the world – he might have been walking from a restaurant. And he smiled, oh, so charmingly, for the photographers!'

Thalia sat back. She lifted her yellow cigarette and drew on it, slowly expelling the pungent smoke. Her eyes stared straight into Fay's. 'Inez was dead, mangled by a gasoline truck – and he smiled! He smiled!'

Fay shivered, and when a warm hand touched her she

glanced up to see Pat, who had risen and come round to her side. 'Come on, kid,' Pat said quietly, 'let's get out of here.'

Fay rose and without another glance at Thalia walked with Pat from the canteen. She felt dazed. Surely it couldn't be true! Lew – Lew wasn't that callous! She glanced at Pat, at her frowning, disturbed face, not half so boyish now that the wide mouth was no longer curled in a gay smile. 'They're true, then, the things she said?' Fay spoke carefully, keeping her voice pitched to a slow deliberateness. She held out no real hope that Pat would deny Thalia's story; there had been a ring of unmistakable truth in that thin voice; a gloating satisfaction in those green eyes, which no lie could have brought to them.

Pat nodded miserably. 'They were engaged, and then suddenly they weren't, and Inez – Inez was out of a job. And Lew has never denied being responsible. I – I mean, if it wasn't true, he'd be bound to deny the story, wouldn't he?'

Fay's heart grew colder than ever within her; her pain sharper, her nausea stronger. As Pat said, Lew would surely have denied such a despicable story, had he been able to. That he had never done so could only mean that it was true …

When they arrived on the set where Lew was working, directing a scene for *Corn In The City*, Fay stared through the cluster of tall cameras and arc lamps, seeing only the face and figure of Lew. He stood in the middle of the set, which depicted a cheap, sordid pool-room, and he was arguing with a short, wiry young man, whose mop of curly dark hair was all on end where his demonstrative hands had been at it, and whose long, almond-shaped eyes were flashing as he argued with Lew.

Fay saw only Lew, so big and vigorous, the sleeves of his shirt rolled above the elbows of his brown arms, his black hair gleaming under the powerful studio lights, and she wondered how he could look as he did, how it was possible he was so monstrous beneath those wonderful good looks. She wondered, in a dull agony, why Thalia's dreadful revelation hadn't killed her love stone dead. But it hadn't. Even as she watched Lew, she felt the familiar quick tug at her heart, the surge of almost primitive gladness that she was his go sweeping through her – and she despised herself. She was held in thrall by him, even now, when she knew the worst of him, and she silently cried out against her own weakness.

Pat said, speaking with a forced brightness, 'I told you you'd see Jerry again.' A little laugh broke from her. 'They're always arguing, those two. Jerry's a darn good actor, but he doesn't like being told what to do. They've been fighting over this particular scene for a couple of days now; Lew won't rest until Jerry does the scene his way and Jerry will deliberately play Lew to the verge of murder before he gives in.'

'Will he give in?' Fay asked, with dull disinterest.

'Oh, he will in the end,' Pat said, 'because Lew happens to be right about how this scene should be played. But Jerry just likes to be difficult; with Lew, anyway.'

'Another member of the fan club?' Fay enquired bitterly.

Pat stared at her. Then she looked away, saddened by the shocked despair of Fay's eyes. Poor kid! She was learning fast that along with the thrills a guy like Lew Marsh could give a girl, there also went, automatically, disillusion and heartache.

When Lew glanced up and saw Fay and Pat standing to one side of the set, he abruptly dismissed Jerry Kaufmann and came to them.

'Enjoying yourself?' He grinned down at Fay,

She nodded. She even produced a smile, wondering how she could behave with this naturalness, when every shocked aching nerve in her was crying out for expression. For wild tears, washing the nauseated disillusion out of her system. For the courage to turn and run from his callous presence.

'Noisy dump, isn't it?' Lew said, waving a big hand about, indicating the hurrying bustle everywhere. 'Don't ask me how we produce order out of this chaos.' He shot a grin at Pat. 'I'll be spreading a little blood as well, if Kaufmann doesn't soon quit the tantrums.'

Pat looked sympathetic. 'Hang on, Lew, he'll come round to your way of thinking.'

'He's going to have to!' Lew retorted. He turned again to Fay. 'I'll be through in half an hour, honey, then I'll take you home – via Olive Hadley's. I want to call in on her on a little bit of business.' His eyes held a sudden gleam, an anticipatory gleam in which were mingled an amusement and an indulgence that Fay was too far gone in misery to notice; or if she noticed, to wonder at.

'All right,' she said.

'By the way,' he said to Pat, 'did you phone the Brill Agency about that singer?'

She looked disconcerted. 'Shucks, Lew, I forgot! I'll go

and do it now.' She caught hold of Fay's hand. 'You come with me, honey. You might get trampled on if you hang about here.'

'I'll definitely be through in half an hour,' Lew promised, and as he strode back on to the set of *Corn In The City*, Fay turned and went with Pat to her office.

Half an hour later, Lew's car swung out of the gates of the studios and he drove rapidly in the direction of Sunset Boulevard, doing most of the talking and not seeming to notice that Fay was extremely quiet. As they drew in before the swanky façade of Hadley House, he leapt from the car with an eager agility. 'Come on,' he said, holding out his hand to Fay.

'Do you need me?' she asked.

He grinned. 'Not particularly, but you might as well come in, it's damned hot out here in the sun.' He grasped her hand and drew her from the car, and he didn't release her hand as they walked in through the swing doors of Hadley House. She felt absurdly like a child.

'Lew, let me go!' she whispered, as one of Olive's elegant receptionists came across the sea-green carpet towards them. He merely laughed. He said to the girl, 'It's okay, Miss Hadley's expecting us.' And he swept Fay past the girl and her delicately raised eyebrows, continuing to laugh at Fay's pink face as they stepped into the lift.

'You can let go of my hand,' she said. 'I shan't run away.'

'I like holding your hand.' He was in a curiously light-hearted mood, his face boyish as he gazed down at her. 'It's such a small, cool hand, all delicate bones. I could crush it in my paw.' Then, as they stood together in that smoothly flying lift, he lifted her hand and buried his lips against her wrist.

His lips were warm and they seemed to stay for ever against the wild throb of her pulse. Fay watched his bent head. For now – for now, it pleased him to do this! Now she was his whim, his toy, but the whim would die and she would go the way of that other girl, whose name tolled in her head with a funereal insistence. She wanted to say that name, to see guilt strip him of his self-possession. She wanted to scream it, show him that she knew it – but she only mutely bore his kiss.

The lift ceased to ride and they got out and Lew, still holding Fay's small hand a prisoner within his, made straight for Olive Hadley's private office. The impetuosity of his stride made Fay glance up at him in some puzzlement.

'Your business with Olive Hadley must be important, Lew,' she said.

'My business with Olive is important.' He grinned as he spoke.

CHAPTER FIVE

OLIVE HADLEY was behind her big desk, busily dictating to her secretary, when Fay and Lew entered her office. She immediately dismissed the girl and came round the desk to them, very smart in a black suit, with a glittering diamond pin upon the lapel. She wasn't a particularly shapely or handsome woman, but the air with which she wore her superb clothes helped enormously to give her a handsome appearance. To Fay, and to dozens of other women, she always appeared the quintessence of enviable smartness and self-assurance.

'Hullo, my dear,' she said to Fay. 'Let me see, I've got to wish you many happy returns of the day, haven't I?'

One of Fay's hands flew to her startled mouth. Of course, she was twenty-four today – and she had forgotten! Forgotten her own birthday! 'Why – why, yes,' she stammered.

Lew laughed. 'Go and get the coat, Olive,' he said. 'I can't wait to see Fay in it.'

Olive went across the room to the door. She opened it and Fay heard her say to the girl at the desk outside, 'Paula, run downstairs and fetch me that mink coat of Mrs Marsh's.'

Fay turned to look at Lew, who was lounging against Olive's desk, casually pressing on and off the onyx cigarette-lighter that stood on the desk. His eyes grew mocking as they surveyed her perturbed face. 'You don't have to look as though I'm buying you a piece of rope to choke yourself with,' he drawled.

But when the girl Paula brought the big lilac-coloured box that held the coat, and when Olive drew it out in all its dark, gleaming luxuriance and helped Fay to put it on, Fay did indeed feel as though a piece of rope had been put around her throat, choking her.

She stood very still as Lew came over to her and stood behind her, watching their reflections in the long mirror she stood in front of. She felt his hands on her shoulders, felt him smoothing the wonderful fur of the coat. His voice came softly to her ear. 'Many happy returns of the day, my dear,' he said.

Her eyes met his in the mirror. She felt a sensation of helplessness, of almost overwhelming weakness. She was glad of the support of his chest at the back of her, the holding of his hands. She felt certain she would have toppled to the floor without them. Today she had learned to what cruel depths he could sink – and today he made her this beautiful present. Such bitter irony moved her dangerously closer to those tears she had wanted to shed at the studios.

'Thank you for the coat, Lew,' she said carefully. 'It's beautiful.'

But he frowned as she made her formal little 'thank you' speech. He was abruptly irritated by the lack of enthusiasm in her voice, in her eyes. Couldn't she see what the coat did for her? Couldn't she see that her face nestled like a pale flower in the rich darkness of the collar? Had she no vanity, this funny kid he had plucked out of the plush stuffiness of Laurel Bay; rescued from the plaintive sickrooms of the elderly?

'I wanted to cheer you up a little,' he murmured.

She turned to him then. She could see that he was disappointed in her reception of his present and she was moved to reassure him. She was genuinely touched by his realization of how upset she had been by Cleo Nixon's departure from Hollywood. 'I really do like the coat, Lew.' She touched tentative fingers to his sleeve. 'I'm just a little bowled over, that's all.'

'Of course she is,' Olive Hadley broke in amusedly. 'Any woman would be staggered by a coat like that, Lew.' She watched them, thinking, with a rare touch of sentimentality, that they were a well matched couple. Many people disagreed with her. They called Fay a bloodless little nonentity, but she personally considered that Lew Marsh had picked himself a winner.

There was heart and courage in the girl's face, and if that storm-tossed guy had any sense, he'd hang on to her for all he was worth. She'd give him the things he needed, the things he should have; a real home, a gentle, constant love – and children. There was no chittering, modern nonsense about Fay; she wouldn't think that providing a man with a happy home was a bore. She wouldn't put the preservation of her figure and her time before a man's natural desire for children.

It was only to be hoped, for both their sakes, that Lew realized her worth. If he were only playing with her, he'd surely live to regret it!

She watched Fay as she reached out her hand and pressed

Lew's arm. She wondered at the look of shock in her eyes. Surely being given a mink coat, even one as fabulously expensive as this, hadn't put that look in the girl's eyes?

Lew swung round to Olive. He was grinning. 'She looks kind of cute, eh?' he said.

Olive nodded. 'I must say Fay's air of fragility blends very well with mink. So many women merely make it look bold and expensive.'

Fay coloured at the compliment and when Lew turned to study her with renewed interest, his fancy caught by Olive's remark, she shrank from the admiring possessiveness suddenly very much alive in the depths of his dark eyes. She wasn't thrilled by the look. She wanted, instead, to turn and flee from it.

She knew a deadly, bewildering sense of disenchantment.

Lew had toppled from his mountain top. He no longer dwelt in solitary splendour in her heart. Now there stood at his side the shadowy image of that tall golden girl, who had died because she, too, had been foolish enough to love him.

She took off the coat and Olive came over and carefully replaced it in the lilac box.

'We'll christen that tonight,' Lew said, wrapping a boyish arm about Fay and pulling her to his side. 'I've got tickets for *A Touch of Heaven.*'

'It's a great show, Lew.' Olive gave him a quick smile of enthusiasm. 'I saw it the other night. The music and the dance numbers are really something!'

'Swell!' He tipped Fay's face up to him. 'That'll put a nice finish to a nice day, eh, sweetheart?'

Fay tried hard to forget what Thalia Van Deen had told her about the terrible death of Inez Holden, but she never really succeeded. Now everything seemed spoiled. When she looked at Lew across a restaurant table, watched his dark, handsome face crease in laughter or grow animated in conversation, she was no longer moved to the old spontaneous pride in his looks. She no longer thought, 'This man, whom people turn to watch, is my husband.'

When, at a party, he stood among a group of film people and she watched him argue, saw him impatiently flick ash off his cigar, his arrogant head thrown back, his chiselled mouth scornful, she saw him almost as a stranger.

Even when he kissed her, she was remembering. She was thinking, 'Once he kissed Inez Holden. Once he held her in his arms. But he left her – he'll leave me.'

And in this mood of disillusionment and perplexity, she met Jerry Kaufmann again.

It was down on the beach. She still went quite often, though a little sadly, remembering the happy hours she had spent there with Cleo and Eric.

She sat thinking about Cleo and the various times she had borrowed Eric when Cleo drove in to Pasadena to see an aunt. Taking him back to the apartment with her and feeding him melon and jelly buns. Letting him thump on the piano, and lying on the carpet with him, as equally absorbed as he in an enormous jig-saw puzzle. Once Lew, arriving home early from work, had joined them on the carpet, a cigar clamped in his teeth as he winked his eye at Eric and carefully fitted in the pieces that formed the white kepis of a line of French Legionnaires firing upon a band of charging Arabs.

Fay sighed and ran the glistening sand through her fingers, her melancholy eyes fixed upon the incredibly blue sea, dotted with swimmers and surf-board riders and tall girls tossing huge rainbow balls to one another. Not entirely unaware that on this gay stretch of beach, alive with bronzed, lounging gods and goddesses and noisy with their talk and their laughter, she stood out a little quaintly, even a little forlornly. A lone, slim figure in a lemon bathing suit that revealed only a slight bust, pale, slender legs and ankles so delicately boned they looked as though they'd break if she ran too hard on them.

When a quick, amused voice said behind her, 'Is it okay if I join you – you look a little in need of company?' she almost jumped out of her skin, turning a startled face to the speaker. She recognized Jerry Kaufmann at once. His dark curls, now, were wetly plastered down where he had been in the sea and his almond-shaped eyes, surrounded by lashes as long as a girl's, were smiling.

He threw himself down beside her on the sand, stretching out his wiry, tanned body in swimming trunks of a bright, brazen green. 'Boy, what a day!' he exclaimed. 'If only that molten sky would open up and pour with beautiful rain!' He lounged back on his elbow, grinning sociably. 'What are you doing all on your own on a Saturday afternoon?' he asked.

'I'm always on my own on a Saturday afternoon.' She smiled slightly. 'Lew plays golf.'

'I'll remember that!' His almond eyes travelled her face, friendly and warm. 'Tell me you don't mind me hustling in on you.'

'I don't mind.' And it was true, she didn't mind. She rather liked him, she realized. Liked the sturdy, independent set to his shoulders, the frank friendliness of his eyes.

'You seemed so blue, I just couldn't resist coming over,' he said. 'I always think that being alone on a beach is the next worse thing to being alone at a hot-dog stand.' He grinned. He had a very engaging grin, showing small, square teeth. 'Hollywood can be a very lonely place for a stranger.' He spoke sympathetically.

'It reminds me of a jungle,' she said, moved to impulsive frankness by the friendly way in which he was regarding her. Though he was a perfect stranger, he didn't seem like one. He had a naturalness of manner that set her quite at ease, an open, confident glance that won her confidence without any effort. 'It's so hot and sultry; full of strange noises and handsome, dangerous creatures who pounce.' She smiled. 'I know I'm silly to let it scare me, but it does scare me.'

'You've no mad ambitions to break into movies, then?' he asked.

She shook her head, her dimples arriving in her cheeks to give her a roguish look that Jerry Kaufmann found very alluring. 'Lew would probably toss me out of the sitting-room window if ever I develop the fever to be a film star,' she said.

Jerry grinned. 'That would be a pretty drastic remedy. Why would he do that, d'you suppose?' He watched her, her delicately curving cheekbones, her mouth like a flower, her throat that was as sweetly hollowed as a child's.

'Why, I'd develop a temperament to match my mad ambitions, wouldn't I?' she said. 'Lew prefers me without one. He says he gets his share of temperament all day long at the studios. Anyway, I'm not the film star type.'

'That's true,' Jerry agreed. 'You strike me as – as retiring, shall I say?'

'You don't mean placid and mediocre, do you?' Her smile was rueful. She had, in these weeks in Hollywood, grown to think of herself in those terms. Everyone here seemed possessed of enormous talent, or tremendous vitality, or extraordinary good looks. People still gaped when they saw her with Lew and were told she was his wife, and Fay was slowly but surely learning to be blasé about the incredulity of these people.

'I think,' Jerry Kaufmann said, with a flattering promptness, 'that you're a very refreshing change from the overflow of lush opulence that one sees around here at every turn of the head. You're as cool as rain – don't you know it?'

As cool as rain, he thought, and sweet as a spray of mimosa. A gentle, timid kid who stirred an unexpected protectiveness in him. Who stirred, as well, a kind of shocked recoil when he thought of her imprisoned in the powerful arms of Lew Marsh, at the mercy of that hard, insolent mouth. To escape the thought, he said to her, 'Do you swim?'

'Not very professionally,' she admitted. She knew, just by

looking at him, that he'd be superbly proficient in the water. He had the tough, well knit body of the good swimmer, and when he leapt to his feet, pulling her up with him, he moved with the easy grace of a dancer.

'Let's go swim,' he suggested. 'This sand is as hot as a grill.' He held her hand and ran her down the beach and into the sea, laughing with the gay abandon of a boy, his wet curls flopping on to his forehead.

That night, over dinner, Fay told Lew that she had spent the afternoon swimming with Jerry Kaufmann. She was curious to see how he reacted to the information, sensing that he disliked Jerry, but she was unprepared for the quick flash of anger that came into his eyes.

'The devil you did!' he exclaimed. 'I suppose the little swine scraped an acquaintance?'

Fay, in her turn, grew rather angry. 'That isn't a very nice way to talk about him,' she said. 'I thought he was quite nice.'

'Kaufmann!' Lew laughed. 'I could tell you things about that guy that would make that pretty gold hair of yours stand on end. You'll stay away from him, if you don't mind.' He looked straight into her eyes. 'I'm not merely asking you to, Fay, I'm telling you to.'

She was taken aback by his tone. She stared at him, half expecting him to break into a smile and reveal that he was joking with her, but when he didn't she grew defiant. 'You could tell me to go jump out of a window, but that doesn't mean I'm obliged to do it,' she retorted, rather childishly.

His eyes narrowed as he looked at her across the table. 'As it happens, my baby, where Kaufmann's concerned, you'd do better to jump out of a window. It's quicker that way.'

'Quicker?' She didn't understand him.

'I'm implying, baby, that Kaufmann's sheer murder.' He poured himself a glass of wine and he grinned at her over the rim as he lifted the glass to his lips. 'What are you thinking, that I'm no spotless angel myself? Now that strikes me as a little sad. You used to hold such touching optimistic views about me, Fay. What's happened to them lately?'

She looked across at his dark, quizzing face. He was sipping his wine, his eyes mocking her. 'I don't think I really care any more whether you're capable or incapable of improvement,' she told him. 'You're what you are, aren't you? I'm accepting you for what you are.'

He raised a black brow at her. 'That's a somewhat ambiguous remark, my pet,' he drawled. 'Would you mind amplifying it a little?'

'Tigers don't change their stripes, do they?' Her soft mouth twisted. 'I was under the delusion that they did, that's all. Now I've grown up; I've shed my childish illusions.'

'I see.' He studied her, her set face and her rather defiant eyes; the funny little question mark caught in their blueness. 'What's gone wrong, Fay?' he asked quietly. 'What have I done?'

And something in the way he said those few quiet words got right under Fay's guard, sent such a thrill of pain through her that she gave a little gasp and gripped the edge of the table.

'Don't take any notice of me,' she murmured. 'I'm a little fool, that's all.'

His brows climbed quizzically. 'Why, because you thought you could cover up the tiger's stripes with a handful or two of whitewash?' He smiled and twirled his wine glass, watching the golden sparkle of the wine through the glass. 'I see that you've found out it would take rather more than that to hide my stripes. I'm sorry the discovery has hurt you, Fay.'

He lifted his glass with a cynical flourish and drained it, his eyes intent on Fay's face; slanting, quizzical eyes, still capable of melting her knees and filling her arms with an aching longing to hold him and hold him. Then he gave a short laugh and rose to his feet. He came round to her and drew her up out of her seat. 'Come and dance,' he said. 'You forget to think questions about me when I've got you close to me.'

CHAPTER SIX

FAY TRIED, after that conversation, to do as Lew wished, she tried to keep away from Jerry, but it suddenly seemed that everywhere she went, Jerry was there. If she went down to the beach, he joined her. If she went to the park to listen to the band, sooner or later he came hanging over the back of her seat, thrusting popcorn under her nose.

And at parties, when Lew disappeared to play poker or to talk films, Jerry would inevitably appear at her side, drinks in his hands or an invitation to dance on his lips.

He was always so friendly and casual and entertaining that Fay was at a loss to understand why Lew had spoken as he had about him. No one, she thought, could have treated her with more respect than Jerry did. Even when they danced he didn't hold her right up close to him, as did some of the other men who frequented these parties. He never attempted the shadow of a familiarity.

She began to think that Lew had let the fact that he and Jerry couldn't work properly together distort his judgement, his sense of fairness. Jerry, she decided, was a lot less harmful than Lew was himself, and though the acknowledgement filled her with a painful sense of disloyalty, she held to it. She used it as her excuse to forget, even to dismiss, Lew's injunction that she keep away from Jerry.

She definitely liked him. She never openly encouraged him, but she knew that the pleasure she felt in his company must show in her eyes when they laughed together over some inane joke that he somehow turned into a witticism. Or when they made a thorough mess of surfboard riding. Or when they stood together at a hot-dog stand and he plied her with the peppery things, trying to make her as enthusiastic about them as he was himself.

He had, Fay realized, taken Cleo Nixon's place in her new life; he had become the friend she needed so badly. She accepted him, wholeheartedly, as a friend. It never once occurred to her that he could ever mean, or ever want to mean, anything more than that to her. She never even noticed that in his own zestful, gamin way, he was very attractive, nor was she particularly impressed by the fact that he was one of the most popular young actors in Hollywood. To her, he was just Jerry – Jerry of the boyish grin, the irrepressible spirit. She was so busy being grateful for his friendship that she didn't notice the amused, speculative glances they were beginning to attract at parties.

One Saturday afternoon he took her to a ball game. She had never been before, and though it was all a bit of a mystery to her, she was soon cheering as enthusiastically as Jerry. And it was in the midst of her cheering that the toffee apple Jerry had bought her flew off the end of its stick and landed a couple of rows down, plonking stickily into the ample lap of a rather glum-faced supporter of the visiting team.

When the indignant head swivelled to find the culprit, Fay was obligingly obeying Jerry's swiftly whispered and barely understandable injunction – he was trying so desperately hard not to burst out laughing – to look as though butter wouldn't melt in her mouth.

The poor man, so unjustifiably bombarded with the enormous and revoltingly sticky toffee apple, met big blue eyes so unutterably innocent, so overwhelmingly devoid of anything approaching guilt or the juvenile desire for such a ridiculous thing as a toffee apple, that any consequences, in the form of glum vituperation from this glum-faced victim of so messy an assault, passed Fay by. The glaring, offended eyes searched the row and Fay could feel the shaking of Jerry's body as he fought to control his laughter. 'Stop it!' she whispered. 'He'll guess in a minute if you go much redder in the face.'

'How – how do you do it?' Jerry gasped. 'You look too darn angelic for words. Hell, he's looking at you again!' In a sudden excess of uncontrollable hysteria, Jerry bent as though to fasten his shoe and Fay could hear him sniggering and hoarsely gulping down by her knee. It was all she could do to keep a straight face herself.

She enjoyed that ball game as she hadn't enjoyed anything for a long time, and when they finally drifted out with the bemused and noisy crowd and Jerry casually said to her, 'If you've time, how about coming back to my place for a coke or coffee?' she agreed, almost eagerly.

She had never been to Jerry's apartment before and she was astounded by the prevailing untidiness of the place, its Bohemian atmosphere of chaotic indiscrimination. It was, this sitting-room, with its conglomeration of bizarre furniture and its big windows looking out over the sea, more like a studio than anything else. Especially so since a covered easel stood by one of the windows, in such a position as to catch the streaming light.

'Do you paint, Jerry?' she asked, eyeing the easel with frank curiosity.

He shrugged, grinning at her. 'Let's just say I try.' He walked to the easel and flicked off the cover. 'Want to examine the body?' he queried diffidently.

She went over to him and stood at his side. Her eyes grew very big as she discovered herself – it was herself and yet it was also someone she had never been.

She sat on a white wall, down which trailed a mass of magenta and gold flowers. Her right hand rested in the flowers, while her feet were bare as they dangled against the wall. Her head was thrown back in gay and irresponsible laughter.

'Well?' Jerry asked quietly.

'It's me – yet –' she turned her wondering eyes to his face – 'yet not me at all.'

'Perhaps it's you as I see you – or would like to see you,' he said.

'A sort of – gypsy!' she gasped incredulously. She turned again to the painting. The colours were bold and applied with a bold hand. Jerry had ripened the colour of her hair, made her mouth more daring. Around her left ankle there glinted a slender bracelet, but her left hand was without its wedding ring. She hardly realized the significance of that rejected ring, so taken was she with the painting as a whole. For an amateur painting it was extremely well done and she recognized the fact, though she knew very little about painting. Her pose was gay and relaxed and as warmly appreciative of the sun as a kitten on a wall.

'The eyes aren't quite right,' Jerry said, peering into the painted face. 'I rather thought they weren't and now that you're here I can see where I've gone wrong. Your eyes crinkle when you laugh, but they still stay big.' He turned to her, looking eager. 'If I bribe you with a long, cool coke, will you sit for me for fifteen minutes or so while I put those eyes in order?'

She laughed, going a little pink. 'Keep it to fifteen minutes, then, Jerry,' she begged. 'Lew is taking me to meet his boss tonight and I daren't be late home.'

'K. C.!' Jerry whistled. 'Are you going to his house?'

She nodded. 'To dinner. Is he – is he very formidable, Jerry?'

Jerry grinned as he walked off to the kitchen to fetch her the promised coke. 'He's absolutely indescribable!' he called back over his shoulder. 'I wonder if our green-eyed friend Thalia will be there.'

'Under the same roof as his wife?' Fay gasped.

She heard Jerry laugh. When he returned with two tall glasses of coke, he said, handing her one of the glasses, 'K. C. is such a potentate that even his missus daren't get annoyed if he brings his mistress to dinner. The missus will surprise you. She's a magnificent, synthetic blonde of about fifty. She weighs a good fourteen stone and she adores her delinquent slob of a husband. Why he bothers with a shrill little beast like Thalia when he has a wife like Magda is a mystery to me.'

'Magda?' Fay queried. 'She sounds foreign.'

Jerry nodded. 'She's something Balkan, I think. They both are – I think.' He chuckled. 'Everything connected with K. C. is a bit of a mystery. Some of the things he says will set you wildly running round for a key to their meaning. He talks real jumble, kid, and if you haven't known him half a dozen years, you'll wonder what the heck he's getting at.'

Fay looked a trifle worried. 'I dare say I'll go and give him a silly answer.' She smiled. 'I'll guarantee I'll tread on Lew's toes before the evening's out.'

It was gone half-past six by the time Fay got home, and Lew, hearing her come in, put his head round the bathroom door and demanded to know where she had been. 'You're devilishly late, y'know,' he grunted.

She nervously shed her coat. 'I – I went to a movie,' she blurted out, keeping her head turned from him so that he shouldn't see by her heightened colour that she lied to him.

'Well, buck yourself up, baby,' Lew urged. 'We're due at the Christbels' by seven-thirty.' The bathroom door shut and Fay stood staring rather wildly into the dressing-table mirror. This wasn't the first time she had lied to Lew. As she saw more and more of Jerry, so her lies to Lew increased in number. She dreaded what would happen when he found out, but she clung determinedly to her friendship with Jerry. Why shouldn't she have him for a friend? He was a real relief to be with, a wholly charming and relaxing person. He woke relaxation in her, stirred into life the irresponsible urge to return to childhood, but to a childhood far more colourful than the reality had been.

When Lew came from the bathroom, vigorously rubbing his wet head with a towel, he gave her a quick, rather irritated glance. 'Jump to it, honey, I've run your water. We haven't a heck of a lot of time, y'know. I put in two handfuls of those lavender crystals, that enough?'

She was obliged to smile. 'From the size of your hands, rather more than enough, I'd say.' As she passed him, she put out her own hand and drew her fingertips across his bare back. When he was like this, so boyishly fresh and clean from his bath, his brown skin gleaming, the muscles of his back and his arms rippling with health, he seemed incapable of any despicableness. He seemed like a brown god, come up out of some deep, clean pool of enchantment. He shone with a cleanliness that seemed of the spirit as well as of the body. She could almost believe in such moments that whatever evil things were said of him, they had their foundation only in the minds of the people who said them. It seemed a blasphemy to believe that he had viciously ruined a beautiful girl.

He was dressed long before she was, impatiently prompting her, as she stepped into her dress, to get a move on. 'Well, come and zip me up, then,' she implored, looking and feeling somewhat flustered, her hand groping impotently about behind her for the zip. She was still uncertain whether or not she liked this dress. Lew had wanted something special for her, this being her first visit to the Christbels', and he had told Olive Hadley to dream up something out of the ordinary, something capable of being worn only by Fay. Fay secretly thought that she was the last person on earth who would be wearing it.

It was of pure silk, extremely close-fitting to the hips and a most delicately lovely shade of lilac. From the hips the lilac colour deepened and the skirt became full, cascading with tier upon tier of innumerable petals, edged with tiny, glittering beads. It was a curious but undeniably attractive mixture of innocence and stylish originality, but Fay, gazing at herself in the mirror, knew again that definite distaste the dress had aroused in her when Olive had first fitted it on her.

She felt Lew's hand on the zip and when she saw the lilac silk close like a sheath on her body, she turned from the mirror with a quick, embarrassed gasp.

'What's the matter?' Lew caught and held her elbows, his eyes searching hers enquiringly.

'I – I feel naked!' she gasped.

He laughed, his brows lifting in quizzing incredulity. He stood back to examine her in the dress, slowly and pleasurably moving his eyes over her. 'You look a picture!' he declared, with emphasis. 'You look like pale innocence gone on the rampage. I told Olive nothing "sweet young miss" and she's come up with a winner. You'll turn a few heads tonight, my pet.' He drew her towards him, his big, shapely hands moving caressingly up her sides, but she held herself rigidly back from him, turning her head, shyness storming in her, distressing her. Why must Lew always show so plainly that it was her body he liked?

'Don't kiss me!' she said. 'You'll – you'll spoil my lipstick.'

'I might, at that,' he agreed, grinning and releasing her. He turned from her and walked out to the sitting-room, and Fay eyed herself without pleasure in the mirror. Should she paint her eyes to match this actressy dress? Go all out? Make a real job of impressing the Christbels? It was perfectly obvious that Lew intended she should impress them.

With abrupt decision and a fighting angle to her chin, Fay sat down on the dressing-table stool and opened the big make-up box Lew had given her and which she so rarely used. She took out mascara and lavender eye-shadow and with care, and something of defiance, she made up her eyes, watching the bewitching sparkle the colouring brought to them with an ironical expression of amusement.

When Lew came back into the room, she swung round on the stool and smilingly batted her mascaraed lashes at him. She waited for the verdict as he came across the room and stood looking down at her.

'I've added a little to the rampage, Lew,' she said lightly.

'So I see. Do you feel somewhat less naked now?' He grinned wickedly as he spoke.

She nodded.

Still grinning, he raised her from the stool, turned her so that she stood with her back to him and lightly clipped a slim necklace of diamonds about her throat. The necklace clung against the white skin of her throat, throwing out small fiery flashes as he turned her again and carefully added matching diamond drops to the tiny lobes of her ears.

Her eyes, a deeper blue than ever with their lids feathered with eye-shadow and their lashes darkened with mascara, stared up into his dark, smiling eyes. 'Why are you always giving me presents?' she asked, her voice tremulous all of a sudden. 'You don't have to, Lew. I don't want presents all the time.'

He gently touched her cheek with his finger. 'Maybe that's the reason I give them to you,' he replied whimsically. He went across to the big wardrobe and drew out her mink coat. As he helped her on with it, he held the big collar up about her face, studying her.

'Do I look – expensive enough, Lew?' she enquired.

'Expensive?' He shook his head. 'Rather more than that, my baby, but the exact description eludes me.'

'Does it, Lew?' She stood quietly between his hands, the diamonds he had given her sparkling in her ears, a smile that was just a little sad playing about her lovely mouth. 'How about decorated goose, all ready for serving up on a platter to the Christbels?' she asked.

He put back his head and laughed. 'You'll do!' he exclaimed. 'Come on, baby face, let's go. K. C. has a bit of a complex about punctuality.'

But they were doomed to be late at that dinner party. On the way to the Christbels', in fact, not far from Crystal Court, the car ran out of gasoline and Lew had to turn in at a gas station to get some.

They had been here before and while Lew beckoned an attendant and had the tank refilled, Fay gazed around for the big shaggy dog that roamed this place and which she was in the habit of petting. When she saw him appear in the doorway of the house adjoining the gas station, she gave a little whistle to attract his attention. His ears cocked in instant recognition, but as he bounded down the wooden steps of the house and darted across to greet her, a great salmon-pink car swept into the gas station and Fay's exclamation of horror mingled with the dog's shrill scream of pain, for the wheels of the pink car had smacked into him and thrown him along the gravelled front of the gas station.

Fay was gone from Lew's side in a flash. She ran to the whimpering dog, knelt down beside him and took the shaggy head upon her knee, uncaring of the blood that gushed from the muzzle, staining the lilac skirt of her dress and the side of her mink coat. But Lew had quickly followed and he bent above her, holding her shoulder. 'Watch yourself, Fay!' He spoke urgently. 'If you touch him where he's hurt, he'll turn on you.'

She ignored him, jerking her shoulder free of his fingers. She bent more closely over the dog, tears starting to her eyes at the hoarse, choking noises it was making, and at the way it shuddered and bled and bewilderedly blinked up at her in the flashing neon lighting of the gas station.

But Lew's hands came relentlessly, lifting her away from the dog, and though she struggled and fought him, he determinedly set her on one side. 'Stand there and keep quiet!' he ordered. 'If you interfere, I'll slap you!'

He crouched down by the dog and Fay watched him pass his strong brown hands along the shaggy back of the animal. His touch, careful as it was, made the dog whine hideously; made its eyes roll in its head and its teeth become bared as it sought to turn and bite the hand that touched its fierce centre of pain.

Lew glanced up at the man and woman who now stood

beside Fay. The woman had run out from the house and she stood with rolled sleeves, wiping wet hands on her apron, her face pale and alarmed in the glaring light. 'Is he bad? Is he bad?' she demanded, while the man, presumably her husband, closed rather oily fingers about her arm. Lew nodded in answer to the question. 'The poor brute's in great pain, he should be finished,' he said.

The woman cried out protestingly and her husband turned to her, speaking in a low, flurried voice: 'He's right, Gert, can't you see?' He turned again to Lew. 'Shall I go and get something –'

Lew shook his head. He bent over the dog and Fay's hands climbed to her silently moving mouth, while she shuddered, violently, at the queer, snapping noise that came. She saw the shaggy body kick, then it became still and Lew rose slowly to his great height.

Fay backed from him, backed into the small group of people who had gathered. She stared at them, her eyes suddenly swimming in tears. 'I'm sorry – I'm sorry!' she gasped, hardly knowing what she did say, only aware that she had whistled the lovable old dog under the wheels of the pink car and that Lew had been the final impassive instrument of quick death.

She turned blindly from the group of gaping people and fled across the gravel to the street.

CHAPTER SEVEN

AS FAY FLED, she stumbled in her flimsy high-heeled shoes, the long, blood-stained skirts of her dress held in her hands. She was almost desperate with the need to escape the sight of Lew's hands, curved to destroy – but as she reached the street, he caught her, spinning her towards him like a doll. 'Where the hell do you think you're going, you hysterical little fool?' he demanded. She struggled, fiercely, hating him; hating his insensitiveness, his ability to kill a dog with a face devoid of emotion. Hating his killing hands upon her.

'Listen,' he said curtly. 'That poor tyke was in agony, even a vet couldn't have helped it. I did what had to be done, and the sooner you realize it and stop behaving like a melodramatic schoolgirl, the better I'll like it. Now buck yourself up. We'll be late at the Christbels'.'

'The Christbels!' Abruptly she stopped struggling, staring up into his irritated face. 'But I don't want to go! Not now! Not now!'

He shook her, impatiently. 'You try me to the point of sheer murder at times, Fay! Anyway, to hell with your scruples!' He turned her and forcibly walked her to the car, uncaring that she stumbled in her high heels.

'I'm – all over blood!' she gasped. 'The poor thing bled all over me!' When they reached the car, she stood by the headlights and despairingly showed him the skirt of her dress, splashed with blood and dirtied where she had knelt in oil-stained gravel.

Lew's face was expressive of various emotions in that moment: patience tried to breaking point, annoyance as with a vexatious child, and something also of reluctant sympathy. 'Why the hell did you have to cuddle the brute?' he demanded. 'You honestly are the limit, Fay! Now we'll have to go home and get you a change of finery. Come on, get in.' He helped her into the car and she watched him with big, scared eyes as he walked round the car and climbed in beside her, slamming the door.

Back at the apartment, Fay followed Lew drearily into the sitting-room and said no word of protest when he poured neat whisky into a glass and made her drink it. She coughed as the spirit bit into her throat and brought tears to her eyes.

'Don't make me go with you!' She clung to his arm, lifting imploring eyes to his face. 'Please, Lew! It won't matter if I don't go.'

'Won't it?' His mouth thinned obstinately. 'I beg to differ. Come on, let's get you out of that dress.'

He marched her into the bedroom, drew off her coat and carelessly tossed it to a chair.

'Get that dress off,' Lew said curtly, striding to the wardrobe and jerking open the door. He ran an impatient hand along the rack inside, pulling out a turquoise blue creation with a pattern of rose-pink sequins spreading on one side of the skirt. It was quite pretty, but nothing near as daring and flattering as the lilac dress, and there was a rather dry twist to Lew's mouth as he brought the dress to Fay.

'K. C. isn't a guy who extends invitations to dinner every night of the week,' he said firmly, 'and I'm darned if I'll turn up there tonight without you. He and Magda want to meet you and they're going to meet you. Now wipe that damned paint off your eyes, it's running. And stop looking at me as though I've committed a murder.'

The house was like something out of a Civil War saga: white and graceful, with Corinthian pillars and a black butler with a pompadour of silver hair.

He ushered Fay and Lew into a hall of magnificent proportions, tiled in black and white, with a goldfish pond as its centrepiece and diamond-bright chandeliers flashing high in the painted ceiling. Fay felt as though she had stepped into an extravagant film set, and her very first glimpse of Karl Christbel did nothing to dispel the feeling.

Her apprehension and her nervousness, because she and Lew were late getting to the house, diminished rapidly as she was introduced to this bouncing ball of a man, all glistening bald head, glistening cheeks, and glistening black eyes. He looked neither the supreme power behind the great sprawling studios where Lew worked nor the amatory partner of Thalia Van Deen.

But his wife, Magda, lived up to Jerry's description of her as a magnificent heavyweight blonde in her early fifties.

She wore beautifully draped black and her diamonds were many, sparkling in the synthetic waves of her hair and halfway up her dimpled arms. She laughingly dismissed their lateness, saying to Lew, in a loud, accented voice, 'Better late than not come at all, huh?' She turned her laughing, richly tinted face to Fay. 'How come this big, bad boy bring you so late?' She reached out a plump, heavily ringed hand and pinched Fay's cheek. 'Was busy kissing you, maybe?'

Fay blushed and Magda gave Lew a broad wink. 'Is so, huh?' Her expansive bosom shook with appreciative amusement. 'Ah, well, youth is but a small time. It quickly pass. One day,' she inclined her head towards Fay and swept a glittering hand down her own stout body, 'one day she will look like me, then what you do, you big, bad boy?'

Lew laughed and lifted his brows at Fay, slender Fay, with her wisp of a waist and her delicate wrists and ankles. 'What do you think I'll do?' he enquired of her.

She met his amused glance and she was perversely moved to retort, 'I think, by that time, you'd have long since found yourself a new toy.'

She turned, then, to follow Magda to the drawing-room, where about eight or nine people were gathered, drinking highballs and awaiting the dinner gong. Fay was relieved to find that the dinner party was such a comparatively small one and that it did not include Thalia Van Deen.

Fay's table companions were a tall, auburn-haired girl, who appeared to be at the party on her own, and a man in a tartan dinner jacket, who would keep talking about his gastric ulcer, informing Fay that this dinner (which he was putting away with the gusto of a boiler attendant) would just about kill him in the morning. Fay, drawing upon her nursing experience, had to smile and agree with him.

Suddenly the girl on her left leant towards her and said, 'We're in for a bit of fun after dinner. Magda and Karl have got hold of a real live gypsy fortune-teller, and according to the grapevine, we're all going to have our fortunes told.' Her smile flashed gaily. 'I'm hoping she's going to promise me a present like that one across the table – that big guy, talking to Magda.'

Fay followed her glance across the table and a quick smile moved on her mouth as she bent her head to her duck in aspic. 'That guy,' the redhead continued, 'gives me prickles up my spine.'

'Really?' A twinkle was in Fay's blue eyes.

'Don't tell me he leaves you cold!' the girl exclaimed, looking incredulous.

'Oh, I quite agree that he's good-looking,' Fay smiled.

'He's more than that!' The girl was frankly admiring Lew. 'That barbaric hunk is born out of his century. I see him striding the deck of a pirate galleon, a blood-stained cutlass in his hand.'

'Or racing chariots down the Appian Way,' Fay murmured.

The girl's eyes sparkled into Fay's. 'So you do see what I mean? You do see that touch of the brute patrician? That guy could hurt like hell, but boy, I don't think I'd mind!'

'Wouldn't you?' Fay looked curious. 'Just because he's something out of the ordinary, does that mean he has to be excused an ordinary code of behaviour?'

The girl considered the question, her attention caught by Fay's sudden look of seriousness. 'I guess nine women out of ten would excuse that guy quite a lot. The tenth, in my opinion, would have to be a pretty cold potato.' She grinned. 'Don't tell me you wouldn't make excuses for that handsome brute?'

'I make them all day long.' Fay's lashes swept down over her eyes. 'He's my husband.'

'Wow!' The girl's fork clattered against her plate. 'Wow to that! And you let me pour out my girlish, pounding heart.' She laughed, shaking her auburn head. 'Still, I guess you're well used to listening to the envious sighs of other women, aren't you?'

'Mostly it's their incredulous gasps I listen to,' Fay returned.

The girl looked perplexed for a moment, her eyes wandering the pale earnestness of Fay's small face. Then her good-humoured mouth quirked. 'I'm not incredulous,' she said. 'I'm thinking that you're exactly the sort of kitten that big bold pirate would carry about with him. I envy you no end.'

'Really?' Fay's smile held irony. Such a remark would once have pleased her, now it only seemed to her to underline Lew's mere possession of her. His kitten! His toy! His small piece of plunder!

After dinner, when they were all assembled in the handsome drawing-room, Karl Christbel announced his intention of producing the fortune-teller. Lew looked frankly unimpressed. He turned to Fay, on the arm of whose chair he was lounging. He lazily ran his finger down her arm. 'This is my fortune, Magda,' he said. He grinned at Fay. 'You are, aren't you, baby?'

She met his eyes, sustained their dark, smiling ownership. 'If you say so, Lew,' she replied.

The Christbels' fortune-teller was an awesome-looking creature, tall, cavernous and middle-aged, with glittering, jet-black eyes and a swarthy skin. Her left cheek carried a small tattoo and she wore any amount of cascading coins about her neck and a red bandana about her head. Her hands were large and extremely coarse and as she sat at the table to which Karl Christbel conducted her she shuffled a pack of dog-eared cards in them. Most of the assembled party were looking rather awestruck by her, but Lew was openly grinning and sweeping her gaunt figure with insolent, quizzing eyes.

She sat watching the cards as they ran through her fingers, then abruptly she glanced up and her jet eyes settled on Lew. His open amusement, his sad lack of proper regard for the art as old as the Romany race itself, had piqued the fortune-teller's pride, and she singled him out, made of him her first victim.

She threw out a sudden dirty hand towards him and her deep, harsh voice rang through the room. 'You doubt my ability to read the future, don't you, young man? You think that it lies hidden behind a veil too thick for human eyes to penetrate?'

He nodded, his eyes wicked. 'You mystification quacks don't impress me one little bit,' he replied.

'You won't, then, step to this table and choose two of my cards?' she asked.

'I'll do it, for the fun of the thing.' He rose from the arm of Fay's chair and approached the table. The gypsy sat moving her well-worn cards about the table top, the coins about her neck giving out a low, barbaric jangling. The look she wore as she watched Lew, tall and unimpressed by her, a cigar smoking in his mouth, was wholly malignant. Then, as he drew nearer to her, a curious spasm passed over her face; her top lip seemed to lift away from her teeth and a piercing look came into her eyes. Only for a second was that look distinguishable, then her coarse black lashes swept down, veiling it.

When Lew reached the table, she gestured to him to turn two of the cards and he carelessly did so. A black king and a red joker lay side by side.

'Well,' Lew drawled, 'penetrate the veil, reveal the future, if you can.'

The woman began to laugh a deep, cavernous laugh that again set her yards of strung coins jangling. With a forefinger set with a hard, yellowed nail she moved the red joker on to the black king. She said, through her laughter, 'In your case, young man, it is better that I leave the veil undisturbed.' Her glance went across the room to Fay, who was watching the scene at the table with large, wondering eyes. The yellowed forefinger was pointed at Fay. 'For your sake I'll do this,' she cried across the room.

Lew's hand reached for the woman's shoulder, closing hard on the bony strength of it, closing until her swarthy head swivelled to him once more. 'Don't try to frighten her!' he said, his voice suddenly empty of all amusement.

A curious silence lay over the room as he said that; a watching, bated silence. All eyes were upon him and the gypsy, yet Fay received the strangest impression that all thought was suddenly concentrated upon her. She shrank in her chair and prayed for an end to that scene at the table.

'It doesn't lie in my power to frighten your wife,' the gypsy said, and her beak of a nose was imperious as she stared up at Lew. 'It lies with you.'

Then she jerked her shoulder free of his fingers and snatched up her strewn cards. She began to re-shuffle them, running her eyes round the room. 'Who will come now?' she demanded, and Fay saw the auburn-haired girl who had been her companion at dinner rise and stroll to the table.

Fay was very quiet going home in the car. It had been a strange, nightmarish evening and now she felt drained of vitality, emptied of everything but a weary apprehension. She sat with her face turned from Lew, watching the darkened avenues skim by, the odour of oranges over high, white walls coming to her.

What had the gypsy meant? What lay in the future? Fay shivered and turned her cold cheek against the cold leather of the car. She was suddenly very close to tears, her heart crying out for reassurance. The reassurance that was not available. Her life with Lew stood on shifting sand; any day he might grow weary of her, and though she knew his cruel streak, his untamable arrogance, she shrank from a future empty of him. He might not possess the gentle understanding Jerry gave so unstintingly, but he held her heart – held, too, the power to break it.

CHAPTER EIGHT

FAY CLUNG to her friendship with Jerry, clutching to it as though to a lifeline, feeling sometimes that if it slipped from her she would be irretrievably drowned and lost in this strange, bewildering world she had entered out of love for a man who didn't love her.

But in her innocence she didn't know that people were beginning to talk . . . which talk suddenly reached Lew's ears at a party of Olive Hadley's.

Jerry had danced Fay out on to the terrace of Olive's penthouse and as they stood looking at the fairyland of lights below them, he said, 'What a night for a drive! How about it, Fay?'

'Oh, I couldn't!' she said, but her eyes, meeting his, were openly wistful. The party was smoky and noisy and the thought of a drive on such a clear, still night was infinitely tempting.

'Lew won't miss you,' Jerry pressed. 'He's too busy playing poker.'

'How – how long would we be gone?' She was rapidly weakening and she knew it.

'Half an hour, no more.' He grinned. 'Come on, be a little unwifely for once. You're the talk of the town already with your devotion.'

'You mean – people laugh because I sit in a corner while Lew goes off to talk films or play poker?' she said, her face going pink.

Jerry didn't deny her assertion. 'I guess they do,' he replied.

So Fay went with him. But they were gone a lot longer than half an hour. Jerry's beautiful cream Cadillac ate up the miles so smoothly, so pleasantly, and it was such sheer joy to ride through the soft night, under the enormous stars, that Fay just didn't notice the passage of time.

They took the ocean road and the wind carried with it the salt tang of the sea, while the mysticism of the moon rode high and white above the flowing black sheet of the sea. The radio in the car played softly, dreamily, and Fay gazed up at the stars, flashing points of light in midnight blue velvet – a mysterious world of singing silence, flooding her with a cool release from care as she rode beside Jerry.

'Loosen your hair, Fay,' he said suddenly. 'Let the wind blow through it.'

'Shall I?' Her eyes were big on his face. Then, with a laugh, she complied, pulling the jewelled pins from the chignon she wore tonight and dropping them into her bag.

The needle on the speedometer moved forward as Jerry pressed on the accelerator and the soft wind whipped Fay's cheeks and sent her fair hair flowing back from her face. 'This is lovely!' she cried. 'This is like being in a chariot, flying through the sky.'

'Funny kid!' Jerry muttered, and Fay didn't notice that the

usual merry twinkle was missing from his eyes. She didn't even question his unusual silence when he stopped the car upon a hill and lay back against the leather of the car, the smoke of his cigarette drifting in a thin blue line to the sky. She was content to be as silent as he, wrapped in the sure warmth of his friendship.

Then, after a while, he began to speak – to speak about himself, which was also unusual for Jerry. 'Ever heard of the Bronx, Fay?' he queried.

'Vaguely,' she admitted. 'By way of books and films.'

'Sure.' He grinned slightly. 'The Bronx is notoriously fascinating to the author and the film-maker – only I lived there and I didn't find it fascinating. My folks died when I was a kid and I knocked around after that on the edge of a sprawling Italian family. They weren't bad, but they didn't have much, they couldn't really afford to feed me, so I quit the Bronx when I was thirteen. I hitched out here to California and got me a job on a fruit farm. Then the farm folded and I got me a job mopping floors and serving beers in a poolroom – and that's how it went on, a succession of cheap jobs, too many cheap meals, and my envious eyes following the flashy, expensive cars of the movie stars day in and day out. Why not me? I thought. I had curls, I had muscles, so why not me?' He fell silent for a moment, studying the red end of his cigarette. Then he went on: 'I got to be a movie star and I got me this car – but sometimes I think I've got nothing. I'm thirty-two, Fay. I'm the kind of a guy who should be settled in a comfortable rut with a wife and a couple of noisy kids, but I've got nothing.'

'Haven't you ever been in love, Jerry?' Fay asked quietly.

'Yeah!' Abruptly he tossed his cigarette butt over the side of the car. 'With another man's wife.'

'Oh, Jerry!'

'I endorse that sentiment.' His smile was cynical. 'It's a lonely business, being in love with another man's wife.'

So they sat, and they talked, and the half-hour Jerry had promised became unconsciously extended to two hours – two hours that went like the wind.

They got back to the party after everyone had gone home – everyone except Lew.

He sat in his overcoat at Olive's big piano, idly picking out a tune with one finger, a cigar in his mouth. Olive lounged in a low chair by the fireplace, her eyes, as they rested on Fay and Jerry in the doorway, frankly sympathetic.

Fay's heart was banging as she stood beside Jerry, gazing across at Lew, across this room that was stale with cigarette smoke, littered with smeared cocktail glasses and overflowing ashtrays. Her ride with Jerry had been entirely innocent, but the very set of Lew's shoulders, the aggressive way his cigar jutted from his mouth, made guilt and fear flower in her.

Then he rose lazily from the piano stool. 'Ready to go home now?' he enquired of her, his eyes unfathomable as they rested on her frightened face, roamed her tumbled hair.

'Now look here, Lew,' Jerry broke in, 'don't go getting any ideas –'

'Ideas?' Lew was quietly folding his silk scarf into his overcoat. 'What ideas should I get?'

'We merely went for a drive –'

'How very pleasant!' Lew turned to Olive. 'Well, so long, Olive. We'll see you.' He came over. His hand closed on Fay's arm and he drew her smoothly from the room.

He said not a word as they drove home, and Fay, frightened by his manner, couldn't have put two coherent words together. She knew how it must have looked and she shrank in her seat. The amused glances at Lew when, bored with playing poker, he came looking for her and she was no longer in her corner. Then someone would have told him, undoubtedly smiling, probably glad to see the high and mighty Lew Marsh put out of countenance for once: 'Oh, she slipped out with Jerry Kaufmann – hours ago, my dear!'

With Jerry! Whom he hated!

As the lift rode to the top floor of Crystal Court, as they stepped out and walked to the door of the apartment, Fay shivered. It was a warm night, but she felt cold, inside and out.

Lew unlocked the door of the apartment and they stepped inside, Fay's hand moving automatically to the light switch. She walked drearily forward into the room and stood removing her silk wrap. Then, unable to bear any longer the silence that stood between them like a wall, she spoke. 'Go ahead, Lew,' she said, 'tell me exactly what you think of me.'

He didn't answer and she turned to look at him, her blue wrap half off her shoulders and exactly reflecting the colour of her eyes. She looked strangely lovely then, gazing at him in half-fearful, half-apologetic defiance. 'Oh, go ahead!' she cried. 'I know you're annoyed with me. If we're going to quarrel because I went for an innocent little drive with Jerry, let's get it over with.'

'Innocent drive?' he said, his mouth wry. 'Was it really?'

Her blue eyes flashed. 'If you're implying that it was anything else, then you're wrong. And insulting.'

'You're gone for two solid hours with a guy like Kaufmann and you expect me to believe that it was all sweet niece and uncle?' he demanded.

'I do! We drove and drove. We didn't even talk much.'

'Oh, I can well believe that you didn't talk much,' Lew drawled.

As he said that, Fay began to tremble, but not with fear. Suddenly she was wildly angry. She swung away from him and made for her bedroom. How dared he imply that Jerry had made love to her! How dared he! Didn't Lew know her yet? Didn't he know that she could never, and would never, suffer any man's kisses but his? Another man's sympathy was one thing, but another man's lovemaking something she never even thought about, let alone wanted.

When she switched on the bedside light and looked at herself in the dressing-table mirror, she saw that she was as pale as the lilies of the valley at the neck of her dress. She unpinned the spray with fingers that shook, while Lew stood sternly in the doorway, his hands thrust into the pockets of his overcoat.

'If it had been any guy but Kaufmann, I'd believe you,

Fay,' he said. 'But I refuse to believe that guy kept his hands off you for two solid hours. He isn't that self-controlled or that noble.'

Fay swung round. 'You refuse! You refuse!' she cried. 'Well, I refuse to be accused of something I haven't done!'

But Lew only smiled, slowly and mockingly. 'Why all the heat if you're telling the truth?' he drawled.

Temper flared wildly in Fay, burning away love, discretion, everything. 'You're in no position to take away either my character or Jerry's! You're only the despicable swine who sent Inez Holden to her death!' she cried.

Lew was across the room in two strides then, gripping her shoulders so hard he bruised them. 'Who told you that?' he demanded.

'Thalia Van Deen.' Fay met his glittering eyes unflinchingly. 'Weeks ago.'

'I see. And you believed her, eh?'

'Well, it's the truth, isn't it? Even Pat Merryweather said it was true.' The words broke recklessly, bitterly from Fay as she gazed up into Lew's eyes, gone black and dangerous in a face where a sudden nerve of temper pulsed beside his mouth. 'Thalia intimated that you treated that poor girl like dirt. She said you openly admitted at the inquest that you had – "shown her the door". '

'And your estimation of me now is that I'm an unrelieved swine, eh?' he spoke quietly and his eyes were losing their menacing glitter, cynicism creeping back into them.

'Yes, Lew, that's my estimation of you exactly,' she replied; wanting to hurt him; hoping she hurt him.

'What if I denied Thalia's story?' he enquired.

'You'd be wasting your time!' she flashed. 'I'm not the starry-eyed little bumpkin you brought to Hollywood, Lew. You can't fool me any more. I know you now.'

'You do, huh?' He watched her a moment longer, his face quite expressionless, then his hands dropped from her. He turned away and quietly collected his pyjamas, dressing gown and slippers. 'I'll sleep in the other room tonight,' he said. 'Doubtless you'd prefer me to.'

As the door closed on him, Fay stood very still, staring at the door, hardly daring to believe that he had gone – gone so quietly.

She undressed in a daze of misery; she was too miserable even for tears. She stood at the dressing-table brushing her hair, and her face, staring back at her from the mirror, was quite colourless. Lew would never forgive her – for saying it all – for knowing it all.

She laid aside the hairbrush and sank down on the bed, pressing her cold face to the cold silk of the coverlet. How strange his eyes had looked when she had cried aloud that girl's name! More startled, at first, than angry. Surely he must have realized that she'd get to hear the story sooner or later? In this town, this hotbed of gossip, it was the sort of titbit that was bandied about all the time; if she hadn't heard it from Thalia, she'd have heard it from somebody else.

Yet now, remembering his startled eyes, the mask of awful anger that had come to his face, she knew a sudden regret that she had taunted him with her knowledge of Inez Holden. She lay prone on the bed, full of wild speculation as to how he would behave towards her in the morning. Would he say they were through? Would he tell her to get out of his life? Her heart came into her throat.

Though he often hurt her with his impatience, his inability to understand how she could be reduced to tongue-tied nervousness by men he openly called jelly-bags, and women he scornfully labelled ambitious strumpets, there were other times when he put himself out to please her. Taking her out to dine at one of the quieter, less fashionable restaurants she liked, where they ate dinner in a dusky garden, under swinging lanterns, the scent of heliotrope and orange blossom all about them. Taking her out into the country in the car and chasing her in the tall, sweet grass, thrusting handfuls of it down her back and laughing aloud at her breathless protestations.

She lay motionless, her face in her arms, emotion utterly spent in her. She no longer cared that Lew had chosen to believe that her moonlight drive with Jerry had been motivated by a desire for Jerry's lovemaking. All she knew was that she, swearing she loved Lew, had allowed her love to falter. While he, who had promised no love, had kept scrupulously to his side of the bargain.

Not once, in all the weeks of their marriage, had his interest strayed from her to another woman, yet she had seen exquisite creatures, golden-skinned from the beach, full of vivacious, sensuous appeal, throw openly inviting glances at him. He smiled at them, raising his black brows in quizzing, frank enjoyment of their beauty and their desire to flirt, but he went on holding her to his side with a firm brown hand.

What motivated his strange faithfulness – her likeness to Inez Holden? Her hand gripped the silk bedspread; her nails rasped upon the silk ...

She slept restlessly, lost and lonely in the big bed, missing Lew's hard, warm arms about her. When she awoke it was still very early, but she threw back the bedclothes and left the bed with thankfulness. Her night had been haunted by restless dreams and she was glad to get to the kitchen and busy herself with the making of breakfast.

As she carried breakfast into the sitting-room, she examined Lew's face with apprehension. He was reading the paper and he didn't look up as she put his plate of bacon and eggs in front of him. Why didn't he speak? Anything was preferable to this awful silence. But he didn't speak, he just ate his usual sound breakfast, drank his usual three cups of coffee and once again took up the paper at the sports section.

Fay, in a sudden excess of misery, pushed aside her untouched breakfast and rose to go to the kitchen, to get away from his impassive face. She was at the door when he said, 'Don't forget we're going to the premiere of Bill's film tonight.'

'Do you want me to go?' she asked, not turning to look at him.

She heard his chair scrape back and suddenly he was behind her, swinging her towards him. His dark face wore an irate impatience. 'I don't intend to spoil Bill's bit of pleasure because we've had a row,' he snapped. 'The poor guy's been pretty sick these last few weeks and tonight's mighty important to him.'

'All right, Lew,' she said. 'I'm not exactly keen to spoil Bill's evening myself.'

'Excellent!' he retorted, and strode from the room, banging the door. A minute later she heard him leave the apartment.

CHAPTER NINE

THE FOYER of the big cinema where the film of Bill Symans' novel, *Hunter's Moon*, was to be shown, was noisy and crowded, glittering with expensive jewellery, neon lighting and the dazzle of flashlight bulbs. The air was smoky and perfumed, and the excited burr of many voices rode above the sensuous rustle of silk and taffeta, shimmering under the fabulous gleam of mink.

Fay felt stunned by this wave of noise, brightness and perfume as she entered the foyer with Lew and Bill Symans. And she jumped nervously when a flashlight bulb seemed to explode right into her face. She heard Lew laugh and when she glanced up at him, he pulled a mocking face at her. 'You have got the jumps tonight, my sweet,' he murmured.

Embarrassed colour swept into her cheeks. She rarely enjoyed these glamorous functions, but this one would be harder than most to get through.

She stood tensely between Lew and Bill, aware of painted eyes upon her, appraising her hair, set in a Grecian style at Olive Hadley's that afternoon; the wine-red velvet of her wrap, the jewels in her ears. She wanted to run out into the night. She didn't belong here. She was rejected on every side; even Lew rejected her!

As she lowered her head and bit at her lips to stop them

from trembling, Bill's hand suddenly closed on her hand. He murmured, 'Try pretending you're at the zoo. Pretend they're all a gorgeous set of beasts paraded for your mere amusement. I always do and it always works.' A smile crept into his voice. 'Look, d'you see that tall tigress in lemon and sable, the one who hasn't had any dinner – you can see she hasn't eaten, she's almost snarling? See that little parakeet in emerald? See that delicious squirrel with the turned-up nose and the button eyes?'

Fay had to laugh. 'A few bars around them would make me feel a little easier,' she confessed. 'I'm frightened to death they're all going to pounce on me and gobble me up.' She smiled up at Bill, grateful for his understanding. His thin face was very gentle, but it was also very tired and strained, and immediate concern caught at her heart. 'Are you feeling all right, Bill?' she asked.

'Fit as a fiddle!' he retorted, but with a twinkle in his eye that frankly admitted he knew he wasn't fooling her.

Hunter's Moon was a psychological thriller, a beautifully produced, soundly acted film that would have held Fay's undivided attention had her mind not been on Bill half the time. His eyes wore a febrile luminosity tonight, and once, when he touched Fay's arm and murmured something about the film, his hand burned her dryly.

She watched him covertly, and when, halfway through the film, he quietly quitted his seat, she turned urgently to Lew. 'I don't think Bill's very well,' she whispered. 'He's just gone out of the foyer.'

Lew rose at once and the two of them hurried out after

Bill. He was sitting in one of the low gilt chairs ranged against the walls of the foyer, fighting to breathe and looking so ghastly that Lew said hurriedly to Fay, 'I'll get a cab.' He strode out through the swing doors of the cinema, past the gaping, noisy crowd that had gathered to see the coming and going of the many stars attending this première, and curious glances followed his tall, grim figure. A couple of girls giggled and called out after him, but he didn't hear them; wasn't even conscious of their presence. He saw Bill, half fainting against the wine-red of Fay's wrap.

When they were in the cab, Bill said apologetically, 'I feel a regular wet blanket, but you two chumps needn't have left the film, y'know.'

'To hell with the film!' Lew exclaimed, watching Bill worriedly. There were gleaming fans of moisture in the deep scoops under Bill's eyes and his nostrils were waxen white and taut with pain. A flicker of affectionate amusement came into Bill's tired eyes as he met Lew's worried look. 'You look all het up, old boy,' he murmured. 'Relax, there's a pal, I'm not going to croak, not yet.'

But when they got to Bill's apartment, Lew took up the phone and called Bill's doctor. It wasn't only the look of Bill that prompted him, it was the professional watchfulness in Fay's eyes. He wasn't forgetting that she had been a nurse.

'You're making a heck of a lot of fuss, Lew,' Bill protested. 'I'm often like this. It passes.' But his smile, as Fay carefully loosened his collar and removed his bow-tie, was a mere ghost of his usual cheerful one. 'Where's the stuff you take for this, Bill?' Fay asked. 'In the bathroom?'

'Cabinet! Top shelf!' he gasped.

She hurried to the bathroom, and it was as she reached up for the pills that a sudden frightening feeling of dizziness seized her. She lay back against the cold tiles of the wall, fighting her weakness, breathing deeply, slowly, clinging to a solid world, a world that did not spin and lurch, with all her might. It was minutes before she was again fully aware of the smooth coldness of the wall tiles under her pressing hands, the nervous hurrying of her heart.

She stood like a stone creature, spreadeagled against the wall, and the suspicion of a week or two slowly turned to certainty within her.

She was going to have a baby!

When she returned to the sitting-room with Bill's medicine, she looked pale, but otherwise collected. She attended to him, carefully stroked the fair hair back off his beaded forehead. 'Feel a little easier?' she asked.

He nodded. 'Um, that's very pleasant!' He lifted his own hand and held hers pressed to his forehead. 'You've a nice cool hand, Fay. Cool hand, warm heart, don't they say?' His grey eyes dwelt on hers. 'Lew's a darn lucky guy. Does he know it?'

She coloured fiercely, and was relieved when he turned his glance on Lew, who was sprawled out in an armchair, a whisky and soda in his hand. His vital good looks, his dark vigour, were in strong contrast to Bill's febrile, brittle look, and Bill, as though realizing it, smiled sadly. 'You're so darned healthy, you're almost disgusting, Lew,' he said. 'You make me feel like a weak old lady.'

Lew didn't return Bill's smile. Instead he said harshly, 'God plays damn funny tricks, putting pain and sickness in a guy like you and a houseful of health in a guy like me! I'd give up an arm to remedy that, I'd change places with you right now if I could.'

'Now that's foolish kid talk, Lew, and you know it,' Bill rejoined. 'If I'm not bitter about all this, then you've no right to be so.'

'Bitter!' Lew's chiselled face was a mask of bitterness. 'I'm passionately bitter. I curse the Almighty for what he's done to you.' He stared down into the glass he held gripped in his hands. 'The world's bound to be a rotten place, when everything good is taken out of it.'

'That's a harsh philosophy, Lew.' Bill was frowning. 'It's in all of us to be good or bad, weak or strong and God takes from every category. His is the final word on whatever happens to us and I refuse to question His word. There is doubtless a reason for all that He gives us or subjects us to. Glory in your strength, Lew; be grateful for all the sunshine that comes into your life and bear with the darkness.'

But Lew was shaking his head and his dour glance left Bill and settled on Fay. 'Sunshine merely settles on the skin, it doesn't penetrate, or so I've found,' he murmured cynically. 'Perhaps I deflect it, eh?'

When the doctor arrived, Lew drew Fay to one side and told her that she was to go home. 'You're looking a trifle whacked,' he said. 'I'll hang on here until Bill feels a little better. Have you got enough money for the cab?'

She nodded.

'Go on, then,' he said. 'I shan't be late home.'

As she ran down the steps of the apartment house and walked to the curb to hail a cab, a long cream Cadillac drew smoothly to a standstill in front of her and she found herself looking into the smiling gamin face of Jerry Kaufmann.

'Hullo, kid,' he said. 'Can I give you a lift?'

Fay stared at him, startled and uneasy. Last night he had been her best friend, but now that Lew had chosen to misinterpret that friendship, to see in it something guilty, Fay now felt guilty about it.

'Come on,' Jerry opened the door of the car. 'We've got things to talk about.'

But still she hesitated. 'How did you know I was here?' she asked.

'I was at the première. I saw you and Lew leave with Bill Symans. I followed the three of you. I've been hanging about here, hoping to get a glimpse of you.' His voice dropped into a more intimate key. 'I didn't dare to hope that I'd get to talk to you.'

'Jerry – I daren't come with you!' she burst out.

His smile froze as he watched her. 'Has Lew played heavy with you as well?'

'W – what do you mean?'

'He's had me pulled out of *Corn In The City*.'

Her hand flew to her mouth in shocked distress. 'Oh, no!'

'He's quite a boy, isn't he? Now do you feel like letting me give you a lift?'

She nodded dumbly. He reached over and drew her into

the car beside him and as they pulled out from the curb he said, 'I was going to keep away from you, Fay, then I saw you at the première tonight and bang went my good resolution.' He glanced at her, his eyes almost melancholy. 'I'm in love with you, kid. I've been in love with you for weeks.'

Her hands gripped on her bag. She gazed at him miserably. She didn't know what to say.

'Oh, don't go worrying about it!' He summoned up his old smile. 'It's just one of those things. I'll tell you something, though. I'm a better guy than Lew Marsh. You might give that some consideration.'

She bit her lip. 'I'm – I'm sorry about the film, Jerry. I hope you're not out of work.'

He laughed. 'Lord, no! But I wasn't exactly pleased about being thrown out of that film. It was a darn good part.'

They were silent then, until he turned the car into the circular drive of Crystal Court. But as the engine of the car ceased to purr, Jerry gently touched the wine-red velvet of Fay's wrap. 'Look,' he said, 'are you really happy with Lew Marsh? Are you, Fay? I've got to know.'

She looked away from him. She could feel his hand touching her wrap, smoothing the velvet. He was nice; he was gentle and kind, but his declaration of love had meant nothing at all to her.

'Of course I'm happy with Lew.' She spoke carefully. 'I understand him. I know he seems callous and hard, but – I understand him.'

'You little fool!' Jerry whispered, and suddenly his arms were around her and he was drawing her against him, but when he tried to kiss her, she began to struggle. She pulled fiercely back from him, exerting all her strength. 'Don't! Don't you dare!' she said, in a cold, hurrying whisper. 'I don't want you! How dare you think I want you!'

His hands dropped from her. His gamin, expressive face showed his hurt. 'I'm sorry!' he said. He watched her as she fumbled with the door of the car, as she stepped out on to the gravel of the drive. He watched her walk away, pass in through the swing doors of Crystal Court. He sighed, and sank back in his seat as the doors swung gently backwards and forwards, banishing her slim figure from his sight.

He sat very still for minutes on end. Once he drew out his cigarette-case, and then dropped it back into his pocket. Suddenly he threw open the door of the car and he, too, went hurrying towards the swing doors.

When the apartment bell rang, three times, peremptorily, Fay's nerves jumped.

She thought at once of Bill, that perhaps Lew had sent over a message about Bill. But even as she was hurrying to the door, she was dismissing the thought. Lew would phone, he wouldn't waste time sending messages.

She opened the door and she stared at Jerry. Anger came washing back over her. 'What do you want, Jerry? Haven't you finished pestering me yet?' she demanded.

He put his hand against the door, as though afraid she'd slam it in his face. 'We haven't said everything yet, Fay,' he spoke urgently, his almond eyes a warm, pleading brown. 'We can't just turn away from each other, become strangers. I won't let that happen. Please let me come in! Let me talk to you!' His hand pressed more insistently on the door and he gently forced himself past her into the apartment. He closed the door and stood with his back to it.

'What's happened to us?' he asked. 'We were pals. What's Lew said to you to make you turn against me?'

But she wouldn't answer, nervously twisting a chiffon handkerchief about in her hands, the diamonds of her wedding ring flashing under the gauzy material.

'I want to know, Fay. I've a right to know,' he insisted.

'Well, isn't it natural he should resent your attentions?' She threw back her head and met his eyes. 'He is my husband.'

Jerry's mobile mouth curled scornfully. 'And just look at you – a picture of wedded bliss! A face as pale as a lily and eyes that have forgotten how to smile!' He looked her over, carefully, sadly. She wore a dress of soft, sheer, silver-grey wool, most beautifully embroidered in wine-red at the waist and at the neck. Small rubies gleamed in her ears. She looked delicately smart, delicately expensive.

'I can remember you the way you looked that day on the beach.' Jerry smiled gently. 'You wore a lemon bathing suit and your hair was tied back with a piece of lemon ribbon. You looked like a little kid. I wanted to pick you up, then, and carry you off. Maybe I should have done. I think you'd have come with me then.'

And as he spoke of that day, she too remembered, and remembering, she smiled. 'Perhaps I would have done, Jerry,' she admitted.

'And now it's too late?' he asked.

She nodded tiredly. 'I married Lew. I married him knowing

he only wanted a plaything, so I've myself to blame if he treats me as such. But a bargain's a bargain, so I shall stay with him for as long as he wants me to.'

'But that isn't good enough!' Jerry stepped towards her, took and gripped her hands. His face was rather grim. 'Fay, honey, you were made to be a man's pride, a man's pal! You weren't made to be shut up in a damned expensive apartment like some hothouse flower! Kid, I can give you laughs! A ride on a roller-coaster, an afternoon at the ball game. I know how to be a kid – and you know how to be one.' His eyes implored her. 'Come with me, honey! Come now, before it's too late. Before that guy kills every bit of laughing youth in you.'

'But I love him!' She pulled her hands free of his. She stood before him, slim and fair and strangely poised. Her poise bewildered him. He preferred her shy gaucherie, her little-girl-lost air.

'You're enslaved by the guy!' he declared bitterly. 'You'll wake up when it's too late – just like Inez did. He broke her, he'll do the same to you.'

'I won't listen to talk like that,' she cried angrily. 'What right have you got to disparage Lew? Are you any better than he is?'

He frowned. A kind of wariness came into his eyes. 'What do you mean by that?' he asked. 'What's Lew said about me?'

'He implied that your reputation was on about the same level as his own, if you must know.'

'And what do you think? Do you think that I'm in his class?' Jerry demanded.

She turned away wearily. She shook her head. 'We're not getting anywhere, talking like this,' she said. 'We're only hurting one another. I'm sorry I can't love you, Jerry. I think it's a great pity I can't. But Lew's in my heart, for good or ill. I can't just push him out.'

She felt Jerry's hand on her shoulder. 'No, kid, as you say, it isn't easy pushing someone out of your heart. I'm not going to find it easy, pushing you out. You crept in, with your little face and your big eyes.' His voice softened. 'I thought you liked me, Fay. You always danced in my arms as though you were real glad to be in them; as though they were some safe harbour you'd found in the middle of a storm.'

Her heart seemed to turn right over as he said that. She turned to him in quick commiseration, and when he quietly put his arms round her, she let her head rest against his shoulder.

'I think I should have met you a long time ago, Jerry,' she said.

'I wish to God you had!' For a moment his arms were fierce about her. 'Fay – Fay darling, don't let Lew Marsh hurt you. I shall be frightened all the time that he'll hurt you.'

'Oh, Jerry, he isn't a monster.' She smiled sadly, and then drew away from him. She lightly touched his cheek. 'Now you'd better go. It's getting late.'

'But what about us?' he asked. 'Are only glimpses of you at premières and parties and in restaurants all I'm going to have of you?'

'I – I'm sorry, Jerry. I really am,' she said.

'Okay!' he shrugged. He even produced something of his

old merry grin. He walked to the door. He stood there, looking at her. 'Are you sure you're not sending away the wrong guy?' he asked.

She shook her head.

'I think maybe you are, kid,' he said. Then he quietly let himself out of the apartment.

CHAPTER TEN

LEW WAS late coming in, but Fay was still up, waiting for him. As he strode in, throwing off his overcoat, he stared, seeing her curled up among the scarlet cushions on the big couch. 'Why aren't you in bed?' he asked.

'I wasn't sleepy,' she said. 'How's Bill? What did the doctor say?'

'He's got to go into hospital.' Lew sighed as he came over to her and stood looking down at her. 'He won't come out, Fay. He's going to die in that damned hospital. He's thirty-three. He hasn't begun to live – to do half the things he was meant to do. He's such a good guy. Why should it happen to him?'

'I don't know, Lew. Time and time again, when I was nursing, I've seen it happen, and the sadness of it never lessened for me. I know just how you feel. It's not being able to do anything to stop it. It's such a depressing, impotent feeling, isn't it?'

He nodded.

She rose and touched his arm. 'Would you like some coffee?' she asked.

He smiled at her quietly. 'Yes, please!'

She went out to the kitchen and made coffee and ham sandwiches, and when she carried in the tray, Lew was standing at the window, staring out into the night. He looked very tall, very broad with his back to her. Fay watched him, wondering again at the complexity of his nature. Only tonight she had learned that out of pure spite he had had Jerry Kaufmann taken out of *Corn In The City*. Yet he stood there, staring into the darkness, filled with compassion for Bill, torn with impotent bitterness because there was nothing he could do to hold back the swift wings of death, so soon to close over the gentle integrity of Bill.

'Come and drink your coffee while it's hot, Lew,' she said.

He turned and came to her, throwing himself down beside her on the couch. She handed him his coffee and he stirred sugar into its steaming blackness; he never took cream in his coffee. 'By the way,' he said, 'I'm going to England in a few weeks' time.'

'England?' She stared at him.

'Directly *Corn In The City* is in the can I'm going over.' He sipped his coffee. 'K.C. wants to do Shakespeare's *The Rape of Lucrece*, and I can't help admitting I'm enthusiastic. It's a darned tricky story, of course, but if we bring it off – wow!' Lew's dark eyes gleamed. 'I'm going to Stratford-on-Avon to try and persuade a certain English actor who rusticates there to come out of retirement and play Tarquin.'

'What about censorship, Lew?' Fay asked. 'As you say, it's a tricky story.'

'That is the rub,' Lew admitted, smiling a little and biting into a sandwich, 'but Karl can afford the loss, if it turns out a loss, and I'll have had the artistic satisfaction of directing an expensive box-office flop. It's funny, but Shakespeare, with all its lust, never does too well at the box office. And d'you know why? Because most people are fools. They shrink like violets from good, honest lust, which, if only they'd be honest and admit it, is all they feel themselves in the name of love. They will wrap sex up in pretty, piffling declarations of love. The big, tough hero must carry his mate off into the bush, but by heaven, if he doesn't say, afterwards, "I love you, darling" – cut! The censor is swooning. Or the public are.'

'Well, Lew, it's human nature to like pretty wrappings,' Fay protested. 'A girl in silk, a birthday present in a coloured box, a pair of lamb chops in frilly leggings. Life would be as blunt as the back of a knife without a few pretensions, and well you know it.'

He stared at her, then he put back his head and laughed.

'Right on the chin – whacko! You've quite a punch, baby, for all that you're a featherweight.'

And as he sat laughing, she said, 'Why have you had Jerry Kaufmann taken out of *Corn In The City*?'

His laughter faded abruptly. 'So you know about that?'

'I saw Jerry – tonight.'

'Really? What was his version of the story – that I had him thrown out of the film because he was after you?'

Colour stung her cheeks. 'I imagine you did it out of spite!' she retorted coldly.

'What a delightful opinion you have of me, Fay.' He was smiling quizzically as he helped himself to more coffee. 'I wonder you can bear to sit in the same room with me.'

She turned her head away, biting her lip at the words.

'The truth is,' he went on, 'Kaufmann and I couldn't work together, it was spoiling the film. I don't let damned spite sway me, Fay, and you can believe me or disbelieve me, but I promise you I shan't start crying into my coffee if you do the latter.'

As he sipped his coffee, he studied her averted head, the delicate curve of her profile. He saw her slight breast lift on a sigh. 'Say it, Fay.' He spoke mockingly. 'Say you've stopped loving me.'

Slowly her head turned and her blue eyes bleakly examined his face. 'If it pleases you to take my wings off, do it, Lew,' she murmured.

'Is it guilt or martyrdom induces you to make the offer?' he queried.

She stared at him. 'I wonder why I love you,' she whispered. 'You're as hard as iron, aren't you?'

'If you say so,' he replied. He set aside his coffee cup and as he leant back in the couch, his hand swooped and his fingers closed like springs on her wrist. Deliberately he jerked her to him, so that she fell down upon his chest. Before she could elude him, his other hand was upon her waist and he was holding her immovable against him. 'I'm sorry I can't be the knight in shining armour you seem to want, but I'm as good to you as I know how to be.' His lips quirked. 'I'm nicer to you than I am to a lot of people.'

She stared up into his eyes, above which the black brows curved so wickedly; she felt the strong beat of his heart against her and she was acutely conscious in that moment that she carried his child. She wondered what he'd say, how he would react, if she imparted that fact to him here and now. Would he show her tenderness, or would he be discomfited that their transitory marriage was going to produce a child?

'What are you thinking?' he asked suddenly.

'Nothing.' She attempted to pull away from him. 'I'm tired, Lew. Let me go to bed.'

'A while ago you were claiming you weren't sleepy,' he mocked. 'What's the matter, my darling, are you afraid I'm going to force my passionate attentions upon you? Is my touch less thrilling now that you've sampled Kaufmann's?'

'You're despicable!' She was struggling wildly in his arms, her face white, her eyes tormented. 'Let me go! For God's sake let me go!'

'I'm damned if I will!' Suddenly his face was harsh. 'I've got something to say first; while you stay under my roof, you'll keep away from Kaufmann, understand? You're my wife and you'll do what I say. You once accused me of buying you. All right, Fay, I bought you! I bought your affection, and whilst it pleases me to enjoy that affection, I'll enjoy it, but I'll enjoy it exclusively – and when it suits me to.' Abruptly he turned her in his arms and forced her head back against the cushions of the couch. His lips came to her throat, fierce in the delicate hollow of her throat, and now she lay passive, dumb with misery.

'Is this submission or disinterest?' he murmured, mockery back in his voice.

'How can you believe I want Jerry Kaufmann? How can you?' She almost moaned the words.

'I'm as entitled to believe what I believe as you are,' he replied cryptically.

The following day Fay went to see a doctor and had the fact that she was pregnant definitely confirmed.

The doctor was a youthful, hulking man, who watched her across his desk with friendly, questioning eyes. 'What's worrying you, Mrs Marsh?' he asked. 'Kids can be great fun, you know. I've got three.'

'Three!' Fay stared at him in amazement. He looked so young. He barely looked married.

He smiled. 'Start young and they grow up with you,' he said. He grew serious. 'When I first confirmed your pregnancy your eyes lit up. Now, why are you looking sad?' He leant his elbows on the desk. 'Look, are you thinking that maybe your husband won't want this baby? I know lots of men get these crazy notions. They think that once the kids start coming, they're going to get neglected, no more petting and cooing, the baby getting it all. Is that what you're worried about, Mrs Marsh?'

She picked at the leather of her handbag with her fingernail. If only it were as simple as that, she thought.

'I guess that is my – my worry,' she murmured.

'Well,' he said, a smile breaking over his face, 'you go home and make such a fuss of the darned boob, he'll think it's his birthday. He'll want kids all the time.'

Then he grew a little more technical. He said carefully, 'I'm bound to tell you this, Mrs Marsh, but I don't want you to go getting any silly notions that you're ill or anything. The fact is, some women are made to bear children, it comes as easy to them as whipping pies out of the oven. But others – well, they aren't quite so fortunate—'

'You mean that I'm in the latter category?' Fay interjected quietly.

'I'm afraid so,' he admitted. 'You're definitely going to have to watch yourself. Take exercise, but don't overdo it. Some dancing won't hurt, but midnight balls are out, and so is any extensive travelling. A lot of women can do all these things and thrive on them, but you won't be able to.'

Fay gazed at him in consternation. 'Don't tell me I've got to behave like an invalid!' she exclaimed.

He smiled at once, shaking his head. 'Heavens, no! Just take life a little slower, a little easier, especially for these first few months. And I want you to come and see me regularly.'

Fay walked from the doctor's office in something of a daze. Perhaps it was just as well Lew hadn't asked her to go to England with him. No extensive travelling! The fates were really combining to separate her from Lew – even if he asked her now, she would have to refuse.

Then, three weeks later, Bill Symans died.

Although it was something both Fay and Lew had expected, it still came as a shock. They attended the funeral along with dozens of other people, for Bill had been more than liked, he had been loved, and Fay was disturbed to see people who looked as though they hadn't a tear in them break down and cry when the beautiful coffin was lowered into the dark soil.

Throughout the funeral Lew remained calm, but when he and Fay got back to the apartment, his impassivity broke. He didn't say a word, he just left her, shut himself in the spare bedroom with a bottle of whisky and drank himself into oblivion.

Fay was neither surprised nor disgusted. She had known all along that he wouldn't take Bill's death with equanimity.

She left him alone until about nine o'clock, then she made coffee and took it in to him. He lay sprawled across the bed, his hair in disorder, his tie pulled loose from the collar of his shirt, his jacket in a heap beside the bed.

Fay put the coffee tray down on the bedside table and sat down on the bed, lifting his black head and cradling him against her. She could smell the whisky on his breath, but she wasn't revolted, and when, with an inarticulate murmur, he pressed his face to her and clung to her, she laid her cheek against his hair and gently rocked him.

'I know, my darling. I know how you feel,' she whispered. 'It hurts, losing someone you love. It's desolation – it's bitter eating. I know, Lew.'

They stayed like that for many minutes, then, with a sigh, he drew away from her. He lay looking up at her, his eyes smeared and bloodshot from the whisky.

'I'll be damned glad to get away from this place,' he said, his voice thick. 'I can't wait for us to go.'

She stared down at him. 'You – want me to come?' she asked.

'Of course you're coming!' Impatience moved in his eyes. 'What did you think, that I was going to leave you all alone in this damned place? I'm not that low.'

'I see.' Fay moved thoughtfully off the bed and stood pouring coffee. Dr Forrester had said she was to do no extensive travelling – yet Lew's need of her cried out so hard that all other voices were drowned, lost. For the first time in their relationship he really needed her. It was in the way he sat pushing the rumpled hair back from his face, the hardness gone from his mouth and a boyish, hurt droop in its place. In the way, as she handed him his coffee, his eyes lifted and met hers, a silent pleading in them.

If she told him about the baby, he would go to England alone.

But she couldn't tell him, for his eyes were lonely – lonelier than she could ever have believed they could look. He wanted her to go with him and it wasn't in her to refuse him.

A few days before they left for England, Fay went to see Dr. Forrester. She explained about the trip. She emphasized Lew's uneasy acceptance of his friend Bill Symans' death. 'I can't see him go alone,' she said.

'You'll be risking your child, Mrs Marsh,' he warned.

'Oh, but we'll be flying.' Her eyes begged him to understand. 'It isn't such a very long trip. Surely – surely –'

'If you take my advice, you'll stay home.' He spoke gravely.

But she shook her head. 'Lew comes first,' she said.

CHAPTER ELEVEN

FAY STOOD and watched the fountain that played in the Avon. To her left the very modern Shakespeare Memorial Theatre was reflected in all its clean simplicity of line in the clear water of the lake, but Fay, at this moment, was only aware of the cold English wind blowing along the lakeside and of the leaves scurrying in the grass at her feet.

She shivered and drew the fur collar of her dark red coat closer about her face. How much longer was Lew going to be? When he had suggested that she might enjoy taking a walk around the town instead of sitting in on a boring technical conference, which was taking place in a little hotel just around the corner, she had agreed. But the conference, made up of various film men interested in this Shakespearean venture of Karl Christbel's including the actor Lew had come in particular to see, had now lasted two hours, and Fay was beginning to feel very cold and rather hungry.

She opened her bag and took out her cigarette case. She lit herself a cigarette, nervously aware of the tremor that kept running through her, affecting in particular her legs. They felt, every now and again, as though they were going to buckle up under her. She drew deeply on her cigarette, coughing a little as the smoke sawed her throat.

It was March.

March in England, with clouds like white puffs of meringue blowing along in a rather fitful sky; with a nip in the air that Fay was very conscious of after her seven months in the warm climate of Hollywood.

The smoke of her cigarette drifted away over the Avon and strands of her fair hair were whipped across her forehead by the wind. She didn't hear quiet footsteps approach behind her and when a smiling, well-known voice murmured in her ear, 'I know a shop, kid, where the pastries are works of art and the tea sheer nectar, how about coming with me and trying them?' She was so startled that all she could do for at least a minute was stand and stare – straight into the warm, almond-shaped eyes of Jerry Kaufmann.

Then warmth was flooding her, bringing her back to life, brightening her eyes back to their usual vivid blue. 'Jerry! You!'

He swept her a gallant little bow. 'None other, my queen.'

'Oh, Jerry, you absurd fool!' She laughed, she touched his arm, as though to make sure he was real. 'What are you doing here – of all places?'

He grinned merrily. 'Taking in the wonders of Stratford-on-Avon. Supping a little of its famous air. Why not?' His eyes, moving over her face, were openly fond. 'Gee, seeing you again does me good!' he exclaimed.

'Oh, Jerry!' she laughed breathlessly. 'I can't get over this! I was feeling so – so down – and you turn up!'

'Like a bad penny?' he queried quizzically.

'No! Oh, no!' She caught at his arm. 'I couldn't be more pleased. But what are you doing in England?'

'Come and eat pastries with me and I'll tell you,' he said.

'That would be nice – but I don't know whether I can.' She smiled. 'I'm waiting for Lew.'

'Where is the guy?'

'Winding up a business deal. When Lew gets talking about moving pictures and camera angles, I fade right into the background.' She looked rueful. 'I believe he's forgotten he brought me with him.'

'And you're darned bored and darned hungry,' Jerry finished for her.

She nodded.

Very deliberately then, he took hold of her arm. 'You're coming with me,' he said, in a voice that showed he didn't intend to brook any argument. 'I'm going to introduce you to some solid pudding and beef.'

'But you said pastries,' she objected. 'They sounded lovely.'

'It's red beef and gravy you need, kid.' He eyed her concernedly. 'I believe you're shivering. What's that guy thinking of, leaving you hanging about here in the cold?' And without further ado, he turned her and marched her across the sparse, shaven grass towards the steps that led up to the pavement.

They ate a very solid lunch and then, over coffee, he told her why he had come to England.

'I've landed a very nice contract with Suvia Pictures,' he explained. 'They're a European company. I like the pictures they make and they seem to like me, so it's a real love match. I was kind of getting in a rut in Hollywood, playing the same sort of parts all the time. I'll spread my wings with Suvia.' He grinned at her over his coffee cup. Very deliberately he said, 'D'you know, you're even prettier than I remember you.'

She ignored the compliment. 'What are you doing in Stratford?' she asked.

'I'm here to steal Lew Marsh's wife,' he replied.

'You're what?'

'You heard, honey.'

'Are you mad? I thought you'd forgotten all that nonsense, Jerry.'

'It isn't nonsense to me. I love you, Fay – I'm out to get you.'

'But what I said to you back in Hollywood still goes, Jerry.' She looked earnest. 'Why should you think I've changed?'

He shrugged. 'You're going to one day. The spell that guy's woven about you has got to break one day. I want to be around when it does. That's why, every now and again, I'll pop up at your elbow, like a genie.' He grinned engagingly.

As they strolled back towards the Memorial Theatre, they saw Lew. He stared, his black brows pulling down when he saw who accompanied Fay, holding her arm as they crossed the road.

He strode towards them. 'Where the devil have you been?' he demanded of Fay.

She smiled up at him, fighting her apprehension. He looked in a temper, his mouth thin, his nostrils pulled in imperiously. 'I was cold and hungry, and Jerry appeared out of the blue and offered me lunch,' she explained.

'You could have come over to the hotel – if you were that cold and hungry. Anyone would think I'd deliberately neglected you,' he said curtly. And as colour moved in her cheeks, he turned his irate glance on Jerry. 'What are you doing in Stratford? Getting culture?' he asked sarcastically.

Jerry faced him imperturbably. 'I'm doing a tour,' he said airily. 'I went to see Warwick Castle yesterday. Now that's quite a place! You two ought to go.'

'I doubt whether we'll have the time,' Lew replied coldly. 'We're going back to London tonight.'

'Oh, are we?' Fay broke in. She met his eyes enquiringly. 'I thought we were staying on here a few more days?'

'Well, we aren't!' He reached over and drew her to his side. 'You'd better tell your little playmate goodbye. I've got to get back to the hotel and make a few phone calls.'

Fay bit her lip. She looked at Jerry and saw that his eyes were still unconcernedly smiling. 'Goodbye, Jerry!' she murmured obediently. 'I hope you like working with Suvia Pictures.'

'I shall, kid,' he assured her. With an almost imperceptible wink at her and a final puckish glance at Lew, he strolled away, his hands thrust into the pockets of his raincoat. Fay watched him go, a sharp feeling of pain at her heart. The day seemed suddenly colder now that the warm friendliness always emanating from Jerry had been withdrawn. She turned resentfully to Lew. 'Why do you always have to be so rude to Jerry?' she demanded.

'Why do you always have to care that I am rude?' he countered.

'Because he's a friend of mine. Oh, don't sneer, Lew! Just because you dislike Jerry, do I have to?'

He took her arm and marched her across the road. 'You're just flattered because he's following you around.'

'He's doing nothing of the sort!' She looked indignant – perhaps that much more indignant because there was a certain amount of truth in what Lew said. 'He's here to make pictures.'

'He's following you around,' Lew reiterated. 'You've really made an impression on him, haven't you, baby?' He glanced down at her, his eyes mocking. 'Well, he's going to have to wait just a little longer. I'm not quite ready yet to hand you over to him.'

She flushed and pulled her arm free of his hand. 'Don't be beastly to me because your darned business talk wasn't to your liking,' she said, voicing a suspicion she had had from the moment she had seen him pacing along the lakeside. Although he hadn't been too pleased to see her with Jerry, that impatient, tigerish pacing had been part of something else. She had seen it before – and always in connection with his work.

Now he proved her surmise a correct one. With abrupt apology, he took her arm again and pulled her to his side as they walked towards their hotel. 'I'm sorry, Fay,' he said. 'I guess I am sore. That damned guy Brewster won't play ball.' His voice grew caustic. 'He says acting bores him, it always has, he's now found his true vocation – farming! Would you believe it? The guy prefers to grow cabbages! And Karl isn't offering him peanuts to play lead in *Lucrece*.'

Lew was still on about Ralph Brewster as they sped towards London that evening, in the car he had hired for their trip to Stratford. He wasn't used to right-hand driving and every so often the car gave a sickening jerk, stirring anew in Fay the slight feeling of nausea she had had, on and off, all day.

The feeling worried her. She had grown used to experiencing some discomfort first thing in the morning, but that usually wore off after she had been up and about for an hour, but today it had been present almost continually, along with that weak aching in her legs.

She leant back in her seat, forcing herself to relax, to ignore Lew's rather precarious driving. 'You talk, Lew, as though Ralph Brewster's the only actor who could possibly play Tarquin,' she said.

'He's one of them,' Lew grunted. 'He's got personality, presence and physique. When you can combine those three things, along with experience and talent, you're way inside the box-office, believe me.'

'Well,' Fay said, smiling, 'if that's what you need, play Tarquin yourself. You'd make a perfectly awesome Tarquin. You'd stop a million hearts without any trouble at all.'

But Lew wasn't in the mood for frivolous remarks. It hadn't pleased him in the least that he had been unable to talk Brewster into accepting the lead in this Shakespearean film. He honestly believed that with Brewster playing lead, the film stood a tolerable chance of being successful. He was known in America – half the battle – and he possessed a verve and a dash that was lacking in a lot of English actors of Brewster's eminence. It had been his idea, he had suggested it to Karl Christbel, that they star Brewster in *Lucrece*.

Suddenly he said to Fay, 'D'you know, I'm damned if I'll give up! I've a good mind to go back to Stratford and have another go at that guy.'

'Tonight?' She gazed at him in consternation. She felt tired and sick and worried. And that warning of Dr Forrester's – that if she came on this trip to England she might very well lose her baby – had been in her mind all day. She reached over and gripped Lew's arm. 'Can't we stop overnight somewhere and go back in the morning?' she begged.

He glanced at her, frowning. 'D'you feel tired, then?' he asked.

She nodded.

'Look,' he said, 'I think we're near Thame. How would it be if I got you fixed up at a pub for the night? I can easily go back alone if you don't fancy the journey.'

'But surely that isn't necessary, Lew?' she protested. 'Surely you can wait until the morning?'

But his mouth had set obstinately. 'I like to do things while my mind's made up on them,' he said. 'I'm darned if I'll take "no" from that guy! I'm going back tonight. You can stop in Thame or you can come with me. Suit yourself.'

And Fay, unutterably weary of the jolting of the car, aware that she'd be sick in earnest if she had to bear much more of it, chose to let him find her a decent pub in Thame where she might stay overnight.

As he saw her settled in, as he prepared to leave her, he

said, 'Expect me about lunch time tomorrow.' He grinned. 'I shan't forget I've left you here.'

'All right.' She stood gazing up at him, looking and feeling rather forlorn. 'Aren't you going to kiss me?' she asked.

'D'you want me to?' His eyes questioned her and she saw now that though the problem of Ralph Brewster had predominated in his thoughts all afternoon, he hadn't quite forgotten Jerry Kaufmann's sudden appearance in Stratford. He was still a little suspicious of that appearance of Jerry's, she realized.

'Of course I want you to,' she murmured.

'You don't usually ask me,' he countered.

'I don't usually have to,' she retorted.

He laughed then, and drew her towards him, drew her close into his arms, and as he bent his head to hers, she clasped her arms about his neck and clung to him.

The power and strength of that kiss, exchanged there in that quaint, dim bedroom, smelling of mothballs, left Fay a little dazed. She lay with her head against his shoulder, his arms tight about her.

'You kissed me as though I were marching away to the wars,' he murmured, trying to speak lightly, but in truth, almost as shaken as she was.

'I – know. I wonder why?' She drew back and looked up at him, a strange apprehension moving in her eyes. She wanted to say, 'Don't go, Lew! Please don't leave me!' but she held back the words, though it cost her something to hold them back.

'Are you all right, baby?' he suddenly asked her, watching her and wondering at her pallor, her almost exhausted look. He couldn't make out why she should look so wan. They had done no mad gallivanting. These three weeks in England had been the quietest they had known since their marriage. 'Don't you feel well, Fay?' He touched her cheek, feeling its coldness.

'I'm tired, that's all,' she reassured him. 'You go and see Brewster. Turn on all your charm.'

'You're – sure?' he said.

She nodded.

'Get to bed early, honey,' he urged, then he lightly pinched her chin and left her.

CHAPTER TWELVE

FAY WASHED and tidied herself and went down to the bar parlour to eat her solitary dinner.

The landlord of the pub was vastly concerned that she should be eating alone. 'It's being so early on in the season,' he said. 'We rarely get many overnight visitors this time of the year.'

'Oh, don't worry about me,' she said, smiling at him. 'I'm perfectly happy.'

But he wouldn't be consoled. 'Now it wouldn't be so bad for you if the young American gent was coming down to dinner, but he didn't order any dinner.'

Fay blinked as she digested this. 'The young American gent wouldn't be called Mr Kaufmann, would he?' she asked. And even before the landlord nodded his florid head in confirmation, she knew that the other visitor was Jerry. To have picked the same pub as Jerry!

'I take it you know the young gent, miss?' the landlord said.

'Oh yes, Mr Kaufmann and I are old friends.'

After Fay had eaten her dinner, she sat reading magazines on the leather-cushioned settle that stood near the big fireplace, where a fire roared cheerfully. She was absorbed in an article on old English castles, when the door breezed open and cheery masculine whistling died on a note of extreme surprise.

Fay glanced up, her dimples well to the fore as she examined Jerry's incredulous face. 'Yes, it's me,' she said.

'Where's Lew?' he asked, as he came across the room to her, glancing round as though expecting to see Lew in hiding behind one of the big carved chairs or behind the floral curtains at the windows.

She laughed. 'Lew's deposited me here like a parcel and gone back to Stratford,' she explained.

Jerry stared. 'On the level? What's so interesting in Stratford?'

'Ralph Brewster. Lew wants him under contract, but he's proving obstinate. And you know Lew, he won't rest until he gets his own way.'

'Too true!' Jerry pulled a face. 'Say, let's you and me have a drink. Tomato juice, huh?'

'That would be nice,' she agreed.

He returned with tomato juice for her and brimming rustic ale for himself. He sat down beside her on the settle and she felt his eyes moving over her as she held her tall glass of juice and sipped it. His openly admiring appraisement embarrassed her and she said quickly, 'You haven't told me why you're here.'

'My car broke down.' He grinned at her. 'I said a few cuss words at the time, but I'm blessing that axle now. Lew won't bless it, though, I bet.'

'If you're going to start saying mean things about Lew, I'm

not going to sit here and talk to you,' Fay informed him, with perfect seriousness.

'Okay, okay! We'll talk about you instead. Why aren't you the skinny little thing you used to be?'

The question took her breath, and then she blushed vividly. Lew had not noticed the slight alteration in her contours, but Jerry, not having seen her for some weeks, had noticed, and if was typical of him to frankly comment on the fact.

He watched the quick blooming of her blush and its slow fading and he frowned. Gradual comprehension stirred in the depths of his eyes, growing and becoming certainty as the tremulous movement of her lips on the rim of her glass of tomato juice.

'I'll guess in a minute,' he said.

'Go ahead and guess,' she retorted, smiling.

'Lew, it seems, has all the luck!' Jerry's grin held irony. 'Is he pleased at the prospect of fatherhood?'

'He doesn't know yet.'

Jerry looked astonished. 'Saving the news for his birthday?' he queried.

Fay's glance faltered from his, but Jerry's hand was immediately at her chin, tilting her face up. 'What's up, kid? Aren't things going too well?'

But instead of answering his question, she asked one.

'Did you know Inez Holden, Jerry?'

He nodded and released her chin. 'Yeah, I knew Inez. Why do you ask?'

She nervously twisted and turned the tall glass that held

her drink. 'I – I sometimes wonder if Lew still thinks about her.'

'You think he might have her on his conscience?' Jerry's gamin face was suddenly hard. 'He ought to.'

'Tell me all about it, Jerry.' Fay's hand reached for his arm. 'I must know exactly what Lew did to that girl to make her do – such a terrible thing.'

'You mean commit suicide?'

Fay nodded, her eye big on his face.

And then, abruptly, he set aside his beer tankard and stood up. He began to pace the rather worn strip of carpet that lay in front of the fireplace. 'I haven't much time for Lew Marsh,' he said, 'but I do care for you, Fay. I care to this extent,' he came and stood over her, 'I care enough to say the thing I wouldn't say three years ago, when a verdict of suicide was brought in on Inez Holden.' He held her gaze, his almond-shaped eyes flashing. 'Inez didn't commit suicide.'

Fay stared up at him. 'How do you know?'

'I was with her at the time.'

He straightened up and took his cigarette-case from his pocket. He extended it to Fay, but she shook her head, watching him light a cigarette, noticing that his hand was shaking slightly.

'Inez and I were friends before she ever met Lew.' He spoke quietly dispassionately. 'I wasn't in love with her, but I liked her. Then she met Lew at a party and shortly afterwards they got engaged. From all accounts he wanted to get married right away, but she was eager to get into movies and make a name for herself first.'

Jerry shrugged and drew hard on his cigarette. 'The trouble was, she couldn't act, but she was damned beautiful. I guess Lew was pretty infatuated with her at that time, for he got Karl Christbel to put her under contract. He even got her a part in a film he was directing at that time.

'It was called *Come Tenderly, My Sweet*, but the moment Inez stepped into the film, things seemed to go haywire. She was like a jinx on it. Janie Streeter, who was playing female lead, went down with a virus and had to be replaced. A whole can of exposed film went up in flames, along with one of the projection rooms and a pile of expensive scenery, and it was only Lew's influence with old Christbel that stopped him tossing Inez out on her ear. K. C.'s a superstitious guy, and directly he got it into his head that it was Inez who was jinxing the film, he took to hating her. And it was probably knowing she was in bad with K. C. that made Inez's acting go from bad to rotten.

'Then Casey Anderson, who was playing male lead, did a sit-down strike. He told Lew that if Inez didn't get her walking orders, he'd walk out. It wasn't that Casey objected to Inez's bad acting, it was because she didn't like him and his tendency to make passes at her in dark corners, and she had told him so, in front of the entire cast of the film. But Casey, as Lew well knew, had to be considered. He was sure fire box-office at that time and Lew was never a guy to be swayed by sentiment.

'So Lew told Inez that she'd never be more than a pretty piece of decoration. He told her that the only part she could ever play with anything approaching efficiency was the profile on a penny. He told her that Casey was in and she was out. God knows why he had to tell her in such brutal terms, but Lew's kind haven't a lot of patience with mediocrity and I guess he was pretty well fed up with the way Inez had spoiled scene after scene of *Come Tenderly, My Sweet* with her bad acting. He informed her that he wouldn't have put up with five minutes of it if she hadn't been wearing his ring. So Inez tossed the ring in his face, told him to do what he damn well liked with it. He put his heel on it and ground it to smithereens.'

Jerry lit himself another cigarette, his thumb impatient on the wheel of his lighter.

'I heard all about the fight from Inez, later that same day, when we met in a downtown bar. She was feeling reckless and drinking hard. I didn't try to stop her. She needed to drink. I've sometimes needed it myself. When life gets hold of you by the throat, the only way out sometimes is to drink until fireworks start or black oblivion comes. With Inez it was fireworks. When we left that bar she was like a sparkling, crazy torch, not caring a damn about anything or anyone. We went dancing. Maybe I came close to thinking I loved her that night – I don't know.' Jerry shrugged and tossed ash off his cigarette. 'Anyway, when she suggested I go back to her apartment with her, I went.'

He smiled cynically at Fay. 'She was beautiful. She was also Lew Marsh's girl. I didn't like him, y'see. I never did.

Maybe because everything seemed to come to him so easily. Maybe because he never had to claw his way to the top, like I did. I guess I hated, too, his ability to go through life treading on people's toes and not having them care – or, if they cared, not caring a darn himself.

'Well, it went on like that for a week or more, Inez and I hitting the high spots, and then, all at once, she seemed to come to her senses. One night, we'd been to a movie, and as we left the cinema, Inez suddenly said, quite seriously, that she was going to see Lew. She was going to ask him to take her back. Life was hell without him, she said. So I drove her to his place and waited. Somehow I knew that she was running to a dry wall; that Lew Marsh's high and mighty pride wouldn't tolerate any backsliding in a girl he intended to marry. And I was right.'

Jerry stared straight into Fay's wide blue eyes. Cinders rolled from the fire into the grate and the distant hum of male voices talking in the saloon bar came to them.

'Inez was crying as she came running out of Crystal Court. I was on the opposite side of the road, sitting in my car. I saw exactly what happened. She stepped off the curb to come to me – and went straight under the wheels of a truck. At the inquest, Lew openly admitted that he had thrown Inez out of his apartment. The driver of the truck said that she walked under his wheels, and I was in no mood to dispute the statement. I agreed with it.'

'And they called it suicide,' Fay said quietly.

Jerry nodded.

'Why did you do that to him, Jerry? Why?'

'Because she took her love to him, and her broken pride, and he threw them back in her lovely face.'

Fay shivered, her clenched hands cold as ice. 'Lew has pride,' she murmured.

'He's hard, all the way through.' Jerry bent and lightly touched her cold hands. 'What is it that makes you love him, Fay? What makes you love a man who hasn't an ounce of compassion or understanding in him?'

'I don't know – I don't know.'

'I can be both, Fay.' He spoke quietly, almost wistfully. 'I'll take you now, if you'll come.'

'I'm having his baby, Jerry.'

'I said I'll take you, if you'll come.'

But she shook her head. 'Leave me alone, Jerry,' she pleaded. 'Please leave me alone.'

'All right.' He straightened up, tossing his cigarette butt into the dying fire. 'All right, kid. I'll go for now, but we'll meet again – we're meant to meet again.'

'Are we, Jerry?' She gazed straight up into his gamin face, as though she would absorb every detail – almond eyes, humorous mouth, black curls drifting down upon his forehead. 'Thank you for telling me the real truth about Inez Holden, Jerry,' she said.

'I'd give you the world – you've only to ask.' Then he lightly touched his curls in a farewell salute. 'I'm leaving first thing in the morning, so I'll say goodbye now, Fay.'

'Goodbye, Jerry.'

The door closed and Fay's rather melancholy glance moved back to the fire, and for long moments, enclosed by the silence of the room, she stared into the fire. Lew believed that he had sent that girl to a deliberate death – he lived with that belief day and night – but did it ever really trouble him?

She rose on the thought, wanting to get to her bed and to get warm. Intolerable weariness was back. As she moved from the settle, her foot struck against something and glancing down she saw Jerry's heavy gold cigarette case lying by her foot. She bent to pick it up and, forgetful that he had said he would be leaving first thing in the morning, she carried it up to her room with her.

CHAPTER THIRTEEN

THE FOLLOWING morning Fay awoke, unrefreshed, to the sound of a tea-cup rattling in a saucer and the big, bosomy figure of the landlord's wife at the side of the bed. She struggled up out of the clinging embrace of the bed's huge feather mattress and tried to smile at the big woman who was smiling so pleasantly at her.

But she felt so ill.

'Now what would you like for breakfast?' the woman asked cheerily. 'Haddock and egg? Bacon and egg? Or perhaps a nice pair of kippers?'

Fay shuddered, uncontrollably, at the mention of kippers and just about managed to murmur that toast was all she ate for breakfast. Toast would be fine.

'Toast?' The woman looked openly aghast. 'Well, it isn't very filling, dearie. Are you sure?'

Fay nodded, desperate now with the need to be alone.

'All right, dearie, if that's what you'd like. Marmalade with it?'

'No – just toast.'

'And the eggs are lovely this morning! Such a pity –'

'I'm – I'm not a very big eater,' Fay murmured, longing to tell the kindly soul to take her enquiring eyes and her talk of haddocks and kippers out of the room.

'Well, all right,' the woman began to edge towards the door. 'Nothing on the toast?'

Fay shook her head.

The door closed on the broad back, the yellow print overall, and Fay sighed thankfully, and deposited the cup of almost orange tea on the bedside table. She lay back against the pillows and stared up at the sloping ceiling. She breathed deeply, slowly, fighting her nausea. She was close to tears. She felt so ill. She wanted Lew. She wanted his arms, to rest in them and be eased by them ...

The minutes slid by as she lay summoning the strength and courage to climb out of bed. She was shivering under the sheets.

Oh, this wouldn't do – this wouldn't do at all. She pushed back the covers, swung her legs over the side of the bed and forced herself to stand up. Her head swam, her knees almost buckled and she knew a deadly fear, a fear that filmed her back and her chest with a cold sweat.

She moved woodenly to the washstand and poured some of the hot water the landlord's wife had brought her into the china bowl. She forced herself to wash, to dress, to comb her hair. To dab her cold face with powder and apply a little lipstick with a shaking hand.

When she opened the door of the room and stepped out on to the landing, the stale smell of beer, rising from below, made her retch anew and clutch the side of the door. And as she clung there, feeling so wretchedly ill, fighting for the strength of will to go down to the bar parlour, where the sour smell of beer would be even stronger, the stout, yellowoveralled figure of the landlord's wife appeared at the head of the stairs.

She came hurriedly along the landing, seeing Fay. 'You're not well, dearie!' she exclaimed. She took hold of Fay and helped her back into the room, almost carrying her to the bed. She leaned over her, her eyes enquiring and alarmed. 'Anything I can do for you, dearie?' she asked.

Fay managed to smile at her. 'Could you – wave a wand and conjure my husband?' she murmured.

'Can I phone him for you, love?' the woman asked at once.

Fay shook her head. 'He's probably on his way here now,' she said. 'I'm – just being a little silly. I'll be all right in a while.'

The woman was suddenly nodding and beaming, for she had tumbled to Fay's secret. Her red cheeks bunched up as she said, 'The mornings always play you up, love. Why don't you rest yourself until this wears off? I'll bring your breakfast up to you, shall I?'

'You're very kind,' Fay told her gratefully.

She managed to eat a slice of the toast the woman brought her, then she kicked off her shoes, rolled herself in the eiderdown on the bed and fell into a restless doze.

Many wavering images walked in that curious dream she began to have. Predominating, strangely enough, was the broad and earnest figure of Dr Forrester. She could hear his slow, deliberate voice, she could hear so plainly what he said: 'Are you afraid he won't want this baby? Is that your worry?' Then: 'You'll be risking your child! You'll be risking your child!'

She turned restlessly, trying to lose the voice, the words. Who was he talking about? Who didn't want her baby? She tried to remember – she fought to remember. Someone must tell her! Who would tell her? Thalia? She went running along a white corridor that seemed to echo with voices, for she could see Thalia waiting at the end of the corridor, a strange, bizarre Thalia, who wore the white uniform of a nurse, but who still smoked a cigarette and smiled. 'Who does he mean?' Fay demanded of her. 'Tell me! Tell me! I must know!' She went to clutch hold of Thalia, but the white-clad Thalia moved like vapour out of her hands; she possessed no reality, she wavered and broke and eddied away, and Fay was alone in the corridor, with only the sound of the many voices coming in hollow waves to her ears.

She knew a stark fear. She began to run. She had to get away from this place. She sped along the white corridor, but the voices pursued her, a hollow baying, a dismal frightening symphony of sound, always at her heels. She saw a door and she made for the door. She pushed at the door, but it wouldn't give, it wouldn't yield, it wouldn't open to let her in. She hammered and pounded on the door. She cried out: 'Let me in! I don't want to stand out here! I'm frightened! These people frighten me! Let me in! Please let me in!'

But the door stayed shut, solid and immovable, and Fay sank slowly down on the cold tiles of the floor, and as her head drooped against the door the voices behind her broke into a chorus of derisive laughter. She shuddered where she lay. She held her hands over her ears. 'Let me in!' she beseeched. 'Let me in before it's too late!'

But the door stayed shut.

And the dream faded and a kinder sleep came to her. A sleep empty of phantoms. When she awoke at last it was to the dark, watching face of Lew.

He was sitting beside her on the bed and as she opened her eyes and saw him, a deep thankfulness filled her. 'Hullo!' she said, and her smile was soft and fond and full of peace. 'Is it lunch time, or are you early?'

'I'm early,' he replied, but he didn't return her smile. He watched her speculatively. He said, 'The woman down in the bar told me you weren't feeling too good. She gave me a damned coy smile and a wink.' He hesitated, just for a moment, then he went on curtly, 'What am I supposed to do, Fay, guess the rest?'

'What – what do you mean?' She struggled into a sitting position, pushing the eiderdown back from her slender legs. She eyed him perplexedly. 'Why are you vexed, Lew?' she asked.

His mouth thinned and his eyes swept down her, from her throat to her heels. 'I wasn't born yesterday!' he snapped. 'Presuming the kid's mine, why do I have to be left to learn about it from some damned publican's wife?'

'Presuming?' Fay stared at him, her blue eyes blue shadowed in her face. She watched him lean away from her and pick up something from the cane table beside the bed. He showed her the gold cigarette-case she had put there last night, the gold case engraved with the initials J. K.

'Jerry's case!' she gasped, and all that was uppermost in her mind at that moment was that she had forgotten to give it to him.

'Does it reassure you, my dear? Does it bring back tender memories to have it by you while you sleep?' Lew enquired, his eyes glittering as they ranged over her face, with its sudden look of consternation. She gazed back at him, bewildered, unnerved. She couldn't make out what he was talking about.

'I – I don't understand you, Lew,' she said. 'What's the matter?' She put a tentative hand on his arm, but he shook it off impatiently.

'I'm asking you what this damned cigarette-case of Kaufmann's is doing here.' His voice cut into her, making her flinch.

'He dropped it – last night—'

'He what?'

'He was here.' She spoke quickly, eager to explain. 'His car broke down and he had to put up here for the night.'

'The devil he did!' Lew stood up, towered over her as she lay on the bed, among the rose-pink folds of the eiderdown, gazing up at him like a bewildered child. 'What a bit of luck for you, my dear,' he sneered. 'Did you make the most of your luck?'

'Oh, Lew!' The hurt tears, the tears that were all part of her physical weariness, her joy that he was back with her – her joy turned to bewilderment, flooded into her eyes. They spilled helplessly, rolling down her face. She turned her head from him. 'What are you saying? Do you know what you're saying?' she whispered.

His answer was to throw the gold cigarette-case down on the bed beside her. It hit the bed with a small, deadly thump.

'There's your talisman, my pet,' he said. 'Pick it up, go on. It'll soothe your tears away.'

But she withdrew from the case as from something repugnant. She was trembling violently. What made Lew so cruel? How was it possible she loved this man whose feelings were encased in armour? Whose pride was so overbearing that he burned at the thought that some other man might have cast proprietorial eyes over his flimsy toy; might, perhaps, have taken it into his hands for a moment?

He didn't love her, yet he exhibited this vicious jealousy!

Suddenly she was unutterably wearied of him – wearied of everything, even the effort of searching the cuff of her dress for her handkerchief, so that she might wipe away her tears. 'Oh, think what you like, Lew!' she said, and drearily she fumbled her way off the bed – and fell forward into a bottomless void, falling, falling, but never quite reaching the bottom of that black pit, for strong hands caught her, lifted her and everything died in silence.

That afternoon, in a cottage hospital a mile or so outside of Thame, Fay lost her baby.

And Lew, in a torment he had never known before, paced the waiting-room, cursing himself. Cursing his vicious temper that had made him say the things he had said to Fay. Suggesting – suggesting that Kaufmann ... The recollection turned him sick.

He sank down on one of the tubular chairs in the waiting-room, running restless hands through his hair. God, what was happening? Why didn't the doctor come, or the nurse – anyone to tell him Fay was all right? Supposing she died! He sat in fear, staring at the red linoleum on the floor; staring until it seemed to dance into his brain, washing his brain in a red haze – where was starkly painted the pitiful helplessness which had overtaken Fay in the bedroom of that pub. She had seemed to die as he had caught her, lifted her – all colour fled from her face, all warmth from her body. She had gone floating away into realms where he could not follow, and he had known a stark fear, an unutterable sense of loneliness.

He had thought her dead.

God! Why didn't the doctor come? He rose and walked to the window and stood drumming his fingers on the cold glass, watching the slow fall of rain on the gnarled, barren limbs of the trees that stood in the darkening courtyard of the hospital.

It seemed hours to him before the door opened and the white-coated figure of the doctor entered. He came to say that Fay had lost her baby, that now she was sleeping and all Lew could do was take himself off until the morning.

'She is all right?' Lew's dark eyes were rather wild, and for all his height and breadth, he looked curiously young, almost boyish, to the doctor. 'I mean, I'll stay the night if there's any danger of a relapse or – or anything.'

'Good lord, no!' The doctor shook his head, smiling slightly. 'Miscarriages are nasty, but not necessarily fatal, old chap. Your wife will be able to talk to you in the morning. My advice to you right now is to go off and have a good meal and a good sleep.' He banged Lew's shoulder cheerfully. 'And stop worrying.'

But Lew didn't stop worrying.

He was still worrying when he came back the next morning, following a pert young nurse into a small room where Fay lay in bed, her fair hair tied back with a piece of ribbon.

'Fifteen minutes, no more,' the young nurse said, and as the door closed on her, Lew moved to the foot of the bed, where Fay lay so quietly, all eyes and cheekbones and small, still hands on the taut sheet.

'I'm sorry about the baby, honey,' he said huskily.

She watched him, thinking how dark, how big he looked in this white cubicle of a room, with its white painted chest of drawers, its humming radiator and its acorn on the blind gently tap-tapping the window as the March wind outside filtered in through the open top of the window and stirred the blind.

She wondered why her heart didn't race in the old way, why the mere sight of him didn't quicken her pulse and gladden her eyes. She wondered why she felt so dead – so dead. It was as though all feeling, all emotion had been drained out of her, as though her heart had died with her baby.

'Why should you be sorry?' she asked, in a voice as devoid of emotion as she was. A cynical little smile moved in her eyes. 'The baby was mine, wasn't it? God knows how I came by it on my own, but I must have done, for I certainly didn't come by it in the way you implied yesterday.'

He winced and his hands moved out to grip the rail of the bed. 'You can't despise me more than I despise myself, Fay,' he said, almost passionately. 'I could kick myself from here to Timbuctoo for the things I said to you yesterday.'

But her smile was tired, almost uninterested. 'I wish I could despise you, Lew,' she said. 'Anything would be better than not being able to feel anything at all for you.'

'What do you mean?' His hands clenched on the rail of the bed and his eyes stared down into hers. 'What are you saying, Fay?'

'I'm looking at you, Lew, and I'm feeling absolutely nothing,' she replied quietly.

He came round to her. He sat down in the chair that was beside the bed and he took hold of her left hand, lying so quietly on the coverlet. It felt very small and fine-boned in his hand.

'I don't blame you for feeling bitter, Fay, honey,' he said. 'I've a swinish, jealous temper and I say many things I should be shot for saying. But a bullet in the heart couldn't hurt me more than to hear you say you don't love me any more.'

'But, Lew, what's love?' she half smiled, echoing his own cynicism. 'Stupid sentimentality, isn't it? A puff of air that is here one minute, gone the next? You were very right to say that. I loved you in the first hour I met you, but it's taken me just one day to stop loving you.'

'Fay,' he gripped her hand, 'I can't lose you, my baby. I don't want to lose you. Won't you believe me?'

She heard him. She wondered why she remained unmoved. She had often prayed for him to say these few words, and now that he had said them she felt nothing. No joy. No sweeping gladness.

'Fay,' his eyes pleaded with her. 'I won't let Kaufmann be the cause of a rift between us.'

She shook her head tiredly on the pillow. 'This has nothing to do with Jerry – though he was the one who said that you had woven a spell about me. Now that spell has broken. I'm free! I want to stay free!' Now tears welled into her eyes and she turned her tired face from him. 'Let me go! Let me go!' she whispered.

'Go where, baby?' He reached over and gently turned her face back towards him; he searched her face with dark, distressed eyes. 'You can't mean you want to go away from me – you can't mean that, honey?'

'I do – I do!' Her head turned restlessly on the pillow, while tears slid silently and forlornly down her thin cheeks. 'I shouldn't have come on this trip. The doctor warned me not to. I should have listened to him – I should at least have kept my baby if I had listened to him!'

The words broke on a sob and a spasm of pain went across Lew's face as he bent above her. 'I can't make out why you didn't tell me about the baby, honey. All of this needn't have happened if you'd told me. Surely I was entitled to be told?'

'I didn't think you'd want it.' She spoke the dreary truth, too tired and drained of feeling to care whether she hurt him or not.

But he was hurt. She saw the wry pain come into his eyes. 'Thanks!' he said. 'Your opinion of me continues to be a pretty poor one, doesn't it, Fay? What did you think I'd do to you – toss you out on your ear?' He spoke with a jocular grimness that would surely have moved her to remorse – yesterday. But yesterday she had loved him.

Her tears were suddenly spilling helplessly, and the young nurse, returning at that moment, came hurriedly to the bedside when she saw that Fay was crying. 'You'd better go now, Mr. Marsh,' she said quietly. 'Your wife's still rather weak. She should be resting.'

He nodded, gazing in impotent distress at Fay. The things she had said had hurt damnably, but the way she looked at him, as though at a stranger, hurt even more. He could understand her bitterness – he had earned that. But her indifference hurt.

Then he leant forward and gently kissed her cheek, feeling her tears salt against his lips. 'We'll talk about all this tomorrow,' he said. 'You'll feel better about everything tomorrow.' But her eyes, looking back at him through the raining, helpless tears, were as bleak and uncomprehending as the eyes of a lost child, and she made no answer to his murmured goodbye.

When he returned the following morning he found her restored to calmness. She even gave him a slight, if restrained smile, as he entered the room and came round to sit beside her, holding her small, passive hand.

'Honey, listen to me,' he said. 'Now that Brewster's agreed to do the film – I got him to agree, y'see,' – his smile flashed for an instant, 'we'll be going into production. The exterior scenes are going to be shot in Spain. Don't you want to come to Spain?'

She quietly shook her head.

He looked openly taken aback. 'I can't make you out,' he

said, with a sudden touch of exasperation. 'Spain's a beautiful country, exciting, romantic – you'd enjoy yourself. What will you find to do all alone in England?'

'I'm going back to my nursing,' she replied.

Now the exasperation that had been in his voice spread to his face. His mouth grew thin. 'Is this – this display of childishness because I said something to you in a fit of temper? I've apologized for that. What have I got to do, crawl on to my knees before you'll accept my apology?'

She half smiled. 'No, Lew,' she said. Her voice was quiet and steady. Physically she was much better and this showed in her face. Her exhausted look was quite gone and colour was back in her mouth. She looked perfectly calm and absolutely sure of what she wanted to do and why she wanted to do it. 'I'm not showing off with you, or being childish, Lew. I've recovered my pride, that's all. I can't – I won't be your little Cinderella any more. Your little dressed-up doll! I won't be sent out to walk round the park, or be told what to wear, not any more. I won't come running when you snap your fingers.' Her eyes were steady on his face and entirely absent of any defiance. She spoke with the simplicity of complete and unalterable decision. 'I won't come to Spain with you, Lew.'

'You really mean to go back to your old life?' he exclaimed incredulously.

She gave a firm little nod of her head. 'I've always known I should have to sooner or later,' she replied calmly. And then she did something that showed him how complete was her repudiation of him. She withdrew her hand from his, took off her wedding ring and held it out to him. He sat staring at her, his dark face grim, his mouth granite-hard. She gazed back at him, quite undismayed. She took hold of his hand, turned it palm upwards and dropped the ring into it, closing his fingers over the expensive glitter and the empty meaning of it.

Her eyes didn't show the exultation she was feeling, but it was running warmly, richly in her blood. She had pushed Lew out of her heart. She had closed the gates of her heart on him – on him, the insolent invader. She had regained pride and self-possession. She had won free of her enslavement.

She watched as his hand slowly clenched on the ring, she watched as the meaning of what she had done took hold of him.

'Aren't you afraid,' he asked quietly, 'that I'll make you come to Spain with me? You're still my wife, remember?'

'I'm that, Lew, but I'm not your little dog on a lead,' she retorted. 'You can't make me go anywhere I don't want to go. You can't,' she smiled, 'you can't drag me along by my hair.'

'Ah, but I know another way.' His eyes were suddenly insolent. He smiled at her. He bent over her and quite gently, but with unmistakable possessiveness, kissed her mouth. She felt the familiar warmth and hardness of his mouth, she breathed the clean warmth of his skin, the aromatic scent of his cigars – she was totally unmoved by his kiss. It was as though a stranger kissed her.

When he lifted his head, she saw from his eyes that her cold and unemotional reception of his kiss had shaken him.

He studied her serene face on the pillows, her eyes that no longer wavered from his in shy confusion or gazed back at him with something of fear moving in their blue depths.

'Love is a fickle jade, isn't she?' he drawled. 'Or am I just unlucky in my choice of women?'

'Just unlucky, I guess, Lew.' Then she patted his hand, the one that held her wedding ring. 'Inez Holden didn't commit suicide, Lew. Did you know?'

'Yes, I knew.' He smiled cynically. 'She was too darned selfish to deliberately throw her beauty under a gasoline truck.'

Fay winced at the words. Lew saw and abruptly he stood up, thrusting her wedding ring into his pocket. 'All right, Fay,' he said, 'if you want me to go out of your life, I'll go.'

CHAPTER FOURTEEN

SO LEW went to Spain alone.

Fay saw him go without emotion. Emotion still seemed held in abeyance within her. She no longer cried, even for the baby she had sacrificed for Lew's sake. She felt isolated from the past, from all the feeling she had once known, where pain had mingled with ecstasy, where hate had touched hands with love.

Lew had rented a flat for her in London, but it came about that she occupied that flat for a bare three weeks after he left for Spain.

Still convalescent from her miscarriage and aware that it would be the height of foolishness for her to recommence her nursing yet, she filled in her days with a little walking, a little reading, a little letter-writing. She didn't know many people to whom she could write, but it did occur to her to write and tell Max Forrester that she had lost her child. She had liked Max. He had been warm and friendly and sympathetic and she was now at the stage of her convalescence where she was wanting to talk to a friend, if only through the impersonal medium of letter-writing. She told Max that she intended going back to her nursing and in his answering letter he made a suggestion that at once appealed to her and yet kept her restless and wakeful that same night.

For Max wrote in his letter: 'I think that you would enjoy working at the Anita Hill Hospital, my dear. You know the hospital, I know, for you once told me that your husband's friend died there. Perhaps, if you've sad memories of the place, it wouldn't be a wise move, yet on the other hand I feel that your deep personal problem can only be fought to a satisfactory conclusion in the place where it had its commencement, Hollywood. So I say face your bogy and come back to Hollywood. It was here that your married life was lived, not in England, therefore it is here, you know, where you must search your heart and find out for certain that you're not throwing away something you really want.'

Fay tossed restlessly that night, her sleepless eyes roving the dark corners of this strange bedroom in the heart of a London that had grown strangely alien. Was Max right? Was he?

She threw her arms across her eyes, trying to collect her thoughts racing into some semblance of order. The Anita Hill Hospital in Hollywood, white-stoned and terraced, with orange trees in the meticulously kept grounds and a very modern nurses' home not ten minutes' walk from the hospital buildings. The place where Bill Symans had quietly died.

Fay, after a while, drifted into sleep, and with the arrival of morning there also came decision. Face your bogy, Max had said; come back and search out your heart.

And so, her courage collected about her like a mantle, Fay returned to Hollywood, where Max Forrester used his influence to get her a post at the Anita Hill.

Fay had always been a good nurse and the familiar routine

of a job she could do with great efficiency soon claimed her. The busy days grew into weeks and the weeks passed swiftly, and though Fay had decided upon her arrival to write and tell Lew that she was back in Hollywood, she found herself increasingly reluctant to put pen to paper. After all – what did it matter?

Fay joined very little in the social life of the hospital, uninterested in tentative approaches from one or two young doctors who would have been pleased to take her out, aware that though she was married, she was at present living apart from her husband. She was strangely content with her own company in those days, going for long walks in her free time, occasionally calling in for a cup of coffee with Mimi Forrester, Max's wife. Then, one afternoon, seeing an old film of Jerry Kaufmann's advertised at a local cinema, she went in to see it. She sat in the perfumed darkness of the cinema, staring at the bright, noisy screen, where a Jerry she did not know played a hardbitten newspaperman. Possibly a powerful piece of acting, she thought, rather dazedly – but this was not the gay warm Jerry she had known. The Jerry who had bought her enormous toffee apples and chased her along the warm silver sand of Pacific Beach. She rose blindly and made her way out of the cinema, memories crowding back, walking her dead heart back to pain. Dear, dear Jerry – where was he now?

May passed into June, and then, with the arrival of July, there came a spell of sultry, trying weather, with long days of almost tropical rain and an outbreak of a summer 'flu that filled the hospital to overflowing. Fay was therefore kept extremely busy, with no time for introspection, for a searching of the heart Lew had come so close to breaking, and it was with startled surprise that she glanced at the calendar in the nurses' sitting-room one morning and saw that August had arrived.

One of the other nurses, noticing Fay's absorption in the calendar, remarked, 'How quickly this year's going! This time last year I was on my holidays. My boy-friend and I pooled our resources and flew to Honolulu; we had a swell time!' She smiled at Fay. 'Recalling your holidays, honey?'

'I wasn't on holiday.' Fay's smile was fleeting. 'I was nursing a very rich old lady, in Casa Roche. A Mrs Laura Marsh, full of majesty and mustard and quite a character – you know.'

'A Mrs Laura Marsh – in Casa Roche?' The girl stared at Fay. 'That's funny!' She darted to the table that stood in the middle of the nurses' sitting-room and picked up the morning paper. She rapidly turned the pages, found what she was looking for and brought the paper to Fay. 'Read that, ducky,' she said. 'Might be your old girl – who knows!'

Fay quickly, rather nervously, scanned the item – and her heart turned cold. Oh yes, this was old Mrs Marsh, whom she had nursed. Old Mrs Marsh, tart of voice, quick of eye, full of love for Della, quite empty of feeling for Lew – and she was dead – found dead of a heart attack by her granddaughter!

The skin of Fay's face felt cold and taut. Della had found her grandmother. Della, that handsome, rather lost creature, who had depended so much on the love of that autocratic old lady. Fay's hand closed hard on the newspaper. Then, abruptly, she swung on her heel and hurried from the nurses' sitting-room, making for the matron's office.

'You're asking for leave, when we're so busy?' Matron stared at her.

'Only three or four days, Matron. It's rather important.'

'Well – I don't know.' Matron tapped a pencil on the desk and thoughtfully regarded the small, earnest face confronting her across the desk. A good nurse, this one, and hard-working ... 'Very well, you may take your four days, nurse,' she said abruptly. 'I take it this is family business?'

'Yes, Matron.'

Fay paid off the rather dilapidated taxi that had brought her to Laurel Bay and mounted the four wide steps to the front door. Her hand was reaching for the bell when the door swung open and the gangling, red-haired figure of Will Bronson stood before her. His green eyes were full of surprise. 'I saw you from the window. Lord, Fay, it's good of you to have come.' He ushered her into the dim, flagged hall. 'Lew's here. He got here this morning.'

'Lew!' Fay stared up at Will as they crossed the hall to the drawing-room. 'I – I didn't know he was back in America.'

If this statement surprised Will, he didn't show his surprise, but as they paused before the door of the drawing-room, he said, 'Look, Fay, if – if you and Lew are having a spot of marriage trouble, don't say anything to Dell about it. Lew hasn't. When Dell wanted to know why you hadn't come with him, he made the excuse that you had a bad cold and couldn't travel. You see – well, Dell isn't quite herself just now. She's having a baby and the shock of old Mrs Marsh's death hasn't done her a lot of good.'

'A baby!' Fay's hand reached for Will's arm and pressed it. 'How nice for you!'

The grin he gave her was boyishly pleased. 'Dell is hoping that the baby turns out to be a boy; but I'm more democratic, I'll take whatever comes.'

'Della's pleased, then?'

'She was happy as a lark about the baby, but as I say, poor old Mrs Marsh's death has rather put the damper on everything for her just now. They were very attached, you know – and Mrs Marsh always seemed such a tough old girl.'

He opened the door of the drawing-room and Fay, small and braced, preceded him into the room. Nothing had changed. The massive mahogany furniture gleamed richly, the chandeliers glittered overhead and the heavy plum-coloured curtains gracefully draped their silk skirts upon the silver-grey carpet. Fay crossed the room, aware of Lew rising from a deep armchair, watching her with dark startled eyes.

'Fay!' he said.

'Fay!' Della said.

And it was to Della Fay went, kneeling down beside the couch where she sat, wrapping soft arms about her. 'Oh, Fay!' Della clung to her. 'I'm so glad you came after all! So glad!' Then, the words barely out of her mouth, Della began to cry. She cried with the sudden hurt abandon of a child, gasping against Fay's shoulder. 'I found her, Fay. Sh-she was dead in a ch-chair. I thought – I thought she was asleep. I loved her so … I loved her s-so!'

And during that storm of weeping, Will leant impotently over the back of the couch, his red hair tumbling on to his forehead, his green eyes distressed. Lew remained as he had risen at Fay's entrance; standing outside this tableau of grief and sympathy, a hand slowly reaching into his pocket for his cigar-case. He selected a cigar, carefully lit it, puffed the rich smoke in a blue cloud about his face, and through the cloud he stared at Fay.

The funeral took place the following day and Della, having shed her bitter tears, was quite calm. It was at the reading of the will afterwards that she lost her calm, for Mrs. Marsh had left all of her substantial fortune, which included valuable property holdings, and this house, Laurel Bay, to Della. Lew wasn't mentioned.

'But it isn't fair!' Della cried, jumping to her feet and confronting the lawyer, her face flushed and dismayed. 'Lew and I should share! I don't want the lot!'

Lew rose to his feet. He lazily approached Della and threw an arm about her, pulling her against his side. He smiled at the lawyer. 'I'm perfectly happy with the will,' he drawled. 'I never expected to be in it.'

'But Lew,' Della turned to him passionately, 'it isn't fair! You're entitled to share with me.'

'It's absolutely and utterly and completely fair,' he elaborated amusedly. 'You were always the sun over the tall trees to old Gran, while I was always the bad boy in the corner, so it's perfectly reasonable, my honey, that she should leave you all her worldly possessions. Now stop getting yourself into a stew over it; do what Gran wants you to do, bring Laurel Bay alive with half a dozen gingernuts.' He winked at Will as he spoke. 'I daresay Will will co-operate.'

Della couldn't forget the will, however. She spoke to Fay about it after the lawyer had gone, taking hold of Fay's hand and walking her out to the garden. 'I know Lew couldn't care less about the money part,' she said, 'but it was darned hurtful of Gran, all the same, to exclude him so completely. She never liked him, I know – but to do that!' Della's fingers suddenly tightened upon Fay's, then slowly she lifted Fay's hand and stared at it. 'Where's your wedding ring, Fay?' she asked.

'My – wedding ring?' Fay bit her lip, 'Why, I —'

'You don't have to say.' Della broke in. 'You don't have to tell me.'

'Don't I?' Fay withdrew her hand from Della's and turned almost embarrassedly to pluck a Michaelmas daisy from a nearby bush. She stood pulling it to bits. 'I should never have married Lew, should I?' she said. 'But I was unutterably flattered that he should want me.'

'And now?' Della murmured. 'Now what do you feel?'

Fay quietly considered the question, the little mauve petals of the Michaelmas daisy fluttering from her fingers. 'I feel nothing. The magic is all gone and now I can think of him with composure. I never used to be able to, you know. Once he was the sun in the morning for me. The smell of tall trees with the rain on them; the fleeting glimpse of a star falling through the sky. He was everything magical and extraordinary – and then – then the magic died. It fizzled out, like short-circuited lights on a Christmas-tree, and I was left gazing at nothing.'

'Nothing!' Della echoed. 'How sad that sounds.'

Fay shrugged her shoulders and tossed the denuded heart of the little daisy from her. She turned to Della and took hold of her hands. 'Now listen, Dell,' she said, 'you've not to worry about Lew and me. It's best we part.'

'But why – why?'

'Because, my dear, a marriage, like a house, won't stand erect on one wall. I tried for seven months to make it do that, but the inevitable collapse came in the end. Now I've no desire to rebuild on the ruins.'

'Has Lew – has he asked you to rebuild?' Della's dark eyes were curiously wistful as they held Fay's.

Fay shook her head. 'I don't want him to, Dell. I just don't want him to.' Then she squeezed Della's hands. 'How about you and Will? Are you happy with him, my dear?'

'Oh, yes – he's awfully good to me. So – so patient and kind.'

'He'll make a splendid father.'

'So would Lew – don't you think?' Della spoke with a little rush. 'I – I mean, men who haven't been all that happy themselves as children, well, they usually ensure that their own children have a good time.'

'Wasn't Lew happy as a boy?' Fay asked – and in her mind's eye she saw Lew as a boy; tall and imperious, doing all the wrong things and only laughing when he did them; too much like his beautiful Sicilian mother for his grandmother to have any affection for him.

'Lew was kind of wild, you see,' Della said. 'Old Gran never really understood him. I guess she took more to me because I was younger, more able to adapt myself to her ways. Did you know that Lew worshipped our mother?'

'No!' Fay's blue eyes flew wide open. 'No, I didn't know that. I received the impression that he hated her.'

'He did after she remarried and walked out on us. He was twelve, you see; he was of an age to be terribly hurt by something like that. It hardened him; kind of killed all his faith in women; instilled a perpetual mistrust. I – I know he must have hurt you, Fay, for you to want to cut free of him, but don't hate him.'

'I don't hate him, Dell,' Fay replied quietly.

It was at dinner that evening that Lew said to Fay, 'Dell tells me you've got to get back to your hospital on Thursday. I've some business to attend to in Hollywood, so why don't we travel together?'

But before Fay could answer him, Della broke in, 'Say darn to that old hospital and stay here for good! Go on, Fay!'

Fay gave a little laugh, while Lew's expressive left eyebrow quirked amusedly. She saw no active objection to Lew's suggestion that he travel back with her. It was true she shied a little from the thought that the intimacy of a train journey together might induce more personal conversation than that they had yet indulged in since meeting again, yet she also felt that she'd be equal to it. Lew no longer frightened her; she found him little changed outwardly, yet there was a quietness about his eyes, a lack of boldness in his glance, that told her he had changed. He had changed, she thought, in that he had come to accept the fact that she was no longer his, over whom he could cast that sweeping, imperial glance of old.

'I quite like working at the Anita Hill,' Fay said. Then she glanced at Lew. 'Are you sure you have to leave on Thursday? I shan't be dragging you away, shall I?'

'Lord, no!' He chuckled. 'Dell will be glad to see the back of me.'

Della pulled a face at him. 'That isn't true and well you know it, Lew Marsh. I'd like you to stay for good as well, except that you'd be rather a dangerous influence on my nice Will.'

Her nice Will, who was carefully removing brazils from their shells and putting the nuts on Della's plate, shot his lopsided grin at her. 'Eat your nuts and stop insulting me. I was quite a lady-killer before you hooked me.'

Della took a nut and obediently chewed it, her eyes upon the glistening bronze of Will's hair. 'I'm wondering whether I shall enjoy having a red-haired baby,' she said. She smiled at Fay. 'If my son dares to be born with red hair, I'll give him to you, Fay. With your craze for babies, you wouldn't care a darn about the colour of his hair, would you?'

'Not a darn,' Fay returned lightly – unaware that Lew was staring at her. 'Anyway, my dear, your baby will probably be born with a head as smooth and hairless as a billiard ball – had you thought of that?'

When Fay, accompanied by Lew, took her departure from Laurel Bay, a slight mist was hanging over the house, blurring its friendly lights as the cab shot down the drive.

The mist seemed thicker in the country lanes, and by the time they reached the railway station it was beginning to bank into a grey-yellow fog. Lew glanced at his wristwatch as they stood on the platform, awaiting their train. 'This murk is delaying our train,' he remarked.

'Have you an appointment in Hollywood, then, Lew?' Fay asked.

'It's nothing that won't keep. Just a preliminary consultation about the European showing of *Lucrece*.'

'*Lucrece?*' Fay smiled slightly.

Lew joined her smile. 'Karl has decided that the full title is a bit much, so we've cut it down.'

'It it a good film, Lew?'

'I think so. The exterior scenes are great. Y'know, you'd have loved it in Toledo, Fay, where we shot some of the film.'

She didn't answer, and he went on: 'It's a strange place; it stirs the blood with its old, wild secrets and its tall, shuttered houses, built from rock. It's a place that hasn't changed in centuries.'

And then they heard their train, felt the speeding tremble of it under their feet as it bore down upon them. It rushed to a clamorous standstill, an ominous thing, sleek and faintly menacing, with its doors slamming loudly as people jostled to get on their way.

They entered a compartment and Fay sank down into a corner seat – and suddenly, right out of the blue, she found herself saying, 'Tell me, Lew, whatever did you do about Jerry Kaufmann's cigarette-case? It was rather expensive and I shouldn't like to think that it got lost.'

Lew was tossing their overnight cases to the luggage rack and he glanced round at her in some surprise. 'You haven't seen him since?' he exclaimed.

'Why, no!' She sat down, drawing off her gloves and tucking them into the flap at the back of her handbag – in the old neat way Lew remembered so well. 'No, I haven't seen Jerry.' Then she smiled slightly. 'That is, I did see a film of his some time ago, but I haven't seen him to speak to.'

'I – see.' Lew sat down facing her. 'I left the cigarette-case with the landlord of the pub,' he said curtly. 'I wasn't going to put myself out, returning that guy's damn property.'

'That was a pretty miserable quarrel we had over that cigarette-case, wasn't it, Lew?' Fay met his eyes, briefly, remembering that quarrel, all that it had led to. Then she glanced away from him, gazing out at the slow drift of fog past the windows of the train, listening idly to the slamming of doors along the train. It was stirring back into powerful life now, a waking giant uttering shaky groans of protest as it set off on the next stage of its journey, gathering momentum every second, plunging forward into the fog.

'Miserable, my dear?' Lew said, drawing her eyes back to his face, grown darker than ever from the hot sun of Spain, a chiselled mask, out of which the dark eyes glowed with a sudden passion she couldn't fathom. 'Monstrous is a better word, I think! You've every reason to hate me. I haven't forgotten the things I said to you. I haven't forgotten that I struck your baby dead with my brutal tongue.'

'Don't!' She threw out a hand, as though to ward off his words, the memories they evoked. 'Don't, Lew! That's all over, all finished. Don't let's talk about – about the baby.'

'No – perhaps you're right.' He laid his head back against the dark plush of the train seat, the action strangely melancholy, strangely tired. 'Well, how's nursing, Fay? Are you happy at the Anita Hill?'

'Very happy,' she said.

'I'm glad. I want you to be happy.' His eyes moved over the delicate contours of her face, took in the new way she was wearing her hair. Gone was the soft page-boy of their married days, now her hair was cut to a shortness that was almost boyish. She looked, he thought, jaunty and independent – and so pretty! 'I couldn't believe my eyes when you walked into Laurel Bay the other day, my dear,' he said. 'I thought you were still in England.'

'I meant to write and tell you that I was back in Hollywood, but we've been kept so busy at the hospital.' She shrugged slightly. 'There never seemed to be time for writing letters —'

'I quite understand, Fay.' His lips quirked on a ghost of his old derisive grin. 'It wasn't important enough to you, the finding of enough time. Oh, I quite understand!'

'There seemed no point, Lew.' She met his eyes with a candid frankness. 'We had said everything – what could I add?'

'Do you really think we've said everything?' Abruptly he leant towards her, his face grown a little grim, his eyes intent upon hers. 'Where do we go from here, Fay? Do you want me to divorce you?'

'Oh, no!' Her eyes flashed with a shocked abhorrence.

'N-not divorce!' Her eyes searched his. 'You don't want that, do you?'

'I, surprisingly enough, want whatever you want,' he returned quietly. Then he added, 'I take it we go on as we are now? We continue as polite strangers?'

'Isn't it the best way?' She held out a hand appealingly, and for a moment it seemed as if he would take that out-thrown hand, then his own half-raised hand fell back to his knee. He sank back in his seat, watched her broodingly for a second or two. 'You really are happy?' he questioned again. 'You're not lonely in Hollywood?'

She shook her head. 'I'm not lonely. I have two very nice friends – Mimi and Max Forrester. You don't have to worry about me, Lew. Or feel that I'm a distant responsibility – I don't want that.'

'Not that, nor me!' The smile he smiled then was wholly cynical. 'Well, I'm not blaming you. You're wise to clear your house of rubbish.'

'Oh, Lew!' She had to laugh – yet it was a laughter that rose on a rather wobbly note, as though he moved her, despite herself. 'Lew,' her blue eyes were very earnest gazing across into his, 'let's get one thing straight, at least. I – I don't hate you, just because I no longer – well, I don't hate you. I don't!'

'Methinks you insist too earnestly,' he broke in, looking sardonic.

'Lew, I must make you understand.' She passed her hand across her head in a worried gesture, ruffling the shining hair, making it stand up, unaware of how endearing that lapse from neatness made her look to him. 'Love – love made of me a creature without a shell, something that got wounded so easily. Love stripped everything from me – independence – protection. But freedom from love has restored my shell and I don't get hurt any more.' Her chin lifted and her eyes held purpose. 'I'm safe now – and happy.'

Safe! Happy! Free!

The wheels of the hurrying train took the words and they became one with the rhythm of the train. Lew heard them and knew a wild need to escape them. Fay – no longer wanting love, shrinking from it, she who was so made for love! He rose blindly to his feet. 'I'm going out to the corridor to smoke.' He spoke hurriedly, harshly, already moving past her to the door. 'Do you mind?'

She shook her head, watching him as he stepped out into the swaying corridor and strode from her sight.

CHAPTER FIFTEEN

LEW SMOKED moodily, staring into the hazy darkness beyond the corridor window and seeing only the darkness of his own thoughts.

So the drear emptiness of the past four months was to go on – because he had stooped low enough to believe that Fay, gentle, compassionate Fay, with her flower-like sweetness, could betray him as Inez Holden had betrayed him.

Inez – he'd nearly choked the life out of her that night she had come to him and laid claim to still loving him. His angry hands had closed about her throat, but gazing down at her face, so flawlessly beautiful, yet now, to him, only a lying mask covering a cheap recklessness, a weary disgust had replaced his anger. His fingers had caught in the pearls about her throat, the pearls that had been his engagement present to her, and as the string had broken and the lovely, iridescent things had rained to the carpet like tears, he had contemptuously marched her to the door and put her out of his life.

With the slam of the door he had sworn that never again would a pair of blue eyes get under his skin; that never again would any woman be more to him than a means of pleasure.

And he had kept that promise – kept it so well that now

he had lost the best thing that had ever come into his life, he had lost Fay's love.

Fay's love! Small, melting body in his arms; lovely mouth flaming under his mouth.

Fay's love, which he had killed; which he had struck dead with that unutterable insinuation that Jerry Kaufmann had fathered her baby. Lew shied from the memory; from the terrible hurt that had been in Fay's eyes.

Half an hour later, when he rejoined Fay, he found her still sitting quietly in her corner, her eyes turned towards the window. She didn't seem to hear him and he stood watching her from the doorway of the compartment, swaying to the motion of the train ...

And then, like a heart missing a beat, the rhythm of the train seemed to change. A faltering shudder seemed to pass along the entire length of it, to be present under the wheels, in the body of it, and then overhead. It came like a flick of lightning, and Fay, in that moment, did glance up – to see Lew, in whom the instinct of danger was as primitive and as lively as his quick tempers and his quick passions, diving across the compartment towards her, reaching for her with his powerful arms. Covering her body with his body as the train, in that split second, went hurtling off the lines and the whole world became one long, hideous scream of wrenching metal, rending wood and splintering, hailing glass.

Darkness swept down like a black wing; a spinning eternity of darkness, in which was held, it seemed for ever, the high and terrible keening of people in sudden agonizing pain and terror.

And then, as fear pierced through the paralysis of numbing horror that the initial impact, the first moment of shock induced, Fay cried out against the nightmare, fighting to breathe, to ease her lungs of the lifeless weight that seemed to be crushing them, while somewhere in the dark, terrible night a pandemonium of dark, terrible noise was raging – a noise that surely belonged in bedlam or in hell!

She couldn't see. She could only feel – feel her aching, stunned body – feel incredulous disbelief. It chased round and round in her head, a panic-stricken voice crying out an unending stream of jumbled words. 'We've crashed!' 'I must have my freedom – I must – I must!' 'We've crashed!' 'We've crashed!' Round and round.

She moved, she pushed with her hands at the weight that lay so heavily upon her, numbing her, stifling her. She felt that weight give a little and it was warm to her hands – she felt with her hands the material of Lew's jacket. She remembered – she lived again that moment when she had glanced up to see him diving across the compartment towards her, his dark face alive with purpose in that deadly moment of his awareness that the train stood on the brink of disaster. His eyes nakedly revealing his determination to reach her before the racking moment of shock and horror came. She had read something in them that lying stricken, barely able to breathe, she had neither the sense nor the will to truly comprehend. She couldn't think of it now. Very possibly she had dreamed what she had seen, but she couldn't think of it now!

She struggled to release herself from the dead weight of Lew's body. If only – if only she were able to see! It was so dark, everything was so dark! Then her hands came free and she held Lew while she slowly pulled herself from beneath him. She lay in splintered wood and glass, panting with the effort she had made, her throat dry and harsh with dust and the hot, metallic tang of fumes that seemed over everything like a pall.

Having regained a little breath, she felt again for Lew. She could hear the hoarse, shallow drag of his breathing and as she felt impotently about him, praying for a lift in the darkness so that she might see how badly he was hurt, the sudden lurid flare of a fire sprang up outside, bathing the shambles that had been this compartment in red, flickering light.

Fay knelt by Lew, pushing at the rubble that lay over him, pushing it from his back and his sides – her hand coming away wet as she touched the left side of him. She saw, by the high, dancing light of the fire outside, that he lay at a curious angle. The right side of his body, from where she had crawled, lay free of impedimenta, but when she carefully felt along the left side of him, where that ominous wetness was rapidly spreading, she found that his arm was pinned. It was thrown forward, as though he had attempted to ward off the onrush of disaster; pinned just above the elbow, gripped in the jaws of something unyielding and metallic, that refused to give an inch to her exploring, suddenly wrenching fingers.

With the quick, sure hands of her profession, she untied Lew's tie, sought in his breast pocket for the silver pencil and the pocket-knife he always carried there and finding them, rapidly ripped with the knife at the material of his left sleeve, ripped it away from the upper part of his arm, ripped away as well the linen of his shirt, baring the arm so that she might apply pressure. Blood bathed her hands as she worked, pouring from the cut arteries of the arm, and though deadly fear was in her, a cold, numbing fear that turned her sick and ill, she worked with steady, controlled hands.

She tore away the skirt of her petticoat for the improvising of a pad, rolling it as firmly and thickly as she could, applying it to the main artery of the arm and then encircling the arm with the silk tie, placing it firmly over the centre of the pad. Then she crossed the silk in a half-knot at the other side of the arm, laid the slim silver pencil against the half-knot and tied a reef knot, twisting the pencil to tighten the silk tie against the pad, twisting fiercely, exerting all her strength, fighting to stay that red flood.

People were running backwards and forwards in nightmare hysteria, calling out and crying. And above it all there was suddenly the clarion call of racing ambulances, the hellish wailing of police-car sirens, the pealing of fire bells. But Fay felt outside of it all, alone on an isle of distress with Lew. The pain and agony of others meant nothing to her. She was only concerned with bringing aid to Lew, stripped of all pretence for ever, her very soul flaring with passionate thankfulness as she saw that the life blood was ceasing to pump from Lew's veins, puddling in the shambles.

She knotted the silk tie and though her heart was pounding so hard it was shaking her body, her hands did not shake. Now she must bring help from outside. Now she must bring a doctor.

She left Lew. She scrambled from the compartment window,

where the glass had shattered into a thousand fragments, uncaring of the small jagged pieces that remained in the edges of the frame, tearing her legs and her arms as she forced her slender body out on to the railway line. She ran along the line, pushing past the dazed forms of people, who, like herself, had escaped injury.

Fire and fog and hissing jets of water seethed above the broken monster body of the train and Fay ran through the haze like a small ghost – shying once, and averting her eyes from something that was no longer living and warm and whole, but which, like a torn doll, lay thrown across the wrenched, shining line.

Then Fay saw the white-coated figure of a doctor bent above a stretcher on the line, and half stumbling, breathless with the acute need to bring aid to Lew, she made straight for him. He had with him a couple of ambulance men and when Fay reached the group, as though in answer to her wild prayers, the men bore away the stretcher. She gripped the doctor's arm. 'Will you come?' she implored. 'There's some-one – he's trapped! Will you come?'

Her face lifted to his in the white light of the arc lamps that were now playing on the wrecked train was desperate in its urgency, and he said not a word, only turning to follow her.

When they reached the place where Lew lay, the white light of the lamps had replaced the red glare of the fire that had now been controlled and Fay crawled in through the window, the doctor following her. They knelt in the rubble beside the trapped, unconscious figure of Lew and the doctor was brisk, examining the pressure Fay had applied.

'Not bad, at a moment's notice,' he said. 'It's a lucky thing for him you knew how to do this.'

'I'm a nurse,' she replied quietly, watching Lew's still profile resting in the dust and rubble. She could see the black mark of a bruise on his temple and she could hear the laboured drag of his breathing.

She watched as the young doctor sought with firm, knowledgeable hands for some sign of life in that mangled arm, entrapped so firmly in metal. And even before he turned a regretful face to her, she knew what he would say. 'The arm's finished,' he said. 'As far as I can make out, the hand's severed at the wrist and the forearm's completely crushed.' He spoke to her quite dispassionately, though he knew that this man meant all the world to her; it was written plain on her face and in her eyes. 'I'll have to amputate. It would be pointless trying to release a perfectly useless arm.' He watched her. He said carefully, 'Will you help me?'

Fay always thought afterwards that the calmness with which she assisted this doctor was heaven-sent. It had to be a gift from God, for she was as controlled as though she assisted a surgeon in the clinical impersonality of an operating theatre. She was as controlled as though this man, over whose body she and this doctor worked, was a complete stranger.

The agony she was feeling didn't show – the terrible torment of heart and soul was clamped down tight inside her. She made no sound as she witnessed the removal of Lew's arm. She made no sound as he, who had been so physically perfect, was put among the ranks of the crippled and the maimed.

Then the doctor, his work swiftly and skilfully completed,

hurried away to fetch ambulance men, and Lew lay lax and still, his breathing less ragged than it had been, for the state of unconsciousness he lay in had been intensified to a deeper state by morphia.

Fay held him gently, stroking his black hair back off his forehead, beaded with a fine, cold sweat. And though her legs were cramped and cut from kneeling in splinters of wood and glass, her dress stiff and sticky with blood, her head pounding from the noise that continued to rage outside, she would have held him like this through eternity.

He had subjected his body to this torment for her sake – he had taken that dive across the compartment in order to spare her the tear of wrenching metal. He had shielded her; his eyes had held, nakedly, the wish to shield her – or die with her.

The ambulance men came and Lew was carefully lifted from the wreckage, laid on a stretcher and borne away to an ambulance, where the young doctor who had performed the amputation immediately set about matching Lew's blood and starting a transfusion. Then he smiled reassuringly at Fay, leapt from the ambulance and swiftly closed the door. The ambulance then swung away from the nightmare, the tumult and the misery and flew through the night towards one of the hospitals that were receiving the injured and the dying from the train wreck at Farmer's Corner.

CHAPTER SIXTEEN

THE AMBULANCE drew to a standstill in the rear entrance of the hospital and the men came round to carefully lift down Lew's stretcher. Fay followed dazedly as the stretcher was borne in through the doors of the hospital and swiftly transferred to a trolley. Fay watched as the blue-and-white-clad figure of a Sister approached the trolley and spoke to the ambulance men.

Reaction was setting in now, and Fay stood swaying in the clinical brightness of the receiving-room, the odour of drugs stinging her nostrils, the murmur of many voices coming in sing-song waves to her ears. She fought off her weakness, pulled together the remaining shreds of her strength and her self-control as she moved towards the Sister, bent above Lew, lying so terribly still. Lew – with maimed strength! That magnificent vigour, that was like lightning flashing high above tall trees, stilled and stricken!

She forced her trembling knees to carry her through the mill of people – shock cases – men and women with bleeding faces and torn clothing – men and women who waited, as she waited, for a favourable verdict on someone they loved.

She stood by the trolley and listened as one of the ambulance men gave the Sister a rapid account of Lew's amputation. She heard the name, Dr Ransome, and she vaguely realized that the name referred to that quiet, skilfully working person who had knelt with her in that shattered compartment and removed Lew's arm, ligatured what remained with firm rapidity and smiled briefly, reassuringly at her when it was all over.

When the ambulance man ceased to speak, the Sister turned at once to her desk and took up the phone. Fay heard her ask for Men's Surgical. 'I'm admitting an amputation,' she spoke swiftly, her sympathetic grey eyes resting on Fay, who was mutely gazing down at the unconscious face of Lew, chalky under the tan and beaded with the fine sweat of shock. 'Left arm,' the Sister said. 'Yes, I'm sending him up right away.'

No time was wasted then, the usual preliminary of taking the trolley into a cubicle and calling a doctor to make an examination dispensed with. The trolley was wheeled rapidly from the receiving-room, the white doors swinging on it, and Fay turned from watching the doors, mechanically giving the Sister the particulars she asked for, Lew's name, age, address – wondering how she kept upright, wondering how her knees held her.

The Sister eyed her concernedly. 'Are you all right?' she asked. 'You've not been hurt yourself, have you?'

Fay shook her head. 'I'm – I'm only shaken up. I'll be all right.'

'Well, find yourself a seat,' the Sister said. 'I'll let you know how your husband's going on just as soon as I can.'

'Thank you.' Fay turned wearily from the desk and made her way across the room to where a few chairs remained unoccupied. She sank down into one of them, clasping her hands tightly together in an attempt to stop them from trembling.

'Dear God,' she prayed, 'don't let Lew die! Please, don't let that happen! He's borne enough tonight; don't take away all his splendid strength! Please – please!'

'Hullo there!' a quiet voice said.

She glanced up. She stared uncomprehendingly at the thin, serious face, the quiet eyes of Dr Ransome, who had just arrived with one of the ambulances. She attempted a smile that merely moved her mouth a little.

'Don't go worrying yourself sick,' he urged. 'That young man is as tough as a tree. He'll pull through.'

'He's – my husband.' Her eyes were infinitely tragic in that moment. She was remembering, she couldn't stop remembering, that in the train, only a matter of half an hour before the crash, she had exultantly informed Lew that her happiness lay in being free of him. 'He's my husband,' she said again.

The doctor abruptly sat down beside her. 'You've nowhere to go tonight, have you?' His eyes were steady on her wan face. 'Would you care to put up at my sister's? She only lives a few blocks from here. She won't mind a bit having you.'

'But I want to stay here!' She eyed him rather wildly. 'I want to be near Lew. He might die.'

'He isn't going to die.' Dr Ransome took hold of her cold, shaking hands, gripping them, trying to instil into them some of his own warmth and steadiness. 'Where's all that wonderful courage of yours gone to?' he demanded. 'Don't buckle under now. You fought most of your husband's battle down in that wreck, now we'll proceed with the rest. We won't let him die.'

'But I must stay here until I know – until I know!' she insisted. 'I can't – I won't go until then.'

'All right. Anyway, I'll give you my sister's address.' He took a notebook and a pencil from his pocket and scribbled the address, tearing the leaf from the book and handing it to her. He smiled. 'I hope you can understand my writing. Now I promise you Kate won't mind having you. She's used to the occasional strays I send along to her. She's an awfully good sort.'

Fay held the piece of paper and it fluttered slightly, in time with her trembling. 'You're an awfully good sort yourself,' she told him gratefully.

He looked a trifle abashed. 'Now what about money?' he asked quickly. 'You'll need some for the cab.' He took out his wallet and extracted a ten-dollar bill, pressing it into her hand. 'You don't mind taking money from a – a friend, do you?' he queried, his smile a little diffident.

She shook her head.

'Good!' He jumped to his feet. 'You'll be fine with Kate. You'll be better with her than hanging about here all night.'

She nodded. He was right, of course. She would go to his sister's when someone came to say that Lew was going to be all right.

'Doctor,' she gazed up at him pleadingly, 'can't I help? Can't I do something? If I sit here, just thinking, I'll go crazy.'

He hesitated. 'You're hardly in a state—'

'Please!' She stood up. 'Surely there's something I can do?'

'Allright, perhaps you would be better doing something.' He took hold of her arm and led her to the Sister's desk, where people were now milling excitedly, shouting questions and bringing a look of harassment to the grey eyes of the Sister as she tried to speak on the phone. 'Please be quiet,' she cried out to them. 'We'll manage so much the better if you'll all try to be calm.'

Then she saw Dr Ransome leaning forward across her desk and she put her hand over the mouthpiece of the phone, eyeing him enquiringly. 'I've found you a volunteer, Sister,' he said. 'This young woman is going to help with some bandaging. Okay?'

She nodded. 'If you say so, Doctor. Does she know how to?'

His smile at Fay was gently amused. 'Best dab hand at a bandage I ever saw,' he retorted, and turning with Fay he conducted her to the ward that was being used this night as an emergency station.

Two hours later Fay stepped from a taxi outside Kate Ransome's house and pressed the doorbell with a tentative hand. Though Dr Ransome had assured her his sister wouldn't mind putting her up for the night, Fay couldn't help feeling a bit of an intruder.

But Kate Ransome accepted her arrival with an unquestioning calmness that put Fay at her ease right away. She was very like her brother to look at. She was a little older, but she had the same serious sort of face that looked rather melancholy until it abruptly broke into a smile. And the way she drew Fay into the small, square hall, without fuss, merely nodding a calm head when Fay murmured that Dr. Ransome had sent her, revealed how well used she was to receiving into her home her brother's occasional 'strays'.

Her rapid appraisal took in Fay's torn and bloody clothes and she said, 'You're from that wreck at Farmer's Corner, I can see. I was expecting David to send along some poor devil or other.' She smiled and her smile warmed away all the serious reserve of her face. 'I expect you could do with a bath, couldn't you?' she asked.

'Oh, I could indeed!' Fay exclaimed gratefully. 'I feel in an awful mess.'

As they mounted the stairs to the bathroom, Kate Ransome said, 'Have you someone at the hospital?'

'My husband,' Fay spoke quietly. 'He's pretty bad, but he's going – he's going to pull through.' Suddenly her eyes were swimming in tears. She leant against the banister, abruptly giving way, relaxing her hold on the tears she had almost shed at Lew's quiet bedside.

She had been in the midst of bandaging a cut knee when a nurse had come to her and murmured in her ear that she could come up now and see her husband. The process of helping, of occupying her mind with a job she knew so well, had restored to Fay a measure of calm, but as she went with the nurse, hurrying along the white corridor and up the iron staircase that made her footsteps ring hollowly, all the pain, the anguish, had come flooding back.

She had stood at Lew's bedside, with its smell of ether,

and its suspended transfusion bottle giving back the life that had flowed out so freely between her fingers as she had worked to stem it with the crude aid of a silk necktie and a silver pencil, and mingled with her prayer of thankfulness that he wasn't going to die was a terrible despair because she could never recall her words to him just before the crash. She had, with those words, put out of her life the only man she had ever wanted in it. She had told Lew that only in being free of him could she ever find happiness.

She bent to kiss him, touching his cheek with lips that trembled. His face on the pillow was withdrawn into deep sleep, and it broke her heart to see him – the strong, the indomitable – lying so helpless.

The nurse who had brought her to him said quietly, her eyes on the chiselled face, the black hair clinging wetly to the strong, wide forehead, 'What a pity about his arm. He's such a fine-looking man, isn't he?'

Fay could only nod her head, she didn't trust herself to speak. She was clinging to her self-control with all her might. Lew had lost his strength for a while and she mustn't lose hers. He would need her, turn to her in the next few weeks and she mustn't fail him, she mustn't be weak and silly …

But she cried now, in Kate Ransome's house, the salt and painful tears raining down her face, devoured by pain so stark, so overwhelming that even the wild shedding of tears did nothing towards relieving it. If she and Lew had no future together, her pain-torn heart cried out, why, oh, why had God not seen fit to kill her?

'I – I shouldn't be crying,' she sobbed. 'I really shouldn't. Lew's going to get well – so I shouldn't be crying.'

Kate Ransome wrapped a warm arm of sympathy about her shoulders. 'You cry just as much as you want to,' she declared stoutly. 'What did the good Lord give us tears for? They're in us to be shed on occasions like this. You go ahead and cry, my dear.'

CHAPTER SEVENTEEN

SOME WEEKS later Lew sat on the veranda of the hospital, a rug across his knees, sunshine in his eyes and an indulgent smile playing about his mouth as the slim, brunette nurse, Joyce, once again found an excuse to come out to him. She had brought, this time, a tall glass of iced orange juice.

'Are you sure you're not too far out in the sun?' she asked, fussing round him, straightening his rug and eyeing him with such an openly affectionate and maternal concern that he longed to burst into laughter. He wouldn't, though, because, despite this grand passion she seemed to have developed for him, she was a nice kid and a grand nurse. They were all grand, these nurses, even though they did make him feel a bit like a sheik with a particularly adoring harem.

'I'll tell you what,' he said, 'you can bring me a hairbrush.' He grinned at her. 'I'd like to pretty myself up before my wife gets here.'

She obligingly fetched him the hairbrush and stood watching him as he tidied his black hair. She thought him perfectly wonderful and she was dreadfully jealous of Fay. She could never bring herself to greet Fay with very much enthusiasm and she didn't now, hearing the quick, light steps in the room behind and seeing her step out on to the veranda.

'Good afternoon, Mrs Marsh,' she said stiffly, and went her way with a starched rustle of skirts.

Fay was obliged to smile as she approached Lew. 'I'm dreadfully sorry for that poor girl,' she said. 'She really has got it bad. You're a menace, Lew. You were bad enough with two arms, but you're far worse with only one.'

She leant against the rail of the veranda, slender and very fair in a cool navy blue suit with a crisp white collar.

'You're beginning to look much better, Lew,' she said. It was true. Though his face still wore something of the look of the invalid, gone was that frightening chalky look under the tan; gone, too, that fine-drawn look around the eyes. He had, she thought, recovered from that terrible injury with remarkable rapidity – probably because he possessed such superb health and such nerves of steel. And these afternoons in the sunshine were doing him good.

Her eyes settled on his pinned sleeve, and the familiar stab of pitying regret took her heart. He had taken the loss of his arm with far more coolness than she had. She would never, she knew, forget that morning following the accident, sitting beside his bed in a borrowed dress of Kate Ransome's waiting for him to wake and speak to her.

And his first words to her, as he slowly rose up out of the well of stupor that had held him for so many hours had been, 'I've got – the darnedest sensation – like – like being on a raft.' His eyes, misty with pain and drugs, gazed straight up into hers. 'Are you – all right?' he asked.

She nodded. She couldn't speak, her throat was hurting her too much. She wanted to throw herself down beside the bed, to bury her face in the covers and howl like a baby.

'Why – why am I here?' he asked. 'What the devil am I – doing here?' She watched his eyes travelling round the room. She saw the perplexity in his eyes, the effort to remember, the effort to break through the drug-induced veil. His eyes slowly turned towards his left side, where the pain he was aware of, distant yet distinct, unreal yet real, was localized. Fay saw, then, that he was remembering – that the veil was shimmering to let him through.

His eyes returned to her colourless face. His eyes searched her eyes, read in them the awful truth. 'They've taken off – my damned arm!' he gasped. He lay assimilating the drear fact, and Fay, her heart torn in two for him, sat like stone, barely breathing. She waited, she watched – she saw his lips move and she bent her head to catch what he said. 'Well, it could – it could have been my head,' was what he said. Then his dark eyes drooped and closed and the sleep of exhaustion claimed him once more.

He accepted the loss of his arm with the same imperturbable coolness with which he had leapt to lose it, and after about a week, his strength rapidly flowing back and with it his wry sense of humour, he was actually joking about it with the nurses. And they, one and all, fell for his good looks and the light thing he made of being maimed, playing truant to pop in and out of his room during the day, to see him and have a brief, laughing chat with him. They called him 'the pirate' and they all openly envied Fay.

She came every day; she never missed. Kate Ransome had insisted she stop on with her and Fay was frankly glad to fall in with the suggestion, for Kate's house was much nicer than a hotel would have been.

The news had quickly got into the papers that Lew Marsh had been an injured passenger on the train and Fay suddenly found herself dealing with phone calls, and telegrams of sympathy, all the way from Hollywood, with an efficient self-assurance that amazed her.

There had been one long-distance phone call from – of all people – Thalia Van Deen, and Fay had turned to Lew to ask what she shoud say in answer to Thalia's bitter-sweet demand for a few words from him to put in her column.

'Tell her to go lose herself in the Grand Canyon,' he retorted lazily. 'Or, better still, tell her to go to hell.'

'Thalia,' Fay said into the phone, smiling at the look of distaste on Lew's face, 'Lew says it's very nice of you to phone.' Her smile spread as he began to look indignant. 'Oh, he's a lot better, thanks. What does he say? Oh, he says it could have been his head. Yes, really! I agree with you, he has got guts, hasn't he? Of course you can quote me. Oh, I really can't say when he'll be coming home, but he's definitely on the mend now. Yes, I was extremely lucky, wasn't I? The cause of the accident? I can't really say – there's to be an investigation, of course, but everyone here seems to think that the fog we had that night was the main cause. Oh, it was a hellish experience! Thank God the train wasn't packed – enough poor devils were killed and injured as it was ...'

When she finally replaced the phone, Lew said, 'Why do

you always have to be so soft with everyone – especially her sort?'

She shrugged. 'It doesn't cost me anything, Lew,' she replied.

He watched her, then he turned his eyes from her. 'You're too damned good to live!' he retorted.

And that was the closest he had come, in these weeks of his in hospital, to a remark that could be construed as personal. He openly showed her that he was grateful she stayed on in this little town called Farmer's Corner to be with him; coming to the hospital every day; writing his letters and handling his phone calls; bringing him amusing little presents, but his eyes never revealed anything more than gratitude, and there were nights when Fay lay sleepless wondering about the future – fearing the future.

Were they still as they had been before the crash? Was ultimate separation from him all she had to look forward to? Had she, perhaps, only dreamed the passionate purpose that had blazed in his eyes when he had leapt across that railway compartment; only imagined the exultation that had leapt like flame in them when he had reached her and torn her from her seat and had her close to him as they descended together into the maelstrom?

She said now, bending to flick a small piece of fluff off the side of one of her navy suede shoes, 'I bet you can't wait for Saturday to come, can you, Lew? I was as pleased as anything when Dr Ransome told me you were being discharged.'

'Sure I'm pleased,' he said, but abruptly he was frowning,

looking away from her, out over the grounds of the hospital, where white-coated doctors strolled in the sunshine and patients and visitors sat talking on benches.

'Oh, I know you'll be sorry to leave your harem,' she laughed.

He merely gave a rather moody shrug of his shoulders and she left the rail of the veranda and crossed to him. She put her hand upon his shoulder. 'What's the matter, Lew?' she asked.

'Oh nothing!' he said, 'I guess I'm just a bit – well, everyone'll make such a damn fuss. That crowd back on the Coast! You know what they are. They'll treat this empty sleeve like the book of the month!'

Her hand tightened on his shoulder. 'They'll only mean it kindly, Lew.'

'Sure, I know that,' he agreed, 'but they dramatize everything right out of proportion. This has happened – I've accepted it. But if anyone comes up to me and says, "How too, too terrible, dear boy!" I shall swipe him one.' He gave her a brief moody smile. 'So help me, Fay, I will!'

'You say that now, but once you're home again you'll feel differently.' Fay's smile was reassuring.

'Maybe I'll change my mind and not go home,' he retorted. 'Now I come to think of it, I've all the world to choose from.'

'But there's your work, Lew!' Now Fay regarded him with a dawning anxiety. '*Lucrece* is due for its Hollywood première – didn't Karl Christbel cable to tell you? You can't let the film down, Lew.'

'Can't I?' He shrugged his wide shoulders. 'Don't you know, baby, that once a film is in the can, the director ceases to be of much importance to it? *Lucrece* will stand on its own merits. I think – I think I might go back to Toledo for a while. It's a fascinating place.' He leant his head against the back of his chair and screwed his eyes against the sunshine that was beating down warmly upon the veranda. 'Toledo in September should be quite a place. I might rent a little house – stay till Christmas, then come home to be uncle to Dell's baby.'

'Talking of Dell's baby,' Fay searched her purse with a hand that shook slightly, 'I had a letter from her this morning.' She found and opened the letter. 'The baby's doing fine. Della says he's showing signs of being a bit of a flirt.' She read from the letter: 'Tell Lew that his small namesake has definitely inherited his flirtatious tendencies, much to Will's discomfiture. He smiles at all the women and merely blows bubbles at anything in pants. He's a real poppet, even though I do say so myself, all delicious brown skin and big brown eyes, a real Marsh. I did think he'd have Will's mop of flames, but he looks like being as dark as I am. He's a darling! I'm longing for you to see him. When Will came to see Lew did he tell you that we've had the old rose arbour turned into a playhouse for the baby? It was Will's idea. It looks fine. We've put in a swing and a little roundabout and had the walls painted all over with Walt Disney characters; you'd never recognize it for the old derelict it used to be. Now on the level, Fay, you're going to love this cute kid of mine; he talks with his eyes, so do bring Lew, just as soon as he's well enough to come, and doubtless when he sees Will's son and heir –'

Fay broke off, the quick pink of confusion washing into her face. She avoided Lew's eyes as she returned the letter to her bag. 'He sounds a stunning baby, doesn't he?' she said, fighting to keep her voice steady.

'Why shouldn't he be?' Lew was watching, carefully watching, the sudden little flags of colour flying in Fay's cheeks – and he knew a quick, sharp pain that it should hurt her, perhaps embarrass her, that light remark of Dell's at the end of her letter. There came sweeping back over him the memory of Fay in the bedroom of that little pub at Thame … and wildly he pushed that memory from him, cloaking it in mockery.

'Dell's rather a stunner herself. Poor kid, she was quite upset, wasn't she, that our domestic ship had not drifted into safe harbour with hers and Will's. Dell I fear is inclined to forget that I'm a mere pirate, while her Will is a steady captain.'

Fay listened to him with pain, turning from him so that he might not read her pain, which seemed to hold her heart in a fist shod with mail. She wanted to cry out to him, 'Oh my dear, we both made mistakes in the guiding of our ship. You wanted less than I was prepared to give. I wanted more than you could give.'

When she did speak she said, 'Lew, I don't quite know what you want me to do about – about Saturday. I mean – if you're not going home –'

'Don't worry about me, Fay,' he rejoined carelessly.

'But naturally I'm worried! I'm worried about how you'll manage on your own.' Fay stood tense by the rail of the veranda, her hands clenched on her bag. 'Will you go to a hotel?'

'Sure.' He continued to speak with carelessness. 'I'll get the boots to dress me, and ask the waiter to clean the spilled soup off my waistcoat.' He was smiling quizzically as Fay swung round to him, but when he saw the white torment of her face, his smile died. 'Don't look like that – I was only joking.' His hand moved, almost as though he would stretch it out to her, then it fell again to his rug-covered lap. 'I've tied you to my damned bedside too many weeks already; I want you to fly away into the sun now, honey.'

'Into the sun?' She was at a loss, her wide blue eyes fixed upon his face.

'Into the sun, my dear. Spreading your wings, flying far from the dark web I spread for you. Forget me – forget me very quickly; you'll be doing yourself a favour.'

'Lew – don't!' The words broke from Fay. 'Don't talk like that!'

'It's the truth, isn't it?' He spoke crisply, leaving himself no margin for excuse. 'From this day I'll take no more of your compassion or your time. I'll be perfectly all right on my own.'

'That isn't true and you know it, Lew!' Suddenly Fay was rather angry with him. The idea! Imagining he could stroll out into the world with that one arm and find no difficulties for himself! Her heels rang on the stone of the veranda as she crossed over to him. 'About Saturday.' Now it was her turn to speak with crisp decision. 'I think you ought to go home, and no nonsense about it. I'll come with you – yes, Lew, I'll come with you. Let's say because I'm a soft-hearted fool who won't see you stumbling around on your own, trying to look after yourself. I'll come back with you and I'll be that other arm of yours until you're more able to cope. And if you tell me again that you want no more of my compassion or my time, I'll hit you over the head with this bag.'

He gazed up at her, a reluctant little smile breaking on his mouth. 'I believe you would paste me one, too,' he murmered.

'I would!' She brandished the bag. 'It's English leather, and English leather has plenty of body in it.'

'But honey, I want to go to Toledo.' He spoke a trifle sulkily, like a small boy denied a toy.

'Don't be foolish!' She touched and shook his shoulder. 'In a little while you'll be perfectly well and able to go anywhere you please, but at the moment you're still pretty helpless – and you know it, even though you won't admit it!'

At these words, his derisive grin danced on the edge of his mouth. 'You sound like Nurse Joyce,' he mocked. 'I hope you intend to coddle me like she does. She's a champion coddler.'

'Then you'll be sensible and go home on Saturday?'

'Yes, nurse.'

Fay looked relieved.

Then, somewhere within the hospital, a strident little bell began to ring; the bell that warned visitors their time was almost up. Fay pulled on her gloves. 'I'd better be off,' she said, 'or I shall have your pretty Nurse Joyce out here after me. I'll come again tomorrow, Lew. Oh, and I left some rum and butter toffees on your bedside locker, along with that Kingsley Amis novel you wanted to read.'

'Thank you, Fay.' He watched her go – was still watching the door through which she had disappeared when Dr Ransome stepped out upon the veranda and approached him. There was a lingering smile of unmistakable pleasure on the young doctor's thin, olive-tinted face. 'I've just seen your wife, Mr Marsh' he said. 'She isn't only a very plucky girl, she's also a very nice one.'

Lew eyed him quizzically. 'Plucky? Why, because she married me?'

The doctor looked surprised. 'No,' he said. 'I was referring to the way she worked to save your bacon the night of the train wreck.' His eyes narrowed. 'Didn't you know? You'd have bled to death if it hadn't been for her presence of mind. She applied the crudest but the most efficient tourniquet I've ever seen and she helped me remove that arm of yours as calmly as though we were working together in an operating theatre instead of in the rubble of a wrecked train.' He smiled, gravely. 'Blood on her face, even on her hair, and the most determined little chin you ever saw in your life! That will-o'-the-wisp fought like ten tall men to save your life that night.'

Lew's face had gone strangely still, but his eyes were blazingly alive, full of such raw shock that David Ransome abruptly ceased to smile and reached out to grip his shoulder. 'What is it, man? What's up?' he demanded.

'Why should she – do all that, d'you think?' Lew murmured huskily.

'Lord, she'd do it for anyone,' the doctor explained. 'She's the type.'

'Of course,' Lew nodded. He sank back in his chair, closing his eyes against the sun that shone into them. Blood on her face, even on her hair – he could see her, fighting for him, determined to hold back death; holding it back because once she had loved him, or holding it back because she had been trained to do so, and because it was as natural in her to relieve suffering as it was for her to breathe.

CHAPTER EIGHTEEN

AS FAY and Lew crossed the quiet lobby of Crystal Court that Saturday evening of their return to Hollywood, Lew said casually, 'Where shall we go for dinner? Have you any particular preference?'

She glanced up at him, a trifle embarrassedly. 'As a matter of fact, Lew, I'm going over to see the Forresters. I wrote Mimi, Max's wife, that I'd call in on them as soon as I got back to Hollywood. I'll probably have dinner there.'

'Max Forrester's that doctor friend of yours, isn't he?'

She nodded. 'He and Mimi are very nice. I got friendly with them while I was working at the Anita Hill. They've three of the jolliest kiddies you ever saw. Rollo, the youngest, has hair like white gold.'

'Sounds cute.' Lew's eyes rested on Fay's own very fair hair as they stepped into the lift; the soft curls glinted round a pert jelly-bag hat in dark red and she looked, he thought, like some jaunty pixie. He stood beside her in the lift, longing to touch those funny little boy's curls, yet vigorously restraining himself. She was not his to touch any more, though she stood with him now in this lift that carried them up to the apartment they had once shared so intimately.

His mouth pulled wryly. She was only here because he needed a nursemaid; someone to fix his tie, to lace his shoes, to cut up his dinner, but he'd soon learn to do these things for himself, and then she would go. Just as soon as he got used to living comfortably with one arm, she'd bid him goodbye.

The lift ceased to ride and they stepped out. While Lew unlocked the door of the apartment, Fay – it was an old remembered habit – stood gazing out of the corridor window at the evening-bound streets, the flashing lights that spangled the tall buildings, and Lew watched her a moment. Then he called out, 'Come on, dreamer. You'll be late for your date with those friends of yours.'

When she turned to him, something a little melancholy lurking beneath his smile caught her eye. 'Would you – rather I came out with you?' she asked.

He shook his head. 'Not on your life! I wouldn't spoil your evening for the world. You've spent enough time coddling me in the last few weeks; you go out and have some fun.'

He switched on the light of the apartment and as he put down his suitcases and watched Fay carry hers into the room, his smile went and irritation claimed his mouth. 'Dammit, Fay, I don't like to see you lugging that thing about!' he exclaimed.

She laughed. 'Don't be so silly. I'm not a rabbit, even if I look like one.' She put down the case and came over to him. She touched his arm tentatively. 'Lew – would you – would you like to come to the Forresters' with me?' She knew she was a fool to ask. He'd only look scornful and laugh off her suggestion, but she felt strongly moved to ask him. The thought of leaving him to go out and seek a solitary dinner in a club, where people would stare and offer the condolences he dreaded, touched off her pity and gave her the courage to speak.

But he didn't say anything, he just stood staring at her.

She retreated a little from him, his silence confounding her. 'They're awfully nice people – I just thought you might like to come.'

'I'd very much like to come,' he said at last. His smile flashed warmly. 'It's very nice of you to ask me, Fay.'

'Oh – good!' She laughed, breathless with relief. 'They won't mind a bit, they love company. And I rather thought you didn't much like the idea of dining out alone.'

His face assumed a sardonic expression. 'I must admit I wasn't exactly looking forward to having to ask the waiter to cut up my meat.'

Her heart ached at his words, but she replied to him jocularly, 'You could always pick your meat up in your hand and gnaw it like a cave-man, Lew.' She took up her suitcase. 'I'm having the spare bedroom, aren't I?'

'Naturally!' He smiled slightly. 'It's good of you to want to help me like this, Fay, but I can't help worrying a little about your job. You were longing to get back to it, I remember.'

She shrugged. 'I can always get another job. Nurses are always in demand.'

'Even by incapacitated husbands, it would seem,' he drawled.

She smiled. 'I'm going to freshen up before we go to the Forresters', I feel a bit messy after that long train journey.' She walked towards the door of the spare bedroom, but at the door she turned to eye him a trifle severely. 'Don't forget to call out if you want me for anything. It's what I'm here for. You will, won't you, Lew?'

'Cross my heart!' he promised. But as she disappeared into the room and the door closed, his smile faded, an abrupt look of weariness replacing it. He tossed his overcoat from him and crossed to the sideboard, pouring himself a straight whisky. He drank it down quickly, wincing at the raw burn of it.

Why the hell had he agreed to go to the Forresters'? Not because he didn't like the idea of eating alone, not because he was afraid of making a fiasco of eating in a public place, but because he wanted to be with Fay. That was the plain unvarnished truth – and he knew it. He was crazy about her! He could feel his heart pounding as he stood by the sideboard. He had not known himself capable of such feeling as this, grabbing him by the throat, making him ache with the effort not to go to her and beg her pardon for not loving her long, long ago.

He wanted her – how he wanted her, but still her pity was not enough; still it held him back. Had he not seen that pity exercised again tonight; seen it plain in her eyes when she had asked him if he would care to go and see these friends of hers?

Beware of pity! He scorned pity. He wanted her love. The sweet, warm love he had blasted to atoms with his brutal tongue.

He glanced at his empty sleeve and an ironical smile moved about his mouth. He remembered the dark, scowling gyspy who had pierced the veil that enshrouded the future and seen him as he stood now. She had smiled and thought the loss of his arm the joke of fate. The loss of Fay's love was the joke of fate.

He sighed harshly. Doubtless he had earned the joke!

Fay rang the doorbell of the Forresters' house, smiling at Lew as they stood in the lighted porchway. 'There's no need to look as though you're calling on your dentist,' she murmured.

'I feel a little like it,' he rejoined.

Then the door opened and Max Forrester stood framed against the hall lights, burly and blond, an expression of open surprise on his face as he examined Lew.

'I hope I'm not the skeleton at the feast?' Lew said, following Fay into the house. He held out his hand to Max. 'I'm Lew Marsh.'

Max's eyes took in the pinned left sleeve, revealed under the lightweight coat as Lew shook hands. He met the steady friendly smile Lew was offering him, and he did a quick mental readjustment. He had been prepared to dislike this fellow heartily, if ever he should meet him, considering that any man who could hurt Fay had to be pretty despicable; but now, looking at that empty sleeve, remembering Fay's detailed account of the train crash in a letter to Mimi, he felt animosity die in him. This handsome devil couldn't be entirely despicable; the deep love Fay had once borne him proved it in some message, while his spontaneous leap to shield her from hurt had been an act of selfless gallantry that definitely commended itself to the very masculine Max.

'Come along in and meet Mimi,' Max said.

Mimi had heard the stranger's voice and she was standing up when they entered the sitting-room, an enquiring expression on her face. Fay smiled as she walked across to her and kissed her cheek. 'I brought Lew with me,' she said. 'I hope it's all right?'

'Of course.' Mimi was a little overawed by the dark, smiling man who even foreshortened her own powerfully built Max. 'Are you quite well now, Mr Marsh?' she asked.

'In the pink,' he replied, and his eyes, that couldn't help examining pretty women with pleasure, openly showed her that he thought her extremely pretty. Colour moved in Mimi's cheeks and she understood now why Fay had once said that she had been as incapable of resisting Lew Marsh's charm as a kitten is incapable of resisting the muddling and entwining wiles of a ball of wool.

'Here, let me take your coat,' Max said to him, and Lew shrugged out of it, handing it to him with a murmur of thanks. His glance had settled on a squat teddy-bear astride the television, one orange ear comically askew and a pink paper skirt about its middle. He grinned at Mimi. 'Fay tells me you've got three boys, Mrs Forrester,' he said.

'Three loads of mischief,' she amended. 'Now they're all tucked up in bed, sleeping the innocent sleep of the righteous.' She indicated a chair. 'Please sit down,' she said. 'What do you drink?'

'Tomato juice,' Fay called across from the other side of the room, where she was handing her coat to Max.

Lew settled back in his armchair, his eyes moving over the laughing Fay as she emerged from her coat. She wore pleated coral-pink linen that made her look as cleanly slender as a boy. 'Ignore her, Mrs Forrester,' he said to Mimi. 'She's one of those poor Puritan souls who get giddy on orangeade. She's to be pitied really.'

Mimi laughed as she mixed drinks. 'I'm going to give you a concoction of Max's,' she said. 'And do call me Mimi.'

'Right you are!' he said at once, smiling at Fay as she came across the room to him. She perched herself on the arm of his chair, reaching down to pull his tie a little straighter. 'I don't do these half as well as you used to,' she spoke apologetically. 'I'm not much of a valet, I'm afraid, Lew.'

'You're not doing too badly,' he murmured, watching her bent head.

Mimi brought drinks to them, her eyes widening at the picture of Fay, leaning over this dark, self-assured, rather overpowering person, casually adjusting his tie for him.

Lew accepted his drink and sipped at it, nodding reflectively. 'Um, pretty potent!' His dark eyes sparkled into Mimi's. 'Trying the same on Fay?' he enquired.

'No, Mimi isn't,' Fay said, accepting her drink, which was obviously the much maligned orangeade.

Dinner was an extremely good meal and afterwards they just talked, a pleasant flow of conversation, relaxing and curiously enjoyable. Lew was amazed at the extent of his own enjoyment. He liked this well-lived-in room, with its deep, easy chairs, its spot of crayon scribbling low down on one of the walls, its comical teddy-bear perched on the television, liked the way Fay and Mimi ate chocolate drops with the ease of kids at a picnic.

Fay was fully revealed to him in this comfortable, friendly house – and the revelation delighted him. She was quite without shyness, unafraid to be herself, and once, when Mimi heard one of the children cry out in the nursery, she begged to be allowed to go up to him. 'It's Rollo, isn't it?' she said. 'Do let me go up, Mimi. I'll soon get him back to sleep.'

Mimi laughed. 'Go on, then, as it's Rollo. I know he's your dreamboat.'

Fay hurried from the room and Max said, proffering Lew a light for his cigar, 'Do you have any trouble with what's left of that arm?'

Lew considered. 'I sometimes,' he said, 'get the oddest feeling that I've still got a hand. I go to use it. I actually feel as though I can move my fingers. Weird, eh?'

'You'll lose that sensation by and by,' Max said. 'It's early days yet. Will you try an artificial limb, later on?'

'Hell, no!' Lew laughed, somewhat ruefully. 'I want no phoney attachments, thanks! I'll manage.'

Max nodded. 'I'd feel the same myself,' he admitted.

When Fay returned from the nursery her face was dimpled with a lingering amusement. 'No wonder he couldn't sleep,' she announced. 'He had a fire-engine in the bed with him. A gruesome thing, with ladders jutting out all over it. I had a hard job persuading him to exchange it for a woolly dog.'

'What argument did you employ?' Max enquired, looking interested.

She came across the room and resumed her seat on the arm of Lew's chair. 'I had to tell him a terribly sentimental doggy story. Mind you,' her dimples were well to the fore, 'he didn't believe a word of it. You know Rollo.'

Max looked fond but quizzical. 'I certainly do know Rollo.' He glanced at Lew. 'Takes after his mother, that laddie does. Hasn't an ounce of sentimentality in him.'

'That isn't true!' Mimi protested. 'Don't be mean, Max. Look at the way I cried over that movie we saw last week.'

'What movie was that?' Lew asked with quick interest.

'Oh, quite an old one,' Mimi said, 'a reissue, I think. It was called *Irene Abbott.*'

Fay turned in quick eagerness to Lew, smiling down at him. 'That's one of yours, isn't it, Lew? Surely I've heard you mention it? Of course I have! I saw it while I was at Casa Roche, nursing your grandmother. I mentioned how much I'd enjoyed it and you said, then, that you had directed it.'

'I did direct it, honey.' His eyes smiled into her blue eyes, so candid and lovely, the fair lashes glinting as they curled back. Then he turned to Mimi. 'I must admit I still get a kick out of hearing someone say they've enjoyed that movie. It's still one of my most successful ventures.'

'I loved that ending,' Mimi said. 'The way the rain fell in one great sheet as Irene fled down the drive of that awful house. And that final moment on the cliff edge!' Mimi gave a little shiver of reminiscent pleasure. 'Why did she have to die, though? Why couldn't you let her husband reach her in time?'

'And spoil one of the best shots in the film?' Lew demanded, looking amused. 'I couldn't resist letting Irene jump off that cliff in the pelting rain. Stupendous stuff!'

'You are cold-blooded, Lew!' Fay protested.

'I might tell you,' he said, 'that I was very tempted to let the husband follow Irene to her murky death.'

'He didn't love her enough,' Fay declared. 'It wouldn't have rung true. It's a good job you didn't give way to your temptation.'

'That's true,' Mimi agreed. 'He didn't love her enough to die with her. You'd have spoiled the film.'

'The point is,' Max put in, taking his pipe from his mouth and using it to emphasize his words, 'would a man standing on the brink of death think: "This is love, I must follow!" Would that be a natural reaction? He might reach out, automatically, to save the woman, but if he failed, would he really want to follow her to her death?'

'A spontaneous action,' Lew said quietly, 'is never truly comprehended. It arises from a primitive desire for self-preservation, or from an equally primitive desire for self-sacrifice. Such an action wouldn't necessarily be motivated by love. Even a man passionately in love might balk at dying with his mate, might in the moment of crisis find himself preserving his own life at the expense of the woman's. I honestly believe that it's a purely primitive reaction. A man could leap, quite without thinking, to save the life of a complete stranger.'

'Possibly,' Max murmured. 'But that would surely depend on whether or not the man in question was interested enough in his fellow creatures to put himself out to save one of them, or die for one of them. Not every man has such an overwhelming love of mankind. He'd surely have to be that type, wouldn't he, to leap so spontaneously to preserve the life of a complete stranger?'

Lew was watching Max, a sudden wariness in his eyes. This blond doctor was trying to drive him into a corner, trying to get him to say something that would reveal his own motive in leaping to shield Fay – to shield her or die with her.

That hadn't been natural love of mankind! That had been sheer, primitive desire to be with her in a moment of racking horror, to go down into the bowels of hell with her, or to fly straight up through the gates of heaven. It hadn't mattered which, just so long as they were together, that slender body one with his through all their days and nights in eternity. That was all he had wanted, and he had known it, as he had dived to claim her.

He said now to Max, 'If we examined all our actions and what motivates them, we'd spend half our lives on a psychiatric couch.' He smiled lazily. 'I'll leave Freud to you. I'll take plain D. H. Lawrence. I understand his philosophies a whole lot better.'

When Fay and Lew had gone and Max returned to the sitting-room, Mimi, who was collecting up glasses, swung round to him. Her eyes were eager. 'What do you think, Max? Do you think they'll stay together?'

Max shrugged his shoulders, lounging at ease against the mantelpiece. 'Fay's a soft-hearted little coot, she may not be able to walk out on him. Did she say she was going to?'

'She said she was only staying with him until he's more able to manage with that one arm.' Mimi came across the room to her husband and with a gesture of complete trust in his love burrowed her face into his broad chest. 'Did you like him, Max?' she asked.

Max lightly touched her smooth dark hair. 'Yes, honey, I guess I did. He's been through quite a bit of hell, you know, and it's knocked off the sharp edges, fined him down.'

'I thought that.' Mimi drew a quick little sigh. 'Oh, I do hope they stay together! He must be awfully fond of her – he lost an arm for her, didn't he?' Then Mimi's eyes slowly widened as she remembered the look she had surprised on Lew's face – that look of unmistakable worship, softening away his arrogance, flooding warm and tender in his eyes as he had watched Fay's fair head bent close to his breast, her hands at his tie. 'Do you know what I think?' Mimi declared. 'I think that mixed-up guy is crazy about Fay.'

She heard Max laugh and glanced up at him. 'I do, Max,' she asserted.

'Honey, am I arguing with you?' he laughed.

Going home in the cab, Fay said to Lew, 'You liked the Forresters, didn't you?' She smiled. 'You looked surprised. What did you expect?' She watched his face in the passing lamplight, saw his rather embarrassed expression. 'They've no sophistication, no brittle pretensions. They're just real nice. Two of the nicest people I've ever known.'

'Your sort, eh?' he drawled, amused and touched by her staunch support of Max and Mimi. 'No enamelled glamour. No blasé wit! No vicious ambition.'

'No.' She laughed, laying her head back against the leather of the cab. 'Just relaxed and pleasant and absolutely straight.

My sort, as you say.' Then, as she lay like that, resting her head, she yawned a little and apologetically covered her mouth with her hand. 'I guess I'm a little tired,' she said. 'Aren't you tired, Lew? This is your first full day out of hospital, after all.'

He shook his head. 'I've spent so many hours in bed in the last few weeks, I'm only too thankful to be back on my feet.'

'The harem looked pretty crestfallen when we left,' Fay remarked, smiling.

'I didn't notice David Ransome doing any dance of mad delight,' Lew retorted. 'When you shook hands with the poor guy I thought he was going to burst into tears.' He watched her as he spoke. Her complete unawareness of her own delicate appeal fascinated him. She had no tricks; no flirtatious mannerisms. She just looked sweet and clean; dipped in dew like an early morning flower, he reflected, smiling at his own lapse into poetic romanticism.

And suddenly he was uncertain of himself. How was he going to keep from reaching out after her, when he wanted her so much? Already he was longing to touch quiet fingers to that thin, sweet cheek, those boyish curls, and he doubted his ability to suppress that longing indefinitely. It wouldn't be easy, having to see her around the apartment, acting the impersonal nursemaid, the courteous little friend. It wouldn't be at all easy.

'I like Dr Ransome a lot,' Fay murmured. 'He's a very genuine sort of person.'

'Would it surprise you to learn that I liked him myself?'

Lew laughed slightly. 'I didn't get the urge to wring his neck every time he looked at you, like I used to with Jerry Kaufmann.'

'To wring his neck? Dr Ransome's neck?' The words came in a hurrying surprise from Fay. 'I'm nothing to you, Lew, so why should you want to do that?'

'You're only all the world and every moment I shall spend in eternity.' Then he sat up sharply, realizing what he had said. 'Ignore that, Fay.' Now he spoke crisply. 'It's like a cheap line from a movie.'

'Not cheap!' Suddenly she was clutching his arm. 'Not cheap, but worth a terrible lot, if you meant it.'

A tense silence followed her words, then, almost blindly, Lew reached for her – and the moment he touched her, blown sky-high was his resolve to hide his love and his longing. 'I couldn't bear to take pity from you,' he whispered, 'but if you've anything else to offer me, my darling, I'll take it – grovelling on my knees.'

'Lew!' She held his face in her hands, incredulous with delight. 'Darling, you don't have to grovel.' Then her arms were about his neck, tight and close. 'My dear pirate, I'd hate to see you grovelling.' She laughed tremulously. 'It wouldn't suit you.'

'You call me your "dear pirate",' his arm tightened about her, almost convulsively, 'but don't forget how I've hurt you.'

'Hush!' She stroked his black hair, gentle with him in her love, though pulses throughout her small body were leaping with exultant life at his warm masculine closeness. Gone was the stranger she had said goodbye to in England; she had never really known that Lew, but this one was different – this one was telling her he loved her. 'Nothing that happened before this moment matters,' she whispered. 'This is all that matters, this love we've found together.'

'But you said – you said you could only be happy apart from me. I want your happiness, Fay. I don't want to be the cause of any more pain to you.' He pressed his face to her; breathed the faint perfume of her dress, felt the warm race of her heart under his cheek. 'You're so lovely – so sweet! How can I let you go?'

'I don't want you to let me go.' A husky little laugh broke from her. 'I was very foolish to say that I could only be happy apart from you. I don't live or feel or want when I'm apart from you. I'm a mere automaton, minus her mainspring.' She laughed again. 'Tell me you don't want me merely to valet you – my very dear pirate.'

'I just want you, my very dear angel!' Lingeringly, then, he kissed her mouth; her lovely mouth, that he hadn't known for long, harsh months. With delight and wonder he stepped into the sweet, warm world of her love again. When he finally lifted his head and she snuggled to him with a little murmur of supreme content, he said, 'Fay, d'you know what I'm going to buy you?'

'You and your presents!' She laughed against his warm throat. 'Darling, I don't want a present.'

'You'll want this one.' His lips were against her forehead where the fine, soft curls stirred under his breathing. 'I'm going to buy you a house. Something gay and friendly, like that house of the Forresters', with an enormous garden. What do you say?'

For a moment she was too choked to say anything. Now she knew that in his full reading of her heart and its desires, he truly loved her. Now she knew that no dark clouds would fly over that house he would buy for her; that he would make only sunshine for her. Very tenderly she kissed his cheek. 'I'll let you live in it with me, if you like, my dear,' she said.

DESERT BARBARIAN

Charlotte Lamb

CHAPTER ONE

THE GARDEN of the hotel was dimly lit by coloured lanterns which swung in a faint sea breeze blowing up from the beach below, shedding jewelled circles of red and yellow on the paths, the fringed palm trees and the flower-beds, giving the garden a new fairy-tale prettiness it somehow lacked by day. Now and then, when the wind blew more strongly, the lanterns swung far enough to bring the blue water of the swimming pool alive with shimmering images of colour, as if suddenly filled with exotic little fish. The gay umbrellas beside the pool, their function unnecessary at this hour, fluttered and flapped over their little white tables. The stone terrace running beside the pool was empty. No one sat at a table, no one swam in the bright water.

From the ballroom came the rhythmic beat of a local band, trying hard to imitate Western music but succeeding only in patches, occasionally the genuine echo of their own wailing rhythms sounding like a wraith beneath the regular drum-beats of the modern dance.

Marie had fled from the dance floor to escape the too-insistent attentions of a rather dull young man who seemed unable to recognise polite refusals when they were given. For five days he had haunted her morning, noon and night. She was on the verge of being rude, and had decided it would be wiser to hide from him rather than say the words boiling on her tongue. Discretion, as her father was fond of saying, is the better part of valour.

She leaned on the low stone wall, staring down at the moonlit sea, listening to the low murmur of the waves as they rolled gently along the curve of the little bay, making an ironic background to the insistent beat of the modern dance music. A lighthouse stood on a promontory to the right of the bay, sending out a steady red beam across the water, laying a glimmering red path across the bay which reminded her of the red of a stained glass window. Somewhere beyond the reach of eyesight a ship made a low moaning, warning of fog far out in the distance.

It had been a mistake, after all, to come here. The brochure had promised her a world more ancient, more mysterious than her own, and it had been in search of that that she had flown here, only to find herself imprisoned in her own world of air-conditioning, hot water and fitted carpets, unable to reach the teeming, enthralling secret world she had glimpsed in her visit to the Kasbah. Their visit had been a brief one, closely supervised by a nervous guide who had not permitted them to wander far from the path he chose and who had constantly looked over his shoulder with visible anxiety as if expecting every moment to be attacked. From the main street they had followed, Marie had seen dark huddled alleys leading away into a tortuous maze of tiny dwellings; women in dark veils shuffling away with lowered heads, olive-skinned, striding men moving arrogantly through the crowds, their dark eyes passing over the little huddle of excited Europeans without interest. For a brief moment she had felt her imagination kindle, only to be led away by the guide, whispering to her of unimaginable dangers lurking in the shadows.

Somehow the fortnight in the mysterious desert had become yet another seaside holiday in a luxury hotel, and she was bored with the whole thing. She was tired of carpets and soft beds, expensive food that managed to taste the same every time, the relentless monotony of comfort and idleness. She might just as well have gone to the South of France or even some English seaside resort. It was true that the desert lay there, beyond the town, but the constrictions of the hotel seemed to impose a barrier between it and the holidaymakers. Marie felt as though she were wrapped in transparent plastic, hygienically protected from the dangerous world beyond.

She sighed. Suddenly a voice made her jump, and turning in surprise, she found Mrs Brown beside her, her freckled, healthy face alight with pleasure.

'Isn't this marvellous? Look at that view! Romantic, isn't it? Oh, I'm having such a lovely time here.' The enthusiastic, breathy voice made Marie envious. Mrs Brown and her quiet husband, Don, had never been out of England before and were ecstatic over their trip. They had won two weeks at the hotel in a competition, and could not get over their good luck. After forty-five years of sedate English holidays, life had taken on a more dazzling lustre for them both.

'I'm glad you're enjoying yourself,' Marie said, smiling at her. She liked Mrs Brown. They had shared a seat on the coach trip to local Roman ruins and become friendly over the sand-buried stone columns and broken walls of the old legion city.

'You're enjoying it, aren't you?' Mrs Brown gazed at her curiously.

'Of course,' said Marie, trying to sound sincere.

Mrs Brown's hazel eyes skimmed over the heavy white silk evening dress the other girl wore, enviously guessing at the price of such magnificence. The other visitors to the hotel could not but be aware that Marie was the daughter of James Brinton, the head of a vast electronics firm based in Southern England. Everything the girl possessed was of the same quality: expensive, stylish and worn with unconscious grace. Mrs Brown, on first seeing her, had been nervous of her, but on closer acquaintance had found that Marie was more approachable than her outward manner indicated. Mrs Brown's own blue chiffon seemed to lose its original charm when she stood beside Marie, and the older woman sighed.

'You're so lucky to have travelled all over the world. I do envy you. Don and I have never been able to afford to go beyond England – there were the children to consider. Our Joanne was never a good traveller, even a trip in the car made her sick, and she could never fly anywhere. Mind you, kids prefer the seaside anyway. They never missed anything. But I used to get travel brochures and read them from cover to cover, longing for faraway places. Now that we're on our own we could get away, but somehow we never got around to saving up enough. There's always something we need, a new carpet, a new car ... something more important than a holiday.'

'You must have been thrilled to win that competition, then,' said Marie, nodding understandingly.

'Oh, I was over the moon! My dreams come true.'

'And it's all lived up to your expectations?'

'Oh, yes,' said Mrs Brown eagerly.

'I'm glad.' Marie smiled back at her, trying to imagine the life Mrs Brown had led, the quiet, busy days in her home with her children, the dreams and excitements of travel always at the back of her mind to comfort her. It was a totally different world from her own. In its way it was as interesting to her as the exotic desert world she had come here to see. What we do not know is always as exciting as a dream. The human mind is never content, always looking out beyond the confines of its surroundings to grasp new concepts, new horizons.

'What about you?' Mrs Brown asked. 'You enjoyed that trip to the Kasbah, didn't you? I noticed how excited you looked as we got on the coach. Mind you, I was a bit nervous, I don't mind telling you. Some of those Arab stallholders looked a bit sinister. I mean, they say there are still slaves in some parts of the Arab world. You couldn't be too careful out here. If you went too far away from civilisation who knows what might happen?'

Marie laughed. 'I think I would rather enjoy getting away from civilisation. I'm sick of drifting in the swimming pool, drinking a glass of mint tea over the tables, driving around in an air-conditioned coach looking out at this world through plate-glass windows ... I've half a mind to go off and explore on my own, find out what it's really like here ...'

Mrs Brown looked horrified. 'I shouldn't do anything like

that, dear. I mean, you're a very pretty girl. That fair hair of yours makes you obviously European. I noticed some of those men in the Kasbah staring at you in a very furtive way. If I were you, I'd stay where I was safe ...'

'Oh, safe!' Marie whirled round and stared down at the moonlit sea, her mind restless. 'I came here to see the desert, the wild, empty spaces of the world, not to eat French cooking and dance to pop music. I suppose I had a romantic dream, just as you did, Mrs Brown, but my dream was less accessible.'

'I expect you've seen so many interesting places that you're more difficult to please,' said Mrs Brown flatly.

Marie turned back and gave her a little grin. 'I expect you're right. I'm sorry, I didn't want to spoil your fun by moaning.'

'Oh, you haven't,' said Mrs Brown, smiling again. 'Come back into the ballroom and have a dance with that nice boy who seems so interested in you ...'

'Not just yet,' Marie said quickly, suppressing a shudder of dismay. 'I have a slight headache, actually. The peace and quiet out here is doing me good.'

'I've got some aspirin in my bag,' said Mrs Brown. 'Would you like some? I'll run and get it.'

'No,' Marie said quickly, stopping her with a hand on her arm. 'No, really. A few moments out here in this cool air will do me more good than any pills.'

'Yes, I agree,' Mrs Brown nodded. 'I hate to take pills, myself. Wiser not to. You get dependent on them sometimes. I had to take sleeping pills after my last baby and it was months before I got a natural night's sleep. I never take them now.'

Marie saw her glance towards the brightly lit doors which led into the ballroom, and smiled at her.

'Don't worry about me, I'll be fine. You get back and have a good time. You're missing all the dancing.'

'Well, if you're sure ...' Mrs Brown gave her a last smile and hurried back eagerly, leaving Marie leaning on the wall, inhaling the night fragrance of the garden flowers and the faint, salty tang of the sea.

Silence seemed to wash back like the waves of the sea. She felt herself slowly relax, her eyes feasting on the plum-dark sky arched overhead, lit by a thousand points of silvery light from the stars, with the lemon sickle of the moon pinned upon it like a diamond brooch.

There was a faint rustle in the bushes below the wall which lined the path leading to the sea. Marie glanced down, but saw nothing. It was probably one of the lean-ribbed, starving cats who haunted the kitchens of the hotel, she thought. She had seen them often and pitied them, scavenging around the waste bins for scraps of food, kicked and berated by the kitchen staff.

She reluctantly turned away. If she stayed out here much longer she suspected that Mrs Brown would send the dull young man out to find her.

As she walked between the gently moving fronds of the palm trees someone leapt out at her. She jumped, giving a stifled cry, but before she could see anything something dark was flung over her head, muffling her scream and blinding her. Hard arms then lifted her like a doll and carried her away. She struggled helplessly, panic flaring inside her. Faintly she thought she heard someone laugh.

Realising the folly of struggling in vain, she lay still straining all her senses to guess where she was being taken. She heard the grate of sand beneath feet, smelt the salt of the sea closer and closer, heard the increasing murmur of the waves. They were going down to the sea.

After a moment or two she realised that her captor was actually walking in the sea – she could hear the wet slap of water against cloth, the splash of feet moving through the waves. What on earth was the lunatic doing? she wondered dazedly.

Suddenly the arms holding her lifted, then lowered her body, and she found herself being placed on something firm. At once, as the hands released her, she began to free herself from the stifling folds of the material. She heard him moving beside her, felt a rocking motion, heard the slap of the waves against wood. Then her wrists were seized and bound together with something smooth and silky.

'Be still,' a deep voice murmured close beside her. 'If you try to escape you will make me angry.'

'Where are you taking me? Who are you?' Her angry words were lost in the heavy material.

'Like all women you chatter foolishly,' the deep voice said with an undertone of grim amusement. 'Be silent now.'

Her mouth was full of dry fluff from the material. Swallowing, she lapsed into silence, listening intently as the boat began to move, the oars rhythmically grated on the iron rowlocks. Inside the cloth she found it difficult to breathe. She grew hot and angry, twisting her hands in a vain attempt to untie them.

Suddenly the boat came to a stop, rasping across sand, bucking to and fro, throwing her helplessly back against the wooden seat. Straining her ears again, Marie heard the oars shipped, then movements, the scrape of feet against the bottom of the boat, then a loud splash. The boat rocked wildly. He had got out, she deduced. The next moment she was lifted and carried again through water which splashed and lapped, on to a beach which appeared to shelve steeply, judging from the way her captor walked.

Gradually she grew conscious of a new sound, the rustle of wind among leaves. The sound of the sea faded gently. The arms which held her seemed tireless. Her captor walked evenly, his long legs striding forward, carrying her without apparent effort.

He halted, and she was shifted slightly in his arms. She heard a metallic click, then the slow creak of a door opening. She was carried through it and heard it slam behind her. Then she was flung down unceremoniously upon something soft. Before she had time to think her hands were untied and the dark cloth whipped away.

She lay, blinking, her eyes dazzled by the sudden flaming of a yellow candle, staring up at a dark figure which loomed above her.

He was so tall that she felt she looked a long, long way to see his face. In his white robes, his head covered by a white headdress bound with a gold cord, he was like a towering column, only the face, half hidden by his headdress, to betray his humanity. Narrowed dark eyes surveyed her insolently. He had a lean, olive-skinned face imbued with arrogance, cruelty and pride.

'Who are you?' she asked, her voice husky with alarm. 'Why have you brought me here?'

His hard mouth parted in a mocking smile. 'Who I am does not matter. I was on the beach while you were talking to your friend earlier. I heard you say you would like to see more of Arab life; what did you say – the wild, free spaces of the desert?' His dark eyes taunted her. 'So I brought you here to fulfil your dream.'

Marie sat up, shivering with fear, her dark blue eyes very large in the oval of her white face. 'You must be mad! How dare you kidnap me like this! As soon as it's realised that I've vanished the police will comb the city for me. My father is a very important man, he'll be very angry ...'

'Ah,' he said softly. 'Your father. How much do you think you would be worth to him? How much would James Brinton pay to get you safely back?'

She stared at him in shock. 'So that's it! You brought me here so that you could demand a ransom from my father? But ...' Her voice broke off as she frowned, thinking hard. 'How did you know who I was? This must have been planned in advance ...'

'How did I know who you were? My dear Miss Brinton, your photograph has appeared often enough in the English glossy magazines. Marie Brinton, heiress to the Brinton fortune, dining out with some handsome and eligible young man ... or dancing, or riding to hounds, or skiing in the Alps ... you are a much photographed, much talked about young woman.'

Vainly she wished she had not gone out into the garden alone, giving this man the opportunity he had no doubt been waiting for ... Her small chin lifted defiantly. 'So you're just a cheap crook looking for a way to make easy money?'

'Not cheap, Miss Brinton,' he said mockingly. The dark eyes flicked over her white silk dress, the naked gleaming shoulders and the proud swell of her breasts beneath the material, half revealed as they were by the low curve of the neckline. 'Neither are you, are you, Miss Brinton? A very expensive young lady, I would guess. For a man who likes soft, useless white-fleshed women you would be a tempting prize. Perhaps I would, after all, get more for you from an oil sheik than from your father?'

She was frightened by the way his dark eyes moved over her body. Trembling, angry, on the verge of panic, she tried to think of a way of distracting him. 'How much are you going to demand from my father, anyway?' she asked huskily.

He gave her an amused, comprehending glance which told her that he had read her motives in asking the question. 'What would you suggest?'

She shrugged. 'I have no idea.'

He grinned lazily. 'Half a million pounds, perhaps?'

'You're mad! Half a million pounds ...'

'I'm sure your father would pay more than that to get you back unharmed.' He reached out a long-fingered brown hand

and lifted her chin to stare down into her blue eyes. 'After all, he must be aware that any man who had you in his power would be very tempted to enjoy the pleasures your revealing dress suggests are available ...'

'Don't touch me, you ... you scavenger of the streets!' She spat the words out furiously, having heard them used by one of the hotel staff to a beggar who had sat by the hotel entrance one day imploring alms of the visitors as they went in and out.

The phrase seemed to amuse him. The hard mouth curved in a smile of mockery. 'To make that sound truly insulting the words should be Arabic,' he told her, his dark eyes full of laughter.

'Then I wish I knew Arabic!' she flung back.

'Perhaps I will have time to teach you,' he returned softly. 'I think it might be enjoyable.'

'Don't bother!'

'Arabic is a language which makes love a sensuous delight,' he said tormentingly. 'It is full of love poetry. Sometimes of an evening the Bedouin sit around the camp fire and recite love poems for hours, capping each other with apt quotations, while the stars make a steely glitter overhead ...'

'You make it sound very romantic,' she said, her eyes held hypnotically by his. 'But I expect it's far from the reality.'

His thin brows rose. 'And I thought you were attracted to the romanticism of the desert! You sounded wistful when you talked of it to your friend on the terrace outside the hotel ...'

'You were listening to us all the time,' she said, half to

herself, her nerves jumping at the thought of him lurking in the shadows watching her while she thought herself alone with the night sky. She tried to remember what she had said to Mrs Brown, but it seemed so long ago. She had said silly, futile things and this man had listened, no doubt with that sardonic, mocking smile.

'You expressed a desire to taste the real life of the Arab world,' he murmured drily. 'Well, you have your wish ...' He moved away, lifting the candle so that the pale light moved around the room. 'A typical Arab house, Miss Brinton. Delightful, isn't it? Romantic and exciting ...'

Her eyes moved around the tiny, low-ceilinged room, taking in the dirty, crooked shutters which covered the small windows, the low table in the centre, around which were arranged thick cushions, the large tapestry-covered cushions which appeared to form some sort of couch, on which she herself had been flung. There was no other furniture but a wall cupboard in a corner. The walls were plastered but had been given a grimy patina by time, and cracks ran across them here and there. In one crack a grey-green lizard sat motionless, only the filmed blink of an eye betraying that he was alive.

The yellow candle beam rested once more on her face. 'You are the only thing of beauty here,' he said softly. 'You are very desirable, Miss Brinton. I would get a high price for that golden hair of yours, that smooth, unblemished white skin and those blue eyes. They admire that colouring here. Your life in the harem would not be hard; it would be as filled with luxury, as idle and spoilt, as your life has always been.

You would merely exchange one indulgent owner for another. The only difference would be that you would learn other arts, more sensuous and infinitely more enjoyable than those of the sports field which you have pursued until now.'

Marie swallowed, digging her nails into her palms, her eyes fixed bravely on his lean face. 'You … you wouldn't dare …'

He laughed at that, a look of reckless gaiety lighting his face and making him younger and even more devastatingly attractive. 'If you knew me better, Miss Brinton, you would not fling out challenges in that light-hearted fashion. Has no one ever told you that the Arabs love a challenge?'

'My father will pay your ransom, anyway,' she said shakily. 'You wouldn't get more … any other way …'

He rubbed his chin thoughtfully. 'I wonder …'

'He will,' she insisted.

He inspected every inch of her again, from her bare shoulders, along the close-clinging silk of the white gown. 'Yes,' he murmured, 'I think he would.'

She felt sick relief in the pit of her stomach. 'M-may I have some water? I'm so thirsty …'

For a moment he did not move, his eyes lingering on her face. She looked at him nervously through her lashes. 'Please … water …'

He moved away to the cupboard. She watched his dark shadow stalk across the wall, the hawk-like profile sharply black against the yellow light. He found a glass and a jug of water, came back towards her, poured water into the glass and handed it to her. Their fingers touched briefly in the exchange, and Marie felt herself shiver. She sat up and sipped, then slowly rose as if to give him back the glass. As he bent to take it from her, she flung the rest of the water into his face.

He swore under his breath, his hands going to his eyes, blinded by the cold sting of the water.

While he was preoccupied she darted to the door behind him, wrenched it open and stumbled out into a dark alley. She ran, holding up her long skirts, doubled round a corner and stopped dead, finding herself in one of the crowded bazaar streets, lit by smoking flares beside stalls and noisy with the calls of the stallholders as they tried to attract attention.

Her appearance immediately attracted notice. Within seconds she was surrounded by a crowd of excited Arabs, all shouting at her, some of them touching her silk gown or the gleaming whiteness of her bare arms with grimy fingers, exclaiming over her, while others babbled at her in pidgin English, trying to sell her souvenirs or offering to guide her back to her hotel.

She was terrified, trembling, completely hemmed in and unable to escape. 'Please,' she asked, turning to one of the older men in appeal, 'will you take me to the Marina Hotel?'

'Yes, lady, yes,' he said eagerly, beginning to quote a price to her.

But then a voice spoke behind them all, in fierce hard Arabic, and the men fell back in silence, backing away from her.

With a feeling of dream-like inescapability Marie saw the

white headdress, the gold cord, the hawk-like face. He grasped her by the elbow and shook her, barking angrily at her. 'Silly little fool!' Then he spoke again in Arabic, his face glaring down at her. The crowd, watching from a distance, their faces curious, began to laugh. One of them shouted something to him, and the others roared in wild amusement. Marie looked round, bewildered and frightened.

The hard arms lifted her again, threw her over his shoulder like a sack of coals, and while she lay helpless in this undignified posture, she was enraged and humiliated to feel a hard slap across her bottom. Kicking and struggling, she seethed as he strode back into the darkness of the alleys while the other men cackled with delighted laughter behind them.

A moment later he carefully locked the door and then flung her back upon her sushions.

'You ... you bastard!' she seethed. 'You enjoyed that!'

He grinned, showing those hard white teeth. 'Yes,' he agreed shamelessly. 'And you deserved it.'

'What did you say to them?' She was sore where he had hit her, and rubbed herself self-pityingly, although it had been her pride which had been most hurt. There had been something so humiliating about the way he flung her lightly over his shoulder and slapped her. She had felt suddenly like a naughty child, a toy in the powerful hands of this dark-visaged stranger. At that moment the full realisation of her helplessness had come home to her.

'I told them you were my woman who had run away from me. They advised me to beat you and then make violent love to you. They assured me such treatment would be certain to make you more malleable in future.' He gave her a taunting glance. 'I've followed one half of the advice. Perhaps I should now follow the other?'

'If you touch me I'll scream,' she muttered in impotent rage.

He laughed. 'Empty threats, Miss Brinton.' He knelt down beside her, his eyes holding hers, and a wave of weakness swept over her. He had a magnetic strength, a primitive personal magnetism, which made her suddenly deeply aware of her own weak femininity, and his physical power. What if he did make love to her? What could she do?

'How long are you going to keep me here?' she asked, again trying to distract him. 'When news of my disappearance gets out, some of those men in the bazaar will put two and two together. There'll be a reward, no doubt. They will inform the police and this district will be thoroughly searched.'

'By then we will be safely miles from here in the heart of the desert,' he said coolly.

Her heart sank. 'In the desert?'

He gave her a mocking smile. 'I thought you longed to see the desert. Aren't you eager to ride across the empty sands with me, lie beneath the stars, wrapped in my burnous, with only the wind for company? I will show you the great wastes of sand and sky, teach you to appreciate the beauty of the emptiness ...'

'Oh, shut up!' she cried bitterly, seeing that his smile was full of wry mockery.

He laughed, pushing back his white headdress to expose

thick sleek black hair. 'You are contrary, it seems, Miss Brinton. Are you tired of the excitements of Arab life already?'

She longed to burst into tears, but determined to show him no weakness. She sensed that any hint of fear would make him despise her, so she had to pretend to a courage she did not possess.

He moved away, searched in the cupboard and came back with a long woollen garment like a tent. 'Put this on ...'

'Why?' she asked dubiously, eyeing it without favour. It was a grey-white colour, crudely woven and shapeless.

'Miss Brinton, don't argue. Put it on. If you do not obey me instantly whenever I give you an order I shall be forced to render you unconscious, and I am sure you would not wish me to do that.'

She stared into his face, finding it as grim as carved stone, the dark eyes unyielding.

Reluctantly she lifted the garment and let it fall over her head and down to her feet. Inside it she was very warm. 'I feel like a tent,' she said sullenly.

He grinned wickedly. 'You look like one. No man will look twice at you now.' He put a hand to the back of the garment and lifted an all-enveloping hood over her head so that only part of her face could be seen. 'Now! You could be any Arab woman.'

'Thanks a lot!'

He laughed. 'You sound like a sulky child.'

'I detest you,' she muttered under her breath, half afraid to let him hear.

His strong fingers gripped her wrist. 'Come,' he said. 'We

must leave now. The desert night is cold. You will be glad of your tent-like clothes later.'

He led her out of the back door into a close-set palm grove and along a winding path to the back of a low stable. An Arab boy in a dirty white djibbah sat on the floor asleep, his bare heels together, his legs loosely crossed. He jumped up, blinking sleepily, as they approached.

Speaking in Arabic, her captor gestured to the stable. The boy nodded and darted inside. Marie heard the jingle of harness, the stamp of horses' feet. After a few moments the boy led out two horses, saddled ready for a journey. She was lifted on to one of them, a fine spirited little white mare. For a moment she thought of galloping away to escape, but her captor read her thoughts and gave her a cool, tormenting grin.

'I would catch you up in two minutes, Miss Brinton,' he said softly. 'And I would beat you with my riding crop until you begged for mercy.'

She glared at him from below the hood of her garment, saying nothing.

He laughed and leapt into the saddle of the other big black horse with a grace and agility which she could not help admiring. Devil though he was, he had a physical appeal she could not resist. She had always admired men who rode well.

They rode away under the sweeping fringe of palms leaving the boy staring after them. There were a few scattered houses on the outskirts of the little town, most of them surrounded by palm trees, a sandy road running between them and winding out inland towards the darkness of the desert.

'We shall ride towards Wadi Aquida,' he said.

Marie was surprised that he should name the place to her, but already she knew him well enough to guess that knowing the name would be of no help to her anyway.

The moonlight showed her an emptiness ahead, an emptiness so bleak and yet so beautiful that it took her breath away.

The horses rode silently over the soft, flat sand. The cool night air was gentle on her face, blowing through her loose garment and refreshing her. The moonlit sand seemed without shadows so that there were no landmarks for her to pinpoint. She wondered how he knew which way to go. The horses occasionally snorted, the saddles creaked. To the east she saw the dark outline of a low line of hills, and once the horizon was specked by a small ring of palm trees circling a gleam of water, lit by the smoky flame of a camp fire.

'Bedouin!' he remarked, nodding as he saw her stare in that direction.

She was growing tired. They seemed to have been riding for so long, and she was longing for her bed. Her back ached, her hands were icy cold on the reins.

Suddenly she saw a swelling ridge ahead which seemed to have sprung up out of the ground. They were riding straight towards it, and soon the horses began to climb it, their feet slipping and sliding on blown sand.

As they crested it, she saw another ring of palm trees and the faint, illusory gleam of water under the moon.

'Wadi Aquida,' he said, riding down towards it.

When they reached the palm trees Marie saw that the sand

around the water was well trampled, and a kicked-out camp fire still smouldered. For a moment her captor squatted, studying the ashes. Then he looked at her calmly.

'Bedouin. They probably left here an hour ago – the ashes are still warm. Find some scrubwood.'

'I'm tired,' she said sulkily, sinking down beside the fire and extending her frozen hands towards the faint warmth which still came from it.

He bent and jerked her to her feet, shook her like a rag doll. 'Do as you are told!'

'My back aches and I'm stiff,' she muttered, on the point of weak tears.

'We are all tired,' he said. 'The horses need watering. Find as much wood as you can and get that fire going again ...'

Marie stumbled away and began to search under the date palms. She found a few branches of thorn trees, withered and dried by desert suns, and hurried back to feed the fire with them, blowing on it and watching it anxiously. After a while she managed to get a few sparks, then a little flame, then eventually a blaze, which she continued to feed with thorn sticks until the fire was adequate. Wrapped in her loose, warm garment she sat beside it, huddling like a child at the hearth.

Meanwhile he had watered the horses, fed them from the saddle bags and then he moved towards the fire, a battered old iron pot in his hand.

'Fill this from the pool,' he ordered.

She reluctantly stood up and took the pot, returning to the gleaming water with it, filled it and went back to him. He had produced two tin mugs, a flat loaf of Arab bread and some oranges from the saddlebags. He thrust the pot of water into the edge of the fire with a practised hand.

'We'll have coffee soon,' he told her. 'Sit and eat.'

She looked at the unleavened bread with a grimace, but when he had wrenched it into two halves and handed her one, she found the taste quite appetising, hunger being an excellent sauce. She ate two small oranges as well and began to feel much better, although sleepiness was becoming a nightmare to her. Her head kept nodding down upon her chest. She had to force herself to stay awake, afraid to sleep. The warmth of the fire was so comforting that she longed for sleep with an almost passionate longing.

When he had made strong, black coffee he poured her a cup. 'It is unsweetened,' he warned her.

Marie cupped her hands around the mug, enjoying the warmth of it, and sipped, scalding her mouth.

He laughed as she spluttered over it. 'Good coffee?'

Warily she sipped again. 'Very good,' she said, suppressing a yawn.

He crouched beside her in the smoky firelight, his face carved into strange, disturbing hollows, the high cheekbones and ascetic lines of the face emphasised by the shadows around them.

'Sleep now,' he said, taking the empty mug from her. He laid a woven mat on the sand, taken from the back of his black horse. 'You will find this comfortable enough.'

She slowly lay down, watching him nervously as he walked away out of the firelight, his back as straight, his walk as steady, as if he had not spent the night riding across the desert.

Her lids began to flicker, to sink. She listened to the singing of the thornwood on the fire, the soft sifting of ash in the desert wind.

Another sound brought her suddenly awake. A muffled slithering across the sand ... her eyes moved nervously around the fireside ... then she gave a scream, freezing immediately afterwards. A small black snake was lying close beside her, forked tongue quivering on the air, one eye watching her.

'What is it?' He had spun round from where he was attending to the tethered horses under the palm trees.

'A snake,' she whispered, not taking her eyes off the ghastly thing.

'Don't move,' he said, slowly coming back towards the fire. 'What colour is it?'

'Black,' she whispered. 'Very small and black.'

He swore under his breath, adding again, 'Don't move an inch. Don't even breathe.'

She lay rigid, her eyes fixed on the snake. It suddenly began to writhe towards her with an undulating slowness that terrified her. Then there was a deafening explosion and the snake was in two bits – blown into half with one shot.

Marie leapt up then and broke into scalding sobs, shaking from head to foot.

He pulled her into his arms, one hand on the back of her head, pressing her close against him. She wept softly, trembling like a leaf, clinging to him.

His hands moved against her back, stroking her calmingly,

soothing her, while he whispered consolation. 'It's all right, it is dead. You were very brave. It's all right now. It can't hurt you now ...'

'It ... it was so silent,' she whispered. 'It ... slithered towards me ...'

'They come in search of the warmth,' he said gently. 'Sometimes they get into your blankets during the night. You have to search the ground before you get up. But there's no need to be afraid. I'm used to them.'

'Are they poisonous?'

'Very,' he said bluntly.

She raised her head, shuddering, but laughed helplessly. 'Oh, you're so damned honest! Why couldn't you lie to me?'

He pushed the hood back from her hair, his fingers lingering on the gleam of gold which framed her white face. 'I'll lie to you if you want me to, Miss Brinton ...'

A slow, warm sweetness was spreading through her body. She hung in the shelter of his arms, relaxed to the point of physical collapse, aware in every nerve of the hardness of his body against hers, the muscled easy strength which had carried him through these last hours of hard riding across difficult terrain yet left him still unwearied at the end. Her own physical exhaustion, coupled with the recent shock and the insidious warmth of the firelight and his closeness, made her head swim.

She looked up into the enigmatic dark face, her smile wry. 'You'll lie anyway, no doubt. After all, what do I know about you? I don't even know your name. I only know you're some sort of kidnapper. You saved my life just then and I'm grateful, but it was you who put me in danger in the first place.'

'My dear Miss Brinton,' he murmured mockingly.

'Don't keep calling me that!'

'What shall I call you?' he asked at once. 'Marie . . .' He said the name with soft pleasure, dwelling on it in a musical voice which sent shivers down her spine.

'If you wish,' she shrugged with a pretence of indifference. 'What shall I call you?'

He looked into her eyes thoughtfully. 'The Arabs call me Khalid.'

Her curiosity was aroused. 'What do other people call you? Or wouldn't it be polite to ask?'

He grinned. 'The desert Bedouin have a saying ... a woman stabs with her tongue or with her eyes ... It fits you well, Marie.'

'If I had anything else to stab with I would use it,' she said tauntingly.

He laughed. 'I believe you.' He released her and moved a hand down his white clothes, producing a curved damascene dagger which glittered wickedly in the firelight. Offering it to her gravely, he bowed.

She took the weapon, feeling a helpless rage. He knew she would not use it. It was useless to her out here in the desert. If she did kill him she would never find her own way back to safety; she would die out here of exposure or be captured by nomad Bedouin.

She threw the weapon away, watching the bright arc of light as it fell. 'You know I can't use it. You were quite safe to give it to me.'

'True,' he agreed smoothly. 'Now find it and bring it here to me.'

'Find it yourself!'

He gripped her shoulders with two hard hands, staring down into her uplifted face with compelling eyes.

'Find it.'

Fear leapt up inside her. She knew that stony, commanding face. When he released her she angrily moved away to pick up the dagger and bring it back to him. He took it from her and slid it back into concealment among his clothes.

'Now, sleep,' he said calmly.

Marie lay down, facing the fire, and curled round to sleep again. Gradually her nerves stopped jumping and she felt a deep sleep dragging her down to oblivion. Just on the point of submersion, she became aware of him settling down beside her on the rug. Her eyes warily flicked open and found his face close beside hers, the dark eyes watching her.

'Go to sleep, Marie,' he ordered with dry amusement. 'I have no interest in a forced lovemaking.'

She felt hot colour run into her cheeks. Slowly her eyes closed again, but she lay listening to the regular sound of his breathing, aware of every move he made, every breath he drew. She wondered what it would feel like if ... then she jerked herself away from that thought, hating herself for entertaining it for a second. Despite herself, she risked another look at him. He was still watching her as attentively as before.

'What now?' he demanded instantly. 'Are you disappointed that I've made no attack upon your virtue, Miss Brinton? Of course, if you insist …' The dark eyes mocked her. 'I can force myself to make love to you if you cannot sleep until I have …'

'Can't you sleep on the other side of the fire?' she demanded. 'You make me nervous.'

He rose suddenly and began to kick out the fire. She watched him, baffled and alarmed.

Then he turned and jerked her to her feet, pulled back the long golden strands of her hair until her face was exposed to him and bent his head. Marie gasped helplessly as the hard mouth silenced her, parting her lips and filling her with a totally new realisation of her own femininity. The hands holding her were fierce and remorselessly compelled her submission, bending her backward so that her head spun and she was dizzily forced to cling on to him or fall. The kiss deepened, grew hot and demanding. Her closed eyes seemed dazzled by an explosion of brilliant light. She knew she was kissing him back, she felt the hot response of her own senses, but she was too helpless to fight, overwhelmed by new sensations. No man had ever made her feel so weak, so female, so much at the mercy of a superior strength. One part of her was furiously angry, scornful at herself for weakly submitting, the other was almost rapturous, glorying in the way he made her feel.

Suddenly she was free. He moved away. Dizzily she stared after him as he collected up the various objects strewn about the sand. He packed them all away into the saddlebags, then returned and lifted her on to the back of her horse.

'Where are we going now?' she asked despairingly. 'I'm too tired to ride any further.'

'We're going back,' he said tersely, mounting. 'We should be there soon after dawn.'

She was incredulous. 'Back?'

'To your hotel,' he said grimly, wheeling his mount away and galloping towards the sandy ridge behind the oasis.

Marie stared after him, disbelief freezing her for a moment, then she followed. When she caught up with him she stared sideways at the enigmatic hawk-like profile.

'Why?' she asked very quietly. 'Why have you changed your mind?' Was it because of their lovemaking just now? she wondered. Had he softened towards her? Or was he sorry for her? Why had he changed his mind?

He didn't answer, riding hard, his gaze fixed on the sky. She rode in silence beside him, hardly conscious of the ache of her back, the weariness in every limb.

'I won't tell anyone about this,' she offered meekly a little while later. 'I won't tell the police anything. I'll say I went out riding alone and got lost.'

He glanced at her briefly then, his face unreadable. 'Perhaps we both got lost,' he said ambiguously.

'What do you mean?' she asked, her face doubtful.

He shrugged. 'It doesn't matter.'

They rode on, across the moonlit sand, and then in the growing greyness of dawn they came in sight of the little seaside resort, with its palm trees and outlying mud-walled houses whitewashed by the sun. They passed into the outskirts, skirted a palm grove and were back outside the little stable. The same Arab boy sat sleeping beside the wall. He got up, rubbing his eyes, held the horses while Khalid lifted her down.

Her legs collapsed beneath her, she sagged against him, so cramped and tired that she could not stand.

He lifted her into his arms again, and she cradled her head against his strong chest with a thankful sigh. For a second or two he looked down into her pale face.

'Allah knows why I am giving away the prize of a lifetime,' he said softly. 'You are as beautiful as the sunrise.'

She flushed, touched by the compliment. 'Thank you.'

He carried her down through the palms to the beach, where the small boat lay beached out of the curling waves. Marie lay sleepily watching him as he rowed along to the other end of the bay, marvelling at his ability to look as if he had just got out of a bed after eight hours' sleep whereas in fact he had been physically working all night, riding across the desert.

When they reached the beach below the modern, palm-fringed hotel, she said quickly, 'Leave me now. I can get into my room without being seen, perhaps, and it would be better if you weren't seen.'

He nodded and watched her clamber out, lifting her skirts clear of the water, then walking slowly up on to the sand.

She glanced back, half reluctant to leave him. He had pulled his headdress down around his dark face, and the dark eyes glinted at her from the shelter of the headdress's shadow.

'If you need money, Khalid, I might be able to help,' she said nervously.

The hard mouth straightened and an angry redness came up into his face. He looked at her furiously. 'Goodbye, Miss Brinton,' he spat bitterly. 'When I first saw you I thought you a typical product of a decadent society; idle, vain and silly. It seems I was right.' His hands moved on the oars and the boat began to pull away. Marie watched, hating herself for having made such a tactless and stupid remark. Then she turned and walked into the hotel.

She met no one as she padded softly along her corridor. She slid into her own room and sank down on the bed. Presumably Mrs Brown had concluded that she had turned in early because of her headache. There was no sign that anyone had missed her. She guessed that if she had been missed the hotel would be swarming with police.

She took off the loose white garment Khalid had given her and laid it carefully over a chair, then slid out of her white evening gown and went into the shower. The warm water fell on her like desert rain, refreshing and reviving her. She put on a brief, transparent lacy nightgown and dropped into bed.

As sleep overcame her she briefly wondered if the events of the night had been a dream. They faded into sleep, a sleep in which she lay once more beside a desert campfire in Khalid's arms and sank into the delirium of his kiss without a second's hesitation, unshackled by the barriers of class or race, moving to claim him with the freedom and certainty a dream confers upon the human mind.

She did not want to wake up.

CHAPTER TWO

IT WAS raining as they drove away from Heathrow. Cold, grey spears lashed down around the car with a relentless ferocity which made Marie shiver. After the heat of the Arabian sun England seemed unbearably chilly, a colourless land of leaden skies and mournful landscapes. She thought of the oasis at Wadi Aquida; the flamelit palm trees and glimmering moon-reflecting water, and a curious pain began to ache around her heart.

'Something wrong?' James Brinton asked gently, looking sidelong at her, one hand touching hers as it rested on her lap.

She smiled at him. 'No, just the weather ...'

'Good old English weather,' he grinned. 'It always comes up trumps! Every continental holiday I've ever had I've come back to find weather like this – laid on specially, I suspect.' He was a small man, his silver hair brushed to cover the balding spot at the front of his head, his grey eyes quietly reflective. He had built up his firm from a small affair started by his father between the two world wars to a giant which was spreading across Europe at an alarming rate. Sometimes his harassed expression made his daughter afraid that James Brinton was a man who had lost touch with reality—his firm was growing too fast, beyond the grasp of one mind.

'You look tired, Dad,' she said, her expression anxious as she surveyed him.

'I've just been to see your mother,' he replied grimly, his eyes on the rain-wet windows.

'Oh.' She bit her lip. Her parents had been divorced when she was in her teens. Her beautiful blonde mother had eloped without warning with a South American millionaire, leaving a brief note for her husband. Marie had cried in secret, but in public had affected an indifference which had gradually become second nature to her. From time to time her mother reappeared in London, always looking incredibly young and beautiful, draped in expensive furs and dripping with diamonds, her eyelashes fluttering madly every time an attractive male passed by, bringing armfuls of ludicrously inappropriate presents for Marie. Once it had been a large doll which talked in three languages. Another time it had been a party dress four sizes too small. Her mother persisted in believing that she was still a little girl long after she had grown up. Marie had protested about this to her father, only to see him smile a little sadly and say 'My dear, your mother is terrified of growing old. While she can believe that you're still a little girl, she can believe that she's still young. Once she's forced to admit that you're a young woman she'll age mentally, and that will destroy her'.

She thought of this conversation now, watching her father's face. Did he still love her mother? He seemed to have a sensitive insight into the workings of her mind, anyway, and he had never betrayed any bitterness or hatred towards her in Marie's memory. He always saw his ex-wife when she came to England, but he gave no indication of his feelings normally, and she had no idea how he felt about her.

'She wants to see you tonight,' James Brinton added quietly without looking at her.

Marie grimaced. 'Must I?'

'She's your mother,' her father said gently.

'Whenever she remembers the fact,' Marie said with bitterness and clarity.

'All the same I think you must see her,' said James Brinton with a loving glance. 'Try to be kind to her, Marie.'

Something in his tone made Marie stare at him. 'Why? What do you mean?'

'Her husband is dead,' said James Brinton carefully.

'I see.' Marie remembered the large, perspiring, cheerful South American without fondness.

'His sons have inherited everything,' James Brinton added without expression.

She almost laughed. 'Oh, no! So that's why she needs some kindness? She's lost the fortune she expected to inherit!'

'I don't like to hear you talking like that,' her father said at once. 'I want you to be kind to her. She's very upset.'

'Upset? Not because her husband is dead but because she doesn't get the money after all!' Marie said bitterly. 'How long is it since I last saw her? A year! And since then I haven't had a letter, not even a postcard. Did she remember my birthday? Did she send me a Christmas present? You know she didn't. Dad, why on earth should I feel anything for her?'

'I don't know any reason why you should,' he said gravely. 'It's harder for you to forgive her than it is for me, I realise that. A child always feels more strongly about such a desertion. But she's still your mother and she's unhappy, whether you recognise the validity of her reason for being unhappy or not. Marie, you're old enough to know that no human being is perfect. Your mother was never a maternal woman. She was terrified of having babies. She was always terrified of growing old. You were a sort of index by which others could calculate her age. After all, a young woman who has a twenty-year-old daughter can't be thirty-five, can she? She was never a real mother to you, I know, but if you can be adult enough to forget that, she could still be your friend. And she needs a friend at the moment.'

'Oh, Dad! Why are you so saintly?' Marie laughed, close to tears.

'Perhaps because I realise that I should never have married Clare in the first place,' he said. 'I was always older than she was, not just in years but in mind. She wanted parties, dancing, a host of admirers. I was engrossed in the business, building it up and expanding everywhere. I had no time to squire her around every night. So I just ignored the problem and let her do as she pleased. Of course, we drifted apart. When she left me it was only the inevitable outcome of our incompatibility. I felt responsible, in a way. I talked her into marrying me. Clare always had doubts, but I steamrollered her into marriage.'

'You must have loved her very much, Dad.' Marie felt half embarrassed at these revelations.

'I was crazy about her,' he admitted with a little grimace of self-derision. 'I couldn't rest until I'd persuaded her to marry me. Then, of course, I turned back to my work and left her to get on with a life she had never really wanted. She just wasn't cut out to be a dutiful wife and mother. She wanted the glamour of high society, and she got it in the end.'

'And now she's lost it,' Marie said thoughtfully.

'That's why she needs your help,' he said, patting her hand. 'Be a good child. Go to her tonight – have dinner with her at her hotel. Listen to her troubles and try to be sympathetic. Try to see her, not as your runaway mother, but as a complete stranger. If you do, I think you'll find her charming and pathetic, a lost little girl in a hostile world.'

'Dad, you're still ... fond of her,' she said in a smothered tone of wonder.

He smiled faintly. 'You sound surprised. Perhaps you're not as grown-up as you think, my dear.'

The car drew up at their block of flats. While the chauffeur struggled with the luggage, Marie and James went up in the lift to their penthouse, talking now about Marie's holiday. James laughed at her confession of boredom.

'I'm afraid you're spoilt. Tired of luxury hotels indeed! What would your reaction have been if you'd arrived to find you were expected to sleep in a filthy little room with dirty sheets and no sanitation? Which is probably how many of your romantic Arabs live in those little mud-walled houses they build.'

'I saw someone building one of them,' she said. 'It was

quite fascinating. He was so deft! He made the bricks out of damp mud, patted, then cut the mud into bricks with the aid of a special little piece of apparatus made out of wood and string. It was so quick and simple. They leave them to dry in the sun which bakes them as hard as iron – a cheap method of building houses.'

'Would you want to live in one, though?' he teased her.

She laughed, recognising the justice of his irony. 'No, I suppose not.'

'I don't suppose you ever even went into one!' he said with amusement.

Marie thought of the little house behind the bazaar, remembering the yellow candlelight which had illumined it for her, and a slight shiver ran down her spine. She did not reply. Her dreams had been haunted since that night. A dark face, eyes that mocked, hands that were hard and yet unbelievably gentle ... his image remorselessly filled her mind whenever she let the barriers down. She might have said to her father, 'I did meet an Arab. An Arab called Khalid ...' and the words would be threadbare, unable to convey a hundredth of the truth.

She looked around the muted luxury of the sitting-room, with its pale blue carpet, white walls, modern paintings, and deep, comfortable brocade-covered chairs. It was all a thousand miles away from the palm-fringed oasis and the firelight beside which she had experienced the most traumatic moment of her life. The two worlds could never meet. In a strange way, this world was the more unreal of the two.

She was still conscious of a feeling of being isolated, cut off from her old life, as though she had been away for many years instead of a mere fortnight. Everything looked strange.

'Mrs Abbot will look after you,' her father said abstractedly, glancing at his watch. 'I have an urgent meeting at three o'clock, so I must rush. I ordered lunch for you. You didn't eat on the plane, did you?'

'No,' she said. 'It was the usual salad and plastic ham. I suppose you haven't got time to have lunch with me?'

'Sorry. I'm lunching in the board room with MacIntyre and Hamley. We're in the middle of trouble.'

'Oh?' Marie glanced at him in concern. So his grey look and furrowed brow had not merely been the result of seeing her mother again? 'Is it serious?'

He gazed at her in silence for a moment, then shrugged. 'At this stage I can't say.'

'What's wrong? Not another strike?' A strike had crippled one of their electronics factories last year for six weeks, losing them millions of pounds in overseas orders.

He shook his head. 'No. A take-over bid.'

She was immediately intent, knowing how such a bid would worry and disturb him. Although he had originally owned most of the shares in Brintons the rapid development of the past ten years had been fuelled by the sale of shares, and control of the firm had passed out of his hands financially, although he was still managing director and a major shareholder. 'Who's making the bid?'

'The Unex Group,' he told her.

She frowned. 'What do they do? I've only heard the name, I know nothing about them.'

He glanced at his watch again, hesitated, then said, 'They're a multi-national company, partly owned by Arabs.'

She started, staring at him. 'Arabs?'

He nodded, not apparently noticing her expression. 'They have a finger in dozens of pies … electronics, food, oil, manufacturing … they actually own a number of English companies. They swallow firms whole, stripping the assets and trimming them down as they go. They're offering my shareholders a price which I doubt if I can match. That's why I must see Hamley for lunch today. I have to ask if the bank can back me if I try to fight this take-over.'

'Surely they will?' Marie was aghast at the idea of her father losing the company he had spent his life building up.

He shrugged, his eyes expressionless. 'We'll have to wait and see.'

'You don't sound very optimistic,' she said anxiously.

'I'm not,' he said, moving to the door. 'Don't worry, Marie. My personal fortune is not involved in this and I won't let you suffer.'

'Dad!' She was blazingly angry at that. 'I'm not my mother, remember! What do I care about the money? By all means use it if it will help you. I can always get a job if things go wrong.'

He smiled then, his face lightening. 'My dear girl, what do you think you could do?'

'I'll think of something,' she said lightly. 'I'm not altogether helpless, you know. I've had a good education and I'm not stupid. You never know, I might even get married one day!'

He laughed. 'I certainly hope so. I want to be a grandfather, you know. Look, I must rush, I dare not be late for that lunch appointment. I'll see you later tonight. Don't forget – your mother expects you at her hotel for dinner at seven thirty.'

'I'll be there,' Marie promised. 'And I'll be sympathetic, I promise.'

He blew her a kiss and left, slamming the front door behind him in a way which was not at all like him. He usually closed doors gently with care. She sensed that under his quiet exterior her father was seriously disturbed.

She ate her lunch without noticing much of what she ate, and her father's housekeeper, Mrs Abbot, clucked disapprovingly over her half-eaten meal.

'You hardly touched a thing. Are you sickening for something? I told you you'd catch something nasty if you went to that foreign place. When my late husband, Stanley, was in Cairo he had trouble with his tummy the whole time. That was during the war, of course. Army food was nearly as bad, he said, and he wasn't one to grumble ...'

'I brought you back something,' Marie said, as the other woman stopped speaking. She picked up a brightly wrapped parcel from the bureau behind her and handed it to Mrs Abbot, who stared at it with overdone amazement. This ritual was proceeded with every time Marie came back from a trip abroad. She always brought Mrs Abbot a present, and Mrs Abbot always pretended to be taken aback.

Now she turned the parcel over and over, saying, 'You shouldn't have bothered. Why, my goodness, what is it? You shouldn't have bothered, you know. I wonder what it is?'

'Open it and see,' said Marie, as she always did.

Mrs Abbot got as much fun out of the parcel first as she could, pinching it and fingering the corners, trying to guess what it was, before at last she untied the string.

Marie had bought her a little Arab statuette of a cat, about five inches high, carved in creamy ivory, with green gem eyes. Mrs Abbot was crazy about cats and kept two Siamese in her own part of the flat. Now she exclaimed delightedly and thanked Marie several times before she departed with her gift.

Marie watched her leave the room with an affectionate smile. Mrs Abbot had looked after her ever since her mother ran away. She was a kind, warm, caring woman without relations in the world since her own husband died. In her early sixties, she was still active and hardworking, with no intention of retiring, although Marie knew that she had plenty of money invested in a building society for the 'rainy day' she had been expecting all her life. She ran the flat with impeccable skill. Her cooking was plain but excellent. She tended to bully both Marie and her father at times, but otherwise she kept herself to herself, preferring to sit in her cosy living-room at the far end of the flat with her two cats rather than go out or meet friends.

What would we have done without her? Marie thought. Then she walked over to the window and stared out at the London skyline, thinking over what her father had told her.

What would they do if her father lost control of Brintons? Would he be forced to retire from the board? She could not imagine what he would do with the rest of his life if he lost the mainspring of his existence. Despite their close relationship, she had always been aware that Brintons came first with him. From time to time she had minded that, but she had learnt to face facts.

She thought of the Unex Group with bitterness. Why were they so greedy, like great sharks devouring everything in their path! The impersonal face of big business hid a cruel ruthlessness every bit as harsh as the bleak wilderness of the desert.

She remembered Ian MacIntyre, chief accountant of Brintons, once saying to her father that it was dangerous to grow much bigger. 'You'll attract the sharks,' he had said. And her father had only smiled and shrugged the warning away.

Marie spent the afternoon on the telephone to her friends, telling them bland lies about her holiday. She would never tell a soul about her night in the desert, she thought, as she hung up for the last time. Let them all imagine that she had spent a blissful fortnight swimming in blue water and lazing on the beach. The reality was a secret locked in her own mind.

For the first time she felt restlessly wistful about her lack of occupation. She had never got a job because her father had insisted it was not necessary. She was supposed to run the flat for him, arranging his dinner parties and lunch parties, writing the personal letters which had to go to friends and doing all the jobs her mother would have done had she not run away.

In fact, of course, she had very little to do all day for most of the time, and filled in the hours with idle leisure; shopping, visiting friends, reading books and playing the piano.

Until now that had rarely bothered her, but now she wished she had a proper job, something to take her mind off the images which continued to haunt her. Every time she relaxed her guard that face flashed into her mind.

Oh, well, she thought, time would solve that problem. In a few weeks she would be unable to remember what he looked like. That time could not come too soon.

She slowly dressed for dinner, choosing her dress with care; a pretty blue dress she rarely wore because of its childlike simplicity, the bodice demurely sprinkled with very tiny white lace daisies, the skirts full and calf-length, swaying around her as she walked. With her hair styled in loose waves around her face she looked like a teenager, she thought wryly, gazing at her reflection.

Well, that should suit her mother. She could hardly manage to look much younger.

Her mother was staying at a large luxury hotel near one of London's parks. Marie asked for her at the reception desk and was immediately directed into the lounge bar. Pausing in the doorway, Marie saw her mother at once. She had hardly changed a hair. At a casual glance one would have put her down as a woman of thirty-five, but in fact, as Marie knew perfectly well, she was in her late forties. The miracle was accomplished invisibly. Her make-up was carefully applied, her clothes expertly chosen. Her beauty remained intact by some magical act of will.

She turned, as Marie entered, a glass in her hand, and for a fleeting second Marie saw an unmistakable look of apprehension on the flower-like face. The blue eyes widened, the mouth trembled, then Clare raised a hand in greeting, smiling brightly. 'Darling! There you are!'

There were, naturally, some men hovering in vague attendance, their faces wearing the sheepish look Marie always associated with men whom her mother took in tow. But Clare calmly dismissed them all with a few sweet words, saying, 'Darlings, you must run along now. This is a very private meeting ...' The smile which accompanied the words left the men bemused as they drifted away.

'You haven't lost your touch,' Marie said lightly, brushing her mother's raised cheek with her lips. 'How are you, Clare?' Her mother preferred to be called that. She said the name Mother was 'ageing'.

'Hasn't James told you? Poor Arturo ... so sad. And those horrible sons of his, grabbing everything, even my cars and my house. All I had left was the clothes I stood up in, I swear.' Clare looked tragic, her lower lip trembling, her wide pansy blue eyes filmy as though with tears.

Marie glanced at the flat pearl studs in her mother's tiny ears; at the diamond bracelet clasped around that slender wrist, at the diamond and pearl brooch discreetly pinned into the elegant black dress into which her mother's slender youthful body had apparently been poured so that it clung to her from the neck to the hem, accentuating the delicate sway of her hips, the alluring uplift of her breasts.

She vividly recalled the other jewels which Arturo had showered upon Clare over the years, and suspected that Clare's poverty was by no means as drastic as she wished people to think.

'I'm very sorry, Clare,' she said, however, mindful of her promise to her father. 'You look marvellous, in spite of your grief . . .' then hoped her mother would not take the words as irony.

Clare, however, was ready to accept her words at their face value, eager to be friends, apparently.

'Thank you, darling.' The blue eyes scrutinised her, approving of the blue childlike dress. 'You look very sweet yourself. I like to see you dress your age. I thought, last time we met, that you were in that tiresome stage of trying to be very sophisticated, which doesn't suit the young, you know. What will you have to drink?'

'Something cool and refreshing,' Marie said demurely.

Clare ordered her a glass of lemonade, adding mischievously, 'With just a dash of gin, barman. We don't want to overdo it, do we?'

Marie saw the barman eye her curiously, and lowered her lids. It would become tiresome, she thought, if she had to keep up the fiction of being sweet seventeen for hours. But it was all in a good cause if she was to keep her mother happy and satisfy her father.

After their drinks they repaired to the dining-room to eat. Clare gazed at the menu with glazed despair, then ordered melon and salad. Marie decided to follow suit to keep her company, and was rewarded with another smile.

'Very sensible. You must look after your figure.' Clare studied her with knowledgeable eyes. 'Tell me about your boy-friends.'

Unconsciously, Marie wrinkled her nose, thinking of the men she knew, her escorts in past months: Nigel with his bland smile and passion for cars; Daniel who talked obsessively of cricket and danced like a rogue elephant; Stephen, the shortest man she had ever met, who was aggressively masculine and carried a chip on his shoulder the size of a tree.

Clare saw the expression and laughed suddenly, her eyes bright. 'Darling! I know just how you feel! Dull, are they?'

'As ditchwater,' said Marie.

Their eyes met in a smile of entirely new sympathy. Clare leaned her elbows on the table in an attitude of confidentiality. 'Poor girl! Has there never been anyone who ...?' Her carefully pencilled brows rose enquiringly.

Marie, caught off guard, thought of Khalid, and at once her mother's face reflected an amused curiosity.

'I see there was someone. Who was he? Was he exciting?'

Marie laughed ruefully. 'Very.'

'English?'

'No,' Marie admitted.

'No, darling, they rarely are,' her mother mourned. 'Are you still seeing him?'

Marie shook her head, her lower lip caught between her teeth, and Clare's blue eyes shrewdly assessed her.

'Serious?'

Marie shrugged. 'I don't know. But ...' words failed her and she broke off the sentence, unable to put into words what she felt.

Clare sighed sympathetically. 'I see – like that. Well, if you want my advice, darling, which of course you don't, but I'll give it all the same ... go after him if you want him. They say men are the hunters, but that's just a myth invented by women to flatter the poor deluded creatures. Of course it's the woman who pursues, but she does it so subtly that he always imagines it was his own idea.'

Marie laughed aloud, and as she did so her laughter attracted some attention from a party just entering the dining-room. They halted to look at her, and she, looking up, aware of being watched, saw her father smiling at her across the room. She smiled back at him, delighted to see him. Then her glance moved on to his companions, and something happened to her heart. She felt a quick fierce pain, as though someone had squeezed her heart in a vice. Her breath seemed to stop and her pulses to accelerate.

For what seemed an endless eternity her blue eyes looked into the mocking dark eyes of Khalid.

Then he bowed, and Clare, who had turned in her chair

to see what Marie was staring at, gave a little cry of amazement.

'Why, there's James, and he has Stonor Grey with him. Now what are those two doing together, I wonder?'

'Which one is Stonor Grey?' Marie asked with an effort, trying to silence the thunder of her pulses, her eyes moving around the little group of men who were now advancing towards them with polite smiles. She recognised Ian MacIntyre, a stooped man of fifty with a tired smile, but the other two men were strangers to her. One was in his early thirties, with short curly brown hair and trendy clothes. The other was plump, smooth, cordial, his dark suit cut on fashionable lines.

'Darling, you must have heard of Stonor Grey,' said Clare in scornful disbelief. 'He's the whizz-kid behind Unex; of course, he started with an enormous personal fortune. His mother was the granddaughter of an oil sheik, so he had a lot of money from her, and his father was Sir Ronald Grey, the stationery king. You know, they make paper and office equipment by the billion ...'

Clare had said all this very fast, very softly, while she kept smiling towards the men. She had just finished before they joined them, and she extended her hand to Stonor Grey with a charming, eyelash fluttering smile.

'Stonor! How are you?'

He bent his black head to kiss the back of her hand with a courtly gesture. 'Clare, you look as enchanting as ever. What magic spells do you say? You look about twenty-five.'

'Ssh, don't mention age!' she pouted. 'I'm old enough to have a daughter who's nearly grown up ... Marie, this is Stonor Grey. Stonor, my little girl.'

Marie coolly offered him her hand. He took it, turning slightly away from the others, so that only she could see his expression. The dark eyes mocked her as he bent over her hand. The courtly gesture was somehow different this time. As he brushed his lips over her hand he let them slide down until they touched the little blue pulse beating with telltale speed at her wrist.

She was so angry she could scarcely breathe. Rage sent sparks into her blue eyes; made her fingers shake and her lips tremble so that she had to bite at their inner skin to stop them from visibly trembling.

No doubt he thought himself a great humorist. The full situation burst upon her gradually, like a series of wild explosions. He had pretended to kidnap her in order to make her look a fool. All that stuff about a ransom ... carrying her off into the desert for a few hours ... just to teach her a lesson!

'Stonor is an original,' Clare was saying. 'You must get him to do some of his imitations of politicians. He's so funny.'

'Oh, a comedian?' said Marie, her tone involuntarily touched with acid.

Stonor laughed, and Clare looked puzzled, while James Brinton stared at his daughter with anxious bewilderment.

'Sometimes I get carried away with my little jokes,' he said, the dark eyes on her face.

'That can be dangerous,' Marie snapped.

He smiled wryly. 'Very true. I gather you've just come back from a trip to my mother's country, Miss Brinton. How did you like the desert?'

She had a hard job to fight down her first reaction, which was to slap his face. With a great effort she managed to say sweetly, 'The desert was ... sandy, Mr Grey.'

'And the people?' he asked still in the same courteous, detached voice.

'I met some very pleasant people. Only one person seemed at all objectionable.'

'And who was that, Miss Brinton?' he enquired suavely.

She shrugged one slender shoulder, her oval face scornful. 'Oh, no one of any importance. Just one of those silly men who think they're irresistible ...'

Clare gave a soft chuckle, but James Brinton looked astonished. 'Marie? What happened? You never mentioned it to me.'

'It really didn't matter, Dad. I got away from him without any trouble. He was the sort of pest who's so consumed with vanity that he's merely laughable.'

Stonor Grey's eyes were filled with shameless laughter. She saw that, far from having offended or shocked him, she had merely amused him. Gravely he said, 'I hope you slapped his face, Miss Brinton. Men like that have to be taught a lesson. The trouble is, so many girls get taken in and swoon helplessly in their arms. I'm sure you were far too level-headed to be swept off your feet merely by a handsome face and a charming manner.'

She glared at him, silenced by sheer awe-stricken rage at his effrontery.

Her father gestured to the other two men, introducing them to her. 'These are two gentlemen who work with Mr Grey, my dear. Stephen Brent and Henry Carr. My daughter, Marie ...'

She smiled and shook hands with them. Stephen Brent was the younger of the two, his hazel eyes pleasant, his smile admiring.

'As you seem to have finished your meal, may I suggest you join us and drink your coffee at our table?' suggested her father.

Clare cheerfully agreed to this, so they moved over to a table large enough to accommodate them all. The men ordered steaks and salad with a purely cursory glance at the menu.

'Are you sure we won't be in the way?' Marie discreetly asked her father as they moved. 'Aren't you here to talk business?'

James Brinton gave a little sigh. His face had the weary grey look which had worried her earlier. 'It's all over bar the shouting,' he said flatly.

She gave him a quick, anxious look. 'What do you mean?'

'Unex will take over Brintons,' he said in the same dull voice. 'Hamley tells me I can't raise the capital to match their offer, let alone outbid them. I'm overstretched as it is. He couldn't help me.'

'Oh, Dad!' She put a hand over his and squeezed his fingers helplessly. 'Not even if you used your own money?'

He shook his head. 'Even if I mortgaged or sold everything I had I couldn't pull if off, and if I did manage to do so by a superhuman effort I would handicap the firm for years to come with a massive burden of debt. The game isn't worth the candle.'

She was stricken, looking at him with miserable anxiety. She could see that this had been a terrible blow to him. His whole life had been destroyed overnight. She looked at Stonor Grey as he seated himself at the table, the lean ascetic face as hard and immovable as flint while those dark eyes were lowered, his powerful body sheathed in elegantly cut evening clothes which disguised the predatory virility of the man in a way which the Arab robes had not done.

He had done this to her father. Like some hawk of the desert he had flown down with cruel talons and ripped her father's life to pieces for a mere whim.

Suddenly the dark eyes lifted and met the bitter, accusing glare of her blue eyes. He glanced down at her hand, tightly linked with her father's, and a cool comprehension came into the intelligent face. It was, she thought, impossible to hide anything from this man. His mind was as quick as lightning, flashing into and illuminating the dark places of thought. He would always be able to read her expression. Grimly, she determined to learn to control her features so as to leave him no clues.

While the men ate their meal, Clare talked, sipping cups

of black coffee. She held them all captive, yet her talk was neither sparkling nor witty. Somehow she managed to captivate without effort. Marie marvelled at her ability. Only James Brinton seemed immune tonight, eating dully without interest, his mood too grim to respond to Clare's charm.

A band began to play on a raised dais in one corner and some of the diners got up and began to dance on a tiny wooden floor just in front of the band.

Stonor Grey flung down his napkin and rose. Before Marie had realised what was happening, he had bent and raised her to her feet with one compelling hand, in a grip she instinctively recognised.

'Let's dance,' he said briefly.

She would have protested had she not wished to preserve the peace, but tonight she was afraid to do anything which might further upset her father.

So she allowed him to lead her on to the floor and pull her into a close embrace, his hand warm in the small of her back, while they moved to the deep rhythmic beat of the pop tune.

'Better get it out before you explode,' he murmured drily into her ear.

'What?' She turned her head to look at him and then looked away, her body springing wildly alive as she became aware of his closeness and the touch of his hand against her body.

'You've been sitting there seething for the last half hour,' he said. 'You have a very expressive face, you know.'

'What do you expect? You played a dirty trick on me. You made a fool of me ...'

'You were bored, so was I,' he said lightly. 'I thought we might have some fun together.'

'I can imagine your idea of fun,' she snapped.

He ran his hand along the full length of her spine, and she stiffened and glared at him. 'Stop that!'

'Don't snarl at me, then,' he said blandly. 'You were lamenting the fact that you hadn't seen any of the wild, romantic side of Arab life, so I supplied it for you, free, gratis and for nothing. You ought to be grateful.'

'Oh, I am, thanks a million,' she said sarcastically. 'You scared me out of my wits, you made me ride for miles across a barren desert, kept me up all night and told me a string of ridiculous lies ... and you expect gratitude!'

He laughed softly. 'Come on, admit it. You had the time of your life. Wasn't it romantic? The desert, the moonlight, the campfire?'

'That evil-smelling cloth over my head stifling me, nearly being bitten by a poisonous black snake, riding until my back nearly broke in half ... oh, it was certainly romantic! Like taking a bath in sheep dip.'

His black eyes danced with amusement. 'Scorpion,' he murmured softly. 'You've had your revenge, haven't you?'

Marie looked at him blankly.

'You very thoroughly chastised me in front of them all just now and I couldn't do a thing about it,' he said teasingly.

'Don't lie! You didn't give a damn what I said,' she said furiously.

He laughed again. 'You looked so incredulous when you

saw me! Rather like your expression when you saw that snake out in the desert.'

'Snakes always make me look like that,' she said meaningfully. 'What were you doing in the hotel garden anyway? Why were you lurking about at that hour of the night?'

'I was on my way to bed,' he confessed.

'You were staying in the hotel?' She was astounded. 'I never saw you.'

'I wasn't exactly a guest,' he admitted. 'I own it.'

'I might have known it!' She looked at him with loathing.

'I own a lot of hotels,' he told her. 'I visit them all once or twice. It just happened to be that one on that particular night.'

'Why did it have to be while I was staying there?' she lamented to herself. 'Why not some other night of the year?'

'It is the will of Allah,' he said mischievously.

She looked up at him. 'That isn't how I would describe it. Why were you wearing Arab dress?'

'I'm half Arab,' he said flatly. 'Why not? When I'm visiting my mother's country I always wear Arab dress. Don't you like it?' The dark eyes rested on her face.

'It suits you,' she said, suddenly breathless.

Stonor Grey smiled.

For a few moments they moved in silence, with the harmony of people who habitually dance together, their steps moving easily and gracefully.

Then Marie remembered, and looked up at him. 'You'll kill my father if you go on with this take-over bid, do you know that?'

His face grew sombre. 'You exaggerate,' he said. 'Business is only business.'

'Not to Dad. That firm is his life.'

'Then he's a fool. He has you.'

'He has always put the firm first,' she admitted.

'No man should put his work before his family. People matter more than things.'

'All the same, it will kill him to lose Brintons.'

'I hope not,' he said flatly.

'You could stop the deal,' she said huskily.

There was silence. Marie looked up and found him watching her intently, a curious look on his face.

'Couldn't you stop it?' she asked him in pleading tones.

'Are you asking me to do this for your sake?' he asked in a neutral voice.

She flushed hotly. 'No, of course not. For my father's sake.'

He shrugged. 'Unex controls dozens of firms like Brintons. We took them all over in the same way, and none of their previous owners died as a result.'

'Dad is different,' she said despairingly. 'He ... has nothing to put in its place.'

The music stopped, and the other dancers clapped. Stonor Grey guided her back to the table, his hand under her elbow. They found an argument going on between the other men. James Brinton was flushed, his eyes hot and weary. His voice rose above the others.

'You'll put hundreds of workers out of a job if you close down the Birdley factory. Don't you care about that?'

'It's uneconomic to run the plant,' said Henry Carr brutally. 'It overlaps with one of our others. We don't need it.'

'Asset-stripping ...' James Brinton ground the word out, rising, one hand at his collar, his breath coming in a ragged, uneven fashion that terrified Marie.

'James!' Clare was at his side, her face pale, staring at him as she tried to catch him.

He made a choked sound and fell forward on to the table. People at a nearby table screamed and the waiters came running, while the whole restaurant rose to stare. Marie ran and knelt beside her father, tears hot in her eyes.

Behind her she heard Stonor say in decisive, icy tones: 'Get an ambulance here at once.'

She looked round at him, white-faced and shrivelled with pain. 'You've killed him!' she whispered hoarsely.

CHAPTER THREE

HIS DARK eyes looked into hers, the blackness of the pupils seeming to dilate with anger. Then he pushed her unceremoniously out of the way, bent and lifted her father with an ease that reminded her of the way he had carried her through the gardens of the Hotel Marina and down to the moonlit beach. Shouldering his way through the staring crowd, he paused to ask the head waiter: 'Is there a room we can use?'

They were directed to a room on the ground floor. Clare and Marie followed the tall, striding figure, their eyes on his burden with the tension of terrified anxiety. James lay with head lolling back over Stonor Grey's arm, his silvery hair ruffled, pale pink patches of scalp showing through. One arm trailed along behind, the hand curiously, painfully, lifeless, the fingers loosely dangling.

Stonor gently laid him on the narrow single bed in the room, while Clare stood, staring at the still body. She scarcely seemed able to breathe, her hands caught stiffly at her breast in an attitude of terror.

A stir at the door heralded the doctor. He looked at them all impersonally. 'What happened?' As he spoke he was already beginning to examine James, and he cut short Stonor's curt explanation with a nod. 'Right, everyone out of the room now. Where the hell is that ambulance?'

The next moment, it seemed, the ambulancemen were there, carrying James past on a stretcher, his face covered by an oxygen mask, while the doctor walked beside him.

'I must go with him,' Marie cried, hurrying after them.

Clare stood staring after her, her white face drawn. Stonor laid a hand on her arm and she looked round at him.

'I'll drive you to the hospital,' he said gently.

She nodded, silent and tearless, yet visibly on the point of tears.

Then Stonor moved fast, catching up with Marie, his hand descending on her arm. She looked round at him in anger and shock.

'You can't go in the ambulance,' he said.

'Let me go! Who do you think you are?' She flung him off with a furious gesture.

He caught hold of her again, with renewed force, his fingers biting into her wrist. The dark eyes were flintlike.

'You can't go in the ambulance,' he repeated.

'Who says I can't? You?' Her voice was contemptuous.

'Yes,' he said. The simple monosyllable held her, her eyes fixed angrily on his.

'I have a right to be with him. He's my father.' Her voice had lost some of its certainty.

'I'll drive you and your mother to the hospital in my car,' he said.

'Don't bother,' she snapped. 'I'll take a taxi.'

He ignored the childish retort, turning towards Clare, his hand still holding Marie's wrist. 'My car is in the car park below. Would you like to get a coat from your room?'

She silently shook her head. 'Let's go now, quickly,' she said, after a moment.

'Look after your mother,' said Stonor, turning to Marie, his dark eyes suddenly stern. 'She's very upset.'

Marie looked at Clare with wide, incredulous, critical eyes. Her mother had shown no tenderness towards James Brinton for years, yet Stonor seemed to be implying that at this hour of danger for him, her father was more to her mother than to Marie. Then she realised that Stonor could not know that her parents had been divorced. She looked at him scornfully.

'They were divorced ten years ago,' she murmured in an icy undertone, turning away so that her mother should not hear. 'Dad means nothing to her.'

Stonor looked down into her pale face. 'I know about the divorce,' he said coolly. 'Take a look at your mother, a good look. She's in a state of shock far worse than yours. I don't know what she feels about your father, but I do know she needs help.'

Clare was leaning against the wall in an attitude of dispirited patience, just out of earshot, her eyes on the floor, her lips trembling and bloodless. Beneath the careful make-up her face was deadly white. She seemed to have aged ten years in the last quarter of an hour.

Marie stared at her, then her face slowly flushed. She looked at Stonor with dislike.

'You see?' he demanded.

'Yes,' she said, 'I see.' At that moment she hated him for having realised something to which she had been blind.

She moved towards her mother and put her arm gently around her.

'Come on, Clare, we're going to the hospital.' Her voice was soft as she urged her mother along the corridor towards the lift down to the underground car park. Clare looked at her dumbly, her blue eyes like bottomless wells of pain.

'He's going to die,' she whispered. 'James is going to die. What will I do?'

Over her head Marie met Stonor's cold eyes. She hugged her mother and murmured comfortingly, 'No, he's strong. He isn't going to die ...'

Clare shook her head. 'I heard you say I'd killed him ... you said it when he collapsed ...'

'Not you, Clare,' said Marie, aghast. 'I didn't mean you ...'

'It's my fault,' Clare whispered. 'All these years, my fault ...'

'No,' Marie urged, stroking her hair. She hesitated, biting her lip, then said recklessly, 'Dad loves you, he loves you!'

Clare lifted her head then, her blue eyes wild. 'Do you think I don't know that?' Her voice held an agony of pain and self-reproach.

Marie was silenced. The lift purred to a halt, Stonor moved over to his sleek silver-blue limousine, unlocked it, turned and helped Clare into the back. Marie slid in beside her. Stonor got into the driving seat and started the engine.

They sat in the white-tiled corridor staring at a green baize-covered swing door which constantly admitted and expelled a number of medical staff. Above the door a large white-faced clock registered the minutes with a slow, remorseless click as the large black hand moved on. They had been there for two hours. No news had come out. James was in one of the rooms on the far side of that swing door, fighting for his life.

Stonor came back for the second time with coffee in plastic cups. Clare accepted hers without comment, her face frozen. Marie looked up as she took a cup from him. Stonor's eyes were still icy. She knew he would never forgive her for what she had said to him when her father collapsed, but at this moment she did not care. She hated him. She hated everything he stood for: Unex, the impersonal brutal world of high finance, the spiritual desert of business where money meant everything and people nothing, where accountants were masters. She thought of the empty open spaces of the desert, the miles and miles of arid sandy waste. That night beside the campfire she had seen in it a terrible beauty. Now she saw only the bleached bones of its victims, the death and horror of its sterility.

Stonor moved away again. Marie drank her coffee without tasting the plastic, crumpled up the cup and threw it into a waste bin. The slap of feet along the corridor made them all turn their heads. A nurse in clean white apron and cap glanced at them without expression, went through the swing door. The black hand moved on once more with a sharp click.

A tired doctor in a crumpled white coat, stethoscope hanging from one pocket, came out of the door, paused and stared at them.

Stonor rose and moved over to him, speaking in a low voice. Clare rose, her eyes stretched in agony.

The doctor glanced at her, smiled politely. 'Mr Brinton is resting at the moment. I'm afraid there's no point in waiting any longer. No one can see him tonight.'

'He's still …' Clare's voice broke off helplessly, her hands made a pathetic gesture of appeal.

'He's holding his own,' the doctor said firmly. 'That's all I can say at the moment. There's no immediate danger, I assure you. I want you to go home now and sleep. Then you can come back here tomorrow and perhaps by then you may be able to see him.' He looked at Stonor. 'I could prescribe something to help her sleep.'

Clare gestured again, irritably. 'I have sleeping pills, thank you. Never mind me. You swear James is all right?'

He smiled gravely at her. 'Mrs Brinton, he has had a serious heart attack. You must judge for yourself what that means. All I can tell you is that he's holding on … if the will to live is there, he may pull through. It all depends on him now.'

'The will to live,' Marie said huskily. She looked at Stonor, but his face was mask-like. 'But has he got that?'

Stonor took the doctor's arm. 'Couldn't his daughter see him for a moment? Just look at him.'

The doctor looked surprised, glanced at Clare, who stared at the floor sightlessly.

Marie said huskily, 'No, my mother must go in … if anyone can give Dad the will to live it's my mother.'

Clare's head lifted. She stared at Marie, her lips shaking. 'Marie …'

'Go in and stand by his bed, Mother,' Marie said softly. 'Say his name. The firm doesn't matter – you do.'

The doctor and Stonor exchanged glances, then Stonor nodded. The doctor hesitated, then said to Clare: 'Will you come with me, Mrs Brinton?'

Clare followed him through the swing door.

Alone with Stonor, Marie sat down again and folded her hands in her lap. After a moment he came and sat beside her, his long legs stretched out across the corridor.

'That was very brave of you,' he said quietly.

'Was it?' Her voice was savage. 'I was only thinking of him. I know he loves her. She may just pull him back. It was a chance worth taking.'

He put a hand on hers, but she pushed him away. 'Don't touch me! You've done enough for one day. Why do you stay here? Why don't you go? I can't stand the sight of you!'

'I'll drive you home when your mother comes back,' he said, his voice level.

'We can call our chauffeur, thanks,' she said.

'I'll drive you,' he repeated expressionlessly.

Marie lapsed into silence. She would not argue with him while her father lay dying a few yards away.

The door swung open again and Clare came out, looking less tense. She looked at Marie across the corridor and her eyes shone with tears. 'Thank you, darling,' she said in a choked voice.

Marie went to her, put an arm around her. 'Was it … awful?'

'Awful,' Clare whispered. 'But not as bad as I feared. He

wasn't conscious, but they let me hold his hand and his fingers clung ... his fingers clung, Marie.'

The doctor came out, a smile on his tired face. He gave Stonor a nod. 'I think something got through. His pulse is improving.'

'When can we come tomorrow?' asked Clare impatiently.

'Ring us in the morning and we'll decide then,' the doctor told her. 'Things take time, you know. We won't be sure about anything for a long while yet.'

Stonor drove them back to the flat. Clare, without discussion, accepted Marie's suggestion that she come there for the night. Marie felt she could not leave her mother alone in a hotel bedroom at such a time.

Mrs Abbot met them at the front door, her eyes pink from weeping. 'Is it true? Is it true?' she asked. 'Is he dead?'

'Of course he isn't dead,' Marie burst out angrily. 'Who told you that?'

'The newspapers have been ringing up for hours. They said he had had a fatal heart attack over dinner at the hotel ...'

'A heart attack,' Stonor put in coolly, 'but not a fatal one, thank God.'

'Oh, thank God, sir, yes,' Mrs Abbot murmured. 'Come in, I'll get you all some coffee ...'

'My mother would prefer cocoa,' Marie said quickly. 'She must get some sleep. Coffee would keep her awake.'

Mrs Abbot looked at Clare with hostility. 'Oh, Mrs Sebastian, it's you, is it? I didn't expect to see you here.'

Clare seemed unaware of her hostility. The dark circles under her blue eyes, the pallor of her face, lent her a new but fragile beauty. She reminded Marie of a wood anemone trembling in a cold spring wind.

She encircled Clare protectively with her arm. 'My mother will sleep in my father's room tonight,' she said clearly, her eyes reproving Mrs Abbot.

The old woman flushed angrily. 'I don't think Mr Brinton would like that, indeed I don't.'

'Thank you, Mrs Abbot,' Marie said fiercely. 'I'll take my mother there myself.' She led Clare down the hall, her arm around her waist.

Mrs Abbot watched with undisguised anger as the two of them went into James Brinton's bedroom.

Clare looked around the room, flinching as her eyes fell upon a large studio portrait of herself beside the bed. Marie was surprised to see it there. She had not been into her father's room often, and she had never suspected that he kept a picture of Clare beside his bed.

'Mrs Abbot is right,' Clare said huskily. 'I shouldn't be in here. I'll take the spare room.'

'I know Dad would want you to sleep here,' Marie said with a hard certainty. 'I suppose it's silly, but I have a feeling that it will actually help him.'

Clare stared at her, biting her lower lip. 'How can it? I don't understand you, darling.'

'I'm not sure myself,' said Marie, with a faint smile. 'Perhaps your being in this room will give you a telepathic link with him … didn't you say his fingers clung when you touched him, although he was unconscious? How could he know you were there except by telepathy?'

'Do you believe in telepathy?' Clare asked her seriously.

'I've never thought about it before, but I don't see why not. Anything which would help Dad is worth trying. I just have this instinct ... a vague feeling ... that he would like you to be here.'

Clare sighed. 'Then I'll stay. You know him better than I do, darling.'

'Oh, no,' Marie stared at her in distress, 'don't say that! I only know one aspect of him – he's my father. I don't know him the way you do. You were married to him for years, after all.'

'We lived together for years, you mean,' Clare said bitterly. 'For the first year we were married. Then you were born and after that James never had time for me. From a wife I became just the woman in his house. You don't know what I went through ... I felt stifled, excluded, isolated. When I protested, he suggested that I find a life of my own. Make friends, he said, go to the theatre. He said he wanted me to have fun, but he didn't have time to have fun with me – he was too busy.' She shrugged. 'Any fool could have predicted the end of it.'

Marie turned down the bed. 'Clare, put the past behind you for a while. Lie down, try to sleep. I'll bring the cocoa along when you're in bed.'

'I don't really want any,' Clare said thickly. 'I'll sleep anyway – I have my pills in my handbag. Goodnight, Marie. If ... if anything happens, call me, won't you?' Her blue eyes pleaded humbly.

'I promise,' said Marie, kissing her on the cheek. 'Goodnight, Clare.'

Clare turned away, then stopped dead, seeing herself reflected in the mirror. She put a hand to her cheek, grimacing.

'I look old suddenly. I've always felt quite young, even first thing in the morning without my make-up. But when I saw James choking and dying right in front of my eyes time seemed to rush away from me at tremendous speed. I aged inside. James and I were so young once. If he dies part of me will die too. He's the only one who remembers me when I was eighteen ... you don't know yet, darling, what that means ... but when all those who knew you when you were young have vanished, you really feel old.'

Marie smiled at her. 'You're still very beautiful, Clare. Even tonight ... believe me.'

Clare laughed abruptly. 'You must think me very vain and silly.'

'No, just human,' Marie assured her.

They smiled at each other, then Marie closed the door and went back down the corridor. The kitchen door stood open. She went in, prepared to do battle with Mrs Abbot, and found Stonor there alone, putting cocoa into hot milk and whisking it vigorously.

'Where's Mrs Abbot?' she asked.

He glanced at her over his shoulder. 'I sent her to bed.'

'She had no right to say what she did to my mother,' Marie said.

'You're amusingly predictable,' he drawled, pouring the foaming cocoa into two mugs.

'What do you mean?' She stared at him suspiciously, sensing criticism.

'You fly off at a tangent over everything,' he said, leaning against the wall, his hand propping up his dark head as though he were physically weary. The dark eyes surveyed her, a glint of laughter in their depths. 'Earlier you were angry with me, then you were angry with your mother. You're emotionally unstable. You have to be taught how to respond in every situation. The first angry thought that comes into your head dominates you until you're shown the folly of it.'

'I'm sorry I'm so immature,' she snapped, naturally furious with him at once. 'Perhaps you'd better leave now. I'm sure you don't want to waste any more time on someone so silly and childish.'

He laughed, his eyes mocking her. 'You see? There you go again, leaping down my throat because I tell you the truth. My dear child, you've been both spoilt and neglected. Your father gave you every material possession but never had time for you yourself. Your mother deserted you. But all that's in the past, and now you're an adult. Try to behave like one. Think of things in an adult way. Tonight you've swung back and forth like a pendulum. Once I had pointed out that your mother was genuinely distressed, you were both kind and thoughtful towards her. You became over-protective, enraged because Mrs Abbot was hostile towards her ...'

'She had no right to say such things!' Marie burst out.

'I agree, but you see Mrs Abbot is fond of your father, too, and she was just as disturbed by his heart attack as your mother had been. I suspect that your own reaction to Clare surprised her. You haven't always been very friendly towards your mother, have you?'

Marie flushed. 'All right, I get what you mean. I wasn't fair to Mrs Abbot. I'll go and say I'm sorry . . .'

Stonor caught her arm, looking down at her, shaking his head. 'No, leave it until the morning. I've already spoken to her.'

'Oh, have you?' She was indignant. Who did he think he was, arranging, interfering, ordering everyone around? 'And what did you say?'

'I told her you were too upset to know what you were saying or doing, and I apologised on your behalf.'

'You had no business to do so!' She was very flushed now, her blue eyes bright with anger.

'Blessed are the peacemakers,' he drawled. 'Or don't you believe that?'

'I think you'd better go,' she said.

'Without my cocoa?' he asked tauntingly, sipping from the mug. 'I make very good cocoa, by the way. Try it.'

Marie seethed for a moment, then gave in, picking up the mug and tasting it. They drank in silence, then he put his mug down and looked at her thoughtfully.

'Would you like me to stay the night? I can sleep on a couch quite easily.' His mouth curved in a tormenting smile. 'As you know, I'm quite used to sleeping on the desert sand, and a couch is quite luxurious compared to that.'

'I think we can manage without you, Mr Grey,' she said coldly. 'We have done for years.'

He laughed. 'We can always get along without things we've never had,' he said softly. 'It's custom that makes us dependent.'

'Well, I'm not dependent on you, Mr Grey,' she snapped.

'Not yet, perhaps,' he said, in a softly menacing tone which made the hair rise on the back of her head.

Her pulses raced as he moved towards her, but she lifted her chin defiantly, determined not to show him how his physical presence affected her.

He looked down at her from his greater height, the dark eyes flickering, the thick almost feminine lashes half veiling their expression. 'You look tired, like a little girl. Are you sure you wouldn't like me to carry you to bed?'

'Don't touch me!' she snapped, panicking immediately at the thought of being picked up in those powerful arms as she had been before, carried like a child against his muscled chest.

His mouth parted on an amused smile, the white teeth showing briefly. 'What are you afraid of? Me? Or yourself?'

'Why should I be afraid of myself?' she retorted scornfully.

'Because you're alarmed by your own response to me,' he said mockingly. 'I think you're rather inexperienced, for all your outward sophistication. The packaging glitters, but underneath it lies something far more vulnerable.'

'You should be a psychologist, not a tycoon,' she said sarcastically.

'Business requires a great deal of psychological warfare,' he said drily. 'Rather like war … how can you defeat the enemy unless you understand him? That was why Field-Marshal Montgomery kept a photograph of Rommel in his bedroom … he wanted to understand the way the other man thought, so that he could anticipate his every move.'

'Thanks for the warning!'

His eyes teased her again. 'Oh, are we enemies?'

The intimacy of the tone made her feel suffocated for a second or two. She said flatly, 'Aren't we?'

'There's no enmity on my side,' he said softly.

'There is on mine,' she returned frankly. 'You played a trick on me, and I haven't forgotten that. Nor will I ever forget that it was because of the Unex take-over bid that my father had this heart attack.'

'Your father has had a heart condition for several years,' said Stonor coolly.

'What?' Marie was incredulous. 'Who told you that?'

'When I do business with a man I like to know all I can about him. I had a report on your father months ago. I knew about his health, his divorce, even about his spoilt, wayward daughter ... when I saw you in the Hotel Marina I had recently read a hefty dossier on you.'

'You sound like the secret police of some police state!' she said in a voice heavy with rage.

He shrugged. 'Information is the raw material of my decision-making process. I never act purely on instinct.'

'Never?' she asked, remembering that kiss beside the campfire in the oasis.

The dark eyes narrowed. 'Almost never,' he conceded, moving nearer, holding her eyes compellingly.

Marie felt a strange fluttering in the pit of her stomach. She knew he was going to kiss her, and for a moment all her instincts demanded that she forget everything, and let him. Then her pride rose bitterly in revolt, and she moved away from him, backing angrily, her glance daring him to touch her.

'Despite what you say, I blame you for my father's illness. Your take-over brought about the attack. If he dies ...'

She stopped on the word, her voice choking, tears rushing into her eyes. She glared at him briefly, then turned and ran down the corridor to her own room and locked the door of her bedroom behind her. As she leaned on the door, sobbing under her breath, she heard the click of a light switch being turned off and then the quiet closing of the front door. He had gone.

CHAPTER FOUR

JAMES BRINTON continued to fight for his life with increasing strength, helped by Clare's constant presence beside his bed. Marie saw clearly that her father's affection for his wife was growing alongside his return to health. The long, quiet days in his bed were giving him time to think, time to take stock of his situation. He and Clare were happy together, talking quietly or falling silent for a while, learning a new companionship which reaped dividends for James in his struggle with his health.

Marie visited him each day, too, but tactfully left her mother behind when she left the hospital. Clare had moved into the flat fully now, bringing cases of clothes with her. Mrs Abbot behaved towards her with a sort of cool politeness which only just masked a deep hostility, but judging it best to leave things alone for the moment, Marie pretended to be blind to Mrs Abbot's feelings. After all, she thought, there was probably a little jealousy involved. Mrs Abbot had run their home for so long. No doubt she felt Clare to be a threat to her own position in the household.

There had been no sign of Stonor since the night when James collapsed. Once Marie saw some flowers in a vase beside her father's bed, a card from Stonor pushed among them, inscribed in strong, flamboyant writing with his name and a brief message. But she herself had not set eyes on him.

She told herself she was glad.

Several weeks after James collapsed, he came home from the hospital briefly before going away for a long convalescence at a private nursing home. He sat in the sitting-room staring around him in a strangely thoughtful fashion.

'At one time I thought I would never see this room again,' he said. 'Now I realise I never liked this flat anyway. I'm tired of London.'

Marie looked astonished. 'Tired of London?'

Clare smiled at James. 'Yes,' she said to her daughter. 'We were thinking of moving into the country. While James is at the nursing home I'm going to look for a house. Will you help me, Marie?'

'Of course,' said Marie, noting with pleasure the easy way in which Clare was taking charge. 'Where are you thinking of buying a house?'

'Sussex,' said Clare. 'Near the sea. We'll be able to take walks along the beach every day and buy a dog ...'

'Buy a dog?' Marie laughed and looked at her father in sheer disbelief, trying to see him in this idyllic domestic setting. 'You and a dog taking walks beside the sea, Dad? Are you serious?'

James laughed and shrugged. 'Completely serious, Marie. I've spent most of my life chasing success, making money, building up the firm, then suddenly it all vanished like fairy gold. The business, my occupation ... gone! Oh, I'm rich enough now, I can do whatever I like. Clare and I talked it over. We're both ready to settle for a cottage by the sea and some peace. Of course, we want you to come, darling. But whatever you think, we've decided that this is what we want, and we're going to do it.'

Marie smiled at him, then at her mother. 'I just want you to be happy. I'm glad if this is what you want.' She hesitated, then asked, 'What about the firm?'

Her father shrugged indifferently. 'Let Unex have it. I no longer care. Perhaps it was time someone else took over. I'd been running the firm for so long, my ideas were getting stale. I was bored with it all, but I didn't even realise that until I came so close to death. Then I got a new perspective on life. I realised that things just don't matter. People are what matter.'

'You're right, Dad,' Marie said softly. 'And I'm glad you and Clare are together again. It seems so right to see you together.'

James glanced at Clare. 'Marie, I would like you to call Clare by her rightful name again.'

For a moment she was bewildered. 'Her rightful name?'

'She is your mother,' he said gently. 'Call her that.'

Marie looked at Clare enquiringly. 'Of course, if she wants me to, but ...'

Clare was pink and half laughing. 'I know I hated it once, but I would like you to start calling me Mother again. You never know you value something until you've lost it.'

'You haven't lost either of us,' James said firmly. 'We're going to be a family again.'

Marie giggled. 'You'll have to get married first, Dad!'

He looked amused. 'I'd forgotten the legal side. I suppose we will. I've never really accepted the divorce, I suppose.'

Clare looked at him half wistfully. 'Oh, James!'

Feeling very much *de trop*, Marie tiptoed out of the room and left them to discuss the subject alone.

While James was away recovering his strength, Marie and Clare drove around Sussex looking for houses. They saw dozens, but none were suitable. Clare wanted a house small enough to be easy to run, yet with plenty of ground around it to ensure privacy. Just when they were giving up hope of success, they were shown a cottage which had just been put on the market by an artist.

'In rather a ramshackle condition,' the estate agent warned them. 'But basically sound, I assure you. It would cost a little to have some repairs and redecoration.'

Clare sighed and exchanged a look with her daughter. It sounded like another dead end.

The car drove along a narrow marsh lane, winding between ditches and reedy banks, with sheep cropping the soft turf in the fields on either side. The estate agent stopped outside a small blue wooden gate. A crooked sign hung on it. Clare leaned forward to read it and laughed.

'Tom Tit Cottage? How charming!'

Through a tangle of old apple trees Marie saw a thatched roof and faint glimpses of old red walls. They moved to the gate and stopped dead, staring in enchanted silence at the low, rambling little cottage. It was perfect.

'I'll buy it,' said Clare on a breath.

The agent looked taken aback. 'You haven't seen it yet.'

'I've seen enough,' Clare said. 'Enough, that is, to know I want it.'

'I think you ought to look round first before deciding,' the agent pressed her uneasily. 'You'll need a surveyor's report first, anyway.'

Clare opened the gate without taking any notice of him, walked slowly up the narrow rose-fringed little path, which was paved with black and white tiles. A bird-table stood in the centre of an uneven lawn. Blue-tits flew busily around a string of nuts hanging from a tree. Hidden behind high hedges, the garden had a dreamy air, like the garden in a fairy tale. The lead diamonds of the windows glittered in the sunshine.

Suddenly from behind a row of runner beans strung to a string trellis, a head popped up; very short straight fair hair poking out from beneath a wide-brimmed Mexican straw hat, piercing blue eyes and a brown complexion.

'God! I'd forgotten about you coming ...' said a deep, horrified voice.

Clare stared, her eyes narrowing. The estate agent smiled uneasily, shifting from one foot to the other, as though his client embarrassed him.

'This is Mrs Cunningham, the owner.'

'Jess Cunningham,' Clare cried in a triumphant voice. 'Fancy it being your cottage!'

The owner came slowly out of her hiding place, staring at Clare. 'I don't think I...' She broke off with a gasp. 'Good lord! It's Clare. Clare Sebastian! Do you mean that you and Arturo are thinking of settling down in England? My dear good woman, you'll hate this place. It's far too remote. You aren't cut out for country life.'

The agent gave a muffled groan of despair, but Clare merely laughed.

'Arturo is dead, Jess,' she said simply. 'Dead three months ago. I'm just getting married again.'

The artist pushed back her straw hat with a gesture of profound amazement. 'Do I know the new one?'

'I don't think so,' Clare said lightly. 'He was my first husband. We're remarrying.'

The artist stared at her in a fascinated silence, then said with a shrug, 'Well, I hope he likes country life, because there's nothing to do around here but paint or catch fish. It suited me for years, but I've just got a commission to go out to India and paint the illustrations for a book on Indian wild life, fascinating stuff. It will take the best part of two years to do the job properly, they think, so I have to sell. Anyway, I think I've had enough of Sussex. When I come home I'll buy a house somewhere more remote – Wales or Cornwall, perhaps.'

'It sounds fascinating,' said Clare. 'Will you show me round the cottage, Jess?'

'Of course. Come along in and have some coffee.'

Clare introduced Marie to her, and Jess shook her hand with a friendly smile. Marie realised that she was older than she had looked at first. Her casual clothes, old blue jeans, white shirt and a vivid green handkerchief knotted around her brown throat, had made her look young, but in fact she was more or less the same age as Clare.

They entered the cottage and went first into the tiny kitchen, a rectangular room with deal panelling on the walls and blue Dutch tiles set into the worktops. Everything was very modern and bright, scrupulously clean.

'This is the only room I've spent money on,' Jess shrugged. 'The rest I left as I found it. It suited me.'

There were three small rooms downstairs besides the kitchen. One was a square sitting-room, rather dark and old-fashioned, with heavy dark furniture and ornate wallpaper. The second was a tiny room with white walls which contained only an easel, a camp stool and a stack of canvases facing the wall. 'My studio,' Jess said calmly. 'It was originally a larder, hence the white walls. I stripped off the shelves and enlarged the window. It faces north, so the light is good.'

The third room was a dining-room, containing just an oval table and chairs and a large Victorian sideboard on which stood a silver fruit bowl and some candlesticks.

'As you see, it only needs a little money spent on it,' the agent said optimistically.

Clare eyed the furniture with horror. 'It needs a great deal of work,' she said firmly. 'And that's what it's going to get.'

Jess eyed her. 'Going to take it, Clare?'

'Yes,' Clare said certainly. 'I knew that the moment I set eyes on it. The interior is a mess, but the house itself is adorable. I know James will love it.'

'James? Where is he, anyway? In London?'

'He's been ill,' Clare told her. 'Very ill. That's why we want a quiet cottage to live in – James needs some peace.'

'What about upstairs?' asked the agent. 'Shall we take a look up there?'

'Of course,' said Clare, moving towards the narrow, rather crooked stairs with eagerness.

'I'll make the coffee,' Jess Cunningham said. She smiled at Marie and asked, 'Like to help me make it?'

Marie followed her back to the kitchen and helped to get out the cups and saucers while Jess put on the coffee and found some shortbread in a tin.

'How do you feel about country life?' Jess asked her.

'I'm not sure,' Marie confessed. 'Actually, I was thinking of getting a job. I've never done any work, but I think it's time I started. The trouble is, I've had no training at all. I've a sound education, but in the practical sense I have very little to offer an employer. Perhaps I'll learn shorthand and typing.'

Jess turned to study her thoughtfully, the shortbread tin open in her hand.

'Do you like kids?'

Marie looked blank. 'I suppose so. But I couldn't teach – I wouldn't know how.'

Jess shook her head. 'No, I'm not looking for a teacher – just someone to look after Jeremy while I work.'

'Jeremy?'

'My little boy. He's four years old, too young to go to school, but too active to be left in the care of anyone like my mother, who's seventy years old and past child care.' Jess grimaced at her. 'You see, I made the mistake of getting pregnant a few months before my husband was killed in a car crash. I'd barely got over the shock of being pregnant when my husband was killed. We'd been married for years and frankly I thought I couldn't have kids. I was too busy to worry about it much, but Dave always wanted a child, and I was glad for him that I was going to have one. Then he was killed and I had to bring up Jeremy on my own. Out here in the country that wasn't too hard. I looked after him myself when he was a baby. It was easy to paint while he slept in his pram. Once he started getting about under his own steam it got more difficult, then a woman in the village half a mile away offered to have him for a few hours every day. He goes down to her at ten o'clock and I fetch him back at four, so that gives me a clear working run of six hours. She has two kids of her own, so I think he enjoys it more there anyway. He likes company.'

'Children do,' Marie agreed.

Jess sighed. 'Yes, but the trouble is, what happens when I go to India? I can't leave him behind. I would hate to do that, anyway. I thought I might find someone locally to look after him, but if you would consider the job I would be very grateful.'

Marie stared at her incredulously. 'You want me to look after your son while you're in India?'

Jess nodded. 'You could share our house. They're giving me a house of my own, they tell me. I would pay you, of course. I don't know what the market rate is for jobs like that, but we could find out.'

Marie thought about it and felt a sudden excitement at the idea. She had never been to India. She would love to see it, to live there and be part of the life for a while. Cautiously, she said, 'I've had no experience, you realise.'

Jess shrugged. 'Neither had I had when I had him first. I

was a total novice, but I managed. It's common sense, that's all. You just keep him busy and amused all day. Your evenings will be your own, of course – I'll take over whenever I'm not working. There'll be no housework to do because they've promised me someone to do all that.'

'They?' asked Marie curiously.

Jess laughed. 'I'm sorry, I forgot you don't know. I'm going out there at the invitation of the King of Jedhpur. He's just opened a National Wild Life Park on the plain of Massam outside his capital, Lhalli, and he's paying me to paint these pictures. He intends to publish a glossy book on the subject, and also hopes to sell prints of my pictures to the tourists they hope to attract.' She grinned. 'He's a very ambitious young man. His country is poor, but he thinks they can make money through this National Park.'

'And you'll live out in the park?' Marie was not sure she liked the sound of that. It sounded rather dangerous.

Jess shook her head. 'No, I'll have a house in Lhalli, they say. But there's a stilt house out in the marshes by the river which I can use to do sketches in ... they have it all worked out.' She smiled at Marie. 'Well? What do you think?'

Marie took a deep breath. 'I'll come,' she said.

Jess gazed at her, amused. 'You make decisions as suddenly as your mother!'

'Why not?' Marie said lightly. 'I need a job. I need to work, and I believe in fate. You've offered me just what I was looking for.'

'All the same,' Jess warned, 'you'd better discuss it with your parents before you give me a firm answer.'

'I will,' Marie promised. 'I'll talk to them when they're together. Don't mention it just yet. I'd rather tell them my own way.'

Jess eyed her thoughtfully. 'I see. Just as you say …'

Clare came down a few moments later, drank coffee, refused a piece of shortbread and had a short discussion with Jess over the price of the cottage. By the time they left the deal was settled. Tom Tit Cottage had changed hands, bar the shouting.

Next day, as Clare poured out the details to James in his room at the nursing home, Marie listened patiently, awaiting her chance to break her own news to them.

When she did tell them, Clare was visibly shocked. 'But you can't leave home just when …'

James watched his daughter carefully. 'Why do you want to go, darling?'

'It's because of me,' Clare burst out huskily.

'No,' Marie assured her, smiling at her. 'I'd already decided to get a job before I got back from my holiday. I'm tired of doing nothing, tired of drifting. I want to work, to do something. Jess offered me a change of scene, a chance to do something useful, a chance to learn something about myself and the world …'

'But we want you with us,' Clare said shakily, grasping her hand.

James said softly, 'Aren't I enough for you, Clare?'

She looked at him, her blue eyes wide. 'Of course you are!'

'Then let Marie go. She's right – she has been too sheltered up till now. She needs to find out more about life. I've wrapped her in cotton wool. There's a great big world outside there and she wants to find it for herself. It would be selfish of us to try to keep her. Tom Tit Cottage sounds a paradise to us, but to a young girl such isolation would be very boring. Marie isn't ready to retire from the world yet. Her life is only just beginning.'

Clare sighed. 'Very well, James, I suppose you're right.'

'You know I am,' he said teasingly. 'Weren't you hungry for life at her age? We all have essential stages in our lives. When we're young we need to open out to life. Later on we know what we are and we know what we truly want – then we tend to make our own little place in the world and stay there. Marie has to find her place.'

'I'll always have Tom Tit Cottage to come back to,' Marie pointed out gently.

Clare smiled at her. 'Yes, promise you'll do that, if you ever need us.'

'I'll be back,' Marie promised.

'When does Jess leave?' Clare asked her.

'Next month,' said Marie.

'Then when you've gone to India, Clare and I will take a long cruise to the sun while the cottage is put in order for us,' said James. 'How about the West Indies, Clare?'

'That would be fun,' she agreed. 'But first I must plan the decor and furniture for the cottage.' She gazed at him thoughtfully. 'I think I'll throw all those rooms downstairs into one huge lounge.'

'Not all of them,' James demurred. 'Keep the little studio

as an escape hatch. You never know when you'll need somewhere quiet to be alone. I suggest you make the two main rooms into one ...'

Marie tiptoed out and left them to talk it over. She was filled with excited anticipation of her visit to India. This time she would not be living in a luxury hotel behind safe plate glass. This time she would be living among the ordinary people, sharing their daily lives. She must get some books on the little state of Jedhpur. She had barely heard of it.

A few days later she sat poring over a pile of books, learning that Jedhpur was an ancient kingdom in the northern hills of India's continent, ruled over by a dynasty of kings descended from a barbaric creature called Jai. The country was mostly mountainous, barren and stony, but there were fertile plains around the river Mas, and it was the Massam Plain which had been turned into a National Park to preserve both animals and countryside from the encroachments of civilisation, and, of course, to attract tourists. There had been some trouble politically over the new park since local farmers had resented the idea, but the King had allowed most of them to continue to farm their land, although it overlapped the area of the park, since they had done so from time immemorial.

The language they spoke in Jedhpur was a dialect, Marie learnt, difficult to comprehend in the rest of the country. English was also used in the capital, Lhalli, for official communications since the King had been to school in England, and some of his subjects had formed a regiment in the British Army before independence.

Clare was with James in the nursing home on one of her

daily visits. She had left with an armful of scarlet gladioli, the long sheaves lying against her breast like spears. Together in front of the mirror in the hall, Marie had thought, they looked like sisters. When she told Clare that, her mother had smiled radiantly, the blue eyes childlike with pleasure. Age still held its terrors for Clare, despite her new content.

Mrs Abbot opened the sitting-room door and looked across the room at her. 'I'm just going out to do some shopping. Would you like me to get anything for you?'

'No, thank you,' Marie smiled.

'You'll be in for lunch?'

'Yes.'

'I was going to get lamb chops. Is that all right?'

Marie was surprised. Mrs Abbot rarely consulted her about the menu, despite the myth that Marie ran the household. 'That will be fine,' she said warmly.

Mrs Abbot hesitated. Marie sensed that she was about to ask her something, and looked at her encouragingly. Mrs Abbot took a deep breath. 'Do you think you could take over running the flat if I left? Or do you want me to find someone else to take my place?'

Marie stared at her. 'Are you giving in your notice?'

Mrs Abbot shrugged. 'Things have changed, haven't they? I'm not needed here any more. I thought I'd buy myself a little bungalow down at Southend. I've seen one I like, but I have to make up my mind now, as the owners are in a hurry – they're emigrating, and they want a fast sale.'

'I shall be sorry to see you go,' Marie said gently. 'But you must think of your own future. Of course you must buy the bungalow, if that's what you want. We'll manage. My parents are going on a cruise when Dad comes out of the nursing home, and I'll be going to India, of course.'

Mrs Abbot looked at her, smiling wryly. 'You can never be sure of the future, can you? Out of a clear blue sky something falls wham! And everything falls to pieces.'

'I'm sorry,' Marie said shyly. 'I'm very sorry.'

When Mrs Abbot had gone she lay on the carpet, gazing at the full-colour pictures of Jedhpur; white-capped mountains, brown fields and a winding river running between marshlands rich with birds and animals.

The doorbell rang, startling her, and she glanced at her watch. It couldn't be Clare back already? Or had Mrs Abbot forgotten her key?

When she opened the door she stared in disbelief. 'Stonor! What are you doing here?'

The dark eyes were unsmiling as he surveyed her, leaning on the door-frame with the casual grace which was his birthright.

'I came to see you, surprisingly enough,' he drawled.

'Oh.' For a moment Marie could only stare at him. 'I hadn't expected to see you again.'

'Obviously.' His voice was irritated. 'Aren't you going to ask me in?'

She glanced helplessly back into the sitting-room, littered with open books. 'I suppose so ...' She stood back.

'Such eagerness is very flattering,' he drawled, moving past her with an angry glance.

'You took me by surprise. I'm afraid the flat is very untidy this morning.' Hurriedly, with flushed cheeks, she began to pick up the books, wishing she had known he was coming. She would not be wearing dusty pink denims and a short-sleeved white blouse if she had had any idea she would be seeing him. She was angrily aware of her disordered hair, the fact that she was barely wearing any make-up, merely a quick dusting of powder and the palest pink smudge of lipstick.

He bent to pick up one of the books and glanced at it with raised brows. 'Don't tell me you're planning a holiday in India, now? Still chasing the romantic dream?'

She piled the books on the table and faced him, chin defiant. 'No. I'm going out there to work.'

He stood very still, staring at her, frowning. 'Work? You? What on earth do you mean?'

'I've got a job in Jedhpur,' she said carelessly, her pride hurt by his look of disbelief.

'You've never done a day's work in your life,' he said brutally. 'What work could you do?' The dark eyes narrowed. 'And who would be fool enough to employ you?'

'I'm perfectly capable of working,' she said angrily. 'It's none of your business, anyway.'

'I'm curious, nevertheless,' he drawled.

'Then your curiosity must be unsatisfied,' she retorted.

He made a soft sound under his breath, an impatient, infuriated noise. 'Your trouble is that you were never smacked as a child,' he snapped. 'You're spoilt, selfish and impossibly headstrong.'

'That's my problem,' she shrugged.

'I suppose you've given your parents some information about this job?' he demanded. 'They do know about it?'

'Of course they do.'

'And do they approve?'

The blue eyes gazed at him blandly. 'They're willing to let me go.'

'That wasn't what I asked! Do they approve?'

'I think so,' she said lightly. She looked at him between her lashes. 'You haven't told me why you're here. What did you want to see me about?'

Again he made that angry sound, his lips tightening, the lean face taut. 'God knows! I didn't intend to come ...' He turned away. 'I'm flying to America tomorrow. I suppose I came to say goodbye.'

'Don't you know?' Unconsciously her tone was provocative.

He swung round, took three strides towards her and caught her by her slender shoulders, glaring down at her. 'No, I don't know. I must have been mad to come here. You're a maddening, immature little fool. You have a lot of growing up to do before any sane man would want to get involved with you. I knew it was madness to see you again, but ...' He broke off, his face grim.

'But?' Marie's heart was racing, her body turning to water as she stared up at his dark, angry face.

He gave a despairing groan. 'If I had any sense I'd walk out of that door without another word!'

'Then why don't you?' She turned away, her movement bringing her hair flicking across his cheek in a scented swathe.

'God help me, I can't,' Stonor murmured under his breath.

Marie felt a suffocating excitement as he reached a hand up to touch her averted face, turning it back to face him, his fingers moving against her skin with the sensitivity of a blind man trying to see with his finger tips.

Slowly he traced the shape of her features; the slender straight nose with its faint upturning, the modelling of her cheekbones, the curved pink mouth. Everywhere his fingers rested she felt fiery nerves spring up, beating in response.

He stared down into her wide, very blue eyes, with their flickering lashes constantly hiding the expression the eyes held.

'Can you imagine what it feels like to be split in half?' he asked her suddenly. 'One part of me has always longed for the emptiness of the desert, the silence, the space. The other half is drawn to the neon lights and crowds of the cities. All my life I've had to fight down the impulse to leave the modern world, and all that it means, behind me; to spend my days out there in the freedom of the desert. I waste much of my energy fighting myself.'

'Why fight it?' she shrugged. 'Why not go there and give up everything else? You're a very rich man. You don't need to pursue even more wealth.'

He smiled sardonically. 'Why don't I go? Because I'm still a young man and I know that to retreat into the ancient, unchanged world of the desert would be cowardice. There's no challenge in the desert that I can't face, but the challenge of the business world does scare me. Every day I hang on an abyss edge. One false move and I go down, everything with me.' His eyes flashed excitedly. 'That's why I stay.'

Marie understood that. She watched his face, darkly alive and glittering, and knew far more about him than she had before. This was a man who loved a hand-to-hand struggle with destiny, with danger. He liked to risk everything on one throw of the dice, loved the thrill of the danger.

'You're mad,' she said softly. 'You can't go on playing Russian roulette with life for ever.'

He grinned down at her, his eyes leaping. 'Can't I? Doesn't that attract you, too, Marie?'

Her breath caught as she met his eyes.

'That night I heard you talking outside the hotel, part of me leapt in wild excitement,' he said quickly. 'You said things I've often thought myself, things I was feeling right then. I, too, was hankering for the desert. I was sick of luxury hotels and silly, flattering fools who think that money makes a man. I suddenly wanted to play a game, a game of make-believe; live out the role of my life, make you believe it too. I took you out into the desert to fulfil two secret dreams – yours and mine.'

She was breathless, spellbound, as she listened, feeling the hard-muscled strength of his body against the length of hers, his arm holding her captive.

Then his face hardened. 'But the reality of it scared you, didn't it? You're too shallow to meet the challenge of that vast emptiness, too immature to match a man kiss for kiss, hunger for hunger …' His voice was stifled by strong emotion, fires leapt in the dark eyes, there was a sudden terrifying urgency in the strong hands that held her, moving over body and face, touching, caressing.

'You're hurting me,' she protested, beginning to tremble. What had she unleashed? Now, even more than on that night in the desert, she felt a primitive force in him which, once let loose, might sweep away everything that stood in its path.

'I want to hurt you,' he said fiercely. 'I want to sting you to life. You're like an android, an artificial creation shaped like a woman, with all a woman's beauty and desirability, but lacking the vital spark which lights it up. I told myself that it was folly to come here. It isn't in you to respond to any man.'

'Then why don't you go?' she blazed, flushed with pain and anger at what he had said.

He swore under his breath. The hawk-like face was so close she could see every detail in sharp clarity; the dark, mysterious eyes so deep looking into them was like falling down a well, the strong nose and fleshless cheekbones, austerely planed, the cruel mouth which was suddenly moving closer and closer …

'No!' she moaned, suffocating under that ruthless pressure, her hands beating at his chest like white moths against a window.

The world swung in a crazy arc around her, fire sprang up wherever his hands touched her. Her heart beat so fast she thought she must faint, as if her senses were not capable of meeting the demands he made upon them. Stonor ignored her struggles, her stifled protests. Compelling, ruthless, merciless, he kissed her until she was clinging weakly to him as to a rock in the midst of a flooding river, half drowning, half ecstatic.

Behind her closed lids a dazzle of light hypnotised her. She clung to him while he kissed her throat, her ears, pushing aside her blouse to kiss her shoulders and the white softness where her breasts rose, panting, from their confinement.

Abruptly he pushed her away so that she stumbled and fell back against the sofa. Opening her eyes, she stared at him, her hair straying in golden wildness across the cushions, her blouse half unbuttoned, her eyes wide and dazed.

For a moment he stared at her, his face grim. Then he bowed sardonically. 'Goodbye, Miss Brinton. It was an education to meet you. I pity the man who's fool enough to fall in love with you. His will be a frustrating experience, trying to spark a flame from the stony emptiness of your heart.'

Turning on his heel, he slammed out of the room, and Marie burst into scalding tears.

CHAPTER FIVE

SOME WEEKS later Marie sat on an elaborately worked wicker chair watching a small boy in a white shirt and blue trousers frowning over the drawing he had made of an elephant.

'Should it have five legs?' she asked him lightly. 'Can you remember?'

Jeremy's brown eyes lifted abstractedly. 'It's blue,' he said. 'I haven't got any grey.'

'What about its legs?' she pressed.

He slowly counted them. 'That isn't a leg,' he told her scornfully. 'It's a tail.'

'Oh, sorry.' She got up and bent over the picture. 'It's very good,' she admitted. 'We must try to find some grey pencils next time we go to the market.'

His small face lit up. 'Can we go today? I like going down to the market. I like the candy man. I like that stuff he sells that's pink and sticky. It makes my teeth stick together.'

'Yes,' she said thoughtfully. 'But I'm not sure it's good for your teeth.'

'I like the man who sells crocodile eggs,' Jeremy went on ecstatically. 'What do you think people do with them?'

'I hate to think,' Marie murmured. 'It's nearly time for your lunch.'

'Not rice again,' he moaned. 'I wish I could have chips.'

'You know they don't have potatoes here,' she pointed out.

'I can wish, can't I?' His face was rebellious, the pink skin flushed, the brown eyes cross. 'I'm not very hungry, anyway.'

The heat was enervating for him, Marie thought. She always insisted that he took a nap in the afternoon, when the heat was at its worst, but Jeremy found it hard to sleep in the daytime and often got up again and played with his toys while she was not watching him.

She had made his acquaintance in England, before they left for Jedhpur, and they had become friends at once. Jeremy was a very friendly little boy, quite accustomed to amusing himself, and always delighted to have company. On the long flight from England there had been no difficulty in keeping him amused. He sat drawing huge pictures of fluffy white clouds while he stared out of the window. Marie had been filled with trepidation that day, wondering if she had done the right thing, wondering if she would miss her parents while she was in India, wondering if she would ever be able to manage to look after the little boy.

They had driven from the tiny airstrip into the crowded capital of Jedhpur through narrow streets filled with people who had turned to stare at the black palace car. Few people in Lhalli had cars. They were still an exciting event and attracted a great deal of excited attention. Jeremy had waved, mistakenly imagining all the interest to be in him, and the dark-eyed, white-clad people had sometimes waved back, amused by his smiling little face and bright eyes.

The car had taken them to the pink-washed palace first of all, driving through a large iron-bolted door held open by two turbanned sentries who saluted, to Jeremy's huge delight.

The palace was sheltered behind great walls behind which lay first the outer courtyard, filled, surprisingly, with goats and boys, who stared and gesticulated as the new arrivals left the car.

'Is it a school?' Jeremy had asked, baffled but enchanted by the goats, with their belled necks and short horns.

'I expect those goats belong to the King,' his mother had said, shrugging.

They had been met at the arched door of the palace by a fierce, turbanned man in spotless white, his broad silk sash fringed where it fell along one hip. He had bowed, hands laid palm to palm, making a courteous greeting. Then he had led them through a bewildering series of marble-floored corridors, their feet echoing as they walked in their Western shoes.

Everywhere they saw sentries and servants, the latter all clad in the same spotless white as the man who was guiding them.

They had waited in a small antechamber for ten minutes before the King arrived, wearing a blue tunic made of some glittering material, buttoned to the throat and falling to his hips, beneath which were white trousers. He had come in suddenly, smiling at them with friendly dark eyes.

'Mrs Cunningham . . . how delightful to see you! I hope you had a good flight? And this is your son.' Solemnly he extended a hand to Jeremy, who took it as solemnly.

'I am very glad to meet you,' the King said politely.

Jeremy looked pleased. 'Why are there goats in your courtyard?' he asked eagerly.

The King's round dark eyes smiled. 'Ah, that is because they have come in to be milked,' he said. 'Then they will go back into the fields, up the hills where the grass is green.'

'There were boys too,' Jeremy pointed out.

'They look after the goats,' the King explained. 'Each has his own flock and his own pasture.'

'Why do they wear bells round their necks?' Jeremy asked with an air of scholarly interest.

'So that they can be heard if they get lost,' said the King with great patience.

'Why ...' Jeremy began, but his mother cut him off gently, 'That's enough, Jeremy.'

The King smiled at her. 'He asks intelligent questions.' The dark eyes moved on to scrutinise Marie. 'And this is Miss Brinton, your governess?'

Marie shook hands with him, impressed by his direct and interested manner. He was not at all what she had expected.

'Have you been to this part of the world before?' he asked her. 'What do you think of our small country?'

'I've never been to India before,' she admitted. 'But I'm sure I'm going to like it.'

'This is not India, Miss Brinton,' he said flatly. 'Jedhpur is an independent kingdom with its own history, language and traditions. We are very proud of our past and very hopeful about our future.'

She was embarrassed by her slip, glancing at Jess apologetically, hoping she had not offended the King too much. Jess smiled at her comfortingly, giving a slight shake of the head.

The King clapped his hands and the proud-faced servant in white appeared, bowing profoundly.

'Rahaib, take Miss Brinton and Master Jeremy to their bungalow, will you?' He smiled at Marie. 'I wish to have a long talk with Mrs Cunningham about her work. I hope you will excuse us for a while. Rahaib will see that you have everything you need. If you have any worries, please mention them to him and they will be attended to at once.'

Marie was taken aback, but smiled back politely and allowed Rahaib to lead her and Jeremy away.

Back they went along the marble corridors, her eyes dazedly admiring the gilt glitter of some of the mosaics, staring in fascinated confusion at huge barbaric statues of gods or men, the limbs entwined in strange contortions, the faces calm and impassive. Rahaib walked at a calm pace just ahead of them, one hand loosely hovering around his sash. When someone suddenly slipped out of an alcove between two pale pink pillars Rahaib's hand moved like a snake, flying away from his sash with a curved, glittering dagger between the brown fingers.

'Put that away, Rahaib,' commanded an amused voice.

Rahaib relaxed, bowing. 'Lord, I did not see it was you.'

The newcomer was a young man in Western clothes; a white shirt and loose white trousers, wearing white sports shoes on his feet.

Marie looked at him in curious surprise. He grinned at her, his thin brown face full of mischief.

'I've been playing cricket,' he explained, pointing to his clothes. 'You must be Mrs Cunningham. I must say, you look amazingly young to be a famous artist.'

She laughed, her blue eyes dancing. 'That's because I'm not Mrs Cunningham. I'm only her son's governess.'

'Ah, yes, the son,' he murmured, glancing at Jeremy, who was a few feet away, inspecting a wall carving of an elephant with much fascination. 'I had forgotten him.' He turned back to her, smiling. 'I am the King's cousin, by the way. My name is Aziz. May I ask your name?'

'Marie Brinton,' she told him.

His voice dropped confidentially. 'I am delighted to meet you, Miss Brinton. You are the answer to a maiden's prayer.'

Her eyebrows curved in silent amusement. She thought he had misunderstood the phrase, but, seeing her unspoken reaction, he grinned at her.

'I mean that literally,' he said. 'I do not suppose the King mentioned Aissa?'

She shook her head. 'Who is Aissa?'

'His sister,' Aziz said softly. 'She has just returned from a year in Paris and she is already beginning to be very bored here. Like myself, she had had a Western education, but now that we are back in Jedhpur we are expected to return to the old ways because otherwise we might shock the people. It is not so bad for me – men have always had more freedom than women here, but for Aissa it is stifling.'

Marie stared at him, uneasy and perplexed. She sensed that she was about to be involved in trouble, but there was little she could do to dodge out of the situation.

Aziz went on pleadingly, 'Aissa badly needs a friend. There are many things she could do with another girl around that she could not do if she were alone. It would not be permitted for her drive around alone outside the palace, for instance, but if you were her companion her brother would not object.'

'The King seemed very modern-minded,' Marie protested.

Aziz sighed. 'He is, actually, but he can only go so far for fear of offending the diehards who help him run this country. Believe me, plenty of people would make trouble if Aissa was thought to be running wild. She isn't married yet, although she is twenty years old, and to some old-fashioned people that in itself is shocking.'

Marie looked at him in disbelief. 'Shocking?'

'They think she is getting old,' Aziz said grimly. 'A hundred years ago she would have been married at fifteen. The King has held them off until now, but some of them are insisting that he find her a husband without further delay.'

'An arranged marriage?' Marie knew that that was the custom here, so this did not surprise her.

Aziz nodded. 'The Prime Minister is the leader of the old party, the ones who are most determined to have her married off ...'

She glanced nervously at Rahaib, who stood within earshot, his face blank, yet who must have heard every word of this. Aziz followed her glance and smiled.

'Oh, don't worry about Rahaib. He was the King's bodyguard when the King was small. He would die rather than betray any of us.'

Rahaib made no move, no sign indicating that he had heard a word of this remark. Aziz smiled at her again, shrugging.

'You see? He is the eyes and ears, but he does not speak, unless the King commands it.'

'Then the King approves of what you suggest?' she asked doubtfully.

Aziz said softly, 'The King wants his sister to be happy, but he cannot move in the matter himself. He can only permit what she wishes out of his love for her. If she asks to be allowed to visit you in your bungalow, he will agree.'

Rahaib turned suddenly and murmured softly, 'The Lord Hathni approaches, my lord.'

'Oh, gracious heavens,' Aziz said in alarm. He gave Marie a quick look. 'Do not mention that you have seen me. We have never met before.'

Marie was puzzled and alarmed, turning to look down the corridor as she heard the slap of sandalled feet. When she turned back to Aziz he had vanished. She looked at Rahaib in bewilderment. His dark eyes met hers impassively.

Then they moved on slowly, Jeremy still staring at the walls with deep interest. He looked up at Marie, wide-eyed. 'Funny drawings,' he said to her. 'Some of those snakes are all tangled up. Are they fighting?'

'I expect so,' she said, nervously wondering about the approaching footsteps.

The man coming down the corridor was short, rather

slightly built and grey-haired, his richly decorated tunic ablaze with colour, his austere face at variance with what he wore. Behind him marched two men in white turbans and red tunics, their faces wearing the same blank impassivity as Rahaib.

He paused as he came face to face with Marie, his almond-shaped eyes narrowing. Then he smiled politely, without warmth.

Rahaib spoke in the soft local dialect, and the newcomer listened without looking at him.

Then he looked back at Marie and made the usual courteous greeting, hands together, head bowed. 'Miss Brinton! I am Hathni Kundor, the King's chief minister. Welcome to Jedhpur. I hope you had a pleasant journey here.'

'Yes, thank you,' said Marie, slightly nervous in his presence. He had an intimidating eye, cold and clear-sighted, and a soft precision of speech which made every syllable he uttered very formal.

He nodded in response to her reply, glanced briefly at Jeremy and then said politely, 'I hope we shall meet again, Miss Brinton.'

She stood aside, realising he meant to walk on, and with another courteous gesture he and his escort proceeded along the corridor. She let out a long sigh of relief.

'Whew!'

Glancing at Rahaib, she fancied she caught a flicker of something that might have been amusement passing across his face, but the next second he had assumed his usual calm mask.

They made their way out of the palace without further

incident, got back into the black limousine and drove out of the palace gates into the teeming city. Soon they were driving between tiny, white-washed flat-roofed houses threaded with alleys which wound away out of sight. Thin, stark-ribbed dogs scratched in the dust. Women in bright silks and soft slippers, their heads draped against the intruding sun, moved from shop to shop with graceful steps. Around an ancient, stone-walled well sat older women, their faces wrinkled and dried up by the sun, gossiping with the ease of old friends, while children in cotton shirts scampered barefoot around them, chasing each other in some ritualistic game.

The streets grew more and more crowded, and the car had trouble inching its way through them. Street-sellers carrying trays of food shouted their wares. A water carrier waddled along, slopping precious drops on either side of his yoked shoulders, followed by a crowd of thirsty dogs who licked at the wet dust.

From street cafés came the high wail of traditional music. A dancing girl in gold-trimmed skirts and bare feet, her ankles and wrists jangling with golden bangles, came out of a café to stare at them as they drove past.

Marie was delighted by one shop, the flat stall in front of it swathed in rainbow-coloured silks, red, yellow, green, blue, flung across the stall in voluminous folds to catch the eye, the gold and silver threads woven into the material glittering in the sunlight. The shopkeeper, seeing her eager eyes, bowed invitingly, but the car drove on slowly.

Jeremy only really grew interested when the car temporarily halted, to let a flock of goats pass, outside a sweet stall.

Wooden bowls full of sticky pink and white sweets drew the attentions of a horde of black flies, at which the perspiring stallholder slapped with a paper fan. Across the street stood a cookshop from which the odour of spicy curry floated. Outside stood a boy not much older than Jeremy, hawking a woven basket of palm leaves; stuffed with cardamon-scented rice and minced mutton, Rahaib informed them. A smile briefly lit his countenance as he added, 'Most delicious, my lady.'

'Can I buy some?' Jeremy asked eagerly.

Marie smiled at him. 'Another day, perhaps.' She was not altogether certain of the safety of eating food from the market. The flies which pervaded the place worried her. None of the food seemed to be covered from the sun; even the meat lay uncovered, descended upon by black tides of flies.

They moved on jerkily, the driver apparently unflurried or annoyed by the constant stops necessitated by the throngs of people who poured past his bonnet. Soon Jeremy saw something else he liked: a stall selling toys; little wooden birds which pecked at painted corn on a bright green board when you pulled the string below, elephants of bright blue which had nodding heads, peacocks with vivid bejewelled tails that opened and closed like fans, little wooden men who swung over and over a string stretched between two poles, windmills of painted paper which whirled round and round when you blew them.

'When can we come here again?' Jeremy asked her eagerly.

'We'll ask your mother,' she promised.

'Soon? Tomorrow?'

'Perhaps,' she said, not liking to commit herself yet. She must see what Mrs Cunningham thought about the market before she agreed to take Jeremy there.

Rahaib said quietly, 'I will escort you and the child to the market whenever you wish, Miss Brinton.'

She looked at him gratefully. 'Thank you, Rahaib. That's very kind of you.'

He shook his head. 'The King's highness has told me to see that you and the child come to no harm. While you are in Jedhpur I am your servant, miss.'

'Oh. I see.' She was taken aback, wondering how she was going to cope with his constant presence day after day.

He smiled then, his face gravely amused. 'When you need me I shall be in the servants' quarters of the bungalow, my lady.'

She flushed, seeing that he had read her mind. 'Thank you, Rahaib,' she said in faint apology.

He inclined his head. 'It is my pleasure,' he said formally. 'There are certain persons in Jedhpur who do not approve of the King's royal desire to modernise the kingdom. They resent foreigners, and they might make trouble for you if you went out alone. That is why the King's highness has asked me to guard you.'

She looked at him anxiously. 'You mean it's dangerous for us to go out without you?'

'It would be wiser not to do so,' he agreed. 'Most of our people are gentle and hospitable, but there are some who hate the new ways and wish only for things to go on as they have always done ... these people are troublemakers.'

She remembered what Aziz had said. 'And the Prime Minister himself does not approve, I gather?' she asked.

Rahaib's face stiffened. 'My Lord Hathni prefers the old ways,' he agreed politely. He looked at her directly. 'But you need not fear him, my lady. Lord Hathni is a very good man.'

'Aziz seemed afraid of him,' she said, half to herself.

Rahaib hesitated, then said gently, 'My lord Aziz respects his father too much to fear him, my lady.'

She stared at him in astonishment. 'His father?'

Rahaib inclined his head. 'Lord Hathni is the King's highness's uncle.'

'And Aziz is his son,' she said. 'Then why did he hide?'

'Because he did not wish his father to see him speaking with you,' Rahaib explained. 'Lord Hathni might then have suspected when you saw much of the Princess Aissa that it was his son's doing ...'

'I see,' she said, not really seeing very much at all. Clearly, the politics of Jedhpur were involved and dangerous. She wished Aziz had not dragged her into them, and decided that if at all possible she would steer completely clear of anything which even remotely smelt of politics. She did not want to cause trouble here for Jess or for the King.

'Thank you for telling me, Rahaib,' she said, looking at the grizzled old man with gratitude.

'I thought you should know, Miss Brinton,' he said simply. 'Prince Aziz is not always very thoughtful or considerate of other people. He sees only his own desires and seeks a way to achieve them.'

'I suppose it was kind of him to wish to help Princess Aissa, anyway,' she said.

Rahaib's eyes met hers briefly. The old man seemed to hesitate, then shrugged, saying nothing. She wondered what it was he had decided not to tell her.

They had left the market quarter behind them now, and were driving along a wide, dusty road fringed with square-built white houses with the usual flat roofs. Wire fences strung from wooden posts surrounded their gardens. Thickly set rhododendron bushes, deodars, fruit trees and dancing flies inhabited these gardens. Their shade was alluring, and Marie stared at each one, hoping it would be theirs.

At last they halted outside one and Rahaib stood to watch them dismount from the car, then unlocked the high gate and escorted them up the dusty path.

There were two doors; one outer with a mesh-wire covering to keep out flies, one inner made all of glass to let light into the house. A long verandah ran the length of the back of the house. Wicker chairs were arranged around a low cane table.

A small, slender woman in a yellow sari came hurrying from somewhere to greet them politely. Over her palms her dark eyes looked curiously at Marie. A red caste mark in the middle of her forehead enhanced the glowing colour of her olive skin.

'Lispa speaks no English,' Rahaib told them. 'I shall interpret for you if you tell me your wishes.'

Marie smiled at Lispa and indicated Jeremy. 'Tell her the little boy is tired and hungry.'

Lispa's dark eyes travelled to Jeremy as Rahaib spoke to

her. A little smile touched her mouth. She held out one thin-fingered hand to the boy, who trustingly took her hand and let her lead him away.

Rahaib ushered Marie along a corridor to a shuttered room full of cool shadows. 'This is your chamber, my lady. Your boxes are here already.'

Heaving a sigh of delight at the coolness, she looked around the room, gazing at the net-enshrouded bed, the carved chests and the wicker, cushioned chair. 'It's delightful,' she told Rahaib.

'Will you rest or eat, my lady?'

'I think we'd better eat first,' she said.

He bowed. 'I will go and find out if the food is ready. Please, wash and refresh yourself.'

She looked at him doubtfully, and he smiled at her. 'There is a bathroom beyond that door,' he told her gently.

Marie was astonished. 'A bathroom?' She had not expected such a thing here.

'This house belonged once to an American who came to study our old temples,' Rahaib explained. 'He had a bathroom built into the bungalow. Of course, we have no modern sanitation in most of our houses. The American dug a pit for the waste out at the back of the house and laid pipes to carry the wastage out there. It took many months and by the time he had finished he was just leaving to go home.' A faint look of amusement came into the dark eyes. 'He was not pleased.'

'Your English is very good, Rahaib,' she told him admiringly. 'Have you been to Europe?'

He looked surprised. 'Of course I accompanied the King when he went to school and university in England. I spent fourteen years in your country.'

'Fourteen years?' She was astonished. 'No wonder your English is so good!'

'The King's highness was seven when his royal father sent him to school at first. We stayed there until he had finished his whole education. Every year we came home for the summer, of course. I could have married then, but I waited. Until my lord the King was home for good I would not wed.'

'And are you married now?' she asked curiously.

He looked surprised. 'But Lispa is my wife,' he said.

'Oh, I see,' she said, taken aback, remembering the formal way in which he had addressed Lispa, the commanding note in his voice. He had spoken to her as if to a servant.

'Have you any children, Rahaib?' she asked.

He smiled. 'Three sons.' His pride was evident. 'Lispa is a good wife.'

She was amused. 'Is the King married too?'

Rahaib's eyes glowed suddenly. 'The King is married,' he nodded. 'The Queen expects her first child in two months. We all pray it will be a son.' He hesitated and again she was sure he doubted whether it would be discreet to speak, then he said softly, 'The Queen is most beautiful and sweet. Her voice is like melted honey, her skin like silk.'

Marie looked at him curiously. He sounded as if he worshipped the Queen, she thought. He had not had that gentle, adoring ring in his voice when he spoke of Lispa.

Perhaps his love for the King carried over to the King's wife.

'How old is the Queen?' she asked curiously.

'Fifteen,' Rahaib said.

'Fifteen!' Marie was astonished. It seemed very young to be a Queen and expecting a first child, but then she knew that things were very different here. She thought of herself at fifteen, a hockey-playing schoolgirl with white socks and a short gym tunic, and suppressed a smile. Indeed, things were very different.

When Rahaib had left her she went into the bathroom. It was a stark, whitewashed room. The bath was sunk into the floor, which had been concreted, perhaps to discourage insects. When she turned on the taps the water issued in a discouraging brown stream, but after running for a while the water cleared, although occasionally a dead fly fell out with it.

She locked the door and had a brief bath, then dried herself and dressed again. When she returned to her bedroom she found Jeremy there, sitting on her bed, staring around.

'I'm sleepy,' he said fretfully.

'Bed, then,' she said, lifting him down. He was limp and heavy, his eyes glazed with weariness. She carried him through to the tiny room which Rahaib had said was for him, undressed him and popped him into bed. She had barely left the room before his even breathing announced that he was asleep. It had been a long journey, she thought. It was not surprising that he was so tired.

Jess had returned from the palace some hours later, having eaten with the King, her eyes excited as she told Marie about the plans she and the King had laid for the work ahead.

'I'm going to enjoy this,' she said delightedly. 'What about you? Are you settling in?'

Marie had said she was already feeling quite at home here, and Jess had given her an approving look.

Their first day in Jedhpur had ended peacefully as the darkness fell with the swiftness of a hawk, cloaking everything with shadows.

And so their life began to take on a routine. Each day Jess got up at dawn, breakfasted on fruit and warm chapattis, then drove off in a Land-Rover the King had lent her to start sketching in the isolation of her stilt hut in the marshes. While she was gone, Marie amused Jeremy on the verandah of the house.

Drawing elephants and tigers was his favourite occupation. Like his mother, he had a natural talent for it, and a deep curiosity about everything around him.

When he was not with Jess, he liked to play in the kitchen with Lispa's sons, who were close to his age and possessed exciting toys similar to those he had seen in the market. He and Marie had already visited the market with Lispa to help her choose food and to see the fascinating shops at closer quarters. Jeremy had bought some pencils, a wooden elephant with a jewelled head-cloth and bright eyes, and a large plastic ball imported from Europe.

Today as they trailed back into the house for their midday meal Jeremy demanded another visit to the market. Marie promised one tomorrow, with which he was content.

He showed Lispa his drawing of the great blue elephant,

and she admired it, clicking her brightly painted fingernails in delight.

Jeremy eyed the food laid out for them with faint depression – a plate of steaming white rice, a bowl of vegetable curry, a pile of warm chapattis and some fruit in a carved wooden bowl.

'Rice again!' he groaned, and Lispa looked at him anxiously.

Marie spoke to her in the local dialect. 'Good, very good.' She had been learning a few phrases from Rahaib in order to be able to speak to Lispa in her own tongue. The young woman's face cleared and she smiled, amicably making her little gesture of polite recognition.

'You mustn't hurt Lispa's feelings, Jeremy,' Marie said gently. 'She works very hard to make your meals. You must try to like them.'

'They're always the same,' he said crossly. 'Curry, curry, curry …'

'Last night we had chicken cooked in the oven,' she pointed out.

'It didn't taste like chicken,' said Jeremy. 'It was all hot and spicy.'

Marie sighed. At his age it was difficult to adjust, she supposed. She helped him to a small portion of rice and curry and he poked at it with his fork, his face sulky.

Rahaib appeared behind her chair and bent to say quietly, 'An Englishman to see you, Miss Brinton.'

Suddenly her heart leapt on a wild, ludicrous hope. 'An Englishman? Did he give a name?'

'He is an archaeologist called Davidson,' Rahaib explained. 'He is living here while he studies our temples – many archaeologists come here to study them. They live in a bungalow near them and rarely come into Lhalli.'

'Davidson?' She did not know the name, but she said that Rahaib might show him in, and the old man departed to do so.

'Miss Brinton? I'm so sorry to disturb you during your meal!' The voice was young, cheerful, with the unmistakable burr of a West Country accent running beneath the English.

She smiled, holding out her hand. 'Mr Davidson? Do sit down and join us. There's more than enough for three.'

'Well, thanks,' he said at once, taking a chair. 'I must admit, I'm hungry. I've been trailing around Lhalli all morning trying to see the King, but they won't admit me to the palace. That's why I'm here, to tell you the truth.'

She was puzzled, staring at him across the table. He was in his late twenties, fair-faced, with wiry brown hair and clear, friendly hazel eyes. She liked him on sight. He had a direct and cheerful manner which was appealing. 'How can I help you?'

'You work for Mrs Cunningham,' he said, accepting a plate from Lispa with a smile. 'And she works for the King. She could get him to see me.'

Marie laughed. 'Oh, I don't know about that. She hasn't seen the King since we arrived. They talked for a while on the first day, but he's been busy ever since.'

'All the same, if she wrote to him I think he might take some notice of her.'

'Why do you want to see him so badly?' she asked.

He forked some curry into his mouth, chewed and swallowed, then looked round at Lispa, who was discreetly hovering within earshot. He spoke in quick dialect for a moment, and Lispa's face beamed at him.

'Mr Davidson, do you speak the local language?' she asked him curiously.

He nodded. 'I've learnt it since I got here.'

'How long have you been here?' she asked.

'Three months.'

'Three months?' She was astounded. 'But ... you sound quite fluent ...'

He shrugged modestly. 'I have a flair for languages – I speak eleven. It's just a knack.' Then he grinned at her. 'By the way, my name is Peter.'

She acknowledged the invitation with a smile. 'Mine is Marie, Peter. So why do you need to see the King?'

He leaned forward. 'I want to see a temple some miles out in the jungle and apparently it's forbidden to go anywhere near it. It's sacred, or something. I'm not sure why there's a taboo on it, but when I tried to drive there the other day I was forbidden to go any further by a very officious village headman, so I want to see the King to ask his permission. He's usually very good about these things—he's a modern-minded chap. But they denied me entrance to the palace, too. Probably old Hathni. He hates the sight of me and makes no bones about it. If I could get a message to the King I'm sure he would give me permission.'

Marie glanced at Rahaib's impassive face. 'Well, I'll

speak to Mrs Cunningham, but I can't promise anything.'

Peter Davidson looked at Rahaib, too. 'What do you think, Rahaib?'

'I cannot say, sir,' Rahaib returned blandly.

'Hmm . . .' Peter looked at Marie and grinned. 'That means he refuses to get involved. Discreet chap, Rahaib.'

'You've met him before?'

Peter laughed. 'Anyone who meets the King meets Rahaib. He's the King's shadow.'

'He's our shadow for the moment,' said Marie, smiling at Rahaib. 'He's been very kind to us.'

Peter looked across the table at Jeremy. 'Enjoying your lunch, young chap?'

'No,' said Jeremy sulkily. 'I'm fed up with rice, and with curry and chapattis ...'

Marie frowned at him. 'Jeremy! That's rude!'

'No,' said Peter cheerfully, 'just honest. I tell you what, Jeremy – why don't you come to dinner with me tonight and I'll give you real English food?'

Jeremy's face lit up. 'Chips?' he asked eagerly.

'I don't know about chips,' said Peter, scratching his chin. 'I could give you new potatoes and sausages, though.'

'Sausages?' Jeremy's face shone with delight. 'Honestly?' He stared at him as if at Santa Claus. 'And potatoes? Marie said there were no potatoes in Jedhpur!' He glared at her accusingly.

Peter winked at her. 'I've got a secret supply. Will you come?' He looked at Marie appealingly.

'Oh, please,' Jeremy begged.

She smiled. 'I suppose I can hardly refuse. Jeremy would never forgive me.'

'Neither would I,' Peter assured her.

CHAPTER SIX

WHEN JESS returned from her day out in the marshes she was hot and grimy, her feet plastered with black mud, her shirt sticking to her back after the heat of the day. She paused, to say hallo, before going to the bathroom to take a quick bath. Jeremy giggled at the sight of her.

'You're dirty, Mummy!'

'Filthy,' she agreed cheerfully. Under her arm she carried a bulging portfolio. 'But I've done a lot of work today. I saw a tiger down by the water hole, a splendid brute with enormous muscles, in fine condition. He stayed there for half an hour very obligingly and I was able to make several good sketches of him.'

'Jess, we've had an invitation,' Marie informed her.

Jeremy chimed in excitedly. 'Yes, we're going to have potatoes for supper tonight.'

Jess laughed. 'Potatoes?' Her brows rose. 'That sounds very unlikely, darling.'

'We are, aren't we?' he claimed indignantly, giving Marie a look of appeal.

'Yes,' she agreed. She looked at Jess and smiled. 'A young man called today and invited us all to supper. He offered us potatoes and sausages – Jeremy couldn't believe his ears. I'm afraid I could hardly turn him down once Jeremy had heard that.'

Jess laughed again. 'Who was this conjuror?'

'An English archaeologist,' Marie told her. 'Peter Davidson. He was rather nice.'

'I see,' said Jess with amusement. 'Well, in that case, I suppose you'd better go to your orgy, the pair of you.'

'Oh, you must come too,' Marie urged.

Jess shook her head. 'I'm too tired. I'll send my apologies – I want to go to bed early.'

'Mummy, when can I come and see your house on stilts?' begged Jeremy. 'I want to watch tigers and elephants.'

'Why not tomorrow?' she replied easily. 'You and Marie can both come. But you'll have to be very quiet while I'm working, Jeremy, you know that.'

'Promise!' he breathed ecstatically.

Jess laughed and went on to have her bath while Rahaib drove Marie and Jeremy along the dusty roads to the bungalows near the temple clearing where the English archaeological party were living.

They were passing through wilder country than they had ever seen before. The houses out here were smaller, thatched with dried grass, their mud walls baked hard by the sun. Thin cattle with great bells around their necks roamed the fields. The jungle was never far away, gloomy with shade, hung with creepers which festooned the struggling trees like Christmas chains. Jungle fowl with red combs and orange necks flew up squawking as they drove past, then settled again to scratch in the leafy dust. Strange red flowers made patches of brightness in the green of the jungle. Among the leafy branches sat parakeets of many colours, mocking them raucously, their round bright eyes following the car out of sight.

'It's rather creepy in there, isn't it?' Jeremy whispered, his small fingers clutching at Marie's hand.

'I'm afraid it is,' she agreed gently. 'But we would be quite safe with Rahaib to protect us.'

Rahaib turned his huge head to grin at Jeremy, his teeth white except for several sheathed in glittering gold. His fierce moustaches bristled proudly. 'I have shot many tigers,' he told Jeremy. 'No need to be afraid while I am there.'

Jeremy looked at him thoughtfully. 'You're very strong, aren't you, Rahaib?'

Rahaib laughed. 'Very strong,' he agreed.

They came to a clearing in the jungle where the ornately carved cupolas of temples reared like mirages against the encroaching green gloom. Nearby stood a wire fence surrounding several roughly constructed bungalows. On the verandah of one stood Peter Davidson, a glass in his hand as he waved to them.

Rahaib followed them on to the verandah and stood impassively while Peter greeted them, then, when they were led into the house, sat down on the steps of the verandah and stared out into the swiftly falling dusk.

'My friends wanted to get in on the act,' Peter said cheerfully, pouring Jeremy a glass of lemonade and a glass of lime laced slightly with gin for Marie, 'but I told them to clear off. This is my party, I said. Find your own visitors.' He glanced at the darkening windows. 'I expect they're watching us sulkily right now.'

'Oh, what a shame,' said Marie, almost laughing. 'How many of you are there?'

'Four of us,' he told her. 'Our leader is Grant Williams, a choleric Welshman of advancing years. Then there's Duffy, who's Irish and addicted to poker, Saintsbury, who's of rather monkish habits, never drinking or having any fun—and me.' He grinned at her. 'I'm the pick of the bunch, believe me. I didn't want you to meet the others yet in case they frightened you off. En masse they can be pretty horrifying.'

Jeremy was gazing around the room with a disillusioned air. 'I don't see any potatoes and sausages,' he said.

Marie gave Peter a warning glance. 'I hope for your sake that you weren't just having him on, because he's set his heart on those potatoes of yours.'

He bowed. 'When I promise something I mean every word I say.' He picked up a brass bell and rang it with abandon. A few moments later an old man in a turban and dhoti came into the room bearing a large brass tray. While Jeremy watched with glee he laid the table with three plates, lit the candles and then placed some covered dishes in the centre.

'Right-ho, Ramji,' said Peter cheerfully. 'We'll do the rest.' He waved them to their seats, then whipped the covers away. Jeremy gave a sigh of rapture. Nestling in one was a pile of small new potatoes shining with butter, faintly dusted with what appeared to be chopped chives. In the other was a mound of sausages swimming in baked beans.

'How did you do it?' Marie demanded as Peter piled the food on to Jeremy's eager plate.

'Tins,' he said succinctly.

She burst out laughing, then her eyes brightened. 'Where did you get them?' If Peter could buy tins of English food, she thought, so could they.

Peter shook his head. 'Brought them from England,' he admitted. 'They were shipped out with our heavy equipment, strictly for special occasions. We could only bring a small supply or I'd give you some.'

She sighed. 'Oh, well, it's wonderful to have a change, as Jeremy says.'

'You might be able to get them from one of the larger towns,' he suggested. 'Of course, there's no demand for such stuff in Lhalli, but in Delhi or Calcutta there's an English population who have such food imported for them.'

'It doesn't matter,' she said, enjoying the buttery taste of the potatoes.

They had fruit and custard to follow, the custard also coming from a tin, Peter informed her. Then they had coffee, strong and milky. Afterwards while Jeremy looked through some coloured books of photographs of India which Peter produced, Marie and Peter played records and talked by candlelight.

Suddenly their peace was interrupted by the tramp of feet on the verandah. Peter looked round, grimacing.

'Blast them! I might have known they wouldn't keep out ...'

Then three men came into the room, eagerly looking at

Marie. Peter sulkily introduced her to them. They surrounded her, talking all at once, making her laugh.

'I've discovered why you aren't allowed out near the Satmu temple,' Grant Williams, a short dark man in his thirties, said to Peter.

'Oh?' Peter asked impatiently.

'Apparently Mrs Cunningham is behind it,' said Grant, smiling at Marie.

'Jess?' Marie was puzzled.

He turned to her, his dark eyes twinkling. 'It seems she doesn't want any visitors out there for the moment in case they scare away any of the animals who visit the waterhole. The temple is just a few hundred yards away in the jungle.'

'So that's it!' Peter exploded. 'Well, it seems simple then. All I have to do is get her to take me out there with her.'

'We're going there tomorrow,' Marie told him.

Peter's face lit up. 'That's terrific! I'll come, too.'

'Oh, I don't know,' she protested. 'You'd have to ask Jess.'

'I'll come back and ask her tonight,' Peter said.

'How are you going to get back?' Grant asked him sarcastically. 'I need the Land-Rover to get into Lhalli to send some telegrams.'

'You can give me a lift back,' Peter said confidently.

Grant shook his head. 'I have a better idea. Strange as it may seem, I'm still in charge of this expedition. I'll see Mrs Cunningham for you and ask her permission for a visit to the temple.'

Peter looked at him unwillingly, and Grant grinned. 'Don't

argue, old man. You can't descend on Mrs Cunningham at this hour and foist yourself on her until I get back from Lhalli. You know how long it takes to send a telegram here.'

So they drove back to the bungalow with Grant Williams driving behind them, and he came into the bungalow to have a few words with Jess.

She was startled to see him. Wrapped in a cotton dressing-gown, her short hair hair damp from her bath, she flushed as she shook hands.

'I'm sorry to intrude at this hour,' he said uneasily, and explained his mission.

'If Mr Davidson comes along tomorrow he must be very quiet,' Jess said. 'I don't want any disturbances near the waterhole. The animals scent any intruders and keep clear for hours until they're sure the coast is clear.'

'I'll bring him myself,' said Grant. 'I think I can vouch for his discretion if I'm there beside him.'

Jess lifted amused blue eyes to him. 'I see,' she said, her glance measuring him.

'Will you trust me?' he asked.

'I think I will,' she said softly.

Next morning at dawn they all set off in two Land-Rovers. Jess, Marie and Jeremy drove in one, Peter, Grant Williams and Rahaib came behind them in another. The journey was slow and painful. The roads were soon nothing but cart-tracks through the jungle, jolting roughly over them they clenched their teeth at each great bump, their faces soon grey with dust.

Soon they left the Land-Rovers parked in a clearing and went the rest of the way on foot, walking carefully in single file through dark jungle paths, listening to the screech of green parakeets overhead, watching the flicker of wings as greenshanks and golden orioles flew between the branches.

'We shall be coming to the river soon,' Jess said softly.

The heat was oppressive, steamy, humid. High grass whispered on all sides of them under the shade of the twisted creepers. At dawn the mist was still slowly clearing from the river banks; a luminous pearly whiteness hung around them everywhere.

Suddenly a kingfisher flew out, a silver fish in its beak, the flash of bright blue making them jump.

'Here we are,' Jess whispered.

They emerged on a river bank, the sides stony with pebbles. A few feet away on the other side some roe deer, small spotted deer with liquid eyes, were grazing. They shot away, vanishing into the mist with a silent speed that was very impressive.

Jeremy froze, clutching his mother's arm. She followed the stare of his round eyes and smiled.

'It won't hurt you, darling. It's only a monitor.'

The lizard slowly moved into the safety of the jungle again, his green skin merging with the trees.

They moved on towards the stilt hut the King had had built for Jess. Thatched with dry grass, open-sided, it was reached by a rickety series of bamboo steps, like a ladder. Below the stilts it stood on the grass was trodden flat and yellowing.

'Doesn't look too safe to me,' Grant Williams observed with a frown.

Jess laughed. 'It does very well for me.' Then she surveyed them all with a little grimace. 'But you may be right. I doubt if it would support the weight of a small army like you. Some of you must stay below for a while.'

'I'll take Marie off to see the temple,' Peter said eagerly.

'I'll stay with you, Mummy,' Jeremy insisted, clinging to her hand.

She looked at Rahaib, who inclined his head politely. 'If you will permit, my lady, I will visit the village and see if I can find fresh milk and eggs.'

'That would be nice,' Jess thanked him. 'You know where it is, Rahaib?'

A look of dry amusement crossed his face. 'Yes, my lady.'

Grant Williams laughed. 'Rahaib knows where everything is,' he told Jess.

Peter took Marie's hand. 'Coming? The temple must be along here somewhere ...'

'No, sir,' Rahaib interrupted. 'It is along that path over there ...' His brown finger pointed confidently to a very narrow, overgrown path.

'Thanks,' said Peter, with a grin. He and Marie took the path indicated, finding it heavy going because it was so overgrown. Peter slashed at the creepers with a sinister-looking knife he had carried with him from the Land-Rover. The river ran to the right of them, chuckling over great grey boulders.

They came out in another clearing, facing the temple, which

was in a far more ruinous state than the ones Peter and his colleagues were working on, its steps crumbling away, the jungle growing in upon it closer and closer, creepers strangling the ornate pillars which decorated it, grass growing through the stone flags of the courtyard.

'What a mess!' Peter said reflectively.

'How old is it?' she asked him, staring at it with great interest and fascination.

'Looks older than the ones we're working on,' Peter shrugged. 'Perhaps third century.'

'As old as that?' she demanded.

He laughed. 'India is a very ancient country. Let's take a look inside.'

They walked up the steps and entered the temple. The sunlight died as they went inside and cool shadows thickened the air. The smell was nauseating.

'Something rather dead in here,' Peter said, grimacing. 'An animal has got in and died, presumably.'

'I'll wait for you by the door,' said Marie, feeling sickened by the smell.

Peter glanced at her. 'Are you all right?'

'Fine,' she said. 'I just prefer the open air.'

He laughed. 'I know what you mean. Look, I won't be long, then I'll guide you back to the others.'

'There's no hurry,' she said. 'It's quite pleasant here.'

Peter plunged further into the gloom, leaving her by the door, staring into the oppressive jungle. She saw a giant spider's web glistening with silvery mist drops stretched across from one pillar to the other. The carvings were so unfamiliar, so contorted and strange, that her eyes wearied of tracing them, trying to make sense of them. She knew nothing of the ancient legends that lay behind them, the mysteries and secrets of the religion that had caused this place to be built.

Suddenly she froze, her whole body shaken with horror. Facing her, between the creeper-straggled trees, stood a huge tiger, sleek, muscled, poised for movement, his tail lashing from side to side, the green eyes staring at her unwinkingly.

She was so frightened that she merely stared back, swallowing on a terror so great she felt sick.

She opened her mouth to scream for Peter, but no sound came. She felt her limbs turn to water.

The tiger's head slowly drew forward. She saw the great body tense for a spring, every muscle beneath his shining coat.

She remembered Jess describing a tiger who had visited the waterhole beneath the stilt house. This must be the same one. Jess had said he left pug marks so big that she had measured them with disbelief.

A sudden crash among the trees drew her attention from him. The tiger too turned to stare, distracted from her.

Someone was moving among the trees, and Marie realised that the newcomer might walk straight into the tiger. She screamed then, her throat relaxed from the grip of terror.

'Tiger! Don't come any further … there's a tiger here …' The words seemed to float mistily on the morning air. For a wild moment she wondered if she had actually said them, then she heard Peter racing towards her from the back of the temple, his feet stumbling on the stone floors. At the same time the unknown person began to run through the jungle, but incredibly towards her, not away into safety.

The creeper-hung trees swayed noisily, then a figure emerged, just a few feet from the tiger's crouched body. With incredulous dismay Marie recognised the tall, dark man in white shirt and casual beige slacks, his head cocked as he took in the scene confronting him.

The tiger flicked his tail with a lazy motion, turning his head to survey the new arrival on the scene, and Peter panted up beside Marie, flinging a protective arm around her.

'What's up?' he demanded. 'I heard you scream ...' Then his eyes flashed down into the little clearing and he swore under his breath.

'God!' He fumbled at his belt and gave a groan of dismay. 'My pistol! I left it in the temple ...'

As he turned to go and get it, she said quickly, 'I'll go. Try to distract the tiger. Keep it occupied. Make a lot of noise – try to frighten it away.'

She ran into the darkness, searching the gloom with eyes that at first could take nothing in, then she saw the scuffed trail of Peter's footsteps across the centuries of leaf mould which had fallen down through the open arches in the walls and made a carpet across part of the floor. She ran forward, following the trail of Peter's feet, until she came to a fallen block of masonry on which lay an open notebook, some pencils and the pistol. Light reflected back from the metal of the pistol as she picked it up and turned to run back.

She heard Peter shouting, stamping his feet. The tiger made a deep menacing sound in his throat, then gave an appalling roar of rage.

Peter shouted again, in alarm. 'Run … get back!'

Terror chilled Marie's blood. It seemed an eternity until she could reach the door, and her eyes, accustomed now to the gloom inside, had to adjust to the dazzle of sunlight before she could take in what was happening.

Stonor was on his back, wrestling helplessly with the huge animal, while Peter was gallantly slashing at its eyes with a bamboo stake. She saw wet stains of sweat spread across the back of his shirt.

She had once been shown how to fire a pistol. Instinct made her now fling up her arm, her eyes narrowing on the tiger's head. The recoil of the shot made her deaf for a moment, then she was able to hear and see again.

The tiger had vanished. Her shot had missed, somehow, but it had frightened the beast away. The leaves swayed in the jungle, testifying to his departure. She ran down the steps and flung herself down beside Stonor. He was clasping one shoulder, a red stain spreading from beneath his fingers.

'Let me see …' she said anxiously.

'No!' His voice bit out curtly. 'Leave it alone!'

She felt hot colour run up under her skin, and drew back. Peter looked at her sympathetically. He lifted her, a hand under her elbow, and put an arm around her waist.

'Look,' he said gently, 'that tiger may come back. I can't go and leave you two alone here, and I can't let you run back to the others alone, so we'll have to help this fellow back there together. If he isn't hurt badly he may be able to walk with our help.'

Stonor ground out harshly, 'Lift me. I can walk without help once I'm on my feet.'

Peter gently helped him to his feet. Stonor swayed, still holding his torn shoulder. There was blood running down his arm and along the side of his ripped shirt now.

'Here, take my arm,' said Peter.

Stonor drew back, frowning. 'I'm all right.' He began to walk steadily, with that upright loping pace which was so characteristic of him, and Peter, giving her a wry grimace, followed him. Marie came after them more slowly, her mind in confusion.

What was Stonor doing here? Had he been looking for her? She looked at his straight, graceful back, the dark hair ruffled by the fight, the broad powerful shoulders held tensely in pain. Of course he must have been here looking for her. Hadn't she known, all the time, inwardly that he would come? When Peter arrived suddenly unannounced, hadn't she thought it was Stonor? She had known that sooner or later Stonor would turn up.

'What on earth were you doing strolling through the jungle in that lighthearted fashion, anyway?' Peter was asking him. 'I was staggered when I saw you. Where did you spring from?'

'Lhalli,' Stonor said grimly.

'What's your name? I'm Peter Davidson, by the way. I'm with the British archaeological expedition in Jedhpur.' He looked back at Marie. 'This is Miss …'

'I know,' Stonor interrupted in that curt fashion. Was he in much pain? Marie wondered anxiously.

Peter looked from one to the other of them, his brows raised. 'Oh, you know each other.'

'My name is Grey,' Stonor told him.

'Friend of Miss Brinton?'

'We've met,' said Stonor.

Peter was baffled, glancing back enquiringly at her, as if to ask her what he was to make of this laconic, tightlipped stranger. But she glanced away without revealing anything.

'Are you an artist like Mrs Cunningham?' Peter asked, struck by a sudden thought.

'No.'

Peter glanced back at Marie again, then shrugged, seeing that he would get no help from her in his interrogation. They came out beside the river. At their abrupt arrival a gaggle of white egrets made a hawking sound of rage and vanished from their fishing in the shallows of the waterpool below the stilt hut. A peacock stalking on the far bank rattled with irritation at them. Far along the river bank came the loud splash as a mugger slid down the mud into the water, his wicked little eyes blinking above his long snout. As if it had been some sort of signal the other muggers basking on the bank in the sun, for all the world like a row of grey-brown logs, came to life and slid down after him, making a series of splashes which awoke the monkeys in the tree tops and sent them chattering and swinging across the jungle.

From the stilt hut they saw faces peering crossly at them.

Then heard an exclamation of alarm. Soon Jess, Grant Williams and Jeremy had descended to them to investigate, having seen the blood on Stonor's shirt.

A few moments later Rahaib came swinging through the jungle at an easy pace carrying a woven basket of eggs and some goat's milk in a wide-lipped jug.

Calmly, despite Stonor's displeasure, he made him take away his hand from the mauled shoulder, frowning over what he saw. Stonor had turned so that Marie should not see his wound, but she saw Rahaib's face, and knew at once that it was far more serious than Stonor had been prepared to admit.

Soon Stonor was in the Land-Rover being driven back to Lhalli by Rahaib. He had arrived in a small, battered Mini which, he said, he had hired in the city. Grant Williams promised to drive it back to its owner for him. Jess accompanied him, and Peter drove Marie and Jeremy back to the bungalow.

'That's the last time I go into the jungle without a gun,' Peter said grimly. He shot her a look. 'Come on, who's that fellow? A bit taciturn, isn't he?'

'He told you his name,' Marie said evasively. Since Stonor had not given Peter any information she hesitated to do so. She might annoy Stonor if she told anyone who he was – she knew him well enough by now to know that his trip to Jedhpur was probably basically a business trip. Whatever he was planning, he obviously did not want anyone to know about it.

'Yes, but who is he? What does he do? What on earth was he doing out in the jungle?'

'He's in business,' she said carefully. 'I met him through my father. They ... did business together.'

'What sort of business?' Peter asked.

'I think he's in the hotel business,' she said truthfully enough. A lie of omission was not altogether wrong, she told herself.

'But why should he be wandering around the jungle?' Peter asked insistently.

She hesitated. 'I expect he was looking for me. He knew I was out here, and my father probably asked him to look me up. Dad was a bit worried about me coming to such a remote spot.'

Peter shrugged. 'I suppose that must have been it. He was pretty annoyed about the tiger, wasn't he? A grim sort of chap. I didn't take to him.'

'He's ... rather alarming,' she agreed quietly.

Peter gave her a furtive glance. 'You ... like him, do you?'

For a moment she did not answer, then she said evasively, 'He can be a bit overwhelming at times.' It seemed an enormous understatement, but it was honest as far as it went.

CHAPTER SEVEN

NEXT MORNING when Jess had gone to the stilt hut to work, Marie took Jeremy into Lhalli to do some shopping at the market, as she had promised. Rahaib and Lispa came too, so after she had brought Jeremy the new pencils he needed and a stick of chewy liquorice toffee, Marie left him with Lispa while she walked through the market to the modern hospital which the King had built some years earlier.

The tall Indian nurse at the reception desk in the low-ceilinged lobby smiled at her, listened to her question and pointed to a room at the far end of the corridor to the left.

'Mr Grey is in room 12,' she said. A mischievous twinkle came into her eyes. 'Be warned, Miss Brinton, he is in a very bad mood. The nurse who took him his medicine an hour ago came out looking as if she, too, had been mauled by a tiger.'

Marie laughed. 'As bad as that?'

'He is most irascible man,' the receptionist said sadly. 'But men make bad patients – we all know that. They hate being in bed for hours with nothing to do.'

'How is his shoulder?' Marie asked.

The receptionist glanced at her carefully. 'He is as well as can be expected. He was lucky to get off so lightly. A tiger can kill quickly. He might have lost the use of his arm had he not been rescued so soon.'

Marie walked down the corridor and tapped on the door softly. A sharp voice growled, 'What is it?'

She pushed the door open. Stonor lay in a stark little bed, his shoulder swathed in bandages, the dark head turned to survey her.

'Come in and shut the door,' he said after a moment, his voice expressionless.

Marie obeyed and came towards the bed, depositing on his little bedside table the bag of fruit she had brought him. He stared at it.

'What's this? Occupational therapy?'

'Fruit,' she said. 'I hear you've been giving the nurses a lot of trouble.'

His dark brows lifted ironically. 'Gossiping with the nurses, were you? Did they tell you that you saved my life?'

She flushed. 'Nonsense.'

'It's true,' he said crisply. 'Another minute and I would have been a tiger's dinner.'

'Peter would have done something,' she said.

He laughed drily. 'Peter? That's his name, is it? A rather ineffectual young man, isn't he? He ran around the beast trying to drive it off with a stick ...'

'It was his pistol I shot at it with,' she told him.

'Oh, you shot at it, did you?' he mocked. 'Well, I hate to tell you, in the circumstances, but you missed.'

'It drove him off, anyway,' she said indignantly. 'You're very ungrateful.'

'Is that what you want? Gratitude?' He lay back, watching her with amused eyes.

She looked at him directly. 'What are you doing here, Stonor? Why did you come to Jedhpur?'

'Why do you think?' he retorted.

'You tell me,' she said.

'I suppose you think I followed you out here?' he asked her softly.

Marie felt herself going pink. 'Did you?'

He laughed. 'As a matter of fact I'm here on business. It's a very delicate matter, and I don't want any hint of it to get out for the moment, so by all means let everyone believe I followed you here.' His eyes mocked her again. 'I don't mind being gossiped about as a lovesick suitor.'

'Perhaps I mind being made the object of gossip,' she pointed out. 'How do I know you really are here on business? You've told me so many lies I don't know what to believe.'

His face hardened. 'I'm not lying now. Very well, I'll tell you. I'm after the hotel concession for the new National Park. This place could be a great tourist attraction if it was built up in the right way. Safari holidays are fashionable. We could make a lot of money here.'

'So that's it,' she said, flatly.

'That's it,' he murmured, watching her face.

'You turn everything to your own advantage, don't you?' she accused him. 'You hadn't even thought of the idea when I told you I was coming here. You got the idea from what I told you about the place.'

'That's right,' he agreed.

'Have you seen the King?'

'I can't approach him directly,' Stonor said. 'It would cause too much talk.' He looked at her sideways. 'I need a go-between.'

'And that's why you came looking for me yesterday,' she said quietly.

'And met a tiger,' he drawled.

'Serves you right! I wish he'd bitten your head off!'

He laughed. 'Temper, temper! What have I done to make you so angry?' The dark eyes taunted her.

Marie turned away. 'You won't get much business done lying in a hospital bed, anyway.'

'Oh, I don't know,' he drawled. 'The perfect excuse for the King to visit me ... who would question a visit to a wealthy visitor badly mauled by a tiger? You only have to see the King and let him know I want to have a few quiet words with him.'

'Just like that?'

He grinned at her. 'Just like that, Marie.'

'And if it's embarrassing for me to have it known that you followed me here? That doesn't matter?'

He was silent, watching her face intently. 'Is there something I don't know? Like another man, for instance?'

She looked down, biting her lip. 'It's possible, isn't it?'

'This Peter?'

She shrugged. 'Possibly.'

'For God's sake, Marie,' he exploded, 'either you're involved with him or you aren't. Make yourself clear.'

She was blazingly angry with him for using her as a shield

in one of his business deals. Her pride and her feelings were both hurt. At least, she thought bitterly, she could retrieve her pride by lying to him.

'All right,' she said stiffly, 'I don't want Peter to think I'm involved with you.'

For a moment Stonor didn't move. Then he said grimly, 'That's a pity. Because I'm going to need your cooperation.'

'Who do you think you are, riding roughshod over other people's lives in this way? Why on earth should I help you?'

He made a shrugging movement and gave a stifled groan, his free hand rising to his bandaged shoulder. She was anxious, moving to help him. He waved her away with a grim face.

Marie drew back, watching him, seeing the new whiteness in his lean face. 'Oh, very well,' she said wearily. 'I'll try to see the King.'

'You'll need an excuse,' he said. 'You can't just walk in there and demand that he visit me.'

'I'll be discreet,' she promised irritably.

'What will you say?' he demanded.

'Leave it to me,' she said, turning towards the door.

'Thank you for the fruit,' he called as she opened it.

She looked back angrily. Stonor grinned at her and lifted one hand in farewell, and she closed the door with a bang.

The receptionist watched her walk back and grinned at her. 'Did he bite your head off too? You look as though you've had a bad time in there.'

'He's impossible!' Marie said with feeling. 'I suppose being one of the richest men in the world makes him above ordinary human customs like courtesy.'

The nurse's eyes widened. 'Is he really one of the richest men in the world?'

'Oh, yes,' Marie said with a shrug. 'Didn't you know? He's a multi-millionaire. But he's travelling incognito.'

'What is he doing in Jedhpur?' the nurse asked.

Marie made a little fluttering movement with her hands. 'He came to see me,' she confessed, looking down with a little smile. Then she walked out, feeling the nurse's eyes on her back with intense curiosity.

Having sown the first seed of her plan, she got Rahaib to drive her to the palace and asked to see the Princess Aissa. She sent in a note, reminding the Princess that she was the governess of Mrs Cunningham's little boy. Aziz's plan to bring the two of them together had not yet been fulfilled, but Marie was sure the Princess would see her.

After a wait of half an hour, she was conducted down endless marble corridors to a beautifully furnished room where she found the Princess seated on a silk-cushioned couch. Slight, graceful and dark-eyed, the Princess gave her a friendly smile, holding out her coral-tipped fingers.

'Miss Brinton? Aziz has told about you. I am so pleased to meet you. I would have arranged a meeting before today, but I have been away on a visit and have just returned. Please be seated. Will you take tea?'

'Thank you,' said Marie, seating herself on a low silk-upholstered stool next to the table.

The Princess clapped her hands, and a plump woman in blue silk hurried through the door and bowed.

'Tea,' the Princess commanded.

A few moments later the woman returned with the large silver tea tray. She poured tea for them both, handed a plate of tiny sweetmeats to Marie, and was then dismissed by Princess Aissa.

'Now,' said the Princess, 'can I do something to help you?' Her dark eyes smiled. 'I suspect your visit was not entirely altruistic.'

Marie flushed. 'I would have come anyway, but it's true that I need your help. A friend of mine is in the hospital ...'

'Mr Grey,' the Princess nodded.

Marie looked at her in surprise. 'You've heard about it?'

'My brother had a report immediately it happened.' The Princess smiled at her. 'Dear Miss Brinton, Lhalli is not London. Nothing happens here that is not observed. My brother likes to keep his fingers on the pulses of the country. The arrival of a very rich and famous man causes interest wherever it happens, and when he is mauled by a tiger that is serious. My brother heard about it at once.' The Princess glanced at her, her dark eyes amused. 'He also gathered that Mr Grey's visit was apparently in connection with you, Miss Brinton. Mr Grey's first action on arrival was to find out where you were living and set out for the bungalow. Then he apparently followed you into the jungle. So my brother deduced that his visit here was therefore a personal one.'

Marie flushed and looked down. 'Yes, but ...'

'Otherwise my brother would have gone to the hospital himself to see if there was anything he could do,' the Princess went on, nibbling at a sweetmeat. 'However, he felt he might be intruding if he went there today.'

Marie hesitated. It was difficult to phrase her next remark. How could she ask the King to visit Stonor without betraying Stonor's reason for being in Jedhpur? His real reason?

'My brother was afraid Mr Grey might be annoyed if he knew how much interest his arrival had caused,' the Princess added. She smiled at Marie. 'Even the very rich have a right to privacy where matters of the heart are concerned.'

Marie felt her face glowing. 'I … I'm sure Stonor would be very glad to see the King,' she said nervously. 'I have my job to do, your Highness. I must be at the bungalow with the little boy. Stonor is alone all day.'

The Princess paused to stare at her. 'Were you hoping I could find someone to take your place looking after Mrs Cunningham's son? I am sure Lispa would be very happy …'

'No,' Marie said quickly, 'thank you. It isn't that. But … Mr Grey does not have a telephone in his room, you see. He needs to make telephone calls overseas rather urgently. I wondered if one could be installed … he has so many business matters to look after, you know …'

The Princess considered. 'I am sure something could be arranged. Indeed, I don't see why Mr Grey should not be transferred from the hospital to a room in the palace. He could have daily visits from his doctor here, and a nurse could accompany him. Do you think that would suit him?'

Marie was certain it would, but she said courteously, 'Oh, I don't think we could put you to so much trouble …'

'It would be no trouble,' the Princess shrugged. 'Mr Grey is a very wealthy and influential man, Miss Brinton, and we need the help and support of men like him. My brother would be delighted to have him to stay with us. We thought of it at once. We only hesitated because we were not sure of his wishes.'

'I think he would be most grateful for your kindness,' Marie said quietly.

The Princess smiled at her. 'And you could visit him as often as you wished. Lispa will look after the little boy. I would be very pleased to see you here. I have so few friends, and I miss the life I led in Europe. Now that I am back home I am so constricted. I think Aziz told you how we feel ...'

'Your cousin did mention something of the kind,' Marie admitted.

Aissa's small face lit up. 'Aziz is always so thoughtful!'

Marie remembered what Rahaib had said about him, and she wondered how well the Princess knew her charming but irresponsible cousin. She listened as Aissa poured out her longings for Europe, her fear of an arranged marriage to someone she could not love.

'Love has another meaning here. It stands for duty and family affection. Romantic love is suspect.'

'I'm sure your brother would not force you to marry someone you didn't like,' Marie soothed.

Aissa sighed. 'My brother is not a free agent. His Council is divided. My uncle and his friends wish to halt our movement towards progress. They want to stop the clock. They fear our new ideas.'

'And Prince Aziz? He is on your side?'

Aissa smiled, her dark eyes eloquent. 'Yes, Aziz is with us.'

Watching her, Marie suddenly guessed that the Princess was in love with her cousin. Was he, perhaps, also in love with her? He had shown much concern for her, yet she had felt at the time that Aziz was not acting solely out of cousinly affection, and she was sure that Rahaib had suspected something behind his desire to help Aissa find freedom.

She left the palace, much relieved to have had her task made so much easier. Now Stonor would have plenty of time in which to talk to the King. She determined that she would not visit him. He had played his last trick on her.

She spent that evening with Peter, who arrived unannounced at the bungalow, and invited himself to supper. Jess, amused, left them alone after the meal.

Peter moved to sit beside Marie on the sofa, his arm stealing along behind her shoulder. 'You're awfully pretty,' he told her awkwardly.

She smiled at him. 'Thank you.' But she felt no interest in him whatever. The shadow of Stonor Grey cast every other man into the shade. Even now, sitting here beside Peter, her only thought was somehow connected with Stonor, wondering what he was doing, what he was thinking.

Peter leaned towards her and she watched him abstractedly, hardly caring whether he kissed her or not. When his mouth clumsily sought and found her lips she sat there without responding, as if she was in a trance. Why should I let Stonor come between me and life like this? she asked herself furiously. On an impulse she slipped her arms around Peter's neck and began to kiss him back, curling close to him.

'Oh, Marie,' Peter breathed as he released her. 'You're fantastic! I could be crazy about you ...'

She laughed. 'Oh, could you?'

'Don't tease,' he said sulkily.

He moved to kiss her again, but she averted her head. 'No,' she said, already sorry she had encouraged him. 'No more ...'

'You're like a will-o'-the-wisp,' he complained. 'One can't get hold of you.'

'Time you went,' she retorted. 'I have to get up early in the morning. Young Jeremy rises with the dawn, and I need my beauty sleep.'

'I suppose I ought to be going,' he said reluctantly. 'I have to get up early too. When can I see you again?'

'You know where I am,' she said lightly. 'Tomorrow Jess and I are going out to the stilt hut again, but this time alone—no men invited. Jeremy didn't see much of the animals, thanks to our little excitement.'

'How is that chap going on?' Peter asked, staring at her.

'Fine, as far as I know,' she said evasively.

Next day Jess, Marie and Jeremy drove out to the stilt hut and spent the daylight hours there. Jess worked while Marie and Jeremy watched the animals, then Marie prepared their picnic meal and they all sat down on the straw mats inside the hut to eat it.

'I'm afraid that tiger has a short life expectancy since he attacked your friend,' Jess sighed.

'What do you mean?'

'The villagers are nervous about him. He's too close to their huts. Sometimes a tiger takes a child – and they're all terrified it will be one of their children. They've asked the King to arrange a tiger hunt, Rahaib says. They want him shot.'

'Oh, poor tiger,' Marie said sadly. 'He was so beautiful, too.'

Jess smiled at her. 'You can't blame them. It's unusual for a tiger to come so close to a village – they usually hunt deep in the jungle and keep away from men. This one must be a man-eater, and they're too dangerous to be allowed to live. Usually, they run away from men, but this one deliberately attacked. That makes him savage.'

Jeremy was peering down river, his straw hat crooked on his little head. 'Mum, what's that?' he demanded.

Jess peered over his shoulder. 'What's what, darling?'

He pointed. 'That black hump, in the water down there.'

Jess laughed. 'That, my darling, is a rhinoceros wallowing in one of the shallow pools at the edge of the river. See, there's his horn sticking up …'

'At least men don't hunt rhinoceros for their skin,' Marie said with a sigh. 'The beautiful animals always seem to be hunted.'

'Oh, men hunt the rhino, too,' Jess said sadly.

'What for?' Jeremy demanded. 'Do they make handbags out of him like they do with the crocodile?'

Jess shook her head wryly. 'No, they saw off his horns and

use them in a sort of medicine.' She glanced sideways at Marie and added quietly, 'They believe it acts as an aphrodisiac. Rhino horn costs five hundred pounds a ton.'

'Nothing is safe, is it?' Marie muttered.

They were tired when they drove back home. Marie put Jeremy to bed early, his small body limp in her arms, and then went along to Jess to join her for dinner. Later she washed her hair, had a bath and went to bed early. She heard Jess turn in about half an hour later.

Next day, she and Lispa went to the market with Jeremy, to buy a chicken and some fruit. Jeremy watched a market conjuror with excited fascination. He found the exotic sights and smells of the market enthralling even now and enjoyed nothing so much as a visit there.

After lunch, she settled down on the verandah with Jeremy to play snap. Jeremy thoroughly enjoyed this and became hysterical with laughter. Jess came home early because a sudden brief storm had made the stilt hut temporarily uninhabitable. The rain had driven in through the open sides and left it awash with water which was immediately filled with frogs and insects driven to shelter from the storm outside. Her Land-Rover was splashed with mud so thick and dark it looked like a mud pie on wheels. Jess herself was filthy and immediately took a bath.

They were just finishing dinner when Rahaib entered the room with his customary impassive expression. He bowed, glancing at Marie.

'A message from the palace,' he said, handing her an envelope with great gravity.

She opened it, guessing who it would be from. Stonor had not wasted words. The scrawled, impatient writing merely said: Come here at once. There was not even a signature.

Marie looked up, flushing. 'How did the message get here?'

'By car,' Rahaib told her. 'It waits outside to take you to the palace.'

'To the palace?' Jess raised her brows. 'To see the King?'

'No,' said Marie. 'Stonor Grey wants to see me.'

'Is he at the palace now? He must have some pull.' Jess stood up, pushing back her chair. 'It's rather late to issue invitations, though.'

Marie hesitated, longing to say she would not go, but knew she could not rest in peace until she had discovered what Stonor wanted.

'I think I should go,' she said. 'He may need help.'

Jess shrugged, 'Do as you like, Marie.' She sauntered away, losing interest, and Marie glanced down at her denims and shirt.

'I must change first,' she told Rahaib.

'Yes, my lady,' he said. He did not approve of her jeans – he made that clear every time he saw them, without saying a word.

She went to her room and found a cream silk dress which looked very good on her without making it seem as if she had particularly dressed up for this visit. She brushed her hair up into a chignon, applied new makeup and put on shoes which matched the dress.

The car sped to the palace along the dark, dusty roads. In

the distance a jackal howled, making the hair stand up on the back of her neck. The headlights lit up the road ahead, making ghostly circles in the white dust.

When they entered the market area Marie was surprised to find it still crowded, despite the late hour. The stalls were lit by naphtha flares. The hawkers still shouted their wares, and the smell of food was stronger than ever. Only the old women no longer gossiped around the well, and there were fewer children about to stare at the car.

She was escorted through the marble corridors of the palace to a room on an upper floor. The servant indicated the door, bowed and took up a crouching position opposite it, apparently prepared to sit and wait until she appeared again.

Marie tapped on the door.

'Come in,' Stonor called.

She went into the room and found him lying on a low couch, his head and shoulders cushioned, the shutters covering the windows and a lamp burning softly beside him, making a dim circle of yellow light around the couch.

She stared at him hungrily, tracing the shadows under his eyes, the hint of weariness in his posture. He still looked ill, but there had been an improvement since she last saw him.

'Well, come here,' he said sharply. 'I can't see you over there.'

She moved over towards him, halting a few feet from the couch. 'What did that rather peremptory message mean?' she enquired coldly.

'What do you mean by staying away me for two days?' he demanded in return.

Her heart thudded. 'Did you expect me to haunt your sickbed?' she asked huskily.

'I expected you to keep up our little fiction about my presence in Jedhpur being on your account,' he retorted.

'Oh,' she murmured, feeling angrily disillusioned. 'That's it.'

He eyed her enigmatically. 'Don't loom over me like that. Sit down.'

Marie looked around, but there was nowhere to sit. He patted the couch invitingly. 'Here ...' he commanded.

She hesitated.

'For God's sake, sit down, girl!' he barked.

She sat down where he had pointed, and Stonor lay back, relaxing, his dark eyes fixed on her face.

'What have you been doing with yourself?' he asked.

She shrugged. 'Nothing much. Today I did the shopping and then played with Jeremy.'

'And yesterday?'

'I spent the day at the marshes watching the animals feed with Jess and Jeremy,' she told him, then added deliberately, 'In the evening I had dinner with Peter.'

The dark eyes narrowed. 'How romantic! How far has the affair got? Does he make love to you?'

She flushed hotly. 'We've kissed,' she flung defiantly.

He bared his teeth in a grim smile. 'Now I wonder why you feel the need to be so belligerent about it?'

'You make me nervous,' she said defensively.

'Do I?' he asked very softly. 'Why?'

She shifted uneasily. 'I don't know. You just do.'

He put his free hand over her fingers. 'Stop fidgeting like that. You're like a cat on hot bricks.'

The touch of his hand made her bones turn to water. 'How ... how are you getting on with the King?' she asked.

'It was easier than I'd imagined,' he said calmly. 'As it turned out, he needs me as much as I need him. He lacks capital, and he was eager to work out a deal. I think we shall both make a lot of money.'

'And Jedhpur? Will that benefit?' she asked cynically.

The dark eyes lifted to her face. 'Sarcasm doesn't suit you. Yes, Jedhpur will benefit a great deal. It needs investment. It needs industry. It needs tourism. I'll supply all three.'

'Then if you've already made your deal you don't need to keep up the pretence of being here to see me,' she said.

'More than ever,' he told her. 'The King wants to keep our deal a secret for the time being. He's afraid of trouble from the conservative element, and he wants to present them with a fait accompli.'

Marie tried to withdraw her fingers from his grip, but he tightened it. 'Let me go, Stonor,' she said breathlessly.

'No,' he murmured.

Their eyes battled, then hers dropped away. Once again she felt that strange, weak helplessness which she had first felt when he kissed her; overwhelmed by the realisation that she was physically his inferior, unable to win a fight against him.

'I can't stay much longer,' she said. 'It's a long drive back.'

'I like that dress,' he merely replied. 'The colour suits you. It's gently understating your femininity.'

She looked at him through her lashes. 'Thank you.'

'Don't do that,' he said abruptly. 'You don't need tricks like that.'

'Tricks?' She was blazingly angry. 'Why, you …'

He laughed at her expression. 'My dear girl, I've known too many females to be taken in by any of those age-old tricks: the eyelash fluttering, the sidelong glances, the tossed head …'

'How about the slap in the face?' she said furiously.

His mouth twitched. 'Try it and see.'

'I bet you'd hit me back,' she said sulkily.

'You'd win your bet,' he answered mockingly.

Marie moved to rise, but he was pinioning her down with his one hand and she dared not struggle too hard for fear of hurting him.

'I've got to go,' she said crossly.

'Kiss me goodnight, then,' he said softly.

She glared at him. 'I certainly will not!'

'Walls have eyes in this place,' he said. 'I'm pretty sure that servant doesn't speak much English, but I know he watches me through the keyhole because I've seen him at it.' The dark eyes flicked over her mockingly. 'So be a good girl and give me a kiss.'

Marie hesitated, then bent slowly forward. His hand left her fingers and came up to clasp her head, pulling her down towards him, until their lips met. The kiss was gentle for a moment, his mouth warmly coaxing. Then fire blazed between them and she felt her self-control slip from her like a straw in a tidal flood.

Against her mouth he whispered, 'You drive me crazy, do you know that?'

'Do I?' Her voice was husky, she pulled away from him to stare down into the brightness of his eyes. 'I hadn't noticed.'

'You're too busy convincing yourself you hate me to notice anything,' he drawled.

'What are you saying? What do you really mean?' She knew she was on the point of tears. He was tormenting her with this cat-and-mouse game, aware that she found him irresistible, enjoying the ability to arouse her whenever he wished. 'I never understand you, Stonor.'

'Oh, you understand me,' he drawled, kissing the curve of her naked arm inside her elbow. 'You know how I feel about you.'

'I don't ... I wish I did ...'

His dark eyes grew hot as he stared at her, his mouth deliberately lingering on her white skin, travelling slowly down towards her wrist.

'I want to take you to bed,' he said thickly. 'You're lovely and desirable and I want you. It's my misfortune that this time I've fallen for a girl who's only half alive, who prefers to be treated like a pretty doll than to be treated as a woman ...'

'This time?' She picked up the words jealously. 'Yes, how many other times have there been, Stonor? How many other women in your life?'

'Did you imagine I'd led the life of a monk?'

'Any man I married would have to intend to be faithful to me for the rest of his life,' she said miserably.

'Were we talking about marriage?' he asked gravely.

She flushed. 'I know you weren't, but I'm not going to bed with you as casually as I would choose a hat, Stonor. When I fall in love it's going to be for keeps.'

'And I don't qualify,' he murmured.

'You don't play the game by my rules,' she said.

'Love has no rules, darling,' he said.

'It has where I'm concerned.'

'You've a lot to learn.'

'Not from you!' she flung.

'From who, then? This ineffective young archaeologist you've picked up? He looked as inexperienced as you are.'

'Then perhaps we'll learn together,' she retorted, standing up and moving away towards the door.

Stonor swore under his breath and she looked back at him. 'Careful! At your age you have to watch your blood pressure.'

'Vixen!' he muttered.

'Goodnight, Stonor.'

'Come back tomorrow,' he said quickly as she opened the door, but she did not answer.

CHAPTER EIGHT

EACH TIME she visited Stonor, Marie afterwards took tea with Princess Aissa, either in her private apartments or in a small walled garden shut away from prying masculine eyes on the women's side of the palace. This part of the building, Marie soon realised, was far more elaborately decorated, far more beautifully furnished than the public rooms only visited by men. The Kings of Jedhpur, in past years, had created a scented, silk-draped paradise for their queens. Marie gazed around these marble-floored, gilded cages and wondered what it had felt like to be the bird of paradise imprisoned here. She remembered that Stonor had once threatened her with harem life – on that evening when he played kidnapper for his own amusement. He had said that she was already, in fact, the prisoner of luxury; indulged, petted and spoilt but shut away from ordinary life. In a sense she knew it was true. Her father had protected her from the problems and pains of life, but in protecting her had walled her up away from the free winds of the world. Now she knew just how much she had missed.

She had looked at her hands with dismay, hating the softness and whiteness of her unscathed palms. Lispa's brown hands were rough from work, and they had a beauty of their own, a beauty and dignity Marie envied. She longed to have

Lispa's deft agility, her quick graceful skill in household tasks. She longed to have Jess's artistic skills, too, or to use her brain in the challenge of industry, or learn even any basic industrial skills.

Anything, in fact, but be useless.

The job Jess had given her was really only a space in which to find her true métier. She spent hours thinking about the future. What could she learn to do? What could she train for? Nursing? That had an appeal. You did not need to be brilliant in order to take up nursing, and her education had been a sound one. Or should she go to a teacher training college? She rejected that idea after some thought as it did not appeal to her. She rejected a business training, too. One by one she considered various jobs and always came back to the idea of nursing. It was an alarming prospect, but she wanted to do something really useful, and it seemed the best way to do that.

She discussed the problem with Princess Aissa and Aziz, during their tea parties. Somehow Aziz always contrived to be on hand for these occasions. He would knock on the door, look surprised and say cheerfully, 'Well, well, Miss Brinton … may I come in?'

Aissa would turn her sleek black head on the long column of her swanlike neck and the almond eyes would smile at him, the corners of the pale pink mouth turn up.

Now and then, as she passed him a cup or a small sweet cake, her fragile, pink-tipped fingers would brush his hand. Once, as Marie was gazing with enchanted eyes at the intense blue of the afternoon sky, she turned back suddenly and caught Aziz kissing Aissa's fingertips, his adoring eyes on the Princess's shy, averted face. Marie felt her own heart quiver at the look on their faces. There was something intensely exciting about the small gesture. In their formal world Aziz's delicate kiss took on the quality of an explosion of passion.

When she met Lord Hathni, as she sometimes did, leaving the palace with Aziz beside her, talking lightly as they walked, she felt herself tense with alarm at the quick, shrewd glance she received from the Prime Minister's eyes. Aziz would bow his head, his palms together, in that graceful gesture of submissive greeting, and Lord Hathni would give him the same shrewd glance.

Once it occurred to her that Lord Hathni suspected Aziz of having an interest in her. She gently suggested this idea to Aziz, who grinned shamelessly.

'But of course he does! He is a man. He knows that no young man of passion could see your enchanting beauty and be unmoved.'

Marie saw the twinkle in his eye as he made this teasing remark. 'Unless, of course, he happened to be far more interested in another girl?' she suggested.

Aziz looked at her sideways, his slanting eyes amused. 'That would, of course, make a difference.'

She hesitated. 'But your father doesn't seem worried by the interest he appears to think you have in me,' she said with some embarrassment.

Aziz looked down at the marble floor, and for a second she thought that he, too, was embarrassed. Then he looked up and shrugged. 'Miss Brinton, my father does not believe

I would so jeopardise my position as to marry an English girl,' he said gently.

She flushed, then laughed. 'I see. He trusts your common sense.'

Aziz spread his brown hands. 'Yes.'

'Then what does he ...' She broke off, flushing, even more hotly. 'Oh!'

Aziz looked at her uneasily, seeing her eyes grow stormy. 'My father may put what construction he wishes upon the evidence, but we know, do we not, that he is wrong? That is all that matters.'

'Not to me,' she said indignantly. 'Your father can't be allowed to go on imagining that I'm permitting you to make love to me . . . I'm sorry if it interferes with your little conspiracy, but in future I can't allow my reputation to be used as a shield for you and the Princess ...'

Aziz stiffened and gazed at her angrily. 'The Princess and I have never seen each other alone, Miss Brinton. Either you or one of her women have been present on all occasions. Do not suspect anything else. I give you my word that nothing I have ever done could harm the Princess.'

She looked at him directly, her blue eyes wide. 'Except that what you're doing is going to come out, sooner or later, and then there'll be terrible trouble for her.'

Aziz frowned, biting his lip. 'What else can we do? Our lives are made intolerable by the present situation. We are snatching what tiny crumbs of happiness we can. The future is grim for both of us.' He looked at her, his eyes miserable. 'Did you know that I am betrothed to a girl of thirteen, Miss

Brinton? My father arranged the match ten years ago. I have never seen her. I will not see her for two years. Then it will only be on my wedding day, when the veil is removed from her head after we have taken our seven steps around the fire.'

'Seven steps around the fire?' she asked in bewilderment.

He nodded. 'The fire is the centre of our wedding ceremony, you see. We take seven steps around the fire, and on the last step the ceremony is complete. We are man and wife. Only then does the bride throw back her veil and reveal her face.'

Marie felt sorry for him. It was a terrifying thought . . . to be tied for life to an unknown person, committed to them whatever their character—a form of Russian roulette which could have lifelong consequences.

'It has been our custom for so long,' Aziz sighed. 'My father honestly cannot understand why I resist it. He only met my mother on their wedding day, and it is true that theirs was a very happy marriage until the day she died.'

'Perhaps your marriage will be happy too,' Marie said gently. 'Surely if you've known about it for so long, you must have adjusted to the idea?'

'Aissa is my beloved,' Aziz said quietly. 'She always has been. In Europe we saw each other frequently, and we learnt to love. Now that we are back here life has grown bitter for us.'

Rahaib was waiting for her outside the palace. He had been shopping in the market for a gift for Lispa, who had just told him that she was again expecting a child. Rahaib was unusually gay, singing softly under his breath as he drove back to the bungalow. A package lay on the seat beside him. It was, he had informed Marie proudly, some fine silk from which Lispa could make herself a new sari.

'Red as the pomegranate, red for passion,' he said delightedly. 'Gold as the sun, gold for joy.'

'That's very poetic, Rahaib,' Marie said teasingly.

He smiled at her over his shoulder. 'Lispa is a good wife. She has borne me three sons. Perhaps she will bear me a fourth.'

'Wouldn't you like a girl this time?'

'If the gods desire it I will have a girl,' Rahaib said carelessly, and added, 'but I wish for a son.'

Marie laughed. 'You're a chauvinist,' she said.

He was puzzled. 'What does that mean?'

'It means you think boys are more important than girls,' she told him.

'They are,' he said in bewilderment. 'Look around you. It is obvious.'

'Yes,' she said drily, 'I'm afraid you are right.'

Rahaib flicked a glance at her apologetically. 'In your world I know it is different, but here we do things as we have always done.'

As he turned back to the road he gave a soft exclamation of surprise. 'There is a car across the road ...'

'Someone has broken down,' said Marie, leaning forward to stare ahead.

A dark car was slewed across in their path, and beside it a young man in a thin shirt and trousers was waving at them. Rahaib slowed down and stopped just in front of the car.

The young man came round to speak to Rahaib. 'Please, sir, would you look at my engine? It is not working.' He spoke in heavily accented English, but he looked Indian.

Rahaib gave him a scornful glance. 'Certainly I will look,' he replied. 'You should learn to mend your car before you begin to drive it, though.' He climbed out and walked to the other car. The bonnet was raised already, and he bent over to look at it. Immediately the young man raised a heavy wooden club and struck him down with one carefully placed blow on the head.

Marie gave a scream of dismay, as Rahaib slumped forward silently. The young man dragged his body away, flung him on to the side of the road. Marie fumbled for the keys in the dashboard, but before she could move over and start the engine there were several young men climbing into the vehicle beside her. One of them held a small gun.

She looked at them, shivering. This was no romantic game, like the one Stonor had played. This was real.

'We must blindfold and gag you, miss,' one of them said. 'Please make no trouble. We do not want to hurt you.'

Their eyes were implacable. She looked round at their faces and felt icy cold.

One of them bound a piece of cloth over her eyes, then stuffed a handkerchief into her mouth. Then she was led away, stumbling awkwardly, and placed in the other car. The engine started and the car swung round, churning dust and small stones, and drove away at breakneck speed.

The drive lasted for what seemed to her a very long time. When the car stopped at last, she was asked to get out. Guided by the hand of one of the young men, she was led into a house, then she heard the door close behind her.

The gag and blindfold were removed, and she put up a hand to her trembling lips. Pieces of lint were adhering to her inner mouth. The young men gestured for her to walk into a small room, and Marie obeyed silently, staring around her. Shutters had been placed over the window. The room was lit by an oil lamp. The only furniture was a small camp bed covered by some blankets and a pillow; two wooden chairs of great age, a low round table and a heavily carved chest with a domed top.

'Why have you brought me here?' she asked shakily, looking at the men.

The one with the gun said politely, 'You are a hostage, Miss Brinton.'

'A hostage?' She felt incredulous disbelief. 'For what?'

'We have grievances which we wish to have heard,' he said. 'Until they are heard, you will remain here.'

'But I'm nothing to do with your country,' she protested.

'You are the woman of the chairman of Unex,' he said clumsily. 'All of Jedhpur know you visit him at the palace. He will wish you to be released. He will persuade the King to hear us.'

'What if it doesn't work out like that?' she asked. 'What if the King refuses to come to terms?'

They looked at each other, then the man with the gun shrugged. 'Too bad for you.'

Marie sat down suddenly on the edge of the bed. Her legs had turned to water.

The men withdrew towards the door, staring at her. They had a quick, whispered conference, then the one with a gun came back to her and said roughly, 'You will wish to have a woman to help you. One is coming, but is not here yet. Is there anything you want?'

She glanced at him. Not quite inhuman, she thought wryly. 'I would like some water,' she said quietly.

He gestured to one of the others, who went out and came back with a large earthenware jug of water and a tin mug.

Marie drank thirstily, then began to wonder if she had been wise to drink unboiled water. One of the first things she had learnt since arriving was that it was dangerous to drink unboiled water since so many of the rivers were heavily polluted.

'When the woman gets here, there will be food,' the man with the gun said.

One of the others said something in his own tongue, and the man with the gun looked at her.

'It will be curry. We have no English food.'

Marie smiled at him slightly. 'I eat your food every day,' she said. 'I'm quite used to it, thank you.'

He seemed taken aback, as if her courtesy disturbed him. After a moment he and the others moved out of the room and closed the door. She got up and went to the windows. There were small holes in the shutters. She peered through them and saw only blue sky.

Hearing sounds outside, she quickly returned to the bed and sat down on the edge again, her back very upright.

The door opened and the man with the gun came in, his

thin dark face alert. Behind him came a young woman in a gay blue sari, her forehead decorated with the red mark Marie recognised as the sign of a married woman. She was carrying a large earthenware bowl covered with a white cloth. A savoury smell floated from it. She carefully laid it on the low table, then turned and made a polite bow.

'Will you eat?' Her English was careful and precise but not fluent.

'Thank you,' said Marie, forcing a smile.

She felt instinctively that she must try to make friends with them. It was useless to protest or make a fuss. They had a grimly determined look which made such protests merely pointless.

The young woman went out and returned with a plate. She laid it on the table, gestured to one of the chairs. 'Please sit.'

Marie obediently sat down, and the young woman took away the white cloth. Marie looked hungrily at the meal revealed – spicy, thick and fragrant, the curried lamb lay in one half of the bowl, white rice lay in the other. The young woman took up a ladle, enquiringly looked at Marie.

'What?' she asked thickly.

Marie pointed to both curry and rice. The young woman ladled some of each on to a plate. Then she paused, biting her lip, and asked quietly, *'Tarkeean?'*

Marie looked at her, recognising the word, trying to remember what it meant. The young man with the gun behind her said, 'Do you wish to have vegetable curry also?'

Marie shook her head. 'Thank you, no.'

The young woman handed her a spoon and stepped back from the table. Marie looked round at the two of them.

'Aren't you going to eat with me?'

The young woman stared at her, then looked at the young man. He spoke quickly in his own tongue. She made a frightened motion of her hands. *'Kubbee – kubbee nahin!'*

Never, no, never, thought Marie, translating mentally. She knew enough of the language to recognise that phrase. Why would the woman not eat with her? she wondered.

The young man looked at her and shrugged. 'She will not eat.'

'Why won't she eat with me?' Marie asked him quietly.

His eyes shifted. 'It is forbidden to eat at the table with one whom one may kill,' he said uneasily.

Marie shivered. 'I see.' There was something chillingly direct about the way they said that.

Her appetite had vanished suddenly, but she forced herself to eat. The food was good and as she ate she recovered some of her spirits.

Afterwards she lay down on the bed and slept. The others withdrew, leaving her alone in the lamplit room. She heard the chirping of crickets outside, a lively, cheerful sound at most times, but tonight it had a melancholy which depressed her.

If only she could see the outside world, she thought. The silence surrounding the building made her suspect that they were in an isolated place. Why would they not let her see outside?

The next morning she lay on the bed with her eyes open

listening to the sounds of cows mooing somewhere in the distance. They were in the country somewhere, then, she thought, not in Lhalli.

The door opened and the young woman came in with a bowl of warm water. She gestured to it. 'Wash …' She hung a rough cotton towel over the chair, placed a cake of scented soap on a small bowl. Marie had already discovered that the only sanitation was primitive, and she was relieved to find that she was going to be allowed to wash and brush her hair.

The day wore on slowly. She attempted to talk to her female guard, but found that the young woman's English was extremely limited. To amuse herself, Marie began to ask her the names of objects in her own tongue, pointing to something and asking, 'What is that?'

The young woman, presumably as bored as Marie was by now, was not unwilling to play this game. She seemed to like to be Marie's teacher. Carefully she would pronounce the word, then smile slightly behind her hand at Marie's attempt to repeat it.

'I … learn English … at … *madrissah* …' she stammered once during their game.

'Madrissah?' Marie frowned.

The young woman nodded. *'Madrissah* in Lhalli … King's *madrissah* …'

'School?' Marie guessed.

The young woman smiled. 'School,' she repeated, nodding. 'Me go to the school one year …'

Marie gestured to the woman's round red forehead mark. 'You are married woman?'

The other woman hesitated, frowning.

Marie pointed to the ring she wore on her foot, a broad gold band which shone when she moved her toes. 'Married?'

The other woman's face cleared. 'Yes … married.'

Marie pointed to herself. 'My name … Marie.' She pointed to the other woman. 'Your name?'

There was a slight pause, then the answer came reluctantly, 'Me … Sarwana …'

'You have children, Sarwana?' Marie asked her, smiling.

Sarwana's dark eyes lit up. 'One baba.'

'Boy or girl?'

'Boy child,' Sarwana said in clear English. She suddenly giggled. 'Like hymn … Mary's boy child …'

Marie laughed back, realising that this was a joke. 'You learnt hymns at the *madrissah?*'

Sarwana made a faint grimace. 'Teacher Christian woman, sing hymns.'

Her tone was disgusted, and Marie was forced to smile. 'You did not like hymns?'

Sarwana hesitated politely then said, 'No good. Bad noise.'

Then the young man with the gun came into the room with a small notepad and a pen. He laid them on the table. 'Please write a message to Mr Grey as I dictate,' he ordered Marie.

Marie sat down and picked up the pen, staring at the paper with eyes that saw little. She was wondering what Stonor was doing now, what he was thinking, how her disappearance was affecting him.

'Write that you are a prisoner,' the young man said. 'That we will release you unharmed only when the King has released the political prisoners from jail and when he has promised to stop the negotiations with Mr Grey and end the National Park scheme for ever.'

Marie looked at him incredulously. 'You are against the National Park?'

'Write what I tell you. Do not ask me foolish questions,' he snapped, waving his gun at her.

'But the scheme will bring thousand of tourists to Jedhpur and bring employment to many of your people. Think how much money will flow into the country, money you badly need.'

'The King is turning our country into a Disneyland for rich foreigners,' he said bitterly. 'We are a land of peasants. If all these foreigners come here, the peasants will leave the land to earn big money working as servants for them, and we will lose our dignity and freedom.'

'You want Jedhpur to remain backward for ever?' she asked him quietly.

His eyes flashed. 'Write! You know nothing.'

Marie looked down at the paper and obediently wrote the message he wished to send. He snatched the paper from her and read what she had written, then he looked at her. 'It is not signed. Sign it with your name.'

The young woman spoke softly, quickly. He turned and looked at her and nodded, then he said to Marie, 'She is right. You must put some words of your own, words of love which will make this man want badly to get you back.'

Marie flushed. 'I've written what you asked me to. I will not write anything else.'

The young woman spoke again, smiling, and the man laughed. He looked at Marie rather more kindly.

'Do not be embarrassed. This must be done. Sarwana says you do not wish to have strange eyes looking at your words. See, I shall not read. You may seal envelope yourself.'

Marie looked down at the paper. Words seemed to burn on it, words she knew she would never write. If she never saw Stonor again these would be the last things she said to him. There was so much to say, so little that could be said.

She wrote slowly. 'Stonor, do what you have to do. Don't worry about me. They've been kind.' Then she quickly sealed the envelope and handed it to the young man. He looked at her searchingly, seeing the flush on her cheeks, the wildness in her eyes.

Gently, he said, 'Soon you will be free. When your man reads this he will move heaven and earth.'

When he had gone Sarwana made tea and they sat and drank it quietly. It was served, of course, in Indian fashion, without milk or sugar, but the liquid was refreshing, and it helped to pass the time.

Marie was allowed now to leave the little room and walk outside. It was dark, as it had been last night when she was given the same opportunity; so dark that she could see nothing but the sky and the branches of the trees which surrounded the house. The air was cool and fragrant. It was hard to go back into the stuffiness of the little room.

She lay down and slept later, while Sarwana departed again, presumably to feed her baby or see to her own house.

At dawn next morning the young man with the gun came back. He burst into Marie's room, awaking her from a deep and troubled sleep, and she sat up in alarm, staring at him.

He laughed aloud, waving his arms. Sarwana stood behind him, wreathed in smiles.

'All is agreed,' he cried delightedly. 'The prisoners are already released. The King has announced that for the present he will proceed no further with the National Park, and Mr Grey will leave Jedhpur without the agreement he had been negotiating.'

'You ... knew about that?' she asked, wondering how soon they would release her.

'Why else did we do all this? Oh, the King and Mr Grey tried to keep it secret, but there are patriots in the palace who objected to the plans. Now things will return to normal. The land will belong to the peasants as it has always done.'

'Or to the landlords who live in the palace?' she suggested.

He looked at her sharply and his brows jerked together. 'You do not understand how things work here.'

'When will I be released?' she asked, afraid of angering him any further.

'When it is dark,' he promised, smiling again. 'I will drive you somewhere and release you.'

The hours seemed to pass with appalling slowness while Marie waited for the moment of her release. She could not eat the food Sarwana brought her. She could only sit staring at the thin slits of light filtering through the shutters.

At last it was dark and she was led out, once more blindfolded and gagged. The drive was bumpy and unpleasant, over rough terrain; they were not, she realised, driving back the same way they had come. At last the car stopped. She was pushed out roughly, the car reversed and sped away with a grinding of gears.

Marie hurriedly untied her blindfold and removed the gag with hands that shook.

Then she stared around. She stood in the dark road on the outskirts of a small village. The lights shone with friendly invitation just a few hundred yards away. She stumbled and ran towards them, and knocked on the first door she came to, her body trembling with the long tension of the last few days.

The door creaked slowly open and a dark face peered cautiously out at her.

'Help me,' said Marie, clinging to the door frame. Her knees were buckling under her, as if she could no longer maintain the pretence of being calmly under control.

The face withdrew. Voices chattered inside the house, then someone else came to the door. Marie held out an appealing hand, realising that they could not speak English and were more frightened of her than curious. They were amazed by the appearance of an English girl in their village at such an hour, and suspicious of her reasons for wandering about without masculine protection in the dark.

She had no money on her, no way of explaining her predicament. She held out her hands again, pleadingly.

'Lhalli,' she said. 'Me ... go to Lhalli ... Lord Hathni ...' She began to recite the names of the royal family, watching them intently.

They looked at each other, shrugging. One of them made a gesture to her, speaking loudly to the others, then he ran off into the darkness. A moment later he was back, leading a reluctant and irritable-looking mule by a rope halter. He gestured to Marie to get on the animal.

She managed to climb on to its back, looking at him nervously as he took up the halter. He turned and nodded to her, giving a shy smile.

'Lhalli,' he said, nodding. 'Lhalli ...'

Then they set off into the night along the rough, rutted hill roads in the dark, moonless and haunted by the howls of jackals and the floating wail of hunting owls. Bumping and clinging to the mule for grim life, Marie felt herself wearily wishing she could just lie down and die. It was all too much for her.

The throb of an engine reached her ears suddenly, making her sit up and stare ahead. Like yellow eyes in the darkness, the headlights of a lorry shone straight at them. The peasant drew the mule to the side of the road to let the lorry pass, but instead it ground to a halt with a crash of gears, and from the back of it sprang a dozen soldiers in the palace uniform. Shouting, brandishing guns, they surrounded Marie and the peasant. The peasant cringed in terror, wailing, then Marie recognised Aziz descending from the lorry cab. He was grinning delightedly.

'My dear Miss Brinton! How glad I am to see you alive

and well.' He glared at the peasant. 'You will suffer for this, animal!'

'He had nothing to do with it,' Marie assured him quickly, laying a hand on the unfortunate old man's shoulder. 'He just helped me when the others had dumped me in his village . . .' She told Aziz how she had been released and he spoke more kindly to the old man, drew out a handful of coins from his purse and pushed them into the old man's trembling hand. Hurriedly, with many bows, the peasant vanished into the night. Marie was not sorry to see the back of his mule, which moved much faster now that it was heading homewards, she noticed.

Aziz helped her gently into the lorry. The soldiers climbed aboard and the lorry slowly reversed. Aziz told her as they drove back to Lhalli that his cousin had been quite horrified by her kidnapping, especially since Stonor had been almost beside himself with rage and anxiety. They had searched everywhere they could think of, all the known haunts of Jedhpuri rebels, but they had found no clue as to her whereabouts.

'So the King had to give way. He could not risk your life. Mr Grey would never have been prepared to invest in our country if you had been killed.' Aziz looked at her, and smiled, relapsing into silence.

Marie was fast asleep, her head slumped against his shoulder.

CHAPTER NINE

SHE WOKE up when the lorry stopped outside the palace gates. Aziz smiled at her, his glance mischievous. 'Mr Grey will be jealous when he learns you have slept on my shoulder for so long! Are you stiff? Come, let me help you down.' He lifted her down and put an arm around her as her knees gave way. 'Shall I carry you? Can you walk?'

Marie shook her head. 'It's only cramp.' She flexed her calf muscles, grimacing at the pain. 'I can walk now …'

Lights still burned everywhere in the palace, but curious sentries stared as they passed along the marble corridors. Whispers preceded them. A soldier ran ahead to warn the King, and as they approached the royal apartments the King himself appeared in the doorway, his face tired, fully dressed.

'Miss Brinton! Heaven be praised! You are safe! Those dogs kept their word, then. We had begun to think …' he broke off as Stonor arrived, his bandaged shoulder impeding him.

Marie looked at him, her whole being concentrated on his face. He was white, his dark eyes like bottomless wells in his face. He stood over her, staring down as if he had never seen her before, searching her face with stark intensity.

'You will wish to speak alone,' the King said quietly, clearing his throat. 'Please, use my room.'

Stonor took Marie's arm in his free hand and propelled her firmly past the King into the room. He paused before closing the door to thank the King, then shut the door and leaned against it, staring at her.

Marie was so nervous she could barely breathe. The room seemed to be full of electricity, like the sky before a storm.

'God!' Stonor groaned. 'Oh, God, Marie …'

Then he had moved towards her fast and she was in his arms, held so close she had to cling to him to stand upright. He kissed her with savage hunger, murmuring her name again and again.

'I was beginning to think they'd killed you,' he said, his voice husky. He moved his lips along her throat with feverish intensity, then returned to her mouth, parting her lips, consuming her in the flame of his own passion. 'I've been out of my mind. I wanted to tear this god-forsaken little country to shreds looking for you. I'd have paid anything, done anything, to get you back safely …'

Her blue eyes shone at him adoringly. 'Stonor,' she breathed softly. 'Darling …'

He drew back, looking down at her. 'Say that again.'

'Darling,' she repeated obediently, her hands touching the black hair at the nape of his neck, delving into the thick strands with fingers that seemed to have nerves in every pore, sensitive to his body in a way that made her shiver.

'Tell me you love me,' he demanded arrogantly.

Her happiness was so all-consuming that she was past preserving her pride or her self-respect. 'I love you, I love you,' she whispered.

'Again,' he ordered.

She lifted her blue eyes to his face again, a slightly rebellious expression in them now. 'Stonor?'

'I want to hear you say it,' he said, the lean face filled with the old arrogance.

'I think we still mean different things by the word love,' she said, suddenly saddened.

'Do we?' He brushed her upturned mouth with his lips. 'We'll have plenty of time to find out after we're married.'

Marie stood very still, her eyes fixed on his face. 'Married, Stonor?'

'Yes,' he said lightly. 'You've broken my spirit, damn you. How can I let you roam the world without protection when you keep getting yourself into trouble like this? I'd never have another moment's peace in case someone was kidnapping you. I'm afraid I'm going to have to carry on where your father left off, wrapping you in cotton wool, showering you with expensive presents, spoiling and adoring you ...'

She took his face in both her hands, her pleading palms against his hard cheeks.

'Be serious, Stonor. Don't play one of your games.'

'I was never more serious in my life,' he retorted.

'I've said it,' she whispered. 'Why can't you?'

He was suddenly very grave, his dark eyes full of sombre thought. 'I'm afraid, Marie. Afraid of losing myself, afraid of drowning helplessly in an ocean of love. It's always been there in my nature, a weakness, the need to love with utter abandon, but I meant to fight against it for the whole of my life. I've seen what it does to men. That sort of love saps your strength.

Then I met you, and when I kissed you that night in the desert I felt a terrible warning. I knew that if I let myself fall for you I would fall so far I could never get back. But by the time I'd realised it, it was already too late. I've been trying to escape from the trap ever since. I tried to convince myself you weren't worth loving, but I never quite succeeded.'

'Didn't you, Stonor?' Her blue eyes were gentle now, recognising his sincerity.

He put a hand to her golden hair, running his fingers down the silky strands. 'That hair of yours first drew my eyes – such a glorious colour! I wanted to touch it, to run my fingers through it. That was my first hint of danger. Then your blue eyes flashed at me and I felt the warning signals again – oh, I had plenty of warnings, but I ignored them all. Like a blind man walking into his fate, I let myself be caught. Perhaps I even wanted to be, secretly.'

She let her arms fall away from him and stepped back, watching him through her lowered lashes. 'You're free, Stonor. Quite free.'

He smiled grimly. 'The secret of your power, you witch, is that I no longer want to be free. For weeks I've yearned to be totally enslaved, even while I struggled against the desire to see you again. Of course I didn't come to Jedhpur to make a deal with the King—I could have done that through one of my agents. I came to see you. I had to come. I couldn't sleep at night any more. Your face was haunting my dreams, driving me mad with desire.' He reached out for her, but she evaded him.

'You still haven't said it,' she reminded him.

He stared at her, his chin raised angrily. 'I've admitted it over and over again. What else do you want?'

She did not answer, her eyes levelly fixed on his face.

He half closed his eyes and groaned. 'All right, I love you. I love you, God help me!'

Marie laughed. 'You sound as if it had been wrung from you by torture, Stonor!'

'Hasn't it?' He pulled her close with his one good hand. 'I've been denied a kiss for five full minutes. What's that but cruel torture?'

Her mouth was parted on a smile as she looked up at him. But the smile died on a gasp as his mouth descended in hard possession, melting her bones, making her shake with mounting passion. When they parted he was dark red, she was trembling.

'We've got to get back to England and get married before I lose all my last shreds of self-control,' he said grimly.

'I can't leave Jess without anyone to look after Jeremy,' she protested. 'He needs constant care.'

'We'll fly someone out to take your place,' he said easily, brushing the problem aside. 'That woman who works there can take over until the new girl arrives. After all, she's been looking after the child while you were away.' He looked at her gently. 'Jess was very worried about you, you know. She was intent on blaming herself for what happened. She thought that if she'd never brought you out here it wouldn't have happened, which, in a way, I suppose, is true.'

'Poor Jess,' she said. 'We must go to the bungalow right away and tell her the good news.'

'I think the King wants to ask you some questions first,' he told her. 'They want to try to catch these damned rebels, and any information you can give them will help.'

'But I don't know anything,' she protested. She knew that she did not want to help to catch the young men who had held her prisoner. They had treated her with comparative kindness. Even their threat to kill her had been a muted one.

'You saw them, didn't you? You saw their faces?'

She shrugged. 'Only in a very dim light. I wouldn't know any of them again. They were just ordinary young Indians.'

Stonor stared down at her, his brows drawn together in a frown. 'Marie, are you trying to protect them? Because if you are, let me remind you that the next person they kidnap may not be so lucky. They can't be allowed to get away with this, you know.'

'I'm not hiding anything!' she protested. 'I don't know anything which could help.'

Then Stonor walked to the door and opened it. There was a slight pause as he spoke to the sentry outside, then he came back to join her.

'Better sit down,' he said. 'This will take some time.'

'I'm so tired, Stonor' she said unhappily. 'And I'm hungry. Can't it wait?'

The King came hurriedly into the room. He smiled at them both in a friendly fashion.

'All is well between you? Good. Now, Miss Brinton, I must ask you a few questions, then I will send you back to Mrs Cunningham by car so that you may relax in the peace of the bungalow. Or if you prefer, you may stay here in the palace near Mr Grey.' His eyes twinkled. 'Which would you prefer?'

'I think I'd better join Mrs Cunningham, sir,' she said. 'I understand that she's been very worried about me, and I wouldn't want her to go on being worried for much longer.'

'You are very thoughtful,' he said. He glanced at Stonor. 'Won't you sit down, Mr Grey?'

Stonor sat down beside Marie on the low couch. He leaned over and took her hand firmly.

She looked at the King with caution.

'First, Miss Brinton, can you tell me the names of any of these men?'

She shook her head.

'They did not once address each other by name in your presence? Are you quite certain of that?'

She nodded. 'Quite sure.'

The King looked depressed. 'They are cleverer than I had thought. Well, then, where were you held? Did you recognise anything about it?'

Marie explained that she had been held in a house at which she had arrived and from which she had left in darkness.

'The room was always shuttered. I have no idea where the house was.'

'Was it in a town? Could you hear any sounds which might give us a clue?'

'It was in the country, I think,' she said. 'I heard cows, and the wind rustling in trees.'

'You never heard any sound of vehicles? Any voices outside? Sounds from other houses?'

'Nothing like that. It was very quiet, I noticed that.'

'Was it marshland?' Stonor asked. 'You must have noticed what sort of country you drove through?'

'I was blindfolded,' she explained.

'What sort of roads were they? Main roads or cart tracks?'

'Rough hill roads,' she said.

Then Stonor pounced. 'Hill roads? How do you know they were hill roads?'

She looked at him crossly. 'We were coming down them at that sort of speed and angle. I could just tell we were driving down hills.'

'Good,' said the King. 'That is one solid point, anyway. A village in the hills, an isolated house.'

'It wasn't a village,' she said quickly. 'I'm sure I would have noticed sounds from other houses.'

'A farm,' Stonor said quietly. 'The cows indicate that, surely. A small hill farm.'

The King nodded. 'There are only a few hundred of them,' he said grimly. 'If it takes us a year we will search every one.'

'Did they talk to you?' Stonor demanded of her. 'Surely they spoke?'

'They only spoke when they had to,' she told him. 'In fact, I only saw one of them more than once. He had the gun.'

Stonor swore. 'Did he threaten you? Hurt you?' His eyes were wild with rage.

She shook her head. 'He never hurt me at all. He was really quite polite.'

'So he did speak to you?' Stonor had taken over the questioning, while the King sat silently watching them shrewdly.

Marie glared at Stonor. 'He spoke occasionally. It was he who dictated that letter to you.'

'But not the postscript?' he suggested softly.

She flushed, remembering all the words she had not written but had longed to put down. 'No, I wrote that.'

'Could he read English? Why didn't he cross it out? It was hardly a message to scare the hell out of me.'

'He very honourably allowed me to write a few words which he didn't read.' She hesitated, then said, 'He thought I was writing a love letter, you see. He thought it would make you more anxious to find me. And, don't you see, he was so sure I knew nothing that could help you that he didn't even ask to read it!'

Stonor glanced at the King.

The King sighed. 'That sounds obvious enough, does it not? Why else should he permit her to write a private message?'

Stonor shrugged. 'Then if that is all, your highness, may I accompany her to the bungalow?'

'No,' Marie said quickly. 'Jess will have enough on her plate without you descending on her, Stonor. I'll go alone.'

Stonor looked obstinate, but the King smiled at him. 'She will be safe. I will send six soldiers to guard her.'

So Marie drove back to the bungalow in a car driven by Aziz, who was looking somewhat subdued now. The soldiers rode behind them on horses, two abreast.

'What's wrong?' she asked Aziz.

'Everything,' he told her. 'In all this trouble, somehow my cousin the King has found out about Aissa and myself, and has ordered that I must not see her again under such circumstances. I think one of the servants was afraid that the King might order severe punishments when he found out that I have been seeing Aissa every day, so he hurried to betray us in order to avert the hand of calamity.'

'Was the King very angry?'

'Furious,' Aziz said grimly.

'What will he do now?'

'He has said that he will arrange a marriage for Aissa at once,' Aziz said sadly. 'I begged him to relent, but he was so angry I was forced to leave the room. He threatened to choke me to death!'

Marie suppressed a smile at Aziz's indignant tone. 'Poor Aissa ... I wonder what sort of husband he'll find for her?'

'God knows,' Aziz said miserably.

'I'm sure he'll try to find her someone near her own age,' Marie said comfortingly.

Aziz looked at her with wild eyes. 'Do you say that to torment me? Am I a stone that I can hear such news without bleeding inside?'

'I'm sorry,' she apologised, aghast. 'I ... I thought you would prefer her to have a chance of happiness instead of being forced into marriage with someone twice her own age ... '

They drew up outside the bungalow. Aziz murmured goodnight, his head averted. She went slowly up the path and the door burst open.

'Marie! Oh, my dear girl ... '

'Hallo, Jess,' she smiled.

Jess hugged her tightly, half in tears. 'How can you sound so calm? I've been frantic. Can you ever forgive me? This has all been my fault—I should never have brought you here in the first place. You must have been so scared.'

'Oh, it wasn't so bad!' Marie said casually.

'Are you having me on?' Jess stared at her incredulously.

She laughed. 'No, really. They were quite kind, honestly. I was a bit scared at first, but they never tried to frighten me.' She remembered the moment when they had said they would kill her and shivered suddenly. 'Well, they never threatened me directly.'

'My dear, they said they would kill you,' Jess protested, open-mouthed.

'Yes, they said that to me, too. I'm not sure if they meant it. I thought they did at the time, but now I'm not certain. They were none of them really the violent type.'

Jess gave a low groan of astonishment. 'I can't get over your calmness. You're very brave, Marie. I would have been gibbering inside twenty-four hours. I have a tendency to claustrophobia – that's why I spend so much time in the open. I hate to be shut up inside four walls.'

'Just as well they didn't kidnap you, then,' Marie smiled. 'They kept me locked in one room for the whole time.'

Jess put an arm around her. 'Come and tell me all about it while I watch you eat. You must be hungry.'

'I'm starving,' she admitted.

'Peter has given me a pile of tins of English food,' said Jess, her eyes triumphant. 'He was quite distracted with worry. He wanted you to have an English meal if … when you got back.'

Marie looked at her affectionately. 'How kind of him. I can hardly wait!'

An hour later, full of cream of tomato soup, sliced cold ham, new potatoes and peas, and some tinned peaches to round off the meal, she sat contentedly watching Jess do a rough sketch of her.

'For Peter,' Jess told her with a smile. 'I gather from the palace grapevine that Peter is in for a big disappointment.'

Marie flushed. 'I'm afraid so. I liked him a lot, but … '

'But Stonor Grey is going to scoop the jackpot, as usual,' Jess nodded. 'So Rahaib was telling me. I was amazed, I didn't think you even liked the man.'

'I'm not sure I do,' Marie laughed sheepishly.

Jess looked concerned. 'My dear, are you sure you're doing the right thing? Stonor Grey isn't an easy man to deal with. He would make a rotten husband.'

Marie looked down at her hands, linked in her lap.

'The trouble is, Jess, I'm crazy about him,' she sighed.

Jess watched her shrewdly. 'I see. Like that, is it? And he?'

Marie felt her cheeks glowing. 'He … feels the same way, he says.'

'Rahaib certainly said he was quite demented when you were missing,' Jess murmured. 'He was furious with Rahaib for letting it happen. He threatened to tear him limb from limb if you weren't found.'

Marie laughed. 'His bark is worse than his bite. How is Rahaib, by the way?'

'Fine. He had a bit of a bump on his head, but apart from a headache, he got over that quickly enough.' Jess grinned. 'I think it was his pride that suffered the worst blow. He was taken in by a simple trick like that. Poor Rahaib! He'll never forget it.'

'How could he have anticipated such a thing? He shouldn't blame himself. Anyway, all's well that ends well.'

'Not for Jedhpur, it doesn't,' Jess said grimly. 'The National Park scheme will have to be shelved until they find another rich man to back it.'

'I expect Stonor will see that they do,' said Marie. 'He told me he wanted no more to do with it, but he knows other firms who would be interested. The King will get his tourist centre in the end.'

'You look tired,' Jess sighed. 'I shouldn't let you stay up talking. Off to bed now, my dear.'

'I would love a bath first,' Marie said. 'You can't imagine how much I longed for one in that stuffy little room. The smell of curry seemed to linger for hours.'

Jess made a face. 'How ghastly! By all means have a bath. Then sleep as long as you like. Lispa is so good with Jeremy that you won't be missed.'

Marie hesitated. 'Jess, I ... '

Jess smiled at her. 'I think I know what you're going to say. Mr Grey wants to whisk you away from us?'

'I'm afraid so,' Marie admitted. 'He says he'll send someone else to take my place.'

'I don't think I need anyone,' Jess said calmly. 'Lispa will go on taking care of Jeremy for me. He plays with her boys and has a marvellous time. I can teach him to read and so on when the time comes. For the present I think I'll just let him grow up alongside Lispa's sons.'

'He'll turn into a little Hindu,' Marie laughed.

'He'll certainly learn more tolerance than he would have done back home,' Jess agreed. 'So don't worry. You can go back home with your man and marry him. You deserve to be happy.'

Marie kissed her, then went off to have a long, relaxing bath before tumbling into bed to sleep the clock around.

When she woke up she found Jeremy sitting on her bed staring at her unwinkingly.

'Hallo,' he said. 'I thought you were dead.'

'Well, I'm not,' she retorted.

'Did bandits kidnap you?'

'Sort of bandits,' she agreed.

'Were you scared?'

'Now and then.'

He considered her. 'I wouldn't be scared. I would hide and they would never find me.'

'Good idea,' she said solemnly.

He jumped off the bed. 'Mum said to tell you Mr Grey was coming in an hour, so do you want something to eat?'

Marie sat up. 'Yes, please. I'm hungry.'

Jeremy eyed her. 'So am I. I'll have another breakfast with you, if you like, to keep you company.'

She laughed. 'You'd better ask Mummy first.'

Jess looked at her with pleasure when she entered the living room. 'You look much better this morning. You looked a bit dead last night.'

'I was dead beat,' she nodded.

'What about breakfast? There's fruit and bread and a few eggs.'

'That will be lovely,' she said eagerly.

Jeremy begged to join her in her meal, but Jess drove him away. 'Little pig, he eats far too much in that kitchen. Stonor Grey will be here soon. Apparently he's determined to get you back to England today.'

'Today?' Marie stared at her incredulously.

Jess laughed. 'A man of lightning decisions, apparently.'

'He can't! I'm not even packed!'

'That can be dealt with in a flash,' Jess said easily. 'I'm not sure whether it's a good idea or not. You've had a bad shock, even though you've taken it so well, and I can't make up my mind whether or not it's wise to fly you back to England so quickly. You need some peace and quiet, in my opinion, but I may be wrong.'

Marie stared at the table. 'I think I would like to be back home.'

'Well, it's true that the monsoon weather will be starting soon, and that can be pretty devastating for anyone. Perhaps you should leave before the heat becomes unbearable.'

Lispa came in with the food, smiling warmly at Marie. While she ate her breakfast, Jess talked to her. 'Lispa can pack for you while you talk to your young man.'

'My young man!' Marie giggled. 'It hardly describes Stonor, does it?'

Jess laughed. 'No, not really. He's pretty impressive, isn't he? A bit like a monolith.'

Then Stonor was in the room, and Marie hardly noticed as Jess discreetly slipped away.

He kissed her hungrily, awaking her sleeping pulses. 'Darling, I'm so glad to see you,' she said, touching his face tenderly.

'Are you packed?' he demanded. 'I'm taking you home before all hell breaks loose.'

'What do you mean?' She stared at him in bewilderment.

'Aziz has run off with Aissa,' he said grimly. 'The King is furious. He was swearing vengeance on his cousin when I saw him this morning. I think we should get out today. Life at the palace is going to be very hectic after this.'

Marie looked anxiously at him. 'What will the King do?'

'What can he do? Apparently they flew off in a private plane, nobody knows where, leaving a note which said they were getting married. Lord Hathni is even angrier than the King. He'll lose face because his son is breaking a betrothal.'

'Oh, dear,' Marie said faintly. 'I think you're right – we must go home at once. I think the air here is too stormy.'

Stonor lifted her out of her chair. 'Say goodbye to Jess and the little boy. I want to get you all to myself as soon as possible. I can't wait another week to marry you. We'll get a special licence when we get home.'

'Are you sweeping me off my feet, Stonor?' she teased.

'That's right,' he retorted. 'I'm going to make sure you don't escape me ever again. Consider yourself my prisoner for life.'

She slid her arms around his neck and lifted her face to his. 'You really are just a desert barbarian at heart, aren't you?'

The dark eyes burned down at her. He smiled adoringly and their lips met. Against her lips he whispered, 'There's a saying in my mother's country: what the desert claims, the desert keeps ... remember that, my darling.'

SUMMER FIRE

Sally Wentworth

CHAPTER ONE

THE ROAR of the high-powered engine reverberated harshly against the walls of the centuries-old cottages as the black-leather-clad motorcyclist accelerated down the long hill that led into the quiet Cotswold village of Arbory Magna. The rider slowed down to negotiate the twists in the narrow road between the stone walls of the houses, weathered to a warm honey colour and drowsing sleepily in the still sunshine of an afternoon in early summer. At the Arbory Arms, which served as the village's only pub, two elderly men sat outside at a wooden table, playing dominoes and each with a pint glass of dark brown ale conveniently near to hand. They looked up as the motorcycle came to a stop at the kerb, the noise of the engine dying down, but the big black and silver machine still throbbing with life between the rider's legs, ready to roar away again at the smallest pressure of hand and foot.

The motorcyclist raised a gauntleted hand to lift the dark-tinted vizor of the astronaut-like helmet and regarded the two men. 'Can you tell me the way to Abbot's Arbory?' the rider called in a voice muffled by the chin-guard of the helmet.

For a moment the two drinkers stared silently, taking in the motorcyclist's fronded leather jacket decorated with chrome studs in the shape of a skull and crossbones on the back, the tight trousers and the high boots, then one roused himself to point down the road. 'You go out of the village and up t'hill t'other side,' he answered in a heavy dialect. 'Go on for about half a mile and you'll come t'the gates of East Lodge. You can't miss it. There be big stone pillars.'

'Thanks.' The rider raised a hand in acknowledgement and gunned the machine into roaring life again, surging off in the direction the men had given.

Even before it had disappeared round the first corner the two drinkers had exchanged glances and then began to laugh heartily at some unspoken jest.

Soon after leaving the village the road widened a little and on the right-hand side was bordered by a high wall of the local stone, worn and aged, as if it had been standing for a very long time. Behind it grew a thick belt of tall trees that threw long, dappled shadows across the lane. The noise of the engine altered as the rider changed gear to climb the long, steep hill and then quietened as it reached the Lodge gates. They were, as the old man had said, quite unmistakable—tall stone pillars surmounted by heraldic rampant lions each holding a shield in its claws, the armorial bearings somewhat worn by time, but the lions still proud and defiant, fiercely guarding the entrance.

Pandora Smith lifted the vizor of the helmet again and smiled to herself a little grimly as she looked at them; they were as defunct and out of date as the whole concept of land ownership by inheritance that they represented. Just because some medieval warlord had wrested the land from the local peasants by sword and torture way back in history, that shouldn't give his heirs the right to keep it now, she thought angrily. She turned off the engine and then heaved the heavy bike on to its rest. There were wide, beautifully wrought iron gates between the pillars, again with the heraldic lions picked out in gold, fine examples of the skills of the blacksmith who had made them in – what? – the early seventeenth century, she guessed. Walking across to the gates, Pandora put out a hand to touch them, capable of admiring the genius that had gone into designing and making such works of art even though she loathed the establishment of wealth and privilege that had caused them to be made.

Behind the gates, on the left-hand side of the drive, there was a small one-storeyed lodge house, again built of Cotswold stone, and ornamented by an unusual turret on the wall nearest the gates, which was higher than the house and provided a small upper room that looked out over the lane. The Lodge looked empty and deserted, the neatly laid-out garden round it slightly neglected, and when Pandora called out no one came in answer to her shout. She shrugged and turned her attention to the gates, finding that they were not locked, but fastened by bolts lowered into holes in the ground on the inside. It was something of a struggle, but by putting both arms through the ironwork Pandora was able to raise one of the handles and lift the bolt free of the ground, the gate swinging open on well-oiled hinges. After wheeling the motorbike through, she carefully shut the gate behind her and then sat astride the saddle and rode on.

The drive continued through the woodland for some way before it thinned out just as the drive swung to the right. Pandora came out of the shadow of the trees into the sunlight, then stopped the bike abruptly, sitting astride it and just staring at the view before her. The ground was open now; rolling green parkland with occasional stands of high oaks and elms casting long shadows on the grass, but the dominant feature was a large lake, its waters shimmering in the sunlight, fed by a small river that cascaded over an outcrop of rock at one end, forming an irregular waterfall. At the other end of the lake, where the water was more placid and in places hidden by the spread of white- and yellow-flowered lily pads, there was a white Palladian-style summerhouse, its architecture matching that of a smaller, pagoda-like structure that Pandora could just make out among the trees on a small island nearer the left-hand end of the lake. For a while she looked at the lake, then slowly, almost reluctantly, lifted her eyes to gaze at the original of the house that was mirrored in its waters.

It stood on an eminence above the lake, set among green lawns, and standing as proud and defiant as the lions that guarded it. A magnificent building in the shape of an H, with an elongated central bar, three storeys high, the angles and chimneys of the roof hidden behind an Italian balustrade. Wide shallow steps curved gracefully up to the pedimented and pilastered entrance, set in the centre of the long side of the house, but its exact symmetry of architecture was softened by the texture of the stone and by the creeper which climbed irregularly halfway up the building at one end. An early seventeenth-century house, built at the height of the Restoration period, its beauty and grandeur held Pandora spellbound for quite some time as she feasted her eyes on it. Almost she was afraid to look away, for the house was so beautiful she felt that it must be a mirage, a fairytale palace, and if she closed her eyes it would disappear. But at length she deliberately shut her eyes, held them tightly closed while she counted to ten and then laughed at herself for being so fanciful when she opened them and the house was still there, exactly as it had been for over three hundred years. She gave a long sigh, acknowledging that wealth had at least produced something worthwhile in this magnificent building, but then became angry again when she remembered that the house and the hundreds of acres of land around it were owned by just one man, and that ordinary people were debarred from even seeing it. For this was no stately home, complete with safari park or some other gimmick, its doors thrown open to attract the public; Abbot's Arbory was completely private – and determined to stay that way.

It was several minutes before Pandora continued on along the drive, following its wide curve down towards the lake and the house beyond. She accelerated the powerful engine, going fast through the parkland, only checking in startled surprise when a herd of deer suddenly shot across the road in front of her and headed for the nearest patch of trees. The shock of seeing them appear in front of her made her lose her grip on the handlebar for a moment and the machine backfired noisily, the sound exploding like gunfire in the still air, and making the terrified deer run even faster for the safety and shelter of the trees.

Pandora recovered control of the bike easily enough and continued on her way more cautiously, ready now for any other animals that might be roaming loose in the park. Further on there were some more deer, but these, already nervous from the noise of the backfire, galloped well out of the way before she got near them, and the only other animals she saw were several horses in a paddock nearer to the house, but these seemed to be securely fenced in. After about half a mile she came to a cattle grid across the road, presumably designed to keep the deer out of the grounds surrounding the house and away from the lake, as was the long ditch of a ha-ha which reached out across the parkland on either side of the grid. Pandora took the grid slowly and carefully, then opened the throttle as she headed for the Palladian bridge, its three arches straddling the end of the lake where the river ran out of it and meandered away in lazy S's across the greenness of the park.

Across to the left, on the other side of the lake nearest the house, she saw another road, and on it a vehicle, a Range Rover by the look of it, also travelling towards the bridge, but approaching it from the other side. It was travelling fast, as if the driver was in a tearing hurry, and Pandora slowed, giving it time to get across the narrow bridge before her, as there didn't seem to be enough room for them to pass between the bridge's ornamented parapets at the same time. But to her surprise the Range Rover, instead of turning to cross the bridge, drove right across the end of it, completely blocking the road.

Pandora carried on across the bridge and came to a stop a few yards from the other vehicle, looking at it in some bewilderment. A man got out and strode towards her, a sporting gun under his arm and a pair of dogs at his heels.

'What the hell do you think you're doing here?' the man demanded furiously as he came up to her.

Pandora's mouth fell open in astonishment, but before she could even begin to form a reply, he added angrily, 'Can't you read? These grounds are private – there's a notice at every entrance telling you so. Now clear out, before I have you arrested for trespassing!'

He glared at her thunderously, a tall, broad-shouldered man who looked quite capable of throwing her out personally, and who would enjoy doing it too, given half a chance.

Pandora started to get off the bike. 'Look, I'm not doing any harm. I came to ... '

'No harm? Then what the hell do you call riding that monstrosity through the park and scaring the deer? I heard the noise of it over a mile away. You yobbos are all the same. You see a straight piece of road and you think you can practise your ton-up stunts on it no matter who it belongs to. Well, you're not going to do it at Arbory. You can just turn round and get that thing out of here. *Now!*' he added curtly, his dark brows drawing into a menacing frown.

Pandora stared back at him indignantly through the tinted visor. It was evident that the man took her for a youth, one of the fraternity of young men and boys who thundered through the countryside on their motorbikes and turned any available field into a race-track in their search for high-speed kicks. Well, Pandora enjoyed the thrills of speed-riding as much as any of them, but she certainly wasn't a boy, although she realised that it was easy enough to mistake her for one in her leather gear.

Hastily she sought to correct him. Getting off the bike and pulling it on its rest, she turned towards her accuser and lifted her hands to take off her helmet. 'You've got it all wrong. I only came here to … '

Her voice died away and she stood frozen as she found herself looking into the muzzle of his gun.

'You heard what I said. Clear out! If you're not out of here in five minutes I'll turn the dogs on you!'

Pandora's hands dropped loosely to her sides as she stared at the gun in appalled horror. Slowly her eyes lifted to the man's face and she saw a gleam of triumph in his eyes as he saw the frightened way she reacted. And then, suddenly, she was angry, gloriously, uncaringly angry. She drew her tall, slim figure in the tight-fitting trousers and high boots to its full height and turned to face her assailant.

'You coward!' Even muffled as it was by the visor her voice carried to him quite clearly and he stiffened in surprise. 'Hiding behind your gun and your dogs!' she went on furiously. 'Why, I bet without them you'd run a mile rather than face up to me. You bloated capitalists are all the same,' she added, mimicking his earlier remark. 'You get a preconceived idea about anyone who's the slightest bit different from you and nothing and no one will ever change it – especially if you think there's the slightest danger of upsetting the status quo. Of losing even the minutest fraction of the privileged way you live! As far as you're concerned everyone who looks or acts a little differently to you has to be regarded as the enemy. You didn't even ask me what I wanted here before you started throwing your weight around.' She paused for breath. 'Why, you're nothing but a – but an ill-mannered pig – and a cowardly one at that!' she added for good measure.

The frown had left the man's face, but instead his eyes had narrowed and his mouth set into a thin, cold line, and somehow this was far more menacing than his former anger. With a mere lift of his hand the dogs moved back to the Range Rover and sat down beside it. 'Stay,' he commanded. Then he put the gun on the ground.

Deliberately he crossed the few feet of space that separated them and looked down at her, his face still taut with barely suppressed fury.

'Now,' he said through gritted teeth, 'I'm without my gun or the dogs. So *what* was it you called me?'

Pandora blinked and lifted her head to look at him. She had to lift it an awfully long way. The man towered over her, and she was tall herself. He must be well over six feet – although right now it seemed more like eight feet at least. He was broad, too; she could see the powerful set of his shoulders even under the tweed hacking jacket that he wore, and he looked as if he kept himself in trim; there was no bulge round his middle, no softness of high-living in the lean, hard face that stared down at her with such cold disdain. She took a swift glance down at his hands that had balled into tight fists and decided that she'd definitely gone too far and the time had come to get out – fast. She took a hasty step backwards.

'Er ... I think I'd better be going.'

'What – already?' He followed her, coming up close again. 'Don't tell me you're afraid,' he added sneeringly.

Pandora took a quick look behind her as she backed away from him; the bike was only a foot or so away and she hastily grabbed the handlebars and started to swing her leg over.

But before she could do so her assailant reached out and grabbed the lapels of her jacket, yanking her towards him so that his face was only a few inches above her as he glared down at her through the visor.

'You young punk!' he said forcefully. 'Nobody calls me a coward and gets away with it. Do you understand? Nobody!' He began to shake her, so hard that her teeth rattled and her head banged against the inside of the helmet.

'Stop it! Let me go!' She put up her hands to try and stop him, but she might as well have tried to bend an iron bar.

Suddenly he pushed her away from him so that she lost her balance and fell sprawling on to the ground. He looked down at her disgustedly. 'You chicken-livered young thug! The only time you've got any guts is when you've a mob of your mates behind you – or in *front* of you,' he added with a sneer. 'Now get out of here before I really lose my temper. And tell the rest of your Hell's Angels pack that they'll get the same treatment if I catch any of them here again.'

Pandora didn't wait for a second invitation. She picked herself up as fast as she could and ran to the bike, fumbling in her nervous hurry to start it so that it stalled once before she got the engine going properly. She took one last, frightened glance over her shoulder at the man, the expression of cold disgust still on his face, and then sped back up the drive the way she had come.

He followed her in the Range Rover, of course. To make sure she didn't frighten a rabbit or crush a few blades of grass, presumably, Pandora thought resentfully as she turned her head and saw him driving down close behind her. She had a few nasty moments at the gate when she had to get off the bike and open it, but apart from getting out to watch the man made no attempt to either help or hinder her, even though he saw her struggling with the bolt that seemed heavier than ever now. At last she had the gate open and wheeled the bike through. She turned back to close the gate again, but the man had walked over and clanged it shut behind her. He stood looking at her through the ornate ironwork, waiting for her to go. Pandora suddenly felt a great rush of relief, as if she had just been let out of a prison and he was the jailor on the other side of the bars, watching her. Her chin came up and she tossed her head defiantly; it was he who was in the prison still, a prison of his own making with bars that he had set round himself, the bars being the strict distinctions of class and wealth that separated him from ordinary people.

He continued to watch her contemptuously until she was out of sight, but even then Pandora could feel a prickly sensation in her back as if his cold grey eyes were still boring into it. She went back the way she had come, down into the village of Arbory Magna. The two men were still sitting outside the pub and laughed openly when they saw her reappear. Pandora smiled sourly; evidently they had known full well what kind of reception she would receive. She rode on a few yards further into the village and stopped at a small, bow-windowed shop with 'POST OFFICE' written on the hoarding and a bright red telephone box outside.

Getting off the bike, Pandora reached up to take off her helmet, her long mane of tawny hair swirling round her shoulders as she shook her head to free it. The laughter of the men across the road at the pub stopped abruptly, and Pandora turned to see them staring at her in open-mouthed astonishment. She lifted a hand in derisive acknowledgement and went into the phone box. There were several numbers listed under Abbot's Arbory in the local directory: house, Estate Manager, East Lodge, West Lodge; even a big industrial concern didn't have that many lines, Pandora thought with increasing resentment. Out of curiosity she looked under Arbory, but although there were four entries with that surname, none of them was for Sir James Arbory, the proud owner of Abbot's Arbory, who had thrown her off his land in such a ruthless and high-handed manner. The sudden thought occurred to her that perhaps it hadn't been the owner, it might have been the Estate Manager. But she dismissed the idea almost at once; an employee of whatever rank would never have treated her with such arrogant contempt and ruthlessness.

Picking up the receiver, Pandora put a tenpenny piece ready in the slot and dialled the number given for the house. The phone rang a few times and then a man's voice, beautifully modulated and in impeccable English, said, 'Abbot's Arbory. Mr Richardson speaking.'

Pandora grinned at the plummy accent, pushed the coin into the slot and answered cheerfully, 'Hello, Uncle Charlie. It's me.'

'Pandora!' The word came out as a gasp of astonishment. 'Where are you?'

'Here, Uncle Charlie. In Arbory Magna.'

'What?' Charles Richardson's voice had a strange, strangled sort of note. 'I thought you were going to France to pick grapes this summer.'

'No, Uncle Charlie,' Pandora answered patiently, 'that was last year. This year I was going to pick peaches in Spain.'

'I don't care where it was,' he returned explosively. 'Just tell me why you aren't there.'

'There was a big storm and most of the crop on the farm we were going to got ruined, so they didn't need so many people,' Pandora explained. 'And then the girl I was going with was offered a job at a hotel in the West Indies, and obviously she couldn't turn it down.'

'Couldn't you go with her?' her uncle asked hopefully.

'No, Uncle Charlie, it was only for one. So here I am.'

'What do you mean – here you are?' he asked warily.

Brightly Pandora answered, 'I mean that I've come to stay with you for the summer, Uncle Charlie.'

'Stay with me?' he gasped, a distinct note of terror in his voice. 'But you can't stay here. You must go back to the college. Yes, that's it – you must stay in college during the vacation and study for your exams. It will do you good to be able to work without any distractions from the other students,' he added, growing increasingly enamoured of the idea.

Pandora let him go on for a while and then interrupted. 'It's no good, Uncle Charlie, the college is closed and I'm broke.'

'What about your allowance?'

'I spent it.'

'Well, you could get a job somewhere, couldn't you?' he asked with a note of despair in his voice.

'Uncle Charlie, *I have nowhere to live.*'

'A live-in job – at a hotel or something,' he urged, with a last desperate try.

Pandora was silent for a long moment, then said in a small voice, 'All right, Uncle Charlie. I realise you don't want me. Even though when Mother died you promised that you'd look after me.' She stifled a sob. 'You're all I've got left, Uncle. I thought I could come to you for help.' She sniffed bravely. 'But I – I'll just have to manage on my own. I'll just walk the streets until ... '

'Walk the streets!' he exploded. 'My God, girl, do you know what you're saying?'

'Why, only that I'll have to go back to London and walk around until I find someone who'll take me in,' Pandora answered innocently.

Her uncle's voice faded into a strangled gasp of horror and it was several seconds before he recovered sufficiently to say weakly, 'You – you can't do that. I suppose you'd better come here while I sort something out for you. I might be able to get you a job with some people I used to be in service with who've now opened a guesthouse on the coast. But it's only for a couple of days, mind,' he added warningly. 'You can't stay longer than that.'

'No, Uncle Charlie,' Pandora agreed meekly. 'I quite understand. It's very kind of you, Uncle Charlie.'

'And stop calling me that,' he said in exasperation. 'You know I dislike it excessively.'

'Of course. I'm very sorry, Uncle Charlie,' Pandora agreed, her hand coming up to her mouth to stifle a giggle, picturing her rather pompous uncle in his black butler's suit, and the devastating effect her phone call would have on him. But she had known that she would get her own way; she always did, ever since the death of her mother when she was twelve and he had become her legal guardian.

Now he sighed heavily and said, 'You'd better come up to the house. You go through the village and up the hill to … '

Pandora coughed. 'I don't think that would be a good idea, Uncl … hmm. You see, I already tried to come to the house, but I … well, sort of got thrown out.'

'You got what?' he demanded.

'Thrown out. By a man with a gun and couple of dogs,' Pandora supplied helpfully.

'What did he look like?'

'Oh, very tall, dark, and arrogant.'

Her uncle had no difficulty in recognising the description. 'Dear God, what have I done to deserve this? That was Sir James himself!'

'Yes, I rather thought it might be.'

'But why did he throw you out? Didn't you tell him you were coming to visit me?'

'Well, I didn't really have a chance,' Pandora explained. 'You see, he sort of took exception to my motorbike and he … '

'Motorbike? You didn't drive up here on that thing, did you?' A sound suspiciously like a moan came over the line. 'He'll never let you stay here now.'

'But does he have to know?'

But her words were drowned by her uncle's mournful wail. 'I knew it was too good to last! I just get myself settled in a decent place and get things running exactly as I like them and you come along and lose me my job – again!'

'Uncle Charlie, it really wasn't my fault I watered all those prize orchids with weedkiller at your last place. The watering can wasn't marked; it could have happened to anyone,' Pandora pleaded, genuinely sorry for her uncle's distress. 'And it *was* two years ago. Look,' she said persuasively, 'Abbot's Arbory is a huge place. If you sneaked me in by a side entrance or something, your boss wouldn't even know I was there. Why, I bet you could hide a dozen people in the attics alone and no one would ever find them.'

It took a lot of persuasion and wheedling, but at last Pandora got her uncle to agree to let her stay at Abbot's Arbory, although she had to make a great many promises, all of which he seemed to think vitally necessary if he was going to keep his job. Personally Pandora thought that if Sir James Arbory was such a tyrant – as her own brief clash with him proved – then she would be doing Uncle Charlie a favour by getting him the sack. But he knew his own business best, so she shrugged and dutifully promised not to approach the house again but to wait until after dark when he would come to fetch her and slip her in by the back door. Although Uncle Charlie didn't put it quite like that, of course, he described it as 'unobtrusively escorting you to the tradesmen's entrance'.

With several hours to kill, Pandora rode into the nearest town and did some envious window-shopping for a while, then found herself walking past the local library and wandered in to read the daily paper and browse through the glossy fashion magazines, all of which were always beyond her allowance. By the time she had paid her rent and bought books and food – in that order – there was rarely any left for luxuries like fashion magazines, or much in the way of clothes at all for that matter. After an hour or so she turned to leave the library, but she had to go through the reference section and her eye was caught by the massive volume of *Burke's Peerage*. An idea occurred to her and she took the book from the shelf and across to a table. Flicking over the first few pages in the A's, she ran her finger over the columns and stopped at the one she wanted. It read:

'Sir James Tristan Wyndham Arbory, 12th Bt., of Abbot's Arbory, Arbory Magna, Oxon. b. 17th Dec. 1945, succeeded his father. Educ. Eton and Oriel College, Oxford. Clubs: Whites, Carlton. Lineage: descended from Sir Edward Arbory, knighted 1417' which was followed by a long line of descendants.

Pandora did a rapid mental calculation; so that made him thirty-five, and there was no mention of a wife or children, so that meant he was still a bachelor.

She slammed the huge book shut suddenly, annoyed that she had let her curiosity get the better of her. What did it matter to her who or what the owner of Abbot's Arbory was?

As far as she was concerned he was just a capitalist leech who was feeding off the backs of the workers. Why, he must have a dozen servants, besides Uncle Charlie, to run a place that size. The whole system was shockingly unfair, and the sooner it was changed the better.

She drove back to Arbory Magna in the cool of the evening, the scent of the hedgerows strong on the light breeze, and waited at a table outside the pub for her uncle to turn up. He didn't come until it was quite dark, trudging purposefully up the lane in the beautifully pressed dark trousers and blazer that he considered to be the correct casual wear for a man in his position. Pandora smiled to herself; much as she loved her only relative, she just had to admit that he was awfully pompous.

He came up to her with a stern frown on his face, but this melted as Pandora jumped up impulsively to give him a hug and plant a kiss on his cheek. He tut-tutted a bit and tried to look askance, but was secretly not displeased at her show of affection.

'Really, child,' he remonstrated, 'what if someone I knew saw us? What would they think?'

Pandora opened her eyes wide. 'I don't know, Uncle. What would they think?'

As usual he was flummoxed for an answer, as Pandora knew he would be. It was one of Uncle Charlie's most endearing traits that he lived in a world way back in the nineteenth century, when all unmarried girls were pure as the driven snow. It made Pandora sigh with exasperation at times, but she often traded on it shamelessly to her own advantage.

'Well, hmm, never mind. Come along. We'd better be on our way.'

Obediently Pandora picked up her helmet and gloves. 'You can ride pillion, Uncle Charlie.'

He immediately looked affronted. 'Certainly not! I wouldn't be seen dead on that contraption. We'll walk and you'll have to push it.'

'But it's over a mile,' Pandora objected.

'Yes, and another mile or so after we reach the gates,' her uncle added, not without a certain satisfaction. 'You should have thought of that before you came here on it. Why you couldn't come by train like any other normal person, I don't know.'

He rabbited on in much the same vein for nearly half a mile while Pandora pushed the bike along beside him, with only an occasional grunt which he could take whichever way he liked. As the hill climbed more steeply she began to pant with exertion, concentrating all her efforts on pushing the heavy bike, but then her uncle lent a grudging hand, then two hands, until they arrived at the lodge gates and rested in a panting but companionable silence.

Pandora had expected them to go through the gates, but Charles Richardson led her on for another couple of hundred yards to another smaller and less ornate gate which he unlocked and which led through trees round to the back of the great house; a way for tradesmen's vehicles which was hidden from the windows of the house or anyone strolling in the park. When they got near the outbuildings he motioned her to silence and led the way almost stealthily to an old coach-house that looked as if it hadn't been used for quite some time.

'You can hide the bike in here,' he said in a low, hissing whisper, at the same time looking furtively over his shoulder.

'Oh, really, Uncle Charlie,' Pandora said in exasperation. 'Anyone would think we were committing a crime!'

He flapped his hands to shush her. 'Quiet! Sir James often takes a stroll in the evening; he might hear us.'

Pandora sighed, but quietly removed her belongings from the leather panniers on the bike and followed him to a side door of the house. It led to a long, plain corridor with brown-varnished doors opening off at either side and at the end of it a flight of uncarpeted steps leading upwards, but her uncle stopped at a door just before the end and opened it.

'Here you are,' he said in a rather more confident tone. 'You can have this room. It's quite clean and aired because we had a maid who left only recently. She only stayed a few weeks – said she couldn't stand being stuck in the country.' He sniffed disparagingly. 'No stamina in today's younger generation. *And* the agency haven't found us a replacement yet. Still, that's neither here nor there.' He looked at her consideringly, seeing her in a good light for the first time. 'You're looking thin,' he remarked, his eyes running reprovingly over her tall slim figure. 'I don't suppose you bother to cook yourself proper meals – just live on convenience foods in that college of yours.'

'Never mind, Uncle Charlie,' Pandora said bracingly. 'While I'm here you can fatten me up.'

'Humph!' He went to draw the curtains across the window for her. 'And why you find it necessary to wear that ridiculous outfit, I fail to see.'

'But it's ideal for the motorbike. I got the leathers cheaply from a student who didn't need them any more.'

'Oh? Did he buy a car instead?'

'No. He just crashed his bike and broke both his legs,' Pandora returned calmly.

Her uncle raised his eyes to heaven. 'Well, I hope you've got some more respectable clothes to wear.'

'Of course I have. I've got jeans and tee-shirts ... '

His face paled and he held up a hand to stop her. 'Don't tell me any more, I don't want to know. When you're ready come down to the kitchen and I'll get you some food. You go back down this corridor, turn left at the end and go through the scullery to the kitchen.'

He left her alone and Pandora looked round the room. It was, as he had said, clean, and to her surprise it was quite amply if plainly furnished with a vanity unit in one corner, a square of grey carpet, a single bed with a navy cover that matched the curtains, and a varnished wardrobe and dressing table. There was also an armchair, again upholstered in navy and which Pandora sank into gratefully while she pulled off her boots; they had never been intended for walking, let alone that long trek from the village. When she went to hang the few clothes she had brought with her in the wardrobe she found two black dresses, two dark grey skirts and cardigans, and two white blouses, all encased in polythene bags, hanging there, obviously freshly back from the cleaners after the maid had left. Pandora looked at the cut of the garments and grimaced; no wonder the girl had left if she had been expected to wear that outdated gear, it was at least two decades behind the times.

Pandora washed and then, bearing in mind Uncle Charlie's strictures, changed into her most conservative pair of jeans, without any patches or badges sewn on, and a tee-shirt that, although bright red, merely had 'I'M INTO THE EIGHTIES' written across the chest and which she hoped wouldn't offend his sensibilities too much.

Apart from a shudder when he saw her, her uncle carefully refrained from comment, merely placing a bowl of soup and a dish of rolls in front of her, followed by a large ham omelette. Pandora ate hungrily while he sat and watched her morosely. Afterwards she sat back and wiped her lips on a napkin. 'That was delicious. Uncle Charlie, you really are a great cook.'

He looked pleased. 'Well, I will admit that I can turn out a good omelette.'

'But you don't have to cook for this Sir James, do you? Surely he has a professional chef?'

'He does when there are guests staying, but when he's alone here the housekeeper usually does the meals.'

'The housekeeper? Does she live in the house too?'

'Yes, but she's away at the moment looking after her mother who's just had an operation.'

'Do any other staff live in?'

'Not in the house itself now the maid's left. There's a groom and a stableboy who live near the stableyard, and various gamekeepers and gardeners who live in tied cottages on the estate, but there's only myself in the house at the moment.'

'And so you're doing the cooking?'

'Yes.' A frown crossed his brow. 'But he's getting a bit fed up with omelettes.'

Pandora burst into a peal of laughter and her uncle gave a wry grin and then laughed openly.

'That's better,' Pandora told him. 'You've been a crotchety old bear ever since I phoned you. I was beginning to be afraid you'd forgotten how to laugh.'

He shook his head. 'I'm sorry, child. It's just that I've really grown to like it here and I don't want to lose my place. And I'm – well, I'm getting a bit too old to keep changing jobs. I'd like to settle here if I can. That's why you must promise to stay here in the kitchen area,' he added urgently. 'Sir James wouldn't like it if he knew I'd let you stay here when he'd already turned you off.'

Pandora's heart was immediately wrung and she put out her hands to cover his. 'Don't worry, Uncle, I'll keep out of his way. After this afternoon I've no wish to run into him again, believe me. I'd rather meet a man-eating lion. Or even a woman-eating lion if it came to that!'

She went to bed shortly after and slept soundly until she was awakened early the next morning by the unusual sounds of birds singing and somewhere not too far away a cock crowing fit to wake every hen for miles around. Pandora turned over and tried to go to sleep again when she saw how early it was, but all the bird population of the Cotswolds seemed to have congregated outside her window and were pouring out their shrill welcome. Giving in to the inevitable, she got up and opened the curtains. The room looked out on to a paved yard, but beyond it, at the back of the house, there were lawns edged with banks of flowers, their bright heads glowing in the dawn sunlight, the drops of dew glistening like diamonds on the velvet petals and leaves.

Pandora turned back into the room and looked at the cream walls and drab carpet and curtains. What this room needed was colour – lots of it. It needed to be filled with flowers. Now, this minute! Impulsively she turned and ran out of the room and down the corridor to the outside door just as she was: barefooted, her long tawny hair falling free, and dressed just in a long, creamy-white full-skirted Victorian-style nightdress, its long sleeves gathered at the wrists.

The air struck cold as she opened the outer door, but she ran on heedlessly across the yard and down some steps to the lawn. The grass was wet under her feet, the morning mist not yet lifted by the sun, so that she felt as if she was running through a cloud. She laughed with delight as the mist swirled around her, happy to be in the country, to be free of work and studying for a while, to be able to relax and to live only for this beautiful morning. Her laughter rang out through the still air as she danced across the grass, twirling round and round so that her skirts belled out around her legs. She bent to bury her head in a mass of roses, drinking in their heady scent, and when some petals came loose in her hands, threw them up into the air and watched entranced as they drifted in the dappled sunlight, the breeze catching them and prolonging their flight in dizzy circles before they came gently down to rest. She reached up to where the lilac blossom hung heavy on the bough, deep mauve and shiny virgin white, and gasped and laughed with delight as the branches showered her with dewdrops. She filled her arms with heavenly-scented carnations, with big white daisies, and irises of every shade, yellow and blue and white and salmon.

She flitted from flower to flower like an exotic butterfly, quite a way from the house, and it was only when her arms were so full that she couldn't hold any more that she turned and ran happily back. Pushing the outer door open with her shoulder, she heard a noise in the kitchen and ran towards it, eager to show Uncle Charlie her treasure trove and demand a dozen vases to put them all in. She burst through the kitchen door and turned towards her uncle, green eyes alight with eagerness, her hair a wind-blown tangle. She began to say 'Uncle—' but then stopped with her mouth wide open, frozen by surprise and alarm.

Her uncle wasn't alone in the kitchen. Sitting negligently on the edge of the table, a mug of coffee in his hands, was the owner of Abbot's Arbory, the lord of the manor, and most definitely the man who had ejected her so violently only yesterday, Sir James Arbory!

CHAPTER TWO

THERE WAS an almighty crash as Charles Richardson dropped the brown earthenware teapot he was holding and it shattered on the stone floor. Pandora gulped, took one look at her uncle's agonised features, and hastily backed towards the door.

'No, don't go.' The tone was as imperative as the order.

She hesitated, giving another beseeching look towards her relative, but he seemed to be as frozen as she had been. Reluctantly Pandora turned to look at Sir James.

Today he was wearing tan riding breeches and a dark brown riding coat, his feet shod in beautifully polished leather boots. A crop and a brown velvet riding hat were nearby on the table. Slowly Pandora lifted her eyes to his face, expecting to see there the frown of anger that he had displayed the previous day, but to her surprise he didn't seem to be angry at all, in fact there was a curl of amusement on his thin, rather sardonic lips, and his eyes when they ran over her held a gleam of appreciation.

Pandora suddenly became acutely aware that she was wearing only her nightdress, that the hem of it was wet, and clinging to her legs.

Sir James put down his cup and standing up, took a couple of steps towards her. 'Good morning. I don't believe we've met. I'm James Arbory.'

He waited, obviously expecting her to introduce herself. Pandora flashed another glance at her uncle, but he still seemed to be struck dumb. She made a strangled sort of choking sound, then shrugged helplessly and opened her mouth to tell him who she was.

But her uncle came to sudden life and interjected hastily, 'She's from London, sir.'

His employer nodded. 'From the domestic agency – so I gathered. It's about time they sent a replacement for the last maid.'

Uncle Charlie looked stunned and Pandora had to stifle a hasty laugh. Dazedly he said, 'Yes, sir. Quite so.'

Sir James looked at her again and said, 'But you haven't told me your name.'

'It's Smith, sir,' her uncle put in before she could speak. He frowned at her mightily. 'But she might just as well go straight back to London without waiting for a month's trial; it's quite obvious that anyone who goes wandering round the gardens in her night attire – *and* picking some of your best blooms – is entirely unsuitable for such an establishment as this. I'll see that she leaves straight away. Go to your room at once, girl, and pack your things,' he ordered dismissively.

Pandora turned to leave, but Sir James' next words halted her in her tracks. 'On the contrary, I think it might make a pleasant change to have so conscientious a maid that she ran out to pick flowers for the house while the dew was still on them. That's the best time to pick flowers, of course. But you knew that, didn't you?' he remarked as he came to take the huge bouquet from her arms and pass them to her uncle.

There was mockery in his voice and in his eyes as he said it. That, and something else as he looked down at her. Pandora followed his gaze and saw that the dew from the flowers had wet her nightdress, clearly revealing the outline of her breasts beneath. Angrily she moved so that the material no longer clung, a flash of fire in her green eyes. So that was the kind of man he was, was he? There had been too many men in the past who had looked at her in just that way for her to fail to recognise it now.

'But we can't call you Smith,' he was saying. 'What's your first name?'

She opened her mouth to speak, but her uncle quickly crossed over to them and said hastily, 'It's Dora, sir. Dora Smith.' Pandora cringed inwardly but made no objection.

There was hidden laughter in his employer's face as he said, 'Well, Dora Smith, from London, welcome to Abbot's Arbory. It's going to be *very* interesting having you here.'

Pandora looked into his cool grey eyes, alight with amusement, and wondered whether that last remark had been intended as a double entendre. Well, whether it was or not, one thing was for sure – she disliked Sir High-and-Mighty Arbory excessively and it would give her great pleasure to wipe that leering grin off his face. An idea came to her and her eyes lit with mischief as she opened her mouth, and in a broad nasal Cockney accent said, 'Ooh, ta ever so. I ain't 'arf pleased to be 'ere, an' all.'

He physically flinched. She could see the shudder pass through his face, even though he concealed it well, and she felt an inner glow of satisfaction which she was careful not to let show, merely looking up at him in what she hoped was a gormless manner. Beside her, Uncle Charlie made a despairing, choking noise, but Pandora carefully avoided looking at him in case she gave anything away.

'Yes, well – er ... ' Sir James seemed to be at a loss for words. 'As Mr Richardson has said, you'd better go and get changed. You can put the flowers in water later.'

Pandora bestowed a bland smile on them both. 'Right you are then, ducks. Shan't be more than 'arf a mo.'

She escaped to her room and collapsed against the closed door, stifling her laughter with her hand. Even if she was kicked out tomorrow it would have been worth it just to see the expression on their faces when she had called Sir James Tristan Wyndham Arbory, Bart, ducks. It was hard to tell who had been the more appalled, Sir James or her uncle. Still chuckling, she began to dress, and going to the wardrobe looked at the maid's uniforms hanging there. Presumably the dresses were worn in the evening and the skirts and blouses for housework during the day. How ridiculous when jeans and sweaters were so much more practical. After putting on the clothes, Pandora came to the conclusion that the previous maid must have been short and plump; the skirt was too big round the waist and barely reached to her knees. She found a safety pin and was able to put a big tuck in the waist, but there was nothing she could do about the length. The blouse and cardigan too were baggy, although the sleeves were too short. There didn't seem to be any sort of cap to wear with the uniform, thank goodness, but she supposed she'd have to do something with her hair; she couldn't imagine Uncle

Charlie approving of it being loose. So she carefully scraped it back off her face and plaited it into a long braid, then coiled it round her head.

When she had finished Pandora looked at herself in the mirror and laughed aloud. She looked terrible! Like a caricature from a theatrical farce. Nothing could hide the fine bone structure of her face, the beauty of her long-lashed green eyes, but without make-up, her hair in this ugly uncomplimentary style, and with the dowdy, badly-fitting clothes *and* that ghastly Cockney accent, then she defied even Sir James to find her attractive. But that he had on first seeing her, Pandora was sure; the arrested look on his face had been unmistakable. The green eyes looking back at her from the mirror darkened with annoyance. It would be interesting to see whether Sir James Arbory would lower his standards or whether he would be too fastidious to contemplate making amorous advances to an employee, and especially to one who was obviously uneducated, vulgar and common at that. Her eyes lit up with mischief at the game she was about to play. She did feel a pang of regret that her uncle would have to play a helpless part in it, but for Sir James she felt no sympathy at all; it served him right for throwing her out so ruthlessly, and for being the arrogant snob that he was.

Before going back to the kitchen, she practised a few inane grins and silly, simpering giggles in the mirror until she was sure she could turn them on at will. It would never do to let her new boss know that there was a brain behind the caricature. This was a game that, once started, had to go on until he just couldn't stand having her around any longer. And judging from her appearance that would be sooner rather than later.

When she went back to the kitchen she found her uncle alone. A pained expression crossed his face when he saw her, then he sighed resignedly.

'Here, you'd better sit down and have some breakfast.'

He put two plates of scrambled eggs down on the table and sat down opposite her. Opening the daily paper, he folded it and perused the columns in a gloomy silence. After a couple of minutes Pandora peered over at the paper and saw that he was studying the Situations Vacant – Domestic columns.

'Are you trying to find me a job?' she asked him.

He lifted his head and looked at her morosely. 'No, I'm trying to find myself one.'

Pandora stared. 'Has he fired you?'

'No, not yet. But he will. Just as soon as the next disaster happens and he finds out you're my niece.'

'But what makes you think something terrible is going to happen?' Pandora protested.

'It's bound to. You're a walking disaster area – always have been,' he answered, his voice heavy with gloomy foreboding. 'I don't know why he even contemplated keeping you on after the exhibition you made of yourself this morning. Fancy coming into the kitchen like that!'

'I didn't know he was in here,' Pandora objected.

Her uncle frowned. 'It doesn't matter who was in here – you shouldn't have come in like that. What on earth possessed you to go out picking flowers – and in your nightdress too? Couldn't you at least have got dressed first?'

Pandora looked surprised. 'It never occurred to me. The sun was shining, I saw the flowers, so I just went out and picked them.'

He studied her face for a while, then set down his cup resignedly. 'It's no use; I've tried and tried, but I shall never understand you. Why it is you can't behave like an ordinary human being and think before you do things instead of acting on impulse all the time, I shall never know. Why, I remember when you were only about ten, you … '

He began to warm to his theme and Pandora decided that she had better interrupt before he really got going; unfortunately he had a good memory, and she had the uneasy feeling that she had committed enough misdemeanours in the past for him to go on for hours. So she said firmly, 'Why did you tell me to stay round the kitchen area when he comes down here for breakfast every day?'

The diversion worked. 'But he doesn't,' Uncle Charlie replied. 'I always serve him early morning coffee in his room at six-thirty, then he goes out riding and comes back for breakfast about nine. And I always serve that in the morning room. In the two years I've been here I've never known him to come down to the kitchen before.' He shook his head wonderingly. 'It must be fate that he should come down today of all days. There must be some malign aura about you that just draws disaster wherever you go.'

Pandora had to laugh at the woeful expression on his face, but she said sympathetically, 'Oh, come on, Uncle Charlie, it isn't as bad as that. Look on the bright side. If I do do something terrible you can always remind him that you said I wasn't suitable right at the start. And I won't tell him we're related – promise. And now you won't have to put yourself out trying to find me a job,' she added bracingly as he showed no sign of cheering up. 'In fact, it's all worked out quite well, really.'

He snorted derisively. 'Quite well! You're bound to do something terrible and get us both fired. Probably break a piece of priceless china or something.'

'No, I won't. I'll be very good, you'll see. I'll be the perfect maid,' Pandora told him optimistically.

'Oh, will you? Then will you please tell me why you found it necessary to speak to him in that terrible Cockney accent?' he demanded indignantly.

'Oh, that.' Pandora flushed guiltily. 'Well, I – I just thought I would,' she said inadequately, but adding more firmly as an idea came to her, 'You see, I thought it would help *you*.'

'Help me? How on earth could it?'

'Well, I thought that if I spoke like that all the time, he'd soon get fed up with having me around and would fire me that much sooner.'

Her uncle grunted, only slightly mollified, but said, 'It won't make any difference. People in Sir James' position don't go around talking to the maids all day! I shall be surprised if he ever bothers to speak to you again.'

'Oh, I see.'

He bent his head to his paper again, and Pandora was heartened to see that he did at least turn the pages and begin to read the news items instead. There had been no way she could tell him the real reason for adopting the phoney accent;

he would have been incredibly shocked and either told her that she was completely mistaken or else insisted on clucking round her like an old hen with its last surviving chick in case any attack should be made on her virtue. Pandora grinned to herself at the old-fashioned term, but that was Uncle Charlie – a throwback to the nineteenth century.

As she finished her breakfast she wondered whether Sir James would, in fact, ever speak to her again. After a few moments' thought she decided that he probably would try to chat her up, but probably not for a few days. He would have to have time to recover from the initial shock before he ventured near her a second time. So she would have to think of something that would really put him off her. She chuckled, imagining several ways she could do it, and her uncle looked up from his paper suspiciously.

'Now what are you planning?'

Pandora smiled back at him serenely. 'Nothing, Uncle, nothing at all for you to worry about.'

'Oh, no!' he groaned. 'When you say something like that I start worrying most of all.'

But after breakfast he recovered sufficiently to show her where everything was kept in the kitchen and set her to cleaning out some cupboards while he prepared his master's breakfast. Pandora was amused to see that eggs played a large part in it and even felt a small twinge of sympathy for Sir James if he had to live on her uncle's cooking for very long. It seemed that he was going out during the course of the morning, so later on Uncle Charlie took her round the house, showing it off with as much pride as if it was his own. And Pandora had to admit that it was magnificent. It was a house that had been cared for through the centuries, with every generation adding to the treasure of furniture, porcelain and paintings that adorned every room. Other stately homes open to the public that Pandora had visited had had a museumlike atmosphere, a smell of mustiness from old, decaying books and hangings, but there was none of that here; the rooms smelt fresh and clean, the curtains looked comparatively new and there were no chairs with the stuffing showing because the last faded and tatty remnants of the original covers had to be preserved and displayed.

They paused in the long gallery, which had several floor-to-ceiling bookcases along one wall and windows looking out across the park on the other. It must have been at least a hundred feet long with a beautifully ornate marble fireplace at each end. These were not lit and it should have been a cold place, but the sun streamed through the windows, warming it and giving life to the family portraits on the walls and the rich polished wood of the furniture. After admiring it silently for a few moments, Pandora had a nasty shock when Uncle Charlie said, 'One of your duties will be to keep this, and all the other rooms that Sir James uses every day, dusted and tidy.'

She looked at him aghast. 'Good heavens, you don't have to keep this whole place clean by yourself, do you? Or with just a maid to help you? Why, that's slave labour! You must be working all day long.'

'No, of course I don't. We have three women who come in to clean every weekday, but they only do the rough work: washing floors and paintwork, vacuum cleaning, polishing, and that sort of thing. It's up to the maid to just dust and tidy up and to prepare the guest rooms if Sir James invites anyone down for the weekend.'

'Is anyone coming this weekend?' Pandora asked, remembering that it was Saturday.

Her uncle assured her that there wasn't and then led her to a cupboard full of cleaning materials and firmly told her to get to work. 'And *please* – try not to drop anything,' he admonished her as he left.

Although Pandora found even the idea of being someone's servant repugnant, she was surprised to find that she quite enjoyed herself that day. It was fun to dust a portrait and wonder what kind of life the sitter had had here in Abbot's Arbory so long ago; would they have sat at the ornate desk to write their letters, have danced in the ballroom with its magnificent chandeliers, or sat in the armchair before the fire with all its ornate carving that made it difficult to dust? And it was a rare privilege to handle some of the delicate porcelain ornaments that adorned tables and sideboards, pieces that normally you were only allowed to stare at through glass cases in museums.

Pandora picked up one beautiful group of a richly dressed man and woman with two spaniels at their heels, the richness of their clothes glowing with life and colour, and lifted it up to look at the maker's mark underneath. As she'd thought; there were the two crossed swords, hilts downwards, which proclaimed that it had been made in the famous Meissen factory in East Germany.

'Good afternoon, Dora.'

The voice coming unexpectedly from close behind her startled her so much that she jumped and dropped the ornament. It fell headlong towards the marble-topped table on which it had been standing, but James Arbory's hand shot out and caught it only a couple of inches from the surface. Pandora let out a long breath and slowly unfroze. She smiled in relief and turned to find her new employer's eyes on her face, studying her intently. It reminded her suddenly of the game she was playing; in her gladness at not breaking the ornament she had almost forgotten and blurted out her thanks in her normal voice.

Now she said, 'Coo, blimey, you didn't 'arf make me jump, creepin' up on me like that! Gave me a proper turn, you did. You're lucky that pot didn't get broken. Still, it's only an old one, innit?'

'As you say, it's only an old one – but rather precious for all that.' He carefully replaced the group on the table and said casually, 'Are you interested in porcelain figurines?'

'In what?' Pandora frowned in perplexity.

'In figures like these.' He indicated the ornament. 'You seemed to be looking at the maker's mark on the bottom.'

'Is that what the black mark was? I thought it was sumthin' that had got stuck on and I was tryin' to rub it orf. Cor, I'd a' been rubbin' all day, wouldn't I, ducks?' And she giggled like a silly, simpering schoolgirl.

His dark brows drew together in a frown, a perplexed look in his eyes, and Pandora hoped that she had fooled him again. She would have to be careful, though; she had had to think quickly over the porcelain mark.

His eyes left her face and ran over her, taking in the baggy clothes. 'That uniform doesn't seem to fit you very well.'

Pandora looked down at herself. 'No. I think that other girl must 'ave been a bit bigger'n me.'

'*Quite* a bit bigger,' he agreed. 'You'd better tell Mr Richardson to give you some time off next week so that you can go into Oxford and get a uniform that fits.'

'Righty'o.'

Pandora went to turn away, but he said, 'By the way, where were you employed before?'

Her mind raced as she turned slowly back to face him: if she said she had been employed by a family he would be bound to ask for a reference which she most definitely couldn't supply. She thought of several other possibilities, but decided it would be better to keep it as near the truth as possible, so she answered, 'I worked in a college; makin' the students' beds and cleaning out their rooms an' that. But it was casual work. I 'ad to find other jobs during the 'olidays, workin' in 'otels and that. But I said t'meself, Dora me girl, I said, you've got ter find yourself a proper job. So I went to the agency and they sent me 'ere. They said this would be a proper job,' she explained helpfully.

'Did they, indeed?' A glint of amusement showed in James Arbory's lean features. 'And what about your family, your parents; do they approve of your coming here?'

A shadow crossed her face. 'I haven't ... ' she stopped and said quickly, 'I ain't got no family. Me parents is dead.'

'I'm sorry.' There was a surprising gentleness in his voice. 'And you have no one else to care for you?'

Pandora hesitated, then said, 'Only me Uncle Charlie,' and added because she couldn't resist it, 'And 'e's inside at the moment.'

'Inside?' He frowned in puzzlement and then said, 'Oh. Oh, I see,' having taken the expression by its slang meaning which was that someone was in prison, as Pandora had hoped he would. Although it was literally true: her Uncle Charlie was inside at the moment – here, inside this house.

'Yes, well – I hope that you'll be happy here, Dora, and if you have any problems please don't hesitate to come to me or to Mr Richardson. Perhaps you could go along to Mr Richardson now and tell him that I won't be in to dinner.'

'In t' dinner?' Pandora looked at an ornate ormolu clock on the mantelshelf. 'But it's 'arf past four. Dinner time was hours ago.'

His mouth twisted wryly. 'Yes, well, perhaps you could just tell him that I won't be in to the evening meal, then.'

'You won't be in ter supper. Righty'o, I'll go and tell 'im right now. Ta-ra.'

She picked up her duster and keeping her face perfectly straight because there were several mirrors in the room, walked out and carefully shut the door behind her, then ran through the corridor leading to the back stairs, gurgling with laughter.

So later that evening she and Uncle Charlie dined in solitary state in the kitchen, and the butler didn't take much persuading to open a bottle of wine from his master's amply stocked cellars. Although it wasn't one of his better wines, as he hastened to point out. But whether one of the best vintages or not, it certainly mellowed him, and as Pandora had insisted on cooking the meal and she was a very good cook, the evening passed very satisfactorily.

They played chess afterwards and Pandora let her uncle win three times out of four and did it so skilfully that he thought he had genuinely beaten her, so that he was *almost* pleased that she was staying on. She told him something of the progress she was making at London University where she was studying for a degree, hoping to eventually get a job as a librarian, and Uncle Charlie in turn told her how he found life at Abbot's Arbory. He wasn't usually so loquacious and in such a good mood, so Pandora let him ramble on, although she couldn't work up much interest in the intricacies of cleaning silver or the trouble he had getting the gardeners to bring the vegetables and fruit he wanted up to the house.

'Of course it will be much better when Mrs Symons, the housekeeper, gets back. What with her being away and Jessop in hospital … '

'Jessop?' Pandora queried.

'He's the man who lives at the East Lodge. He's quite an elderly man, lived on the estate all his life and now just sees to the gate and does a few maintenance jobs round the house.'

'Why is he in hospital?' Pandora carefully placed her knight so that her uncle could take it with his bishop.

He snorted angrily. 'Because a crowd of motorcycling rowdies pushed their way in one night and started to race each other round the park. Jessop called the police. Two of the mares were in foal and Jessop was frightened something would happen to them, so he tried to stop the cyclists himself.' His face darkened. 'One of them knocked him down with his motorbike and he broke his leg.'

Pandora stared at him appalled. 'So that was why he was so angry with me! Why he aimed a gun at me.'

Her uncle smiled triumphantly as he took her knight. 'Who, Sir James? I'm not surprised. I've never seen him so angry as that night. He didn't know anything about it until he got back quite a few hours later, and then he insisted on going off to the hospital there and then to see how Jessop was, and then he went down to the police station and created merry hell until he was sure that every last one of the gang had been rounded up.' He took another drink of his second bottle of wine and added, 'Personally I think he would have been pleased if he could have taken the law into his own hands and taught those punks a lesson they wouldn't forget in a hurry. He could have done it too.'

Pandora remembered Sir James' broad shoulders, and the way he had squared up to her so menacingly, and shivered. 'Yes, I'm quite sure he could,' she murmured feelingly.

She played rather abstractedly after that and her uncle really did win the game, but when he proposed another she refused, saying that she was tired. She helped him to clear up and then said goodnight and went to her room. She kicked off her shoes, but instead of undressing straightaway, sat on the bed for some time gazing pensively into space, and at length she got up and changed into jeans and a sweater and quietly let herself out of the house.

A bright moon illuminated her way as she walked slowly

through the gardens towards the lake and the park beyond. In the distance an owl hooted in the trees, but apart from that the night was incredibly peaceful, not even a breath of wind to disturb the leaves of the trees. The lake was silver in the moonlight, rippled now and then as a fish came to the surface. Pandora walked down to the edge, her bare feet silent on the springy grass, and stood looking out over the park for some time before she turned and looked back at the house. There was nothing dark or mysterious about the place. Even at night, when it was in complete darkness except for a single light over the entrance door, left on as a welcome for its master, the house looked warm and hospitable in the moonlight, as if she had only to say the word and the doors would open to receive her, the lights blaze out, the rooms fill with music and laughter ...

In the distance a horse neighed, breaking her reverie. Pandora gave herself a mental shake and walked over to sit on a wooden seat that circled the massive trunk of a huge old oak tree. She tucked her feet up under her and looked musingly at the house. It seemed that she had been unjust in her first summing up of the master of Abbot's Arbory. Maybe he wasn't such a tyrant after all, if he had thought that she was yet another member of the original Hell's Angel gang who had put one of his servants in hospital. It was just her bad luck that she had happened along only a few days later and had taken the brunt of his anger. So it seemed that she would have to revise her opinion of him. But strangely she felt an odd reluctance to do so; he was rich, titled, and powerful, one of a group she despised, and it suited her that he should conform to type, to be hard and arrogant. That he should have raised hell because his old servant had been hurt meant that she could no longer fit him neatly into his pigeon-hole. If it had been just his precious horses he had got het up about she could have understood; the English were notorious for the way they cared more about animals than they did about people. No, she would much rather not have known that he had a bona fide reason for threatening her; it cheapened the game she was playing somehow. But once started, of course, there was no way of going back.

She continued to sit there, deep in thought, for some time, and didn't notice the twin points of light gradually increasing in size as a car travelled towards the house, its engine running so quietly that it made no disturbing noise to break the quietness. It was only when it ran slowly over the cattlegrid that Pandora heard it and looked up. No wonder she hadn't heard it before; the car was a gleaming silver-grey Rolls-Royce, its engine running almost silently as it whispered its way over the bridge and pulled up at the foot of the double staircase leading to the entrance. James Arbory got out of the back of the car and then it pulled away again, the chauffeur driving it round to the garage block at the far side of the house.

Pandora stayed where she was, waiting for Sir James to go inside so that she could run back to the house herself, but instead of going in immediately, he looked around and paused to light a cigarette, then put his hands in his pockets as he, too, strolled down towards the lake. Shrinking back into the shadow of the tree, Pandora tried to make herself as small as possible, feeling an overwhelming reluctance to reveal her presence. He strolled down to within only about twenty feet of her, then stopped to lean his elbows on an ornate stonework pillar, one of a pair that stood at the top of some steps leading down to the lake. He leant there comfortably, smoking his cigarette, as if he did it often, and Pandora only then remembered her uncle's warning that Sir James often took a late night walk.

She wondered what he was thinking as he gazed out across the moonlit landscape, every bit of which belonged to him, every stick and stone as far as his eyes could see. Was he revelling in his suzerainty, feeding his arrogant pride with this silent survey of his estate, or was he – she smiled to herself – merely deciding that the grass needed cutting or the lake clearing? Somehow she had never associated such mundane matters with the nobility before.

James Arbory threw down the stub of his cigarette and straightened up. He was wearing a black evening suit that made him seem taller and broader somehow. But perhaps it was just a trick of the moonlight, the same moonlight that darkened the planes of his face giving him a lean, predatory look that was both dangerous and menacing.

No, she had no need to revise her opinion of her master, he was as hard and proud as she had first supposed, fully in control of his environment and ruthless in his determination to keep things that way. A man to be afraid of, not to try to fool with silly games.

He turned and looked straight towards where she sat huddled against the tree for a long moment, almost as if he could see her clearly, which she knew was impossible, but even so she shrank deeper into the darkness. Then he turned abruptly on his heel and strode purposefully back towards the house.

CHAPTER THREE

PANDORA MANAGED to get through the next day without incurring her uncle's wrath and without seeing James Arbory, both because it was Sunday and their employer had gone out for the day, leaving early in the morning, so Uncle Charlie relaxed in a chair with the Sunday paper and magnanimously told her that she could have the rest of the day off after she had done all her chores. It was obvious that he wasn't going to stir an inch to help her, regarding this as a rest day, but Pandora merely laughed, rumpled what little hair he had left on his head so that he bellowed with annoyance and then ran upstairs willingly enough to tidy her employer's bedroom.

Her uncle had shown her what had to be done the day before, but somehow it still seemed strange to walk into someone else's room, to handle their things and see the way they lived. Not that you could tell much of James Arbory's character from his room, really; it was too neat for that, with very few things left lying around to give any clues. Just a pair of jade cufflinks on the dresser which she carefully put away in a drawer, a concert programme thrown into the wastepaper basket. Pandora squinted at it sideways: so James Arbory liked Mozart, did he? Interesting. But apart from that she learnt little about her employer; the furniture, though mostly antique, wasn't overwhelmingly so. The bed, for instance, was a wide, comfortable half-tester and not the huge four-poster with heavy drapes that she had expected, so it wasn't too difficult to make with the clean linen that he insisted on every day – a luxury that made Pandora green with envy. The bathroom, though, was ultra-modern and super-luxurious, with a sunken bath big enough for about three people and containing one of those whirlpool devices that made the water bubble up and froth around you as you sat in it. Pandora was strongly tempted to try it out now that Sir James was safely out of the way, but thought of her uncle's face if he ever found out and contented herself with merely cleaning out the room.

With the rest of the day to herself, Pandora decided to explore the grounds and to go in the direction of the paddocks where she had seen the horses on her first day. From conversation with Uncle Charlie, she had learnt that Abbot's Arbory was fast getting a reputation for itself as a stud farm, a side of the estate that James Arbory had built up since coming into his inheritance five years ago. The weather was dry, but there was quite a strong breeze, so she plaited her hair into one long, thick braid down her back, pushed her feet into a pair of serviceable wellington boots, and put on a tweed jacket over her sweater.

The wind struck cold at first; Pandora turned up her collar and began to stride out towards the stables, but from behind her came the sound of barking and she turned to see the two dogs that had been with James Arbory on the day that he had thrown her off his land. She stood still immediately. Their master might not have recognised her without her leather gear, but the dogs certainly would, *and* they would remember her as someone to whom he had been antagonistic.

They stopped a few yards away, eyeing her warily and growling deep in their throats. They were beautiful dogs and in excellent condition; pointers, working dogs that James Arbory would take on shooting parties with him, and presumably they lived in one of the outhouses, because Pandora hadn't seen them in the house anywhere. She stayed very still and began to talk to them gently, using a soft lilting tone that her father had taught her when she was only a small child. Slowly the dogs' growls died away, their stances became less threatening and their ears came up. Pandora carefully extended a hand towards them and first one and then the other came to sniff at it. She didn't try to hurry them, let them take their time in making up their minds about her, still talking all the time in little more than a soft whisper. At last they began to lick her hand, their smooth long tails wagging in friendship. Then Pandora went down on to her knees to stroke and praise them.

'Good boy. Good dogs.' Still petting them, she searched along their collars for their name tags. 'So you're Thor and you're Odin. Very warlike names for such old softies!' She continued to make a fuss of them for a while, then stood up. The dogs immediately came to her heels, looking up at her expectantly. She laughed. 'Okay, you can come along, but don't blame me if your master finds out and gets mad.'

She set off again on her interrupted walk, playing with the dogs as she went, throwing them sticks and making them leap up to take things from her hand, all three of them enjoying themselves immensely, but at the entrance to the stableyard, which was nearly half a mile from the house, she hesitated, wondering if the dogs were allowed in. 'Sit,' she told them. 'Stay!' And they immediately obeyed, settling themselves down to wait for her.

Pandora went through the arched entranceway topped by a bell tower, and found that the stableyard was a big hollow square with looseboxes all the way round. Most of the boxes had the upper halves of the doors open and several horses were looking out, but all the human activity seemed to be centred in one corner where three men were clustered round the open door of a box with number twelve over it. Curiosity being just one of her besetting sins, Pandora walked over to see what was going on.

The men were so intent on their conversation that they didn't notice her crossing the yard and she had time to obserye them. The eldest of them was about fifty, dressed in a worn but serviceable tweed jacket and riding breeches. His face was tanned and leathery as if he worked in the open air all the time and he spoke with a marked country accent. The features of the man who stood next to him bore a striking resemblance, although the man was much younger, and Pandora guessed that they must be close relatives, probably father and son, but the younger man wore jeans and a thick sweater. The third man she instinctively put in a different class, possibly because his clothes, although just as practical, were better cut, or perhaps it was only because the other two men seemed to defer to him, to listen attentively when he spoke. He was about thirty, tall and fair-haired.

They were discussing a mare that was in foal and all three of them seemed to be anxious about it. Pandora came quietly up behind them and looked over their shoulders into the box. The horse inside was a magnificent Arab mare, a grey, with long mane and tail. She shone with health and good grooming, her head held elegantly high, tossing her mane arrogantly at being disturbed.

'Oh, she's beautiful!'

At Pandora's exclamation they all three turned round to stare at her in surprise. The youngest man gave an appreciative whistle as he looked her over, but it was the elder who said suspiciously, 'And who might you be, miss?'

For a moment she was in a quandary, wondering what to say, then thought she had better stick to the diminution of her name that her uncle had saddled her with. 'I'm Dora Smith. I'm the new maid.'

This admission immediately settled her place in the hierarchy and the older man said brusquely, 'Then you shouldn't be here. Your place is up at the house. Unless Sir James sent you?'

'No, he didn't send me. I just wanted to see the horses.'

'Then be off with you. This is a stud, not a riding stable. We don't allow people to stroll around whenever they feel like it.'

Both of the younger men came to her rescue, talking at once.

'She isn't doing any harm, Dad.'

'I'm quite sure Sir James wouldn't object.'

And the third man won as as he went on firmly, drowning

out the other, 'One visitor hardly represents a flood, Mr Langley, and I'm sure it can do no harm to let her look round. He smiled at Pandora. 'I'm Jonathan Thursby, the local vet. And this is Mr Langley, the stud manager, and his son Tom.'

Pandora smiled at them all, her green eyes warm and friendly. 'How do you do. I'm sorry if I interrupted you when you were busy.' She turned the full brilliance of her eyes on Mr Langley, who seemed to be the only one in opposition. 'I didn't mean to intrude. The horses looked so lovely in the field, I just wanted to see them closer to.'

'Well ... ' He hesitated.

'Go on, Dad,' his son urged. 'I'll take her round and see she doesn't do any harm.'

'Or I've got half an hour to spare if you need Tom for something,' Jonathan Thursby put in smoothly, receiving a stabbing look from Tom for the suggestion.

'Well ... ' Mr Langley demurred again, then looked into Pandora's face, her eyes wide and wistful. 'Oh, all right, as it's Sunday and we're not very busy at the moment. But it's only for just this once, mind,' he added, wagging his finger at her.

'Oh, *thank* you, Mr Langley. You are kind. Where shall we start?'

In the end they all three took her round; Mr Langley enjoying showing off his charges as much as the others enjoyed escorting her. Several of the horses were mares brought to be covered by the Arab stallions at stud, but there were also some younger horses coming along and some mares that were owned by the stud itself. They ended up back at the box where the grey mare was in foal.

'What's her name?' Pandora asked as she admiringly stroked the mare's nose.

'Greymist,' Jonathan Thursby told her. 'We're taking extra special care of her. She's a very important lady. Sir James bought her in to improve the blood line and this will be her first foal, so we're all hoping it will be successful.'

'Is there any danger?'

'Not really.' He too came to stroke the mare's neck. 'But mares are always nervous the first time. Especially sensitive beauties like this.'

The tour ended, Pandora thanked Mr Langley and his son warmly and turned to leave, but the older man surprised her by saying rather gruffly, 'As you're here, lass, you might as well come over to the house and meet Tom's mother. I expect she'll have a cup of tea on the go.'

Tom's face broke into a big grin and Jonathan Thursby's eyebrows rose at the suggestion. 'You're honoured, Dora. Not many people get invited to Mr Langley's on such a short acquaintance.'

Pandora smiled warmly. 'I know I am, and I'd love to accept, but the dogs followed me here and I've left them sitting by the gate all this time and I just can't leave them any longer, poor things.'

Tom Langley frowned. 'Dogs? You don't mean Sir James' pointers?'

'Yes, that's right. Thor and Odin.'

They all looked at her in astonishment.

'Well, I'll be—' Mr Langley exclaimed. 'I've never known those dogs to take to anyone but Sir James.' He chuckled. 'The last maid they had up at the house was scared to death of them. But don't worry about bringing them, I expect the wife can find them a titbit or two.'

Whether the invitation had included him or not wasn't quite clear, but Jonathan Thursby tagged along all the same, blandly ignoring Tom's offer not to keep him if he was busy. Mrs Langley was a buxom, friendly woman who had herself once been a parlourmaid at the big house, and Pandora spent a very pleasant hour drinking first tea and then Mrs Langley's home-made gooseberry wine and eating freshly baked scones, still hot from the oven and dripping with butter and strawberry jam.

She learnt a lot about Abbot's Arbory in that hour and quite a bit about Sir James, as Mrs Langley had known him since he was born.

'The estate had run down quite a bit before he inherited,' the older woman confided. 'That was because his father, Sir Edward, that was, had been ill for a long time, but not so bad that he'd hand over completely to his son, as he should have done. But Sir James has done wonders since he took over – built up the farm and repaired all the houses on the estate and in the village that he owns, as well as turning the stables into a stud. Worked all hours of the day, he did, when he first took over, what with putting the estate and the house to rights as well as seeing to all his business interests in London. Did very well, he did, in business, by all accounts. He put all his energy into that, you see, when his father was alive and when he wasn't allowed to help with the estate.'

This began to sound intriguing, but unfortunately Mr Langley overheard and told his wife off for letting her tongue run away with her. Pandora took this as a hint and stood up to go.

'I really must be getting back to the house now or Mr Richardson will think I've got lost or something. Thank you so much, I've enjoyed myself immensely.'

Mrs Langley escorted her to the door. 'You must come again some time.' She didn't exactly say it, but the expressive look on her face said clearly, some time when the men aren't here and we can have a good gossip.

Jonathan Thursby took his leave at the same time and walked along beside her, Thor and Odin at her heels.

'Do you know this part of the country at all?' he asked her.

Pandora shook her head. 'No, I've never been here before.'

'In that case perhaps you'd like to come on my rounds with me one day. I get to cover quite a large area on my different calls, and as you're so good with animals it would probably interest you to see something of my work.'

'That's very kind of you, Mr Thursby,' Pandora began, 'but ... '

'The name's Jon,' he broke in with a grin. 'When you call me Mr Thursby it makes you sound like a customer who owes me money.'

Pandora laughed. 'Okay – Jon.' She smiled at him, liking his typically English good looks and the open friendliness of his manner. 'I'd like to go with you, but as yet I'm a very new maid, in fact I only started properly yesterday, so it might be difficult to arrange.'

'You must get a day off at least.'

'Yes, but I haven't really got round to discussing it with the butler yet. I might have to fit it round whether Sir James is entertaining guests or not. I'm not really sure; I haven't had a job like this before,' she confessed.

'Well, Sir James will make sure you get your share of time off. He's always very fair with his staff. If you like I'll ask him to let you have a day off during the week.'

'Oh, no,' Pandora said hastily. 'I'd much rather work it out with the butler.' He nodded and after a moment she said, 'Do you know him that well, then? Sir James, I mean.'

'Quite well. Mainly through my job, of course. But we're both members of the cricket club and on the board of the local P.D.S.A., that sort of thing.'

They reached his car and he offered to give her a lift back to the house, but Pandora steadfastly refused, merely shaking hands as she said goodbye and then turning to walk back towards the house, the dogs ranging along beside her.

Monday was a busy day, starting with the arrival early in the morning of the three dailies who were all women from the village. They were nice enough, but privately Pandora christened them the three witches, because every time they came together they gossiped inexhaustibly in their broad dialect so that there always seemed to be a babble of noise rising and falling wherever they went. What they thought of Pandora she didn't know, because as soon as they heard that she was from London they treated her as a foreigner, as unlike themselves as someone from Peking or Timbuctoo.

Luckily her duties didn't overlap with theirs too much and she was able to go about her tasks without getting in their way, although Uncle Charlie twice had to tell her off for whistling as she worked. 'Young ladies don't whistle,' he reproved her. 'And Sir James certainly wouldn't like it if he heard it. Here, take this clean laundry up to that big linen cupboard near Sir James' room. And walk up the stairs, don't run up them two at a time!' he admonished her.

'Okay, Uncle Charlie, will do.' She gave him a mock salute and marched out of the kitchen with the pile of linen in her arms as if she was on parade. Her uncle gave a groaning sigh and raised his eyes heavenwards.

Pandora reached the linen cupboard without whistling, running, or dropping the sheets, which she thought was pretty good, considering, and carefully laid the bed linen and towels out on the old oak shelves that smelt of the lavender of a hundred summers. Closing the door, she turned to go back to the kitchen, but noticed that the door of a bedroom further down the corridor was ajar. Thinking that one of the cleaners had left it open, she went to shut it, but couldn't resist looking inside first as this wasn't one of the rooms that her uncle had shown her over. She took one glance at the four-poster bed inside and went in for a closer look.

It was a very feminine room; the hangings on the four-poster were in soft creamy lace and the walls painted a pale pink with a deep-piled carpet in a darker matching tone. A three-mirrored dressing table stood near the windows and there was another, full-length mirror over in the corner. Definitely a woman's room! She crossed over to the big wardrobe and opened it. There were some clothes inside and her eyebrows rose as she went through them: a fashionable tweed jacket and matching skirt, a sophisticated evening dress, a bathrobe, a pair of riding breeches, and, last of all, a slinky black nightdress that couldn't have left a lot to the imagination. All good clothes and in a size not much larger than Pandora's own. In the bottom of the wardrobe there was also a pair of riding boots, and a pair of high-heeled fluffy mules, again in black to match the nightdress, presumably. Pandora stood back to contemplate these for a moment, then pulled out the drawers of the dresser where there were a couple of sweaters and some delicate lacy underwear, the sort that look made out of nothing but cost a fortune. Pandora thought of her own much laundered undies and shut the drawer firmly. On the dressing table there was a bottle of French perfume and some make-up, and she found a few other feminine cosmetics, bath oil and that kind of thing, in the adjoining bathroom.

It seemed that Sir James had a guest, someone fairly young and fashionable, going by the clothes, who came to stay frequently but only for short visits, often enough to lay claim to the room but not long enough to leave any more permanent belongings other than clothes. No photographs or books, for example. Intriguing. Pandora took a last look round the room, trying to guess who the woman could be and what she would look like.

Back in the kitchen she found Uncle Charlie fussing around trying to do three jobs at once.

'Sir James has just phoned to say that he's bringing two guests to lunch. He said anything would do, but I know he'll expect at least a four-course meal. Where's that gardener with the vegetables? I told him I wanted them right away. Oh, and there's the wine still to be brought up from the cellars. And you'll have to set the table, Pandora.'

Pandora looked at him in some amusement, then took pity on him and firmly took the basin he was holding out of his hands. 'Uncle, why don't *I* cook the lunch while you see to the wine and the table? What were you going to use all these eggs for – omelettes? I thought so.' She gently shooed him out of her way and he went willingly enough, raising only a half-hearted protest.

Left to herself, Pandora happily set about preparing the meal – but without the omelettes. She much enjoyed cooking and had taken several specialised courses in the past, mainly so that she could get a job as a chalet hostess in Switzerland during the winter holidays, which she had done for the last two years. When she was about fourteen she had even contemplated taking up cookery as a career, but she had too much intelligence and curiosity to want to be tied to a kitchen all her working life and she had decided instead to go on to university.

The gardener, an elderly man and inclined to be surly, eventually turned up with the vegetables, but after Pandora had sat him down, given him a bottle of beer and got him talking about his beloved gardens, he mellowed quite a bit and confided that 'that there townie butler' didn't know a thing about the difficulties a gardener faced and kept expecting him to supply out-of-season fruit and vegetables 'as if I were a magician with a wand and a top 'at'.

Pandora sympathised with him, gave him another beer and suggested he bring what vegetables he had up to the house every morning and she would adapt her menus accordingly. When he left he called her 'a right good lass' and she rather thought she had made a friend for life.

Uncle Charlie served Sir James and his guests with home-made mushroom soup, grilled trout with almonds, and chicken in wine sauce followed by a strawberry flan and cream. Nothing really elaborate because Pandora hadn't had the time, but when her uncle came down into the kitchen at the end of the meal he graciously informed her that her new employer had sent his compliments. Spoiling the effect rather by adding, 'So you might as well take over the cooking while you're here. At least you don't seem accident-prone in the kitchen.' And Pandora realised she had lumbered herself with another job.

While they were eating their own lunch she said casually, 'Has Sir James got any sisters?'

'Sisters? No, he's an only child.'

'No female relatives at all?' Pandora persisted.

'Only an aunt who comes over to act as hostess whenever he has a hunt ball or a really big house-party. I expect she'll be coming over next month for the Rose Ball.'

Pandora was instantly diverted. 'The Rose Ball – what's that?'

'It's a tradition here,' her uncle explained. 'A ball is held every year when the roses are in bloom. It goes back to when

Charles II was restored to the throne and he came here to thank the contemporary owner of Abbot's Arbory for supporting him in the war against Cromwell's Roundheads. A ball was given for him then and has been held ever since.'

The idea was enchanting and Pandora let her imagination run riot for several minutes as she pictured the original ball with the Merry Monarch and his court here in their gorgeous costumes, dancing in the rooms and gardens, lit by candles and moonlight, the women vying for the King's attention. But this thought brought her mind back to the present and she asked, 'This aunt – how old is she?'

'Lady Townley? Oh, she must be about sixty, I should think. Why?'

'Oh, nothing really,' Pandora answered, trying to sound casual. 'It's just that I saw some women's clothes in one of the bedrooms and I wondered if Sir James had a relative who came to stay.'

'Hmph – those!' Her uncle sniffed rather disdainfully. 'Those belong to Miss Marsden.'

'Who's she?'

'Just a friend of Sir James',' he replied repressively.

'What kind of friend?'

'She has an antique shop in Oxford and Sir James buys pieces from her now and again.'

'You'd think he had enough of them already,' Pandora remarked, remembering the amount of dusting she had to do. 'Is she a close friend?'

'Who?'

'This Miss Marsden you're telling me about.'

'I'm not telling you about her,' her uncle retorted in some annoyance. 'It's you who keeps asking about her.' He tried to change the subject. 'Pour me out another cup of coffee, would you? And then you can put the rest of the dirty crockery in the dishwasher.'

But Pandora poured out two cups of coffee instead of one and sat down opposite him again. 'Well, how close a friend is she?'

He stirred his coffee resignedly. 'I believe they've known each other for years.'

'That doesn't tell me how close they are. I've known several people for years and we're not close friends.'

'That hardly surprises me,' her uncle replied at his most repressive.

Pandora chuckled. 'Come on, Uncle Charlie, spill the beans! Is this Miss Marsden Sir James' mistress?'

He choked on his coffee so that Pandora had to leap up and bang him on the back.

'All right! I'm all right.' He looked at her indignantly. 'Really! The young these days have absolutely no sense of decorum. Why, in my day ... ' He broke off when he saw the look on her face. 'Fancy asking me a question like that! How would I know? I don't go around prying into Sir James' personal life.'

'Oh, come on,' Pandora said persuasively. 'Servants always know everything there is to know about their employers.'

Exasperatedly her uncle said, 'Well, even if I did I certainly wouldn't discuss such a subject with you, young lady, because it's definitely none of your business.'

'Which means that she is his mistress,' said Pandora with some satisfaction. 'What's her first name?'

Automatically he answered, 'Cynthia.' Then in real anger, he added forcefully, 'And now I forbid you to say another word about it. Do you hear me, Pandora? You are not to mention the matter again.'

Having got all the information she wanted out of him, Pandora took the wind out of his sails by saying meekly, 'Very well, Uncle. I won't tell anyone you told me,' and gurgled with suppressed laughter at the expression of surprise and consternation on his face.

But it was Pandora's turn for consternation later that day when her uncle came down into the kitchen after serving dinner and said, 'Sir James has said that you can go into Oxford tomorrow and get yourself a new uniform. You're to meet him in the front hall promptly at nine-thirty.'

Pandora looked at him in surprise. 'What do you mean – meet him in the front hall?'

'Sir James has to go into Oxford himself tomorrow to attend a meeting and he says you can drive in with him.'

'But I don't want to drive there with him, I'd rather go on my motorbike,' Pandora wailed.

'Well, you can hardly tell him that, can you?'

'No, I suppose not.' Pandora looked at him dejectedly. 'And I was looking forward to going to Oxford, too. I've never been there before.'

'Well, you won't have to spend the whole day with him. Only the hour's drive there and back,' Uncle Charlie pointed out reasonably.

But the thought of even two hours in Sir James' company somehow filled her with foreboding and took all the pleasure and anticipation out of the trip. It also kept her awake part of the night, her biggest fear being that during two hours her phoney accent might slip and he would find her out, but by the next morning she had hit upon a way round the difficulty and was waiting for him in the hall on the dot of nine-thirty, dressed in one of her own jumpers and skirts and a navy blue mac left over from her schooldays.

Sir James, too, was prompt. He was wearing a dark business suit and carrying a briefcase, which somehow made him seem more intimidating than in his country tweeds. Perhaps it was because it gave a cleaner line to the hardness of his jaw, sharpened his already lean features. His grey eyes under the slightly arched brows ran over her as she stood beside her uncle.

'Good morning, Dora.'

She didn't answer but fell in behind him as Uncle Charlie opened the door and he went down the steps to the waiting Rolls.

He nodded to the chauffeur who was holding the back door open for him. 'It's all right, Travers, I'll drive myself today.'

'Very good, sir.' The chauffeur sprang to open the driver's door instead and Pandora took the opportunity to dive like a squirrel into the back seat. Sir James looked round for her, his eyebrows rising slightly as he saw that she was already in, but he made no comment, merely starting the softly purring engine and setting off down the drive.

Pandora looked back at the house as they drove away, loving this view of the mansion set among its parkland with the sun glistening on the lake; watched until the trees hid it from view. The Lodge gates were already open, a boy standing by them, and they swept through and turned to the right, away from the village and in a direction Pandora hadn't travelled before. Ordinarily she would have been looking through the windows at the perfect Cotswold scenery of long, undulating hills and picturesque villages, but she had never been in a Rolls-Royce before and was busily taking in all the luxurious fittings. The upholstery was in the softest leather, the seats deep and comfortable and there was a console built into the armrest near her hand with several buttons to operate all the electronic gadgets in the car. Pandora peered at them: windows, air-conditioning, heater, radio, television, bar, telephone. Her eyebrows rose at the last three and she would dearly have loved to press the buttons, but didn't dare. Her fingers stroked the smooth upholstery; impossible not to be impressed with such luxury, but then she thought how much it had cost and how many tractors could be bought for poor farmers in third world countries for that money to help them produce food for the starving, and she was filled with an impotent stab of rage. How *could* one man have so much when hundreds of thousands had nothing at all? She gazed out of the window at the fields rich with crops, the houses with gardens full of vegetables and fruit trees, the shops bursting with goods, and her heart filled with bewilderment and anger at the apparent inability of the world's leaders to set the balance right.

She was so consumed by her own thoughts that she didn't notice that Sir James had pulled in to the side of the road and had stopped the car. He turned towards her, his arm along the back of the seat, a slight smile on his lips, but his expression changed when he saw the unhappiness on her face and he frowned.

'Is something the matter, Dora?'

The sound of his voice made her jump and brought her rudely back to the present. She stared at him for a moment and then shook her head.

'Then come and sit in the front with me.' It wasn't a suggestion but a definite order.

She shook her head again. 'Mr Richardson said as how I was to sit in the back,' she replied hoarsely.

'But I'm telling you to come and sit in the front.'

For a moment longer she gazed at him, wondering how she could get out of it, then reluctantly opened the door and walked round to sit beside him, carefully not looking at him directly.

He looked at her quizzically for a moment, then leant towards her.

Pandora immediately flinched away, but he merely said, 'I'm only going to do your safety strap up for you,' and reached past her to pull the strap down and clip it into place. Then he drew back, but continued to look at her. 'You're not afraid of me, are you, Dora?'

Her eyes flew to his face, to see the slight look of amusement still there, then quickly away again. She shook her head dumbly.

'Good. You certainly weren't before.'

He waited for a moment, but when she didn't answer, her face still averted, he frowned slightly, then turned away to start the car again. 'I hear you went over to the stables on Sunday,' he remarked.

Now who told him *that*? Pandora wondered, but he went on, 'Do you like horses?'

When she didn't answer straightaway he glanced towards her and she nodded assent.

'Then maybe I'll arrange for you to have riding lessons. Would you like that?'

Riding lessons – for a maid? Who did he think he was kidding? Firmly she shook her head.

He frowned, then brought the car to a stop again. 'What's the matter, Dora, cat got your tongue? You're not usually so reticent.'

'I got a sore throat,' she lied hoarsely.

He was immediately all concern. 'Richardson should have told me. But how lucky that we're on our way to Oxford; my doctor has a practice there and we can easily go there first so that he can take a look at you.'

A look of alarm came into Pandora's eyes and she chokily muttered something about 'throat lozenges' and 'be all right'.

But James Arbory said firmly, 'No, I must insist that you see a doctor. Sore throats can often be the first sign of something far worse. Pneumonia, for instance,' he added mendaciously.

Pandora looked at him balefully, hating him. 'It ain't as

bad as that,' she was forced to admit in something approaching her normal voice.

'Good, then you'll be able to talk to me, won't you? Now, you like horses but you don't want to learn to ride, is that right?'

'Yes, Sir James,' she agreed woodenly; no point in telling him that her father, who had been a pilot officer in the R.A.F. before his early death in a plane crash, had taught her to ride almost as soon as she could walk.

'You just like to look at them, is that it?'

'Yes, Sir James,' she agreed, her face expressionless.

An exasperated look came into his eyes. 'Dora, I shall become extremely angry with you in a minute. Why are you being so formal?'

Reluctantly she turned to look at him. Still in her broad Cockney accent she answered, 'Mr Richardson told me off. 'E said I was always to call you Sir James and only speak when I was spoken to.'

'Did he, indeed? And did he also say that you were only to answer yes or no?'

Pandora decided to blame her poor uncle even further. ''E told me to keep me mouth shut as much as I could, 'cos I don't talk proper.'

To her surprise, instead of laughing his face softened. 'So you pretended to have a sore throat so that you wouldn't have to speak to me?' He hesitated, then, 'Are you ashamed of the way you speak, Dora? Because if so I might be able to do something to help you. Elocution lessons, for example.'

So now he saw himself as Professor Higgins to her Eliza

Doolittle, did he? Well, she would squash that idea on the head straightaway. 'No,' she retorted defiantly, 'why should I be ashamed? Just because I don't talk posh like you. I talk the same as all me mates in London, and if you don't like it you can always gimme the sack. They didn't tell me at the agency that I 'ad to speak wiv a plum in me mouth for this job.'

'No more you do.' James Arbory looked at her steadily for a moment, then smiled suddenly. 'And I much prefer your Cockney naturalness to that po-faced formality you tried earlier.'

Which statement so surprised her that she could only stare at him as he sat back with a chuckle and started the car again.

For the rest of the journey he talked to her about Oxford, it turning out that he had been to university there and knew the town well, and she managed to keep up her pretence of ignorance, resisting his attempts to draw her into conversation, although it was sometimes difficult to remember as she longed to ask him about the Bodleian Library and the history of the colleges, when all he told her about was the shops and trivialities about the town. But then she supposed he was talking down to her because he thought that was her level of intelligence – as if not speaking the same way as he did meant that you also lacked a brain! A thought that made Pandora's blood boil so that she was heartily glad when he pulled into a car park at the side of a large hotel.

He took a card from his wallet. 'The shop you want is just off the High Street. Here, I'll write the name and address on the back of my card.' He handed it to her. 'Show them this and tell them to charge the things to my account. Then come back and meet me here at one o'clock.' With a slight smile he added, 'Think you can remember all that?'

Pandora looked at him bleakly: even a complete fool could remember that! But she merely said coldly, 'Yes, Sir James.'

His eyes flicked up to her face and his voice hardened. 'Good. Then don't be late. I dislike being kept waiting.'

Pandora hurried along to the shop, one which specialised in 'domestic attire' as they termed it and had models in the windows wearing a chef's outfit and a chauffeur's uniform. Production of Sir James' card assured her of immediate service, but she took no pleasure in trying on the new uniform and surprised the assistants by the speed in which she made up her mind and completed her purchases. Within half an hour she was out of the shop and into the sunshine, eager to make the most of the little time she had left to explore the town.

For a couple of hours she wandered happily round the streets and the parts of the colleges that were open to the public, but a glance at her watch told her that it was almost one already and she turned regretfully to make her way back to the car park, promising herself a much longer visit on her next day off.

James Arbory was waiting for her at the entrance to the car park, but to her surprise he led her not back to the car, but to the entrance to the hotel.

Seeing her puzzled look, he said, 'I thought we might have lunch here. You can leave your parcel with your coat in the cloakroom.'

Pandora looked round the marble-pillared foyer, busy with richly-dressed people, and through the door to the restaurant, all hurrying waiters, snowy-white cloths and deep plush carpet. Then she remembered her own shabby skirt and sweater and for a moment her heart failed her. She opened her mouth to say, 'But I can't ... ' then looked into her employer's face and the words died away. He was regarding her steadily, his left eyebrow slightly raised and a distinct challenge in his eyes. Pandora's chin came up defiantly, mentally picking up his gauntlet. So he thought she was afraid, did he? Well, she'd show him that she was as good as all those toffee-nosed snobs any day! And maybe she'd make him sorry into the bargain. So she said quite loudly, 'I'll go and 'ang me coat up, then.'

But for all her bravado, in the cloakroom Pandora took care to comb her hair into some sort of order and apply her lipstick carefully. She looked ruefully at the skirt and jumper, and sighed – if she'd only known that he was going to take her out to lunch. Then she shrugged; not that it would have made any difference if he had told her, she still wouldn't have had any suitable clothes to wear. She just wasn't in the habit of being taken out to lunch in posh restaurants by wealthy baronets. Lifting her head, she regarded her reflection in the mirror thoughtfully, wondering if the rich baronet in question was in the habit of taking his maids out to lunch. Somehow she rather thought not. 'Which means, my girl,' she told her mirrored image, 'that you'd better watch it. The man is obviously trying to turn your head so that he can achieve his evil intentions.' And she leered at herself in the glass, so that the woman in the fur jacket standing next to her stared at her in astonishment, then hurriedly picked up her belongings and almost ran out of the cloakroom, which made Pandora double up with laughter.

It seemed that Sir James was well known at the hotel, for the head waiter greeted him by name and himself led them to a discreetly placed table in an alcove with a big window overlooking the river. An underling placed a menu in her hands and her eyebrows rose at the exotic choice of dishes, none of which had the prices by them, she noticed. Did that make the clientele so rich that they didn't care how much they paid? Why, you could probably feed a whole African or Indian village for the cost of one meal here!

Her indignant thoughts were interrupted as Sir James said smoothly, 'Perhaps you'd like me to choose for you, Dora. The veal here is excellent.'

Veal! Trust these bloated plutocrats to eat the flesh of poor, newly-born calves! Her eyes sparking, she said distinctly, 'No, thank you. I would like soup followed by a salad.'

His eyes came up quickly to her face, an arrested look in them, and she realised that she had forgotten her phoney accent. Quickly she tried to retrieve the slip by adding, 'I ain't very 'ungry.'

He nodded and turned to the waiter to give the order, waving away the wine list as he asked for a certain vintage with which he was obviously familiar.

Turning to face her, Sir James sat back in his chair, his dark eyes watching her contemplatively. 'You know, Dora,' he said slowly, 'you're rather an enigma.'

She returned his look warily. So he wanted to play verbal

games, did he? Well, she could serve a few aces herself. Opening her eyes wide, she replied, 'Oh, no, I ain't. I'm a Londoner. I was born in 'Ackney.'

A quick gleam of laughter came into his eyes but was immediately suppressed as he said gravely, 'I'm sure that Hackney was a very good place to be born in, but that wasn't quite what I meant. An enigma means something or someone that is mysterious and puzzling, has hidden depths.'

Pandora picked up her fork and made patterns with it on the crisp whiteness of the tablecloth. 'And why do you think I'm one of these enigma things? There's nothin' mysterious about me.'

'Isn't there? I rather think there is.'

She looked at him uneasily, not liking the turn the conversation had taken. Had he seen through her already?

Without waiting for her to answer, James Arbory went on, 'This is the twentieth century, Dora. Girls who look like you don't usually become domestic servants. They try to get into modelling or acting, often via beauty contests. And if they don't succeed there or don't have that much ambition, they at least try for a more interesting or glamorous job – such as an air stewardess or something similar. Haven't you ever tried for something like that? Or ever wanted to?'

Pandora returned his look angrily. What a typical male chauvinist attitude! Just because a girl had a decent face and figure men thought she ought to be in a job where looks were all that mattered. It never occurred to them that there might be a brain behind a pretty face and that a girl might want more out of her work than just showing herself off until she got too old and crabby to be employable. And personally she would hate such a career; the everlasting fight to keep yourself looking young, the backbiting and spitefulness of other girls fighting for the few jobs there were, having to look glamorous all the time and to be pleasant and smiling even when you felt like death. No, thank you very much, that kind of life certainly wasn't for her. She wanted something with a challenge, where she could use her intelligence and work on her own initiative, to have a career that would last her through life and she could always fall back on, no matter what.

Shortly she answered, 'No. I'm all right as I am,' and glared at him rather defiantly.

His eyes held hers for a long moment, then he said abruptly, 'How old are you, Dora?'

'I'm twenty,' she returned automatically, but had little time to wonder why he had asked because the waiter came up with their first course, making a welcome interruption.

She concentrated on eating her soup, feeling uneasy and wishing that the meal would soon be over, but Sir James took his time over his avocado stuffed with prawns and insisted that she try the glass of wine that the waiter had poured out for her. Pandora sipped it gingerly at first but with growing appreciation; it was far superior to the supermarket plonk that was the usual drink her college friends managed to afford whenever there was some sort of event to be celebrated, usually birthdays or the passing of an exam.

While she waited for him to finish, Pandora looked around

her at the other diners. There were only a few couples like themselves, mostly there were trios or quartets of women, gossiping about their shopping, or of men on what were obviously prolonged and expensive business lunches. And all on their expense accounts, Pandora thought cynically. She watched one man push his plate away, the large steak on it only half eaten, a woman try a mouthful of gateau, decide she didn't like it and call the waiter over to replace it with something else.

Turning to Sir James she said abruptly, 'What happens to all the waste?'

He looked startled. 'I beg your pardon?'

'The waste food,' Pandora said impatiently. 'What happens to it?'

His eyebrows rose. 'I have no idea.'

'No, I don't suppse you have,' Pandora retorted, much incensed. 'You rich people are all the same. You couldn't care less about the other half of the world. They can all starve to death for all you care! Just look at the food that's being wasted in this room. Why don't the people just take enough for what they want instead of being so greedy? And look at them – they're nearly all so fat that it would do them good to eat less. Heaven help them if they had to spend a week on what the people in the third world countries had to live on. Perhaps that would make them appreciate what they've got,' she added heatedly.

'I'm sure it would.' The words were said mildly enough, but it made Pandora glance at her host sharply. She found him watching her closely, the arrested look back in his eyes, an amused twist to the corner of his mouth. She flushed and looked away, taking a long drink of her wine, aware that her tongue had run away with her.

He leaned forward and filled her glass again. 'Are you a Communist, Dora?' he asked calmly.

'No, of course I'm not.' She looked away, playing with the stem of her glass.

'But you believe that the earth's products should be shared out more fairly?'

'Yes, I do.' Her head came up and she looked at him defiantly. 'And I believe that the land should be shared out too. I think it's wrong that only one per cent of the people should own ninety per cent of the country.'

'So you think that estates like Abbot's Arbory should be parcelled up and given away to people to use as allotments, do you?' James Arbory asked drily.

A waiter unobtrusively put the next course in front of them, but Pandora hardly noticed. 'Something along those lines, yes. Not necessarily allotments, of course – it would have to be worked out properly – but it's totally unfair that one person should have so much when others are crowded together in high-rise flats or grotty little houses without even a garden for the children to play in.'

'So you think the house should be pulled down and a housing estate built there, do you?'

That made Pandora pause. She thought for a minute and then shook her head. 'No, it's too beautiful for that. It ought to be preserved, but it ought to be shared. Why, you don't even open it to the public.'

His voice hardening, he said, 'Maybe that's because I believe that everyone has a certain right to privacy. Abbot's Arbory is my home. Would you like people tramping through your home? Going through your rooms and gaping at your most cherished possessions, things that have been treasured by your family and lovingly handed down from generation to generation?' His voice grew angry. 'Would you like to have massive car and coach parks where there was once a garden, public lavatories in the stables, ticket booths and souvenir stalls by the lodge gates and boat rides on the lake? Is that how you'd like to see Abbot's Arbory? Is it?'

Pandora stared at him, taken aback by his vehemence. It had never occurred to her to look at it from the owner's point of view before, and, having come to love the house, even though she had only been there for a few days, she could understand now what an anathema the idea must be to him who loved it so much more. Haltingly she said, 'I'm – I'm sorry. I hadn't thought of it like that before.'

'No. Not you or the countless others who want to nationalise the land, wrest it from those who've nurtured and cultivated it through the ages. The system of land ownership has evolved because it's right for the country and for farming. If it was parcelled up as you envisage we wouldn't produce half the crops and the country would go under in less than a decade.'

He took a long drink of his wine and looked at her consideringly, his eyes narrowed. 'And I suppose you also think that all people are equal?'

Pandora looked at him indignantly. 'Yes, of course I do.'

'Well, you're wrong, Dora, because they're not. It so happens that ... '

But Pandora interrupted him before he could go on. 'Oh, I *know* that,' she said sarcastically. 'In a capitalist society there are always inequalities of class and wealth. People who inherit money and property will always see themselves as being superior to those who have to work for it.'

His mouth set into a thin line at her implied rudeness. 'There is also the basic inequality of being born either with a natural talent or without one. Clever or stupid. No matter how much you try to argue against it, Dora, we are not born equal. All man can ever strive for is the equality of opportunity for those who have the ability to make the most of it. There are always those who will succeed and those who have no ambition or ability who will fall by the wayside.'

'But you can't deny that those who have money have far more opportunity than those who haven't?'

'Not entirely, no. But I believe that a person with brain enough can go as high as he wishes.' He paused, then said more gently, 'What you want will come, Dora, but it will take time. And the last thing we want is a revolution to try and hurry it along.'

He regarded her steadily for a long moment, until Pandora looked away, feeling confused by his arguments; her ideas that had been so clearcut before now seemed childish and immature.

For a few minutes they ate in silence, then James Arbory said, 'Dora, if you believe that all people are equal, then presumably you think that no one should be subservient to another, right?'

Pandora looked at him cautiously, wondering where he was leading. 'Yes, basically,' she admitted.

He leaned forward, his eyes holding hers. 'In that case why did you choose to become my servant?'

CHAPTER FOUR

PANDORA STARED at Sir James speechlessly for a long moment that seemed to go on for ever, completely trapped by his question. He watched her intently, his eyebrows raised quizzically as he waited for her answer.

'Well, I – I … ' she floundered, unable to think of anything that would satisfy him, then gave a gasp of relief as the waiter came up to ask if they would like a dessert.

James Arbory sat back in his seat, a wry smile on his lips when he saw that she had escaped answering. 'Would you like anything else?'

She shook her head. 'No, thank you.'

He glanced at his watch. 'Then I think we might as well leave.'

He paid the bill while Pandora got her coat, and this time he made no objection when she determinedly got in the back seat, quite unable to face another argument with him. Or any kind of conversation, come to that. She had the uneasy conviction that he was the type of man you could never argue with, who would always shoot down your opinions in flames and leave you feeling like a first-form schoolgirl. So she sat alone in the back, still smarting and thinking over what he had said, and it wasn't until they had gone several miles that it suddenly occurred to her that in the heat of the argument she had completely forgotten her phoney accent and had spoken in her normal voice!

Now what was she going to do? Pandora stared malevolently at the back of his head, his dark, well-cut hair just touching his collar. Impossible to hope that he might not have noticed, so why hadn't he said something at the time? Because he was involved in their argument and didn't want to be sidetracked? Because he didn't think it worth mentioning? Or – and this she didn't like at all – because he had already seen through her and it came as no surprise? She stirred uneasily in her seat, angry with herself for having got carried away, and wondering if James Arbory would pick her up on it. No, not if, when. Because somehow she was quite sure that no way would he let her off scot free.

When they reached the house she muttered a hasty thank you and almost ran into the house clutching her parcel, scuttling past Uncle Charlie, who gave her a startled look as he hurried forward to open the car door for Sir James. Later he asked her how she had got on, but she merely told him that she had wandered round Oxford, feeling strangely reluctant to tell him that she had actually lunched with their employer. He had very definite ideas about the line drawn between master and servants and certainly wouldn't have approved, and it would only have raised added complications that Pandora could well do without.

For the next week or so she managed to avoid meeting Sir James, making sure that he was out of the way when she tidied the rooms he used and dodging back to the kitchen by the back stairs when he returned to the house. He was out to lunch most of the time, but she continued to cook his breakfast and evening meal which her uncle served as usual, but several times he passed on a message of appreciation for her cooking.

During the afternoons Uncle Charlie gave her a couple of hours off and she loved to explore the gardens, walking between the long banks of rhododendron bushes, their red, mauve and purple flowers a blaze of colour in the still summer air, or exploring the summer-house on the edge of the lake and spending lazy hours on the seat there, the book on her lap neglected as she watched bright blue dragonflies darting over the lilypads and waited, hardly daring to bréathe, as a heron flew down and patiently looked for a fish to pluck from the water. But mostly she was drawn to the paddocks where she would sit on a fence and watch the horses as they frolicked in the fields, enthralled by their beauty and gracefulness, and to the stables where Mr Langley, to the surprise of everyone, let her help to groom one or two of the less valuable horses under his careful supervision. She enjoyed this immensely and grew fond of all the horses, but her favourite was Greymist, for whom she always had some lumps of sugar purloined from the kitchen and who soon got to know her and would come to the stable door with a whicker of expectant welcome, nuzzling her hands as Pandora stroked her and nudging her until she got the sugar lumps.

'You'll spoil that horse,' Tom Langley told her, coming up to lean against the wall and watch. 'She's really taken to you, though. Usually she's nervous of people. Aren't you, lass?' He reached up to stroke her head, but the mare shied away and went back into the stable. 'There, you see. She doesn't want to know me.'

Pandora laughed. 'Maybe you don't speak to her properly. You have to tell horses how beautiful they are, you know. Flatter them until they eat out of your hand.'

'Is that the trick?' He looked at her, his eyes openly admiring her slim figure in blue denim dungarees, and said in a clumsy attempt at wit, 'I'll have to start flattering you, then. I wouldn't mind having you eating out of my hand.'

'Oh, but I'm not a horse,' Pandora returned lightly. 'And I'd see through flattery straightaway.'

She went to turn aside, but Tom put his arm against the wall, barring her way. 'Flattery or not, you're still a good-looking bird. How about coming to the cinema with me tonight?'

'Thanks, but I have to cook dinner for Sir James,' she replied shortly, and turned the other way, intending to walk away from him.

But Tom swiftly put out his other arm so that she was trapped between them, leaning against the wall. 'So come down to the pub for a drink when you've finished, then. It doesn't take you all night to cook and clear up, does it?'

Pandora looked up at him in some annoyance; she supposed he was nice enough, but she didn't like the way he was trying to throw his weight around, putting on this he-man act in an attempt to either impress or coerce her. She opened her mouth to reject his suggestion, but as she did so he leaned forward to try to kiss her. Angrily she lifted her hands to his chest to try to push him away.

Then from behind Tom a crisp voice said, 'I believe I asked for a horse to be saddled for me at three o'clock,' and Pandora looked over Tom's shoulder to see James Arbory watching them with a disdainful frown on his face. Tom sprang away from her guiltily and Pandora flushed, realising how it must have looked to him.

'I'll get the horse for you now, sir.'

Tom rushed off towards the tack room and left her facing Sir James. For a moment their eyes met and held, then Pandora quickly turned away and hurried through the nearby arch leading out of the stables. As she did so she heard him call her name, but she pretended not to hear and kept on going, feeling completely unable to face him again.

She didn't stop until she got to the house where she sought solace in the library, out of breath from hurrying and feeling strangely agitated. She sank down on a comfortable red leather chesterfield and looked around her at the room which had soon become her favourite of the whole house. It was circular in shape and two storeys high, with three long windows in the south-facing wall so that sunlight streamed in all day long, lighting the rows of bookshelves and the gallery above, again lined with books. It was a room that didn't seem to get used very much and Pandora often sneaked in here for an hour or so after Uncle Charlie had gone to bed, to gaze with awe at some of the titles and to handle with reverent care one or two early editions of famous works. She would dearly have loved to take a book to her room to read, but was so overwhelmed by the rarity of most of the works that she didn't dare in case they should get marked, so she contented herself by just looking at the rarer editions and reading those books which were already well thumbed and which would be difficult to find in an ordinary library, often becoming so engrossed in a book that she stayed curled up in the chesterfield until the early hours of the morning.

But right now she wasn't interested in reading, only in the peaceful atmosphere of the room. Moodily she wandered over to the window and looked out, angry with herself for having got upset. What did it matter what interpretation Sir James had put on that nasty little scene with Tom, and why did she feel so guilty even when she hadn't been doing anything? But strangely enough it did matter; she hadn't liked that cold, disdainful expression on his face when he had looked at her, she had felt an overwhelming urge to blurt out that it was none of her doing, that she had been trying to push Tom away, not return his embrace. But she hadn't, and she was glad. What the hell had it got to do with James Arbory if she wanted to flirt with Tom, or any other man, for that matter? He could frown as much as he liked, but it certainly wouldn't stop her from doing exactly as she liked in her free time. But then she remembered his anger and forcefulness when she had first met him, and she knew that she could never stand up to that sort of sheer animal menace again. A movement in the park caught her eyes and she looked up to see Sir James astride a big black stallion trotting away from the stables. He glanced towards the house and Pandora instinctively drew back, even though he could hardly have seen her from that distance, gripping the curtain, her hand going to her throat as if she found it difficult to breathe.

That evening her uncle brought her another message from Sir James. 'He wants to hold a dinner party on Wednesday of next week and told me to ask you if you feel capable of taking on the cooking. It's for eight people, including himself. He says if you don't feel up to it he will quite understand and get a chef from Oxford in as he usually does.'

Pandora looked at her uncle undecidedly. 'I don't know. What do you think?'

He shrugged. 'It's up to you, my dear. But you seem very capable to me.' He patted his stomach appreciatively. 'In fact I'd say you were almost as good as the chef from Oxford, and certainly a lot better than Mrs Symons, the housekeeper, who's done it once or twice when the chef hasn't been available.'

Pandora considered the idea a moment longer, then nodded. 'All right, I'll do it. Eight people isn't too many and I can always have at least one cold course which I can prepare beforehand.'

In fact she found it a challenge and began to take pleasure in working out the menu and ordering the ingredients to be sent out from a luxury store in Oxford. And even though she wouldn't admit it, she thoroughly enjoyed having the opportunity to use exotic and expensive foods that she had never been able to afford to cook before. Existence as a student meant ekeing out one's grant on the very cheapest of meals, and good food only came your way if you were lucky enough to have a rich boy-friend to pick up the tab occasionally.

'Who's coming to this dinner party anyway?' Pandora asked her uncle one morning just after the delivery from Oxford.

'Apart from Lady Townley, I have no idea,' he replied, picking at a fat bunch of grapes.

Pandora smacked his hand. 'Leave those alone, I need them. Who's Lady Townley?'

'I told you, Sir James' aunt. She always stays the night when she comes, so we'll have to get her room ready for her.' He paused to examine a carton of cream, then said, 'Though I'm surprised she's coming to such a small dinner party, and in the middle of the week. She usually only comes at weekends.'

The day before the dinner party, Uncle Charlie took her menu up to show Sir James and after a while he came back with the list of the wines he was to get from the cellar to go with it. There were almost as many types of wine as there were courses, and after running her eye over it Pandora decided that it wouldn't matter if the dessert turned out to be a hopeless failure anyway, because the guests would be too drunk to notice after getting through that little lot.

What with doing the cooking, helping to clean the silver and wash the best crockery, preparing Lady Townley's room, as well as all her usual jobs, Pandora had no time at all to feel nervous, and as she had been taught to be methodical she had everything well organised and actually had time to arrange the flowers that the gardener had sent up on the afternoon of the party. While she was doing so the door bell rang and Uncle Charlie poked his head through the doorway of the scullery.

'That will be Lady Townley. You'll have to come up with me, Pandora, and take her things up to her room.'

Hastily she took off the coverall she had been wearing and ran up the steps behind him and through the swing door into the entrance hall. As she did so Sir James was hurrying down the last of the stairs and she almost cannoned into him. He put out a hand to steady her, catching hold of her arm. Pandora felt the strength of his fingers through her sleeve, glanced up into his face, muttered a suddenly breathless apology and hastily pulled herself free of his grip.

Uncle Charlie had opened the door and Sir James moved forward to greet his aunt, but Pandora looked at the newcomer unseeingly for a few seconds until she heard Sir James say, 'And this is Dora, our new maid,' and she blinked and was able to focus again.

She found herself being regarded by a pair of lively blue eyes set in a rather lived-in face, a face whose owner enjoyed life to the full and didn't mind getting older and showing it. The eyes twinkled at her suddenly and Lady Townley smiled and nodded as if she had satisfied herself about something. Pandora took her coat and small suitcase up to her room and unpacked for her while Uncle Charlie served her and Sir James tea in the drawing room. Pandora smiled as she hung up the older woman's evening dress, an elegantly simple creation in grey silk; somehow she had the idea that Lady Townley was far happier in the country tweeds and serviceable shoes that she had arrived in rather than this. She glanced round the room at the freshly polished furniture and the vases of flowers, glad that she had taken extra pains to make the room welcoming, for there was something about Lady Townley that had made Pandora take an instant liking for her.

The same instinct that had prompted her to take a liking to Lady Townley made Pandora take an immediate dislike to another of the guests later that evening. She was again standing in the hall with Uncle Charlie wearing her new black evening uniform dress and little lace cap on her head, waiting to take the women's wraps when they arrived and show them to the cloakroom if necessary, and all the time worrying in case the cleaning woman from the village, who had come in to help for the evening, did something stupid and ruined the main course that Pandora had left simmering on the cooker. The first guests to arrive were two middle-aged married couples who had travelled together, and Pandora had hardly finished hanging up their coats before another car drew up and Uncle Charlie ushered in Jonathan Thursby, the local vet she had met at the stables. He smiled and came straight over to her.

'Hello again. I was hoping to see you tonight. You haven't found life in the country too boring yet, then?'

Pandora smiled warmly back. 'No, I'm liking it more than ever.'

'Good. Have you found out which day you're free yet? That's if you'd really like to come on my rounds with me, of course.'

Pandora hesitated for a second and then nodded. 'Yes, I would. Very much. And I'm free tomorrow, as a matter of fact.'

'Fine. Well, I have my morning surgery to do first, but I'm usually finished with that by ten-thirty. Suppose I pick you up about eleven, will that be okay?'

'Yes, that will be fine.'

'I'll look forward to seeing you, then.'

He smiled at her again, and then both of them became aware of a new arrival. They turned towards the doorway and found the last of the guests regarding them. It was a woman of about twenty-seven, tall and slimly elegant in a close-fitting black evening dress, her blonde hair cut fashionably short in a sleek head-hugging style, her face cleverly made up to accentuate her eyes and cheekbones. She was attractive, sophisticated and elegant – and she had the coldest eyes Pandora had ever seen.

Coolly she said, 'Hello, Jon, how lovely to see you,' and held out a hand to him so that he had to leave Pandora and go and shake it, but the woman's eyes never left Pandora's face.

'Hello, Cynthia. How are you?'

Pandora's eyes quickened with interest. So this was Cynthia Marsden, Sir James' mistress. Yes, she went with the clothes that she had proprietorially left in the closet upstairs. And she was the right type to be the mistress of a rich baronet – or to be his wife for that matter. Was there a marriage pending? she wondered. Or was Sir James the type who wouldn't marry when he could get what he wanted without it – or even *because* he could get what he wanted without it? Impossible to say one way or the other. At one time it was clear cut; a man just didn't marry his mistress, but nowadays it was an accepted fact that couples slept together before marriage, if they bothered to get married at all, but surely someone in Sir James' position ...

'Are you going to stand there staring all night, girl?'

Pandora hurried forward to take the mink stole that Cynthia Marsden thrust at her, although she had given no sign of waiting before.

'I'm so sorry.'

The older girl sniffed disdainfully. 'Really, servants these days are absolutely useless!' She turned and put a hand on Jon Thursby's arm. 'Where on earth did James dig that stupid little creature up from?' Then she smiled up at him. 'I haven't seen you for ages. You must be sure to tell me all about your pigs and cows and things.'

Uncle Charlie opened the door into the drawing room for them and they walked in together. Through the doorway Pandora saw Sir James look round and step forward to greet them. Immediately Cynthia let go of Jon's arm and stretched out her hands to her host, lifting up a laughing, glowing face for his kiss.

Pandora took the stole into the cloakroom and threw it viciously on to a chair. Trust that type of woman to have *real* fur, she wouldn't care how many poor little minks had to be killed just so that she could show off with her precious stole! She glared at it resentfully for a moment, then suddenly remembered the dinner and went running back to the kitchen with visions of disaster.

All was well, however, and the meal went without a hitch from the hors d'oeuvres to the home-made mints and stuffed dates. Afterwards she and Uncle Charlie more or less collapsed into a couple of chairs while their helper put the last of the pots and pans into the dishwasher and then went home.

'I think we deserve a drink,' he remarked, and poured her out a generous glass of the wine left over from the dinner party.

'Phew, I'm glad that's over. Are we finished now?'

'I'll have to go up to the drawing room again soon and replenish their drinks and then show them out when they leave.'

'What about Lady Townley, will she want anything?'

'She doesn't usually. She's very good and always tries to give as little trouble as possible.' Her uncle looked at her benignly and gave, for him, fulsome praise. 'You've worked hard the last couple of days and you did quite well tonight. If you're tired why don't you go on to bed; I'll get the women's wraps for them when they leave.'

'Thanks, but I think it's the heat in here and working over the stove as much as anything. I'll go and get some fresh air for a while.'

'All right, but they may not leave until the early hours of the morning and there's no point in us both sitting up.'

Pandora plonked him an affectionate kiss on the top of his head and went out through the yard and into the formal gardens at the front of the house. The sound of music and laughter came from the open windows of the drawing room and Pandora moved nearer the terrace so that she could see in. A record on the turntable was providing the background music while some of the guests sat around talking. At first she couldn't see Sir James and one of the couples, but then a light came on in the long gallery and she guessed that he was showing them round the house. Cynthia Marsden was sitting on a settee talking rather languidly with Jon Thursby, and Pandora wondered wryly if he was telling her about his 'pigs and cows and things'.

For an instant she felt a stab of something very like jealousy that she should be on the outside looking in and not a member of the party. But then she shrugged; such a staid party was hardly her thing, she and her friends at college were into disco dancing and all-night rock concerts at the moment. A dinner like tonight's was a parent-type non-event among her crowd. But even so her face was a little wistful as she continued to watch until Sir James and the remaining guests returned to the room. Cynthia Marsden, who had been looking openly bored, immediately became animated, looking up at Jon and laughing at something he had said, then she turned to her lover and held out her glass to him, but when he came to take it from her, got to her feet and stood close beside him, her arm through his. Just as if she owned him, Pandora thought cynically. Abruptly she turned away, feeling suddenly cold. How could a man let himself be used like that? She certainly hadn't expected Sir James to be the type who would let a woman walk all over him. But she supposed that men in love did silly things; even in her young life she had had boy-friends who had turned from being nice, sensible people into moody, besotted idiots when they thought they were in love with her.

She shivered in the chill air and hurried back to the house, but although she was tired she felt too restless to sleep and decided to go to the library to find herself something to read. Sir James seemed to have finished his tour of the house, and the library was far enough from the drawing room not to have any of the guests wandering in there. Her intention had been to find a comparatively modern novel that she could take back to her room to read, but as usual she couldn't resist examining some of the older books with their leather bindings and gold lettering, the pages often speckled brown with age. She ran her fingers lightly across the shelves, thinking that someone really ought to catalogue all these books and make sure that the more valuable ones were preserved from any damp that might be in the air. A very old-looking book caught her eyes, the title almost faded away, and she carefully drew it from its place. To her delight she found that it was a very early copy of Chaucer's *Troilus and Criseyde* and written in old English too.

Reverently Pandora carried her find to the chesterfield and made herself comfortable in its roomy depths, kicking off her shoes because her feet ached. For a couple of hours she read with avid enjoyment, but the beautiful old language was heavy going in places and gradually her head began to nod and she had to blink hard to keep awake. She yawned tiredly, but no way was she going to stop reading yet; she would lie in tomorrow on her day off. She read a few more pages but started to nod again. Perhaps if she just closed her eyes and rested them for a few minutes ...

Something touched her face gently and she stirred, feeling cramped and cold. Slowly she opened her eyes. James Arbory was standing by the settee, looking down at her. Pandora blinked and hastily sat up, her book sliding off her lap down among the cushions of the chesterfield. Feeling totally confused, she reverted to her Cockney accent and said, 'Oh, I – I must've dropped off.' Hastily she got to her feet.

'Do you make a habit of coming in here in the evenings, Dora?' he asked, his eyes noting her confusion.

'Oh, no, Sir James,' she lied, not wanting him to forbid her to use the room. 'I was just tidying up an' that, but I felt that tired, so I put me feet up for five minutes and must've gone off sound.'

'I see.' His expression was quite enigmatical, but somehow Pandora felt extremely uncomfortable, as if she was a mouse being played with by a cat.

'Can – can I go now, sir?'

'In a moment.' He moved to lean his shoulder against the high fireplace of white marble. For a moment he was silent, his expression unreadable, then he said surprisingly, 'Are you happy at Abbot's Arbory, Dora?'

'Oh yes. Yes, thank you.'

'And you think you'll stay with us for some time?'

She hesitated, knowing that she would be here only for the summer, but there was no point in telling him that. 'Yeah, I 'spose so,' she agreed.

'Good.' He straightened up and Pandora instinctively took a step backwards, but he seemed not to notice as he went on, 'I had intended to see you tomorrow to thank you for the way you cooked the meal tonight. It was faultless and everyone enjoyed it. You are to be congratulated.'

'Oh. Ta ever so,' she muttered awkwardly, hoping that he had finished and she would be able to leave.

But instead he went on, 'You must have had a great deal

of practice to cook as well as that. Where did you learn?'

'I went to evening classes for a couple of years,' Pandora replied, glad to be able to be truthful for once.

'And have you never thought of taking up cooking for a living? There must be many opportunities.'

'No, I – I wouldn't want to be stuck in a kitchen all the time.' She looked at him pleadingly. 'I'm glad you enjoyed me cookin', but can I go now, sir? I'm really ever so tired.'

'Yes, of course. Goodnight, Dora.'

'G'night, sir.'

She hurried from the room and down the corridor towards the servants' quarters, and it wasn't until the tiled floors struck cold to her feet that she remembered that she had left her shoes in the library. Well, never mind, she could get them in the morning. But then she remembered the copy of Chaucer she had been reading and stopped, appalled that she could have treated a valuable book in such a way. Why, the pages might get bent or even come away from the backing if she left it there all night. Damn! It was all Sir James' fault. Why did he have to come to the library at this hour of night? He should have been safely tucked up in bed with the glamorous Cynthia by now.

Looking at her watch, she decided to give Sir James twenty minutes in which to leave the library and go to his room, or whoever's room he was going to, and then she would slip back to the library and replace the book and collect her shoes. The time passed with intolerable slowness, but at last the twenty minutes were up and Pandora made her way back, her bare feet making no noise on the oak floor. Softly she turned the handle and pushing the door open stepped into the room. Then stopped abruptly. Sir James was still there, standing by the fireplace with a book in his hands, slowly turning the pages. It was the copy of *Troilus and Criseyde* that she had been reading!

He looked up from the book. With cold firmness he said, 'Yes, Dora, I think you'd better come in – and shut the door behind you.'

CHAPTER FIVE

SLOWLY PANDORA obeyed. She opened her mouth to speak, but Sir James cut in, 'And please don't insult my intelligence again by using that phoney accent. You're not a good enough actress to keep it up indefinitely.'

She flushed; he certainly wasn't pulling his punches. But she said calmly enough, 'I forgot my shoes.'

He glanced down at her feet, then his eyes came back to her face, probing. 'And I don't think that's all you forgot, was it?'

It took a great effort of will not to look at the book in his hands, but she managed to keep her eyes on his face as she tried to bluff it out and answered, 'No, there was only my shoes.'

His mouth thinned. 'And this? I suppose you just happened to pick it up.'

'That old book? I must have been dusting it when I ... ' Her voice trailed away as she saw his eyes narrow and a dangerous glint come into them.

'Yes,' he said softly, menacingly, 'it's much wiser of you not to try to lie to me. I don't like little girls who tell lies, and you're as bad at that as you are at keeping up a common accent.' He put the book down carefully on a side table and took a couple of steps towards her. 'I think you owe me an explanation. You're no common little ignoramus, Dora, so why the big act?'

Pandora hesitated, wondering how much she could manage to hide from him. One thing was certain, though, whatever she said she mustn't implicate Uncle Charlie. But maybe she was a better actress than Sir James surmised. So she opened her eyes wide and said rather tremblingly, 'I'm sorry if I've deceived you, Sir James, but you see I really only wanted a job for the summer, but I went to several agencies and they all said they only had permanent vacancies and said I was more suited to office work. But I ... '

'Just a moment,' James Arbory interrupted. 'Why did you only want a summer job?'

'Well, because ... as a matter of fact I'm a student and I just needed to work until the end of my vacation.'

'I thought as much,' he said on a note of satisfaction. 'I knew that voice could never go with that face.'

Pandora blinked, then went on hurriedly, 'But I wanted to work in the country and I needed a live-in job, so I – well, I'm afraid I lied and said I was free to take on a long-term position, and I used the Cockney accent because they all seemed to think I ought to do office work. But as soon as I spoke like that I got this domestic job at once.'

She looked at him hopefully, wondering if she had got away with it, and to her relief she saw a look of amusement on his face.

'I see. Very enterprising.' He put his hands in the pockets of his black evening suit and moved nearer to sit on the edge of a big mahogany desk. 'So you're a student. Where?'

'At London University.'

'And what are you studying?'

Reluctantly she answered, 'For my B.A. I hope to become a librarian.'

His left eyebrow rose in surprise. 'So that's why you were looking at the Chaucer. Can you read it?'

Pandora's chin came up. 'Yes, I can read it.'

A mocking look came into his eyes. 'Brains, beauty and cooking too. Is there no end to your talents, Dora?'

Two bright spots of colour came into her cheeks and she said uncertainly, 'You just said I was a terrible actress.'

'Oh, yes.' The mockery deepened. 'But sometimes that can be a distinct advantage.'

'It – it can?' Pandora found that she was stammering, her pulses racing.

'Mm. Especially at moments like this.' Unhurriedly he straightened up and took his hands from his pockets. Then he moved to stand close to her and almost casually put his hand on her waist and drew her towards him. His arms went round her and for a moment he looked down into her face, her green eyes wide and startled. 'Yes, definitely at moments like this,' he murmured softly, then bent to kiss her.

His mouth was firm and hard against hers, his lips insinuating as they explored her mouth with little kisses that promised but didn't satisfy. Pandora's mouth moved under his. She tried to pull away, gasping, 'No! No, please,' but his hand came up to coil itself in her hair and he forced her head back. His mouth became more demanding and suddenly Pandora's head started to whirl. She felt the strangest sensations; as if the room was spinning round and she was sinking down, down into a deep whirlpool. She gave a little moan, her mouth opening. His lips moved against hers, sensuous, exploring. Desire grew deep inside her, slowly at first but then with gathering momentum, until she was filled with longing, an aching need for fulfilment. She wanted to move closer to him, to put her arms round his neck and to return his kiss, to let passion take over. But some instinct for self-preservation held her back and she stood still in his arms, not fighting him but not returning his embrace.

At last he lifted his head and Pandora slowly opened her eyes. He was looking down at her quizzically, awaiting her reaction. She fought to regain her composure, but even so her voice was still unsteady as she said coldly, 'Do you always take advantage of your female servants?'

The ghost of a smile curved his lips. 'Only when they're as young and as incredibly lovely as you.'

Pandora felt the colour heighten in her cheeks. How on earth did she reply to such fulsome flattery as that? Abruptly she pulled away from him. 'Let go of me!'

Unhurriedly he took his hands away, watching her with the same quirk to his lips, as if he found the whole thing extremely amusing. Anger filled her and she said scathingly, 'You're about three hundred years out of date, aren't you? The droit du seigneur thing went out with the Middle Ages. Or hadn't you heard? Nowadays people don't have to put up with that sort of treatment.'

The amused curve deepened. 'So what are you going to do about it?'

Pandora's fists clenched at her sides. 'Leave, of course,' she answered shortly.

James Arbory put his hand on her neck and gently caressed her throat with his thumb. Pandora's heart began to race and it took every ounce of strength she had not to tremble at his touch. 'No, you won't leave,' he said softly.

She tried to open her mouth, to say that she would, but his fingers burned into her skin and somehow the words stuck in her throat.

A little gleam of triumph came into his eyes, and he moved a little nearer to her. 'No,' he repeated, 'you won't leave, Dora, because you want this as much as I do,' and he drew her unresistingly close to kiss her again.

This time when he let her go she kept her head lowered, reluctant to look at him and see that light of triumph again in his eyes. For a few moments he didn't speak, then he said rather thickly, 'You'll stay?'

Slowly, reluctantly, she nodded.

His hand gripped her shoulder suddenly, hurting her as he stared down at her bent head. Then he let go abruptly. His voice suddenly harsh, James Arbory said, 'What a child you are!' He stepped away from her towards the fireplace, reaching up a hand to grip the mantelshelf. For a long moment he looked at her moodily, then he gave an impatient sort of shrug and said, 'You must be tired, why don't you go to bed?'

His sudden change of mood threw her and for a moment Pandora could only stare at him, then she hurriedly bent to pick up her shoes and slip them on. She gave him a last quick glance, but he was gazing down into the empty fireplace, a frown between his brows, so she turned and hurried to the door, closing it gently behind her before running down the long corridors to her room, running as if all the devils in hell were behind her.

But the sanctuary of her room provided little peace of mind; she realised that by submitting to James Arbory's masculine domination, even so little as she had, she had made an absolute fool of herself. The only sensible thing to do now would be to leave first thing in the morning, before anyone was about. She could leave a note for Uncle Charlie with some excuse, say a friend had found her a job—anything! Anything, so long as she got away from Abbot's Arbory and away from its master! She shivered, knowing that if she stayed here a minute longer than necessary she would be placing herself even deeper under his domination. Pandora had been kissed many times by various boy-friends, but never before had her senses been so immediately stirred, her emotions roused so that she was in danger of losing control. The moment he had begun to kiss her she had found herself wanting to submit to a sexual mastery that had almost overwhelmed her, only the strongest effort of will making her hold back from surrendering herself to him completely.

Feverishly she picked up a pen and scrabbled round in her bag for a piece of paper. She got as far as writing 'Dear Uncle Charlie,' and then stopped, the pen poised over the paper. Slowly she put it down and sank down on to the bed. It was no good, Sir James had been right all along; she had wanted him to kiss her—and more, much more than that. She shivered again uncontrollably. Even though she had resisted him, he had known that she was his. It had been like an electric shock running through her, making every nerve in her body tingle and come alive, and she could no more run away from a man who was capable of rousing her like that than she could swim the Channel or fly to the moon. She was on terribly dangerous ground and she knew it, there was every chance of getting her fingers badly burned, but she just *had* to stay, even if only to see whether she had the strength of mind to resist him completely when he tried it again. And that he would try to seduce her again, Pandora was quite, quite certain.

Jonathan Thursby called for her promptly at eleven the next morning. He was driving a blue estate car that had a metal grille between the back seats and the boot. 'In case I ever have to transport any tigers back to the surgery,' he told her jokingly as he helped her into the passenger seat.

'Our first stop had better be to check on Greymist, I think,' he said as he joined her in the car.

'Why, is something wrong with her?'

'No, but I like to keep my eye on her, so as I'm here I thought I'd drop in.'

They walked together into the stableyard and across to Greymist's box. The mare whickered with pleasure and blew softly down her nostrils as Pandora stroked her head.

Jon laughed. 'I see you've made a conquest. It's obviously the feminine touch that does it. I'd ask you to hold her head for me while I look her over, but I've an idea Mr Langley would have a fit if I did.' He looked around. 'I'd better go and find him; he really shouldn't leave the stables unattended like this. These are valuable horses.'

He walked off towards Mr Langley's house and Pandora slipped Greymist the lumps of sugar she had brought with her. 'Yes, you're a beauty, aren't you?' she cooed to the horse as it tossed its mane. 'But it doesn't matter how haughtily you behave, you know I'll always bring ... '

'Dora.'

Her heart lurched and she jumped so much that the horse shied away nervously. Pulses racing crazily, she turned to face the speaker, but then gave a little gasp of relief as she saw that it was only Tom Langley.

'Oh, you – you startled me!'

'I've been up to the house looking for you, but Mr Richardson said it was your day off and that you'd gone out. The way he said it I thought he meant you'd gone right away from the estate. I didn't realise you'd only come over here to look for me. We must have missed each other on the way.'

Pandora shook her head. 'I didn't come to see you, Tom, I only came to ... '

He came up to her, a cocky grin on his face. 'Come off it, you don't really think I believe that line about coming to see the horses, do you?'

'Why not? It's true,' Pandora replied, looking at him steadily.

For a moment he looked disconcerted, but then his natural vanity reasserted itself and he said, 'You don't have to play games; I'm not the type who thinks a girl's cheap just because she encourages a man. Why waste time pretending to be a prude when we could *really* be getting to know one another?'

Pandora looked at him exasperatedly; how on earth did you get through a king-sized ego like that? She supposed he was a little older than she, about twenty-two or three, and he was quite good-looking except that his hair was too long and greasy and there were pockmarks on his cheeks. Not that he could help that, of course, but he smelt of horses and he didn't clean his nails properly. Pandora guessed that he was one of the local young bucks and probably had all the girls in the village trailing after him, so that he was able to pick and choose. And he now expected her to be the same, to fall into his lap when he crooked his little finger. Pandora smiled mirthlessly to herself; like master, like man. Did all the men in the country see themselves as God's gift to town girls? Well, this one at least she definitely could resist.

Coldly she answered, 'Mr Thursby is here. He's gone to find your father.'

Tom swore. 'What the hell does he want to do that for? Now I'll get into a row for leaving the stables.' He started to hurry towards the house. 'Thanks for giving me the tip, Dora. I'll thank you properly some other time.' He winked at her and went to pat her bottom as he passed, but Pandora moved adroitly out of the way.

He came back about five minutes later with Jon and his father, and it was obvious from their conversation that he had lied his way out of trouble. He gave her a triumphant wink which Pandora ignored, trying to show him by her attitude that she disliked him, but somehow she had a feeling that she was just wasting her time.

Jon looked the mare over while Mr Langley held her head, and pronounced himself well satisfied.

'She's doing fine. As long as she doesn't get frightened or upset so that the foal comes prematurely, she'll be all right.' He turned to smile at Pandora. 'So let's get on our way, shall we?' He put a hand under her elbow and nodded to Mr Langley. 'I'll call again in a few days' time, but if you're at all worried about her in the meantime give me a ring, day or night.'

He led Pandora towards his waiting car and she saw with some satisfaction the indignant look on Tom Langley's face. Perhaps *now* he would get the message.

Their next stop was at a farm where Jon had to examine a couple of cows in a field near the farmhouse. Pandora sat on a gate and watched until the farmer's wife, unable to curb her curiosity any longer, came to ask her in for a cup of tea and tried to find out who she was and what her relationship was to Jon. Pandora evaded the questions as best she could without being downright rude, but was glad when Jon came in and she could jump up and signal urgently with her eyebrows at him not to accept the cup of tea he was offered.

He washed his hands and then joined her in the car. 'What was all that about?' he asked as he drove away.

'That woman at the farm; she kept asking me all sorts of questions.'

'What about?'

'About me, and – well, about you *and* me, if you see what I mean.'

Jon grinned. 'Oh, sure, I see all right. Sorry, I suppose I should have thought of that. I've never taken a girl with me on my rounds before, you see.'

'So I gathered,' Pandora returned drily. 'That woman wouldn't happen to be the local gossip by any chance, would she?' And when Jon nodded rather shamefacedly, she groaned and added, 'And now I suppose it will be all over the area that I'm your girl-friend or something.'

He glanced across at her. 'Would you mind that much?'

His tone was casual enough, but there was something in his voice that stopped Pandora from laughing as she had been about to and instead answer lightly, 'It wouldn't be true, would it?'

'But it could quite easily be, if you wanted it.'

She sat silently for a long moment, then said slowly, 'Jon, we've only just met and I – quite honestly I don't know what I want. So, please, don't let's get involved, okay?'

He smiled ruefully. 'Okay. I always was the slow, plodding type anyway.'

Pandora laughed at him. 'I'm sure you're not. Where are we going next?'

'To visit an old-age pensioner in a village a couple of miles farther on. He's got something wrong with his dog.'

They continued on the round with Pandora helping where she could and she found it intensely interesting, but there were times, particularly when they were driving from place to place, when she fell silent and became absorbed in her own thoughts. Jon looked at her, wondering if he were the cause, and would have been chagrined if he had known that they were not of him but of James Arbory. Again and again she went back to that scene in the library last night, remembering the way he had kissed her, the pressure of his mouth on hers, the heat that had seared through her body like a flame. She stirred in her seat, lips parted softly, her eyes far away – only coming back to an awareness of her surroundings again when she realised that Jon had pulled up and was looking at her searchingly.

'Dora? Are you all right?'

She flushed, acutely embarrassed and said hastily, 'Yes, I'm fine, really. It's just that – oh, nothing. I was just thinking about my job, wondering whether I'll stay there.'

His eyebrows rose. 'Aren't you happy?'

Pandora shrugged. 'I don't think it's my scene.'

He smiled at her choice of words, but then became serious as he reached out and took her hand. 'Well, I hope you do decide to stay, Dora, very much. Especially as we've just started to get to know one another.'

Looking up at him, Pandora felt suddenly ashamed; he was so open and friendly that her masquerade seemed cheap and childish. Impulsively she covered his hand with her other one and said, 'Look, Jon, I'm afraid I haven't been altogether straight with you. I never intended to stay at Abbot's Arbory later than September anyway. You see, I'm a student and I just wanted a job for the summer, but I couldn't very well tell Sir James that when he employed me. And my name isn't Dora, it's Pandora.'

Jon looked at her in some astonishment, then said, 'But why, if you went to so much trouble to get the job, think of leaving when you've only been there two or three weeks?'

'Because yesterday I had to tell Sir James the truth. He – he may not want me to stay now.'

'I see.' He thought for a minute and then said, 'Well, look, if he does decide to get rid of you, I can always use an assistant in my practice; looking after the animals at the surgery and that kind of thing. And as you seem to have such a way with animals I'm sure you'd be good at the job, and enjoy it too.'

Pandora looked at him gratefully. 'Thanks, Jon, I really appreciate the offer, but I'm sure you don't really need anyone, and I just couldn't impose on your kindness like that.'

'Nonsense, all the animal owners for miles around will come flocking to the surgery with you as a receptionist.'

She smiled but shook her head.

'Well, keep it in mind. The offer stays open as long as you want it.' He leaned forward and lifted her chin to look into her face. 'And I hope you'll accept, because I don't want to lose you as soon as I've found you, Pandora.'

He moved his head nearer as if he was going to kiss her, but she lowered her eyes and turned her head away.

After a moment he took his hand off hers and sat up. In a rather gruff voice, he said, 'Maybe we'd better be going.'

He drove her round to the tradesmen's entrance of the house and cut off her thanks abruptly.

'It was my pleasure. Will you come out with me again?'

She nodded. 'Yes, I'd like to.'

He reached out and gripped her hand. 'And you won't leave without letting me know? Promise me that, Pandora.'

For a moment she hesitated, but the earnest entreaty in his face made her nod, albeit rather reluctantly. 'Yes, all right, I promise.'

'Good. I'll give you a ring later in the week.'

Pandora had to square her shoulders to go into the house, wondering whether Sir James was at home and if he would ring for her on some excuse and try to kiss her again. But most of all she wondered whether this time she would have the strength to resist him.

But almost as soon as she entered the kitchen, Uncle Charlie informed her that their employer was leaving first thing in the morning to travel to Ireland where he hoped to purchase some new stallions and would be away for a week or so. Pandora's first feeling was one of relief, but it was one that didn't last; almost at once she realised that it had only postponed the inevitable and that now she would have to wait in apprehensive suspense for his return.

Life at Abbot's Arbory was quiet with its master away, almost as if the heart and purpose had gone out of it. Pandora and Uncle Charlie were able to get up later and eat at times to suit themselves instead of fitting in around Sir James, and now she didn't have to keep an ear cocked for his footsteps while she was cleaning so that she could slip away and avoid him. She had more free time too, but spent it more in solitary walks round the park with just the dogs for company rather than going to the stables where she would inevitably run into Tom Langley. It was annoying that the pleasure she derived from the horses should be curtailed because of his unwanted attentions, but it was also pleasant to be entirely alone for a while after living at college where there were always people around her all through the day and where she had to share a room with another girl, so that solitude became a thing to be treasured.

But her attempts to rid herself of Tom Langley proved fruitless, for he came every day to seek her out at the house, waiting – much to Uncle Charlie's annoyance – in the kitchen until she put in an appearance, and no amount of hints or even downright rudeness would get rid of him. That he had a crush on her he made evident, and he was always on at her to go out with him to the cinema, or 'the flicks', as he called it. Pandora found no difficulty at all in refusing, but he was convinced that she was only playing hard to get and that he only had to keep on asking for her to eventually give in.

During the following week Pandora had another day out with Jon which she enjoyed, mostly because he was wise enough to keep the conversation to impartial topics and not again mention his liking for her. This time she consented to go back with him to the nearby market town of Broxford where he had his surgery and see the animals that he was caring for personally. Afterwards they sat round a log fire and ate toasted crumpets oozing with butter and drank mugs of cocoa while they listened to some of Jon's collection of classical records. It was fun, and to Pandora held no great importance because that was the kind of thing she and her friends did in each other's rooms all the time. Perhaps to Jon it held more significance, but if it did he was clever enough not to let it show, but the local gossips had a field day. News of her day out with Jon earlier had already gone the rounds, and as it was the kind of small town where everybody knew everyone else's business better than their own, it was soon common knowledge that the new maid at Abbot's Arbory had spent several hours alone with Jon in his house at night and that she must, therefore, be highly immoral.

No one, of course, mentioned this in Jon's hearing, and it never even occurred to Pandora that rumours might be going round about her, but it soon came to Tom Langley's ears and he descended on the kitchen in an indignant rage.

'What's this I hear about you going out with the vet?' he demanded, a scowl on his face.

Pandora looked at him exasperatedly. 'What do you mean?'

'You know darn well what I mean. Do you fancy him or something?'

'Not particularly, no,' Pandora answered as she turned to put some dishes in the cupboard.

'Why go out with him, then?'

'Because I wanted to, of course.' Then she added more placatingly because she didn't want to row, 'It was interesting going on his rounds with him and seeing the type of work a country vet has to do.'

'I could have borrowed my dad's car and taken you for a drive round the country, if that's what you wanted,' he told her belligerently.

'It would hardly be the same,' Pandora pointed out.

'No, it wouldn't, would it?' he returned angrily. 'Don't think I don't know why you went out with him. It's because he's what they call one of the professional classes. You're just trying to get off with him for what you can get out of him. You town girls are all the same – always going for the bloke who'll spend the most money on them.'

'That isn't true!' retorted Pandora indignantly.

'Then why go out with him instead of me, if you don't fancy him?'

'I've already told you ...' she began, but he interrupted her with a derisive snort.

'Yagh, don't give me all that country vet stuff. I wasn't born yesterday, you know. You're just a snob, Dora. You don't think I'm good enough for you, do you? Why go out with the bloke who mucks out the stables when you can go out with the vet?'

'That isn't so at all,' Pandora answered, shocked that he should think such a thing of her when she had always prided herself on her indifference to class distinction.

'Prove it, then. Come out with me as well as Mr Thursby.'

'All right, if that's the only thing that will convince you, I will,' she retorted before she had had time to think, then groaned inwardly as she saw the triumphant grin on his face and realised she had walked straight into his trap.

'Good, we'll go tonight,' he told her, pushing home his victory. 'I'll borrow Dad's car and pick you up at half past six to go to the flicks. There's an *Emmanuelle* film on; you'll like that. And we'll go for a drink after. See, I don't mind how much money I spend on a girl either. And I bet I give you a better time than that snotty vet does, too.' He gave her a cocky wave as he went out of the door. 'See you later, darlin'.'

Pandora grimaced. *Now* what had she let herself in for? But that thrust about her being a snob had cut home. *Was* that why she preferred Jon? She sighed; well, it was too late now, if she tried to get out of it Tom would make life unbearable, so she would just have to endure the evening as best she could.

But right from the start he assumed an arrogant, swaggering manner and bought her a big box of chocolates she didn't want in an attempt to impress her. The film frankly made her blush, but she was too taken up with stopping Tom trying to kiss her and to prevent his hands groping her to give it too much attention. After the film she refused point blank to go to a pub, reckoning that he would be even more difficult to handle after he had had a few drinks, and told him that she wanted to go home. Fortunately, but surprisingly, he didn't argue and they set off back to Abbot's Arbory in silence.

Pandora began to relax, her mind on other things, but came to with a jerk when she realised that Tom had turned the car off the main road into an overgrown lane and pulled into the entrance of a farm track.

He switched off the engine and turned to her with a lascivious grin. '*Now* we can really start to enjoy ourselves. Let's get in the back seat.'

'Wait a minute, Tom Langley. If you think you're going to get anything from me, you're mistaken. So you can just turn this car round and take me home!'

'Aw, come on, Dora, stop playing hard to get. You know you're hot for it.' He reached out to pull her towards him, his hand searching for the buttons of her blouse.

Pandora pushed him violently away. 'For heaven's sake! Doesn't anything get through that thick head of yours? I don't fancy you, Tom. Now leave me alone!'

'Come off it. Everyone knows you're a tart. If you can do it for Jonathan Thursby you can do it for me.' And again he reached for her, catching her wrist and jerking her towards him while his free hand pulled up her skirt.

'Let go of me!' Pandora balled her hand into a fist and punched him in the mouth as he tried to kiss her.

'You bitch! I'll make you pay for that.' He bent her arm back so that she gave a cry of pain and grabbed a handful of her hair, pulling her head up so that she couldn't get away when he put his mouth on hers. Vainly she tried to get free, but he was as strong as one of the horses he cared for, and he was enjoying hurting her when she struggled.

At last Pandora realised that there was only one way she was going to get out of this situation and she suddenly relaxed, pretending to acquiesce and let him kiss her.

'All right, you win,' she told him when he lifted his head. 'We *will* go in the back seat.'

He laughed insolently and squeezed her breast. '*Now* you're talking! I knew you were hot stuff the minute I set eyes on you. And don't worry, I'll satisfy you more than Jonathan Thursby ever could, you'll see.'

He got out of the car and opened the back door, Pandora picking up her bag and following more slowly. Then, as soon as he was inside the car, she slammed the door on her side and began to run down the lane back towards the main road. There was a furious shout and then the sound of heavy footsteps thundering along behind her. Pandora reached the more open main road and turned left in the direction of Arbory Magna, still running as hard as she could and hoping that either Tom would give up or else a car would come along that she could flag down. But there were no cars and he kept on coming, until Pandora realised with sickening dread that he was gaining on her. His outdoor life and manual work probably kept him fit, while a long winter in college had made her out of condition. Her only chance was to hide and hope that he wouldn't find her, so she ran on to the grass verge, looking for a place to hide, although it was difficult to see in the near blackness. But maybe she could use that to help her. Panting heavily, she came to a clump of trees that looked as if there might be more trees behind them, plunged away from the road and ran in between them, trying to make as little noise as possible. After about thirty yards or so she found a tree with fairly low branches and sprang up, swinging herself on to it and then quickly climbing higher among the concealing foliage of the leaves. She sat astride a branch, clinging to the tree trunk, and trying to control the hammering of her heart and her sobbing, gasping breath.

She heard Tom coming into the wood, searching for her, muttering curses as he stumbled over a root. He came nearer and Pandora hardly dared to breathe, biting her lip hard in case he heard her. He paused almost under the tree, listening, and then she realised that she had lost her bag. Her heart froze; had he found it beneath the tree? Was that why he was standing there, looking up into the branches for her?

But then he moved on, cursing again, and soon after he

began to call for her. 'Dora! Stop being so silly. It's all right, you can come out. I'm not going to do anything. If you come out I'll take you home.'

Humph, if she believed that she'd believe anything.

He searched around for her for another ten minutes or so and then he shouted out, 'All right then, damn you! You can stay here all night for all I care! You little slut!' He passed near her tree again on his way back to the road and then she heard him walk along the tarmac surface until his footsteps receded into the distance. Ten minutes later she heard a car go by in the direction of Arbory Magna and gave a sigh of relief, but even so she stayed on her uncomfortable perch for another twenty minutes; it just might have been a different car that had gone by and Tom was still waiting on the road for her to come out.

For this reason, too, when she did climb down Pandora kept among the trees as she walked parallel to the road for another half a mile before venturing on to the better surface. She judged that she must be at least five miles from Abbot's Arbory, and the shoes she was wearing were definitely not designed for five-mile hikes. Still, she supposed she was lucky to have got off so lightly, things could so easily have gone the other way, so she would just have to put up with it and serve her right for having gone out with Tom in the first place.

She had been going for about half a mile when she heard the sound of a car coming up behind her. For a second she felt fear in case it was Tom and looked wildly round for somewhere to hide, but then she realised that this engine was a soft purr in comparison to Tom's rather noisy one, and hopefully put up her thumb in the hope of getting a lift. The car, a big, sleek job, passed by and she turned to walk on with a sigh, but then it came to a sudden stop a few yards down the road.

Pandora ran to it eagerly and opened the passenger door. 'Oh, please, can you give me a lift to ...' and then broke off as she found herself staring at Cynthia Marsden, and sitting beside her in the driver's seat, an angry frown on his face, was James Arbory.

'I thought it was you. Get in,' he ordered grimly.

Reluctantly Pandora obeyed him and got into the back seat, although she had a feeling that it might have been better to walk the whole way home on bleeding and blistered feet!

CHAPTER SIX

SIR JAMES started the car again and drove on in silence, but Pandora could feel his anger; it hung in the car like something tangible. Presumably because he had wanted to be alone with his girl-friend and had felt obliged to stop and pick her up, Pandora supposed.

She sat quietly, trying to efface herself, but Cynthia Marsden half turned in her seat to look at her. 'Do you always hitch lifts home – Dorothy, isn't it?'

'No, it's Dora. I missed the bus,' Pandora muttered, unwilling to let the older woman get an even bigger rise out of her.

'Really? I thought the last bus didn't leave until midnight. Doesn't it, darling?' she asked, addressing Sir James.

'I've no idea,' he replied curtly.

Pandora looked up and found his eyes, dark with anger, on her in the driving mirror. For a long moment their glances locked and then he lowered his eyes to watch the road again. She turned away, feeling strangely empty and confused, and saw that Cynthia Marsden was staring at her in scarcely contained fury, and realised with a sickening feeling that she had seen.

The other girl's lips set into a thin hard line and Pandora could almost see her inner struggle to contain her rage, then, after a minute or so, she said in a silky voice, 'Why, Dora, your jacket is covered in dirt.'

Glancing down at her sleeves, Pandora saw that they, and the front of her coat, were stained with moss from the trunk of the tree she had climbed. Her skirt, too, was streaked with it and had a jagged tear. Rather hollowly she said, 'I tripped and fell.'

'Good heavens! It looks more as if you've been rolling around on the ground,' Cynthia returned, her tone heavy with implication. 'Did you spend the evening in Broxford?'

'Yes, at the cinema.'

'Oh, that place where they show all the explicit sex films,' Cynthia said disdainfully, for all the world as if she herself was as white as the driven snow.

She opened her mouth to make some other remark, but the car stopped with rather a jerk outside a neat Georgian house standing a little way back from the road, that Pandora recognised as being on the outskirts of Arbory Magna. So this was where Cynthia Marsden lived. How convenient!

The older girl immediately turned her attention on Sir James. 'You are coming in for a nightcap, aren't you, darling? I'm sure your maid can walk from here.'

'Yes, of course I can.' Pandora moved to open the door, but James Arbory said curtly, 'Wait,' then got out to open Cynthia's door for her. He walked with her up the driveway to the house and after a few moments a light came on inside.

Pandora bit her lip, wondering whether to get out and walk the rest of the way as she would very much like to do, but was afraid that it would make her employer even angrier if he came out and found her gone. But if Cynthia succeeded in her obvious intention to keep him with her he might be ages, hours even, if they got really involved. But he surprised her by coming back within a couple of minutes, getting into the car and driving away immediately. He drove decorously through the sleeping village, but put his foot down so that the powerful car seemed to surge up the hill, the trees flicking past as darker shadows in the night. At the sound of his horn someone came running to open the gates and then they were through and speeding down the mile-long drive to the waiting house. He pulled up so sharply outside the entrance that gravel sprayed up from the tyres. Then he got out and jerked her door open.

Pandora hastily scrambled out. 'Thank you for the lift.' She started towards the side entrance, but Sir James reached out and caught her arm.

'Oh, no, you don't. I want a word with you.'

His grip like a vice, he propelled her up the steps and through the big double doors, kicking them shut behind him. Then he half dragged her down the corridor and into the drawing room. Only then, when he had shut the door, did he let her go.

'Now,' he said furiously, 'you're going to tell me what the hell you were doing thumbing a lift at this time of night.'

Pandora automatically began to rub her arm where he had held it. 'I told you, I missed the ...' Her voice faded as she saw the sudden flame of rage in his eyes and she took a hasty step backwards, but he reached out and caught her wrist.

'Yes, it would be much wiser if you didn't lie to me,' he said silkily, menacingly.

Her eyes went to his hand circling her wrist, biting into her flesh, and then she raised them to his face and began to tremble.

'Well?' he demanded.

'I – I was out on a date. And he – well, he got over-amorous, so I got out of his car to walk home.'

'And the dirt on your clothes?' He indicated her stained jacket.

'He came after me,' Pandora admitted reluctantly. 'I ran in a wood to hide, but it wasn't very thick and I had to shin up a tree so he wouldn't find me.'

'And then he drove off and left you to walk home alone, I suppose?' Sir James said grimly. 'And did it never occur to you that by thumbing a lift you might run into the same danger again? That someone else might have tried to have sex with you?'

Pandora shook her head and said rather helplessly, 'My feet hurt.'

He raised his eyes to heaven. 'Dear God!' He looked at her again and his face hardened. 'Who was it, Dora? Some lout from the village?'

She hesitated; although she had no reason to protect Tom Langley after tonight, she was reluctant to get him into trouble because she knew that it was bound to upset his parents, both of whom she liked very much. She had received nothing but kindness from them, especially from Mr Langley, who had let her help groom the horses, and she didn't want to be the one to bring trouble on Tom, who was their only child and the apple of their eyes – and spoiled rotten because of it, she realised.

So she lied and said, 'No, it was someone I met in Oxford.'

His eyes narrowed. 'Is that the truth?'

She nodded, 'Yes,' and lowered her head to avoid his scrutiny.

'Because if it's not ...' he began threateningly, his fingers tightening on her wrist as he pulled her towards him.

Looking up, she saw the dark flame in his eyes and involuntarily whispered, 'No!' But it was as if he hadn't heard; he drew her close against him, one hand low on her hips so that she felt the lean hardness of his body. He bent his head and sought her lips, his kiss soft, sensuous. Only for a moment did she put up a token resistance and then her mouth opened under his and her arms crept round his neck. He kissed her eyes, her throat, sending sensations of delight running through her. She moved against him and could feel the growing tension in his body as he bit the lobe of her ear. Then his lips were on her mouth again, but hard now and demanding. She responded passionately, eagerly, and made no demur when he slipped off her jacket and it fell to the ground. His fingers sought the buttons of her blouse and that, too, fell to the floor, then his hands were cupping her breasts, his thumbs exploring, caressing. Pandora moaned softly, her mouth moving under his. He lifted his head and stared at her for a moment, his breath ragged and uneven, then he stooped to pick her up and carry her to one of the large, deep settees, laying her gently down on its cushioned softness.

He sat down on the edge, feasting his eyes on her youthful loveliness, then he reached out and began to caress her again so that her breasts hardened beneath his fingers. Pandora writhed and moaned, then opened eyes grown dark as jade by desire and lifted her arms to pull his head down, so that his lips, too, could kiss and caress her, holding his head there as wave after wave of desire ran through her, making her groan and bury her fingers in his hair. Then he was lying beside her on the settee, murmuring her name over and over again, and kissing her with a fierce, hungry passion.

Pandora didn't know how long it was that they lay together, until he suddenly pushed himself away and got to his feet, standing with his back to her. 'You'd better get dressed,' he said abruptly, his voice harsh and uneven.

Slowly she sat up, looking at him rather dazedly, unable yet to fully comprehend what had happened. She pushed her hair back out of her eyes with shaking fingers, then looked round for her things.

'Here.' He picked up her blouse from the floor and tossed it to her, giving her only a glance before turning away again.

She held the blouse against her, covering herself as she stared at his broad back, then she slowly swung her legs to the floor and with fumbling hands put it on and did up the buttons while he went to the sideboard to pour himself a glass of Scotch. Getting up, she crossed to pick up her jacket and started for the door, but he said urgently, 'No, wait!' and she slowly turned to look back at him.

His hair was dishevelled, his grey eyes still shadowed by unfulfilled passion. For a few moments he studied her as she stood waiting, then he put down the glass and moved forward to put his hands on her shoulders. 'Goodnight, Dora. My beautiful girl,' he said gently.

She looked up at him wonderingly, bewildered by his change of mood. Slowly she said, 'Goodnight, Sir James.'

He shook his head. 'Goodnight, *James,*' he corrected her, his eyes warm.

Softly she repeated it. 'Goodnight – James.'

He smiled, then bent to kiss her, his mouth gentle. 'Go now. I'll see you tomorrow.'

Pandora went to the door and opened it. She looked back at him standing so tall and powerful, the master of Arbory, and then at the settee. Her eyes flew to meet his and then she quietly shut the door and walked slowly through the moonlit corridors of the great house to her room.

It was late the next morning before Pandora woke, and for once she didn't spring out of bed immediately as she usually did, but lay languidly gazing up at the shaft of sunlight that lay along the ceiling from the gap in the curtains. She knew it was unfair of her to leave getting the breakfast to Uncle Charlie, especially when she had had a day off yesterday, but her mind was a mess of emotions and even a few minutes in which to try and sort out her thoughts was too precious to lose.

Ever since she had come to bed last night she had been

trying to work out just what made James Arbory tick. But last night her emotions had been too coloured by the memory of the way he had made love to her, skilfully arousing her passions until she had been unable to deny him anything he had wanted. But, although she had gone farther with him last night than any man before, he had stopped short of taking her completely, had drawn back before things got out of control and had left her feeling empty and frustrated, her body aching for fulfilment. And that, too, was something that she had worried and puzzled over until the early hours when sleep had finally overcome her.

Now she tried to marshal her thoughts into some sort of order and decided that the most disturbing problem was why, when he already had a mistress, was James Arbory also trying to seduce her. No, *had* seduced her, as near as damn it, because last night she had *wanted* him to take her and would willingly have given him her virginity. She put her hands on her breasts beneath the bedclothes, remembering how he had kissed and caressed them, and her body trembled with agonised longing. Then she turned convulsively and gripped her pillow hard, forcing her mind away from ecstasy and back to being objective. Was he just amusing himself? Was he the type of man who had to try his luck with every reasonably pretty girl who came his way, and once the seduction had been successful would drop her when he grew tired or when the next girl came along? But in that case where did Cynthia Marsden fit in? Perhaps, Pandora thought with bitter cynicism, he also liked to have a permanent mistress, an experienced woman who could cater to his more erotic whims as a young girl like herself could never do. She remembered someone saying that the last maid hadn't stayed long; had she, too, fallen a victim to Sir James' powers of seduction and then been cast aside? He had certainly gone from his mistress to her last night, she remembered.

But if all that were true, why then had he held back, and been so gentle with her when he had said goodnight? Did he, perhaps, intend to get rid of Cynthia Marsden and make her his mistress instead?

Pandora's mind ranged back and forth, finding many discreditable reasons for his treatment of her, but having every theory blown apart by the simple fact that he hadn't taken her when he could have done. In the end she sat up in bed and balled her hands into fists which she beat against her head. It was no use, she didn't know what to think, and she was only getting more and more confused. Only time would tell – that or some decisive action of her own to leave Arbory. But Pandora knew she couldn't do that; she was held here in his power as surely as a fly caught in a web who knows that the spider will eventually come for him.

That morning she went about her duties lethargically, often pausing to stand staring into space, her thoughts far away, but at the same time her nerves were on edge in case James came near, but he was making his rounds of the farms on the estate today and wasn't expected back until the afternoon. During the morning Jon Thursby phoned to ask her to go out with him again, but she made an excuse, feeling quite unable to cope at the moment with his obvious wish for them to be more friendly.

'I haven't upset you or anything, have I, Pandora?' he asked anxiously.

'No. No, of course not. It's just that I'm not sure when I'll be able to get a day off now that the preparations for the Rose Ball have started,' she told him. Which, in a way, was true, because Uncle Charlie was making out lists of things to be done and was already contacting caterers and domestic agencies for extra staff.

After lunch, Pandora decided to take a walk to try to shake off her restlessness; at least it might help to stop her mind going round in circles all the time. The stables, of course, were out; Tom Langley had definitely put paid to any more walks in that direction and in so doing had lost her the solace she might have found there, so she turned her steps towards the lake and the summerhouse at the head of it. This had been built in the eighteenth century for the ladies of the house who would come here for picnics with their children or to read and draw. Several sketches by one more talented baroness had been framed and hung in the small room off the entrance hall where the tenants were shown to wait when they came to the house on estate business or to pay their annual rent in the days before telephones and banker's orders.

She walked slowly along the wide gravel path that ran round the edge of the lake, her head bowed in thought, hardly noticing the flowering shrubs or the sunlight reflected off the water, but when she reached the summerhouse she paused for a moment on the steps to look back at the house, her thoughts, though, still on its master. Then she shrugged her shoulders angrily and pushed the doors open to go and sit in the cool, shady interior. She was being an utter fool, she knew that. Always, since she had left school, she had prided herself on being sensible where boys were concerned, and not let herself get carried away by emotion or even curiosity, but now ...! Now she was behaving like a cheap little idiot. Why, she had hardly known the man more than a few weeks and already she had let him – but it was much better not to think of that. Pandora dug her nails into her palms and tried to concentrate. What was it about him that made all her defences just melt away? He was handsome, yes, but she had been out with other good-looking men and they had never had this effect on her. She thought for a few minutes, picturing Sir James in her mind, and came to the conclusion that it was his arrant masculinity, his complete self-assurance that so overwhelmed her. That, and his sexual expertise. She had never met a man like him before and somehow was sure that she never would again.

Leaning back against the white-painted wall, Pandora sat in the sunlight of the open doorway, feeling warm and drowsy, the silence of the afternoon broken only by bird song and the far-off drone of a combine harvester reaping the first of the summer crop. Then she heard hasty footsteps outside on the gravel and her heart gave a crazy kind of lurch as a tall figure appeared suddenly in the doorway, blocking out the sun.

Pandora blinked, unable for the moment to focus, then stood up hurriedly when she realised that it was Tom Langley.

He crossed the floor and stood glaring at her, his face red

and angry. 'I didn't think you'd dare to come to the stables again after last night, so I kept a lookout from the shrubbery and followed you round here. Why didn't you come when I called you? I told you it was all right.'

Pandora laughed shortly. 'You didn't really expect me to believe that, did you, after the way you behaved?'

'What do you mean, after the way I behaved? It was you who led me on, you little slut!' he retorted angrily. 'You girls are all the same, you let a chap spend his money on you and then get all prim and proper when they want a kiss or two in return.'

Coldly, Pandora said, 'It was you who kept on at me to go out, remember? And it was hardly my fault that you turned nasty when you couldn't get what you wanted.'

An angry flush of colour suffused his face and he took a step towards her.

'You keep away from me!' Pandora exclaimed. 'If you try anything again I'll scream the place down!'

'Huh, I wouldn't want to even touch you again now. I don't want Jon Thursby's leavings,' he said jeeringly. 'He's welcome to you for all I care.'

'Then get out of here and leave me alone.'

'Not till I get what I came for. Have you said anything about last night to anyone? *Have you?*' he repeated, catching hold of her wrist when she didn't answer at once.

'If you mean have I told anyone that you acted like a depraved animal, the answer's no,' Pandora retorted, then gave a cry of pain as he viciously twisted her wrist. 'You pig! Let me go!'

'Not until I'm good and ready.' He twisted her wrist again, smiling cruelly as he did so. 'There are other things you can do to a girl besides what I wanted to do to you last night, and if you dare to tell anyone about it then I'll have to ...'

He broke off suddenly and made a strange gurgling sound in his throat, his hand letting go of her wrist as he was suddenly yanked off his feet.

'To do what? Just what was it you were going to do to Dora if she didn't keep her mouth shut?' James Arbory tightened his hold on Tom's collar and for all his size shook him by it like a dog. Tom yelped and tried to pull himself free but couldn't, his face becoming even redder than it had been before as his collar started to strangle him.

James looked at her. 'I take it this was the man you went out with last night?'

She nodded dumbly and his eyes lit with anger. 'I seem to remember warning you not to lie to me.' Pandora could only look at him helplessly until he said curtly, 'Get out. I'll speak to you after I've dealt with this young thug.'

There was a dangerous glint in his eyes, a look that she remembered seeing when he had accosted her on her motorbike, and she looked nervously from him to Tom, who was tearing at his shirt to try to open the collar. Involuntarily she said, 'Oh, please, don't hurt him.'

His face hardened, his mouth setting into a thin line. 'Get out!' he ordered again, his voice cold as ice.

She looked at him pleadingly, her green eyes anxious. 'But – his parents!'

His eyes came swiftly back to her, a different look in them

this time, and he said more gently but no less compellingly, 'Go back to the house, Dora.'

For a moment longer she hesitated, then, knowing that any further attempt at intervention was useless, turned and ran out of the summerhouse and back towards the house, not stopping until she was out of breath and most definitely out of earshot. She wasn't sure what James had in mind for Tom Langley, but by the way he was holding him as if he didn't much care whether he strangled him or not, she was afraid Tom was in for a lesson he wouldn't forget in a hurry. And serve him right. But she couldn't help but be worried about the effect it would have on his parents. And James had said that he would speak to her after; that, too, wasn't something she was looking forward to at all.

But, although she waited in acute apprehension for a summons, James didn't send for her at all that day, and the next morning one of the cleaning women told them that Tom Langley was leaving Abbot's Arbory.

'Yes,' the woman passed on the gossip with great relish, 'seems he came home yesterday with a nasty black eye and bruises in other places I can't mention. At first his mother thought he'd been in a fight or something, but he said one of the horses had shied sudden when he was grooming it and it had knocked him down against a post. Then he comes out and says that he's been thinking of trying to get a job in a racing stables and that Sir James had agreed to give him a letter to take to a friend of his who trains horses at Newmarket. Ever so peculiar, isn't it? His ma said he hadn't mentioned to her about getting a new job, but then stands to reason he wouldn't tell her, would he? Because she's bound to try and stop him, Tom being her only one. But then his dad went to see Sir James and came back happy enough about it; said the boy ought to spread his wings a bit, so it's all settled and Tom's going on Friday. There's one or two girls in the village who'll be crying their eyes out this week, I can tell you,' the woman added to Pandora in a lowered voice so that Uncle Charlie couldn't hear. 'Several of them had their eye on Tom at one time or another.'

Pandora listened with mixed feelings; feeling inexpressibly relieved that Tom was going, and hoping against hope that his parents didn't know the truth and were blaming her for it. But Mrs Langley herself popped into the kitchen the next day to use the washing machine as hers had broken down, and it was evident from her conversation that she was completely in the dark, so Pandora was able to feel that at least half her fears were allayed.

It seemed that James had forgotten his threat, for he didn't send for her, and in fact she didn't see him at all for the next few days as plans went ahead for the Rose Ball and Uncle Charlie kept finding her extra jobs to do connected with it, so that some of her usual work had to be done later than normal. At first she had been nervous and tense as she waited for James' summons, but when none came she felt a little piqued and instead of being ready to hurry away if she heard him coming, now she lingered longer than necessary about her jobs, half hoping that he would walk into the room while she was there. But when next she did see him it was quite unintentional; because she had been helping to go through the extra linen they would need for the guests who would be staying the night after the ball, she had almost forgotten to take fresh towels up to the master bedroom, and she hastily picked up the pile and ran upstairs with it before he went up to change for dinner.

But James must have come up earlier than usual, for when she hurried into the room without bothering to knock, he was already there, taking off the jacket of the suit he had been wearing to attend a business conference in Oxford.

Pandora stopped short on the threshold. 'Oh! I – I'm sorry, I didn't think you'd be here. I've just brought up the clean towels.' Quickly she crossed to the bathroom and hung them on the rail.

As she emerged into the bedroom again she carefully kept her eyes averted and walked hurriedly to the door, but even as she reached to open it James said softly, 'Dora,' and she stood still, quivering, her hand gripping the knob hard.

'Come here.'

Slowly she turned to face him, her pulses racing. He was watching her enigmatically, his dark eyes narrowed, and instinctively she said, 'No.'

His mouth tightened for a moment, then he thrust forward his wrists and said coolly, 'Undo these for me, would you?' indicating the cufflinks set into his sleeves.

Still half afraid, Pandora moved hesitantly towards him and gave him a quick glance, but his face was quite impassive as he looked down at her, his expression unreadable.

As she began to undo the first link he said abruptly, 'I suppose you've heard that Tom Langley is leaving the stables?'

Pandora nodded without looking at him. 'Yes, I heard it from one of the cleaning women.'

'Why didn't you tell me it was him, Dora? Why did you lie and say it was someone from Oxford?'

She hesitated for only a second, but his free hand came up and clasped her arm fiercely.

'Answer me! Why did you lie?'

'Because – because I didn't want to get him into trouble.'

'You're so loyal, then? To a man who tried to rape you?' His voice sneering, James added, 'If you care that much for him I wonder you didn't let him have what he wanted.'

Angry colour came into her cheeks. 'That isn't so at all! I couldn't care less what happens to Tom, but I like his parents very much and I didn't want them to be worried and upset. It was for their sake that I didn't tell you the truth.'

'You swear it?'

'Yes.' She glared up at him, still hurt and angry. 'Not that it's anything to do with you who I …'

But he interrupted her brusquely, 'Then why go out with him in the first place if you didn't like him?'

'I didn't want to, but he kept going on at me to all the time. And – and he accused me of being a snob.'

'I see.' He let go of her and she went on with her task. 'You should have trusted your instincts, Dora, and gone on refusing to go out with him. He's the type who gets dangerous when he's thwarted.'

She took out the first cufflink and looked down at it unseeingly. Speaking with difficulty, she said, 'And you? Should I trust my instincts where you're concerned, too?'

He smiled mockingly. 'Of course.'

Very carefully she took out the second cufflink and laid them both on the nearby dresser. With beating heart she said as steadily as she could, 'Then I'd better give in my notice and leave at once.'

'Perhaps that would be better.' Her eyes rose swiftly to his face at that and the mocking smile deepened. 'But you won't,' he went on softly. 'Because you've never experienced anything like this before. With me you're discovering a sexual awareness that you were too immature to know even existed. You're attracted to me, Dora, and there's no way you can leave here until I choose to let you go.'

Pandora stared at him in shocked horror, then turned to run away, but he swiftly caught her wrists, holding her prisoner. She made a convulsive movement to get free, but he was far too strong for her.

His eyes darkening, James said brusquely, 'Stop fighting me. You know you want it.'

'No!'

For a moment he was silent and then, to her surprise, he laughed mockingly. 'Oh, Dora, when *are* you going to stop saying no when you mean yes?'

'I don't! I – I ...' Her voice faded and she stopped trying to break free. She gazed up at him, her mouth parting in a little sob of surrender, her eyes wide and dark in her pale face. 'Yes, oh, yes, James! *Please!*'

The next second she was pulled into his arms and his mouth was on hers, kissing her with a fierce hunger, a kiss that Pandora returned with passionate abandonment, uncaring about anything but the aching need that only he could assuage.

It was James who drew away first, again gripping her wrists as he put her from him, his fingers bruising her flesh, but for a different reason now. His eyes glittered down at her, his breathing uneven. His voice thick, unsteady, he said harshly, 'Help me undress.'

Pandora stared into his face for a long moment, then very, very slowly she lifted her hands and began to undo the buttons of his shirt. She reached the last one and hesitated again before opening the shirt and pushing it off his shoulders. He slipped his arms out of the sleeves and tossed it on the bed. He waited then, watching her, and his breathing quickened as she gently lifted her hands and very lightly, with just her fingertips, ran them along the broad width of his shoulders and on down to the hard, firm muscles of his arms. She touched them wonderingly, marvelling at his strength, her hands opening wide to take in their expanse. For a while she lingered there, but then her hands went back to his shoulders and this time moved slowly down the smooth, taut planes of his chest. He quivered, and then made a groaning sound deep in his throat as her fingers found, touched, explored, then trembled convulsively as he guided her head down and her lips, too, began tentatively to kiss and caress.

Suddenly he seized her arms and jerked her roughly against him, his hand coming up to wind itself in her hair as his mouth found hers with savage passion, his lips cruel and bruising.

'Dora! Oh, Dora, I want you. I want to take you, love you!

I ...' He broke off suddenly and then swore. 'Hell and damnation!' Then Pandora heard it too, the strident sound of the phone ringing persistently by his bed. His hands gripped her again and she could hear his heart hammering in his chest. He took a deep breath to try and control himself, then said imperatively, 'Wait! Don't go.'

Crossing to the phone, he picked it up and spoke while Pandora turned away, trying to stop herself from trembling and to collect her scattered wits. She crossed to the dresser and gripped its edge hard, lifting her head to stare at her reflection in the mirror. Her eyes were wide and uncertain, but there was a brilliant light in their green depths, so that her skin looked pale and translucent in comparison, and her lips, the lower one still trembling, were deep red from his assault on her mouth.

She heard James' voice rise in some annoyance. Then he said curtly, 'Very well, I'll be there about nine-thirty,' and rang off.

He came up behind her, putting his hands on her shoulders. Their eyes met in the mirror and for a long moment they gazed at each other, then James gently turned her round and cupped her face in his hands. His eyes warm, tender, he kissed her gently, then said huskily, 'Darling, there's so much I want to say to you, to tell you, but this is neither the time nor the place. I have to go out on business tonight, but we'll talk tomorrow. Come to the library in the morning straight after breakfast.' His lips touched her eyelids, the curve of her cheek. 'Promise me you'll come.'

'Yes, all right.'

His mouth brushed hers lightly, but Pandora pushed herself forward, clinging to his lips so that he had to kiss her properly, and when at last they parted she opened her eyes and gazed at him wonderingly. 'Oh, James!'

'Hush.' He put his finger to her lips. 'We'll talk tomorrow.'

She left him then and went to the kitchen to finish preparing dinner, but she was in a kind of daze, doing the cooking automatically and only mumbling a reply when Uncle Charlie spoke to her. Luckily, however, he was pretty preoccupied himself and didn't take too much notice. But after he had served his master's meal and they were eating their own, he made a sound as if he was being poisoned and hastily pushed the strawberry mousse she had prepared away from him.

'Good God, girl, what on earth have you put in this? It tastes terrible!'

'Does it?' Pandora had been gazing into space, but now she looked down in surprise at her own plate. Picking up her spoon she tasted it. A look of appalled horror crossed her face. 'Oh, no! I put salt in it instead of sugar.'

'*And* you gave the same dessert to Sir James,' her uncle reminded her.

'Oh, lor! Didn't he say anything?'

He shook his head in puzzlement. 'No, he didn't. I wonder why that was? He certainly tasted it. But come to think of it he didn't eat much.'

'Perhaps he liked it?' she suggested hopefully.

Her uncle snorted derisively. 'No man in his right mind would like that!' And he got up to scrape his plate into the waste disposal and make a cup of coffee to get rid of the taste.

Pandora stared down at the mousse with a puzzled frown on her face. What on earth had made her do that? Anyone would think she was in love, or something equally ... Her thoughts tailed off and she sat frozen. Was that the matter with her? Had she fallen in love with James Arbory? She shook her head, trying to clear it. It couldn't be so, it just couldn't! She stood up and abruptly pushed her chair away from the table. 'I think I'll go for a walk.'

Uncle Charlie stared after her in astonishment as she hurried out of the kitchen, but she just had to be alone for a while.

It was high summer now and not yet dark even though it was quite late in the evening. She ran down past the garage block and the high walls of the kitchen garden and into the open land at the side of the house, not stopping until she reached the first of the majestic oak trees that stood sentinel over the park. The evening sun was low on the horizon and lay like cloth of gold over the fields, casting long, deep shadows where the deer grazed slowly across the grass. Pandora leaned against a tree trunk and gazed back at the house, dazzled by the sun's reflection in a hundred window panes.

Perhaps that's what it is, she thought wildly. Perhaps I'm just dazzled by the house and by James' wealth. I can't be in love with him! It's just infatuation. To be in love with him would be all wrong, he stands for everything I despise! She tried to argue herself out of it, but the more she did so the stronger the feeling became. She began to walk agitatedly along the path, not caring where she was going. How could she possibly have fallen in love with someone whose whole way of life was such an anathema to her? It couldn't be love. It was just sex, that was all. The strongest sexual and physical attraction she had ever experienced. She stopped short suddenly, closing her eyes and trying to halt the chaotic thoughts in her mind, trying to let her feelings come through. And then, in that quietness, she knew, with blinding clarity, that she *was* in love with him. There would be no more doubts and questions ever again, and with that knowledge came the most wonderful sensation of happiness she had ever known. It seemed to bubble up inside her and burst out so that she spread her arms and whirled round and round, laughing aloud and wanting to shout and cry out with joy. It had never felt so good to be alive before. And to be young and in love was the most marvellous sensation that could ever happen to anyone. She ran through the park, startling the deer, leaping up to reach the leaves on the lower branches of the trees and throwing them up in the air, jumping over the shadows as her heart sang, 'I'm in love, I'm in love. I'm in love with James.'

She swung round to face the house again and sobered suddenly, face flushed, hair dishevelled. Like every other person since time began who has found themself in love, Pandora's first thought was whether James loved her in return. Her brow creased in anxiety. Their backgrounds, their principles, were so different. And she was only his maid! How could he possibly feel as she did? But then she remembered the way he had looked at her earlier and his promise to talk to her tomorrow. Surely that could only mean that he, too, was experiencing this most wonderful of all feelings?

It was almost ten o'clock and quite dark when Pandora at last turned and began to make her way back to the house. She went reluctantly, unwilling to have this wonderful moment of discovery spoiled by the intrusion of ordinary everyday matters, but hoping that she would be able to just say good-night to Uncle Charlie and go straight to bed, where she could lie and think and dream, longing for tomorrow to come, but half afraid of so much happiness.

A light shining through the open doors of one of the garages helped to illuminate her way, but as she passed the chauffeur, Travers, turned it off and closed the garage doors.

He greeted her and fell into step beside her. 'I'm just going up to the house to have a word with Mr Richardson. Sir James gave me a message for him.'

'A message?' Pandora asked in surprise. 'Why can't he give it to him himself? You have just brought him back from wherever it was he went, haven't you?'

The man shook his head. 'No, I came back alone. I took him to that Miss Marsden's.'

'Miss – Miss Marsden's?'

'Yes,' the chauffeur nodded, adding helpfully, 'She's the one who lives on the other side of the village.'

'But you will be going to pick him up again later, won't you?' Pandora asked tightly.

'No, he doesn't want me any more tonight.'

'But how will he get home?'

The man looked at her in some surprise and then laughed scornfully. 'Use your loaf, Dora. He won't *be* coming back. He's gone there for the night. And not for the first time either.'

CHAPTER SEVEN

IT WAS early the next morning when Pandora let herself out of the side door, her note for Uncle Charlie saying 'Have decided to take today off', propped up on the kitchen table. She wheeled the motorbike out of its hiding-place and along the back drive to the tradesmen's entrance, not starting it up until she was safely outside the gates. The day was fine and sunny, the best kind of English summer morning, the July heat bringing the countryside to life and adding lustre to an already perfect setting. But Pandora was oblivious to it all and, although she had gone there with the firm intention of enjoying everything she saw, found herself wandering around Oxford aimlessly until she ended up sitting on the bank of the river, gazing blindly down into the rippling water.

Some students from one of the mixed colleges came along some time in the afternoon and drew her into conversation. They had stayed on in Oxford to do some extra studies during the long vacation and were all going to a party that night. They took Pandora under their wing and she went along with it more or less willingly, glad to have some of her own contemporaries around her, people who didn't ask questions or make demands of her. She went with them for a beans-on-toast type meal in one of the girls' rooms, and then later to the party which was being thrown at a flat in the town.

The people there, nearly all under twenty-five, dressed and behaved exactly as they pleased; if they wanted to let their hair down in the way they danced, it was okay by everyone else; if they wanted to make love they disappeared into another room for a while, and if they wanted to drink they brought their own bottles and that was okay, too. The music was loud and the room was hot and crowded with people. It was the kind of party that was Pandora's scene and where she should have felt right at home – but as the night wore on she found herself hating every minute of it! She danced with whoever asked her and laughed and drank red wine, ignored several passes that were made at her, and wished with all her heart that she had never seen either Abbot's Arbory or its master.

She left at about two in the morning when the party was still going strong and looked to last the whole night. At first she had been determined to stay till the end, but had suddenly been unable to stand any more and had collected her crash helmet and quietly slipped away. Strangely she wasn't tired, even though she had hardly slept the night before, but the fast ride through the deserted country lanes failed to invigorate her as it normally would. It was just a journey that had to be undertaken from A to B, and no longer the thrill of speed and power that it had always been before.

When she reached Abbot's Arbory she opened the gate, which fortunately was still unlocked, and turned off the engine to free-wheel down the long slope towards the house. She was surprised to see that there were lights still burning, in the kitchen area as well as in the main part of the house, although it was now nearly three o'clock. Her bike and the helmet she put back in the same place, then walked to the side door and quietly let herself in, intending to go straight to her room.

She hadn't thought that she had made any noise, but as she went down the corridor her uncle suddenly opened the door to the kitchen.

'Pandora!'

She jumped and turned rather guiltily. Uncle Charlie was wearing striped pyjamas under a maroon dressing-gown and looked far from pleased to see her.

'Where on earth have you been till this time of night? Don't you know it's three o'clock in the morning?'

Rather unbelievingly, Pandora said, 'You weren't waiting up for me, were you?'

'Of course I was. Otherwise I'd have been in my bed hours ago.'

'But why? I left a note to tell you I ...'

'I've been worried to death about you,' he interrupted her brusquely. 'Ever since I realised you'd taken that hellish machine of yours. At two o'clock I even phoned up the County Hospital to find out if you'd had an accident.'

'I'm sorry, Uncle Charlie. I went to a party and ...'

'A party?' His already angry face went redder than ever. 'And I suppose it never occurred to you that I might be worried and to pick up a phone to tell me where you were and that you'd be late?'

Pandora looked at him in some distress and then shrugged rather helplessly. 'No. No, it didn't.'

Her uncle snorted with rage until Pandora said slowly, 'You see, I'm not used to having someone worry about me,' which made him look rather shamefaced and turn away.

'Well, I wasn't the only one who was worried this time,' he told her, crossing to the house phone. 'Sir James came down here looking for you this morning and when I told him you'd taken a day off he said he wanted to see you as soon as you got in. Then when it got to eleven tonight he rang down and said I was to let him know when you got in, however late it was.'

He reached for the receiver and Pandora involuntarily put out a hand to stop him. 'Do you have to tell him?'

'Of course I have to tell him,' he answered testily. 'He ordered me to.'

'But, Uncle Charlie, I *have* to talk to you before I see him,' she said imploringly.

Her uncle looked at her anxious face, then sighed wearily. 'I don't for a minute suppose he'll want to see you at this hour. And *I* certainly don't want to talk.' He pressed the button for James' study and it must have been answered immediately, for he said almost at once, 'Yes, sir, she's just come in. Yes, quite all right. I gather she's been to a party.' He listened for a few seconds. 'I don't think that would be a very good idea, sir. Perhaps tomorrow. Very good, sir, I'll tell her.'

He put down the receiver. 'You're to see Sir James in his study at ten tomorrow.' He held up a hand as Pandora opened her mouth. 'And now I don't want to hear another word. I'm going to bed and anything you want to say to me will have to wait until morning.' He yawned and said, 'I'm not used to late hours.'

Pandora went to him and gave him a hug. 'I only wanted to say thank you, for waiting up – and for worrying,' she said huskily, then hurriedly turned and ran out of the kitchen and to her room.

The next morning found them both up on time, but neither of them looked very bright-eyed and bushy-tailed. Uncle Charlie was inclined to be short-tempered while Pandora had dark shadows around her eyes that told of another sleepless night.

She waited until her uncle had taken Sir James his morning coffee and then said firmly, 'Uncle Charlie, I have to talk to you. I'm going to relieve you of your biggest worry. I've decided to leave here.'

He looked at her, then poured out two mugs of coffee and put them on the table, motioning her to sit opposite him. 'Why?' he demanded bluntly.

She shrugged. 'I'm bored here. I think I'll go back to London. Today.'

'Where will you live till September? When you came here you said you had nowhere to go.'

Pandora looked down at her cup. 'I'll find somewhere.'

He looked at her searchingly. 'That's your only reason for wanting to go? You're sure?' His voice altered suddenly. 'You haven't broken something valuable, have you? That isn't why Sir James wants to see you?'

'No, it's nothing like that,' Pandora hastened to assure him. 'I told you – I'm just bored here in the country,' she lied, looking away.

He stared at her for a moment, then suddenly got to his feet. 'Well, I think you're being extremely selfish,' he said angrily. 'I've had to more or less deceive my employer so that you could have this job, and now you're throwing it back in my face. You *know* how hard it is to get a maid and yet you want to walk out this minute. *And* just as the Rose Ball is coming up and we're at our busiest. I think you're both selfish and ungrateful!'

Pandora gazed at him in consternation, completely thrown by his attitude. 'But, Uncle Charlie, you don't understand.'

'Yes, I do. It suited you to come here, but now you've changed your mind. Met someone at this party last night and want to go off with them, for all I know. You young people are all the same,' he added indignantly, 'you have no thought or consideration for other people. But I must admit I'd thought better of you, Pandora!'

Biting her lip, Pandora sat in miserable silence; she had fully intended to leave this morning and never see James Arbory again, to run away from this first, disastrous love, and try and put it behind her, but she saw now that that was impossible unless she told Uncle Charlie the truth. She looked at his back as he huffily busied himself at the sink and knew that, much as she loved her only relative, she could never confide in him because he simply wouldn't understand, which meant that she had to either antagonise him, perhaps for ever, or stay. She stared into her coffee cup, longing to take the easy way out, but knowing that she was too softhearted to do it.

At length she said hollowly, 'All right, I'll stay until the ball.'

A decision which mollified her uncle but left Pandora to face her interview with Sir James. As ten o'clock came near she went to her room to tidy herself, pulling her hair back into a severe plait and making sure that her uniform skirt and blouse were clean and pressed. She delayed coming out of her room until the very last second and walked slowly through to the main part of the house, her heart beating loudly, and fighting an almost irresistible urge to turn and run. At the study door she halted as she tried to still her heartbeats, gritting her teeth in an effort to control herself. For a few moments she closed her eyes, willing herself to remember that he had gone straight from her to his mistress. And that helped – it helped considerably. Pandora's face was pale and tense, but her emotions were under control as she raised her hand and knocked on the door.

'Come in.'

James was sitting at a big mahogany desk set under the window, a working desk with neat piles of letters and files on its polished surface. He sat back in his chair as she came in, his grey eyes on her face. Carefully Pandora shut the door and turned to face him, but she kept her eyes fixed on a point above his head.

'You sent for me, Sir James,' she said tonelessly.

James stared at her for a few seconds, then threw a pen he was holding down on to the desk and stood up. 'Yes, I sent for you,' he agreed harshly. He came round the desk and strode towards her as she still stood by the door. A pulse began to beat in her throat, a sure sign that her nerves were at screaming point, but somehow Pandora stood her ground. 'You may recall that you made a promise to come here yesterday. A promise you didn't keep.'

He waited for her to speak, but Pandora continued to stare silently out of the window. Exasperatedly James put his hands on her shoulders and swung her round to face him. 'Why did you do it, Dora? Why just suddenly take off like that?'

Carefully avoiding looking at him, Pandora deliberately misunderstood. 'I hadn't had a day off for two weeks. I'm entitled to ...'

'That isn't what I meant and you know it,' he interrupted fiercely, his eyes blazing with anger. His fingers tightened on her shoulders and for a minute Pandora thought that he was going to shake her, but then he seemed to take a hold on himself because his grip loosened and he sighed and said, 'Are you afraid of me? Is that what it is?' His hand moved up to her face and he began to trace the outline of her features with his fingertips. Pandora's heart lurched and she had to dig her nails into her palms to stop herself from shaking, but still she didn't speak.

'You don't have to be afraid,' he said softly, insinuatingly. 'Don't you know that you can trust me, that I'll never do anything to hurt you?'

Her eyes flew bleakly to meet his and she shook with inner rage; hadn't he already hurt her more than she'd ever been hurt before?

He must have felt the tremor that ran through her and mistaken it for desire, because he bent his head to brush her lips with his. 'Oh, Dora, my darling, I …'

Pandora jerked her head away and stepped back. 'Will that be all, Sir James?' she demanded flatly.

For a moment he could only stare at her incredulously, then he said fiercely, 'No, damn it, that will *not* be all! Why are you behaving like this? What's happened to make you change so suddenly?'

Again he waited for her to speak, but she just stood there woodenly, her mouth stubbornly closed, her face set.

'For God's sake, Dora, answer me!' He went to reach out and catch hold of her again, but saw the sudden flash of contemptuous anger in her green eyes and stopped short. He stared at her, then said urgently, 'Dora, what is it? You *must* tell me.' Adding rather bitterly when she wouldn't answer, 'Does what was between us mean so little to you, then?'

Pandora slowly turned her head to look at him, realising that he had handed her a weapon with which to wound his inflated egotism. She shrugged disdainfully. 'A few kisses? Why should they mean anything?'

His eyes narrowed. 'They seemed to mean something to you at the time.'

She sniffed disparagingly. 'This is the twentieth century; petting sessions mean nothing to girls nowadays, not when they've been the whole way so often.'

A muscle jerked at his jawline and he flinched as though she had struck him a physical blow, and then a look of such murderous rage came into his eyes that for a moment

Pandora's courage failed her, but she managed to add insultingly, 'And older men get so boring after a while. They always take themselves so seriously.'

His face tightened, went white, and if Pandora hadn't known that it was only his vanity that had been hurt, his manhood denigrated, she would almost have thought that it was pain that darkened his eyes and made him turn abruptly away and stand staring out of the window, shoulders hunched, his hands balled into fists in his pockets.

It was some minutes before he turned towards her again, and it seemed suddenly as if she was face to face with a stranger. His features were set into a stony mask, his eyes giving away nothing of what he was feeling. Only his voice betrayed him a little as he said harshly, 'I'm sorry you found my—attentions so boring, Dora. I gather you preferred those of the young men at the party you went to last night?'

'Yes,' Pandora lied boldly, desperately wishing that he would put an end to it.

'Well, you needn't worry, I shan't be bothering you again.'

She looked up then, surprised by his tone of voice, and for a brief second saw the mask slip as a look of bitter defeat came into his eyes. Then it was gone as he said icily, 'Very well, you can go back to your duties – and tell Richardson that I'm going in to Oxford and won't be in to lunch or dinner.'

Pandora obeyed him rather blindly, remembering that Cynthia Marsden had an antique shop in Oxford. So he was running back to her for solace already, for balm for his bruised ego, she supposed – and then cursed herself for a stupid fool as she felt bitter tears running down her cheeks. Fiercely she told herself that she had been right to do what she had, that he deserved nothing better, but then the racking, hollow pain of loss filled her heart and she wanted to turn and run back and tell him that it was all a lie and that she'd do anything he wanted, anything, so long as they weren't apart any more. And share him with another woman? Would she be willing to do that, too? Pandora's steps had automatically taken her to the library and she curled up at one end of the chesterfield, biting her knuckles as she tried to control herself. She had read of women, lots of them, who had loved a man so much that they were willing to sink their pride and tolerate another woman – or women – in his life, live for the few scraps of affection he was willing to show them from time to time.

But Pandora found that no way could she accept it. Okay, a love affair with him might not last for very long, perhaps only for a few months or weeks until James got tired of her, but in that time she would have to know that she was the only one, could never give herself with all the uninhibited passion of which she was capable if she knew there was someone else. She sat there for a long time, wishing desperately that she had someone to turn to for advice, to confide in, but there had been no one, not since her mother had died, and she suddenly felt as lonely now as she had done in those first terrible months of grief when there had only been Uncle Charlie, who had never had to cope with a child before, and had rather thankfully packed her off to boarding school because he thought he was doing the best thing for her. But somehow that memory helped; she had had to learn to live with loss then and she would do it now. She would be sure to always keep out of James' way, and although she owed it to her uncle to stay while he needed her, the moment the ball was over she would leave and find a job somewhere else for the rest of the summer.

If Uncle Charlie was curious about her interview with their employer, he took one look at her set face and refrained from questioning her, probably guessing that she had been told off for staying out so late. A lifetime of serving other people had made Uncle Charlie nothing if not tactful. He immediately gave her a job to do and kept her busy all day long, for which Pandora was profoundly grateful; the last thing she wanted right now was time to think.

But even though she had lots to do, the next two weeks to the ball dragged interminably. She managed to keep out of James' way, in fact he seemed to be out a great deal, but even so the house was full of his presence; it was impossible to go into a room without seeing some personal possession of his and she found it almost unbearable to go into his bedroom or the drawing-room with all the memories they evoked. Even her beloved library she entered with reluctance, because it was here that he had first kissed her.

Inevitably her unhappiness showed; she grew quiet and withdrawn, her gay laughter no longer ringing round the kitchen to brighten up the dullest day. Although she continued to cook appetising meals for Sir James and her uncle, she only toyed with her own food, and this, together with throwing herself into cleaning the house and preparing it for its great day, made her lose weight and look tired and drawn. At first her uncle had been convinced that she was just indulging in a fit of sulks because he hadn't let her leave when she wanted to, and decided to ignore her behaviour, he had enough on his plate with all the preparations without having to worry about a sullen niece. But after a few days even he began to realise that there was something wrong and clumsily tried to ask her what was the matter.

Pandora looked at him out of rather wistful, lost green eyes and shook her head. 'I'm fine, Uncle. Just rather tired, that's all.'

'Well, perhaps I have been working you a bit too hard. Why don't you take your day off tomorrow?'

She gave a small smile and looked away. 'There's too much to do.'

'We'll manage. You don't even go down to the stables for an hour or so any more. And Mr Thursby phoned up again for you yesterday, didn't he? Why don't you go out with him? You said you enjoyed it when you went before.'

'Yes, but I don't want to go again.'

'You haven't quarrelled with him, have you?'

Pandora gave a short laugh. 'Oh, no, Jon's too nice a person ever to quarrel with.' She stood up abruptly. 'There's just time to finish the job I was doing before I have to start getting dinner,' and she walked out of the kitchen with her uncle staring after her in bewilderment.

Now that Tom Langley had left there was nothing to stop Pandora going down to the stables, but, as Uncle Charlie had said, she never went there in the daytime in case James might be there. She found it difficult to sleep, often not dropping off until late or else waking in the early hours and not being able to get to sleep again, and sometimes then she would get up and dress in sweater and jeans and go quietly out of the house and down to the paddocks where the horses were out grazing, or to the stable block to feed sugar lumps to Greymist and the other mares in foal.

One night, only a couple of days before the ball, it was particularly bad; she woke in her little room and heard the soft patter of rain on the window, tried to go to sleep again, but could only toss and turn and think, think of nothing but James and everything she was trying so hard to forget. At length, when the light coming through the curtains grew stronger, she got up and washed and dressed, brushing her hair but leaving it hanging long and loose on her shoulders. She slipped on a mac and filled the pockets with sugar-lumps, then let herself out and ran down to the stableyard, unheedful of the rain on her bare head, her hair flying out behind her.

The sky was grey overhead, but in the distance the clouds were thinner with just a touch of blueness in their depths, giving the promise of dryer weather and sunshine later in the day.

Greymist came as soon as she had opened the top half of her door and Pandora spoke to her lovingly. 'Hello, my beauty, how are you today? It's your kind of day this morning.' She stayed talking to the mare for about ten minutes before moving on and then stood at the arched entrance looking out over the park to the mist-hung hills beyond. A frustrated restlessness filled her, adding to her unhappiness; she longed for something, anything to happen, what she didn't know. Suddenly she turned and ran to the tack room where she took down a bridle and exercise saddle, then went back to the stables to the stall of one of the new stallions that James had brought back from Ireland. He was a beautiful creature, a big three-year-old chestnut with a white blaze and powerful shoulders, who had won several races. Pandora talked to him, but he snorted a little and moved impatiently while she saddled him, eager to be off.

Leaving her mac in the stall, Pandora swung herself up and the horse started to move even before she had got her right foot in the stirrup.

'Hey, wait for me!' she laughed, and patted the horse, leading him out of the yard and down between the paddocks towards the rain-shrouded hills. Once clear of the fences she let him break into a canter and set him at a fallen tree trunk, to find out if he had been a steeplechaser. He cleared it with feet to spare and went over a stone wall dividing the park from the open ground beyond as if it was a kerb.

Pandora brushed rain from her face and bent low over the horse's neck. 'All right, boy, let's go!' And she kicked him into a fast gallop, thundering over the undulating countryside in a long, powerful stride as if he was once again competing in a race. Pandora laughed aloud, loving every minute of it, the rain on her face, the wind blowing her hair out behind her like a second mane, almost the same colour as that of the horse.

After a mile or so she turned the horse's head to make a

gradual half circle and slowed down a little, her shoulder and thigh muscles aching after not having ridden for years, realising that if she wanted to get the horse back and groomed before the stables came to life she ought to turn back now. She turned the horse towards Arbory, and then stiffened. Another rider was coming fast towards her, cutting across from the stables in a diagonal line that would bring him directly to her. Pandora had no difficulty in recognising either rider or horse. It was James Arbory on the big black hunter he always rode.

Her heart gave a wild jolt that communicated itself to the horse, because he plunged to one side suddenly, almost unseating her. Blind panic at the thought of having to face James again took over and she gave the horse his head, steering him in the direction of a pinewood with the crazy idea that she might be able to lose him there. She reached the trees first and dived through the thick undergrowth of bracken that reached up to her stirrup in places, bending low over the saddle to avoid the branches that brushed against her. The wood was very quiet, there was no noise except the startled cries of birds who flew up into the air as she passed, the heavy noise of the stallion's breathing, the thud of his hooves on the soft ground, and the echoing sounds of her pursuer coming up fast behind her.

Pandora pushed the stallion as hard as he would go; he was probably much the faster horse of the two, but he wasn't used to this soft, uneven ground and he had already had one good gallop and was tiring, although he gallantly pushed himself to his limit when she urged him on. They weaved their way through the trees and jumped a wide, fast-flowing stream as Pandora tried to shake James off, but then she came unexpectedly on a clearing where rain made whirlpools on the surface of a large pond, and she had to swerve to avoid dashing into it, breaking the horse's stride and slowing him down for a few precious seconds.

It was all James needed. The next minute his horse was alongside and his left hand reached out for her bridle, pulling the stallion up so suddenly that the animal reared and plunged and it took all Pandora's skill to stay in the saddle.

She turned on him, eyes blazing. 'Let go of my bridle! Damn you, how dare you …' Her words were cut off abruptly as James put his arm round her waist and lifted her bodily out of the saddle. For a moment she was held firmly against him, but then he had scooped her rein out of her hand so that he had both horses and dropped her unceremoniously to the ground.

Pandora cried out as she landed, but it was her dignity that was hurt far more than her behind. She yelled at James angrily, but he had dismounted himself and was tying the reins to a tree. Then he turned and came purposefully towards her.

Pandora took one look at his face, stopped yelling and turned to run. He caught her before she had even gone two yards and dragged her back.

'You crazy little fool! You could have killed yourself in this wood!' He shook her violently, his hands gripping her arms. 'I ought to put you over my knee and give you the hiding of your life!'

For a terrified moment Pandora thought that he was going to carry out his threat and she started to struggle.

'Let me go! Damn you, let me go!' She raised her hand to hit him, but he was too fast for her and caught her wrist. Furiously she opened her mouth to yell at him again, but was suddenly still. James was staring down at her, his face set and tense, the anger still there but subdued before a deeper emotion.

His fingers tightened, biting into her flesh. 'Why did you run away from me? Why?'

'I – I don't know.' The rain was falling heavier without the protection of the trees, wetting her hair and plastering it to her head. A drop trickled down her face. Almost absentmindedly James put up a thumb to brush it away, then put his hand on her neck as he studied her face.

In little more than a whisper, Pandora said shakily, 'Please don't – touch me.'

'Why not?'

She didn't answer – couldn't.

'What is it, Dora? Why have you changed towards me so suddenly?'

Her hands began to tremble and she turned her head away, biting her lip.

Immediately, roughly, he pulled her back. 'Don't turn away from me. Tell me, Dora. *Trust me.*'

He said it urgently, persuasively, but her eyes darkened as she stared into his face. How could she possibly trust him now? Lifting her arm, she knocked his hand away, her green eyes glaring defiance. 'I said don't touch me!'

It was the wrong thing to do. His face hardened and he grabbed her round the waist, pulling her against him and forcing her head back as his lips found hers. It was quite some time before he released her mouth and even then he didn't let her go, holding her head close against him so that she could hear the rapid beating of his heart in his chest.

'Is this the only way I'm going to get through to you?' he demanded raggedly. 'Won't you ever learn to trust me?'

'No!' She tried to pull away. 'You're just playing with me. Just amusing yourself by trying to make me fall for you, but ...'

'So that's it! I thought as much. Oh, Dora, if you only knew the half of ...' He bit off what he was going to say and instead said urgently, 'Listen, I want you to do something for me. I want you to try and remember how you felt when I kissed you – now and before. Just your feelings, nothing else. We had something good going for us – I know you felt it too. Just think about it, Dora, and let your heart guide you, not all those stale prejudices you've had indoctrinated into you over the years. Promise me you'll try.'

Pandora stared at him, then looked away wretchedly. Did he really dare to ask so much of her? 'I don't know. I don't see any point.'

'But you'll try?'

Grey eyes gazed earnestly into green and she found herself capitulating against her will. She nodded. 'Yes, all right,' she agreed huskily.

'Good girl.' His eyes warm, he bent to kiss her again, but she deliberately turned her head away and after a moment he let her go, then turned and walked to the horses. 'Who taught you to ride?' he asked.

Pandora accepted the change of subject thankfully. 'My father. I was riding almost before I could walk.'

James raised his eyebrows as he brought the horses over and handed her the chestnut's rein. 'I thought you said you were an orphan. Or was that, too, part of your Cockney charade?' he asked quizzically.

Pandora flushed. 'No. My father was killed when I was only eight.'

'He was killed?'

'Yes. He was in the R.A.F. Something went wrong with his plane and it crashed.'

'And your mother?'

'She died of cancer a few years later.'

Pandora thought she said it quite matter-of-factly, but James gave her a swift glance and covered her hand with his. 'I'm sorry.'

'Don't be.' Deliberately she moved her hand away. 'It was a long time ago and I'm quite capable of looking after myself now,' she told him with a defiant toss of her head.

'Of course,' James agreed smoothly. He looped his own rein over his arm and joined his hands together to make a step for her, hoisting her easily into the saddle. 'And didn't you mention a relative, an uncle or something?'

An imp of mischief came into her eyes and made her smile. 'Oh, yes, I have Uncle Charlie.'

James swung himself up into his saddle and came close up alongside her. 'Do that again, would you?'

Her eyebrows rose questioningly. 'What?'

'Smile.' He leaned forward and took her hand, carrying it to his lips. 'Because you so seldom smile for me, and because you look so very lovely when you do.'

But Pandora didn't smile, she could only stare at him as he bent to kiss her palm, then closed her fingers so that the kiss was like a tangible thing, held close in her hand.

They were mostly silent as they rode slowly back through the wood and down to the stables. The rain had stopped now and a weak sun was pushing aside the clouds to make the raindrops sparkle like diamonds on the leaves and the grass. The house, too, had a scrubbed clean look, the golden stone soaking up the sun and looking brand new, and yet as old as time itself. Unconsciously Pandora reined in as she gazed across at the house, never tiring of filling her eyes with its beauty.

James, too, stopped, but he was looking at her, not the house. In a rather strange tone he said, 'You've fallen in love with it, haven't you?'

She shot him a swift look and said lightly, 'How can you fall in love with a pile of stone and mortar?'

'Very easily. My family have been doing it since it was first built,' he told her with a rather wry twist to his mouth.

Curiously she asked, 'What does it feel like – to own all this? To be the master of Abbot's Arbory?'

He shrugged. 'Sometimes it feels like a millstone around my neck; when the harvest is bad and the roof leaks yet again. And it can be a lonely place when you have no one to share it with. But at other times, times like this, you realise that you've been granted a great privilege in being able to live in it and take care of it until it's time to hand it on to the next generation – or to the nation if they keep up their iniquitous taxes or decide to nationalise the land as you'd like,' he added drily.

Pandora flushed, remembering that conversation in Oxford, but before she could speak, he went on, 'We'd better be getting back. You're soaking wet. Why did you come out without a jacket or a scarf?'

'I don't know – I didn't think about it. Anyway, I like the rain.'

When they reached the stables he took the horse from her. 'I'll see to him. You go back to the house and get into a hot bath.'

'Oh, but I ought to groom him and see that he's ...'

'Dora,' he said in a tone that made her stop short, 'do as you're told.'

Her eyes lit with amusement. 'Yes, Sir James,' she agreed demurely.

She turned to go, but his voice stopped her. 'And Dora – remember what we agreed.'

Her face grew serious again, and she gazed at him for a long moment before nodding briefly and hurrying back to the house.

But there was little time to think over the next two days as the house seemed to be invaded by an army of outside caterers, florists and musicians. And impossible to dissociate herself from the air of excitement and bustle that seemed to fill Uncle Charlie and everyone else as the time for the ball drew near. The house shone inside as well as out, every room cleaned and polished, the ballroom and all the reception and guest bedrooms filled with flowers, the doors open and welcoming.

Sir James' aunt, Lady Townley, arrived the day before and went over the house with Uncle Charlie following anxiously at her heels, but she had no fault to find and was unstinting in her praise, which pleased him immensely. She also chatted to Pandora when she brought her evening dress up after pressing the creases out.

'Such a pity you're only here for the summer, Dora. You seem to be settling in so nicely. When do you go back to college?'

'In September. But how did you ...?'

Lady Townley raised her eyebrows. 'How did I know you were a student? James told me, of course. He's told me quite a lot about you. He does confide quite a few things to me, you know.'

Pandora had left then, but the remark had puzzled her. She couldn't understand why Lady Townley had said it, or why James had bothered to tell his aunt anything about herself. You would have thought he would have kept his sexual affairs from his relatives.

On the evening of the ball she dressed in her best uniform, expecting to take the women's wraps as they arrived, but James told Uncle Charlie that she was to stay in the kitchen quarters and that a hired maid could see to the coats. Pandora was first astonished, then angry. 'Did he say why?' she demanded.

He shook his head. 'Probably wants you to keep an eye on the caterers while I'm upstairs,' he remarked, too busy to be really bothered.

Pandora's face fell with disappointment. For what seemed like weeks she had been helping to prepare for this party, and now she wasn't even to see it. Not that it was her kind of scene, of course, but she had been looking forward to seeing the clothes the women wore and that kind of thing. But there was plenty to do in the kitchen and she had no time to be more than mildly resentful until after the buffet supper had been served, then she sneaked up the back stairs and round on to the main landing which ran round the entrance hall and where she could see several of the guests and hear the distant sound of the band. The big front doors were wide open and many people were going outside to stroll through the lantern-hung rose garden. As Pandora watched, a foursome, two women followed by two men, came back into the house and one of the women turned to catch hold of the arm of the man behind her, her laugh ringing out as she spoke to him. The other three were strangers, but Pandora would have recognised that laugh anywhere. It was Cynthia Marsden.

She stiffened with shock. Was that why James had ordered her to stay in the kitchens? Because he didn't want her to know his mistress was here? Or even vice versa? For the first time it crossed her mind that Cynthia Marsden might be suspicious of James' new maid, might even have told him to get rid of her, so that she, Pandora, was being kept out of the way to keep his mistress sweet. Rage soon gave way to a need for revenge, and without stopping to think she ran to the back stairs and down to her own room. She yanked off her uniform, tearing it in her hurry, and with hands which she had to force herself to steady she drew her hair back and coiled it into a sophisticated style, then made up her face with eyeshadow, highlights, blusher, the whole works. Then she crossed to the wardrobe and took out The Dress, an haute couture creation that she and three of her friends had, in a mad but never regretted moment, clubbed together to buy from one of those little shops in Chelsea that specialise in good secondhand clothes that have been worn for a season or until the original owners get tired of them. It was a beautiful thing; in a burnt orange with diamanté straps and a low back, but cut so well that its simple lines clung and yet covered, revealing nothing and yet suggesting everything. With Pandora's colouring it looked superb, and she thanked her stars that it had been her turn to use it for these holidays. She fished out the bag that went with it and put on her only pair of decent evening shoes, then for good measure splashed on the last of the French perfume that she had been carefully hoarding. If she was going to spoil James Arbory's game she might as well go the whole hog!

Picking up her skirts, she hurried through the back way to the main house again, waited for some women to go down the staircase and fell in behind them. Her heart was thudding with anger rather than trepidation, but her face was serene as she walked, head held high, into the ballroom.

It was only just midnight, people had finished supper and the dancing was beginning to be in full swing again. Pandora glanced round but couldn't see anyone she knew, so she began to walk round the room towards the other end. Almost at once a young man came up to her and said that he was sure they'd met somewhere. She let him get away with the lie and accepted his offer to dance; it was as good a way as any of looking round the room and finding out where James was.

They went slowly round the dance floor, the young man trying to arouse her interest, but Pandora looking round all the time and answering him abstractedly. He wasn't a very experienced dancer and twice they bumped into other couples. The second time the woman tutted with annoyance and Pandora turned her head to find herself only a foot away from Cynthia Marsden. The older girl looked at her for a moment with a slight frown, as if she was trying to place her, then gave a little nod and a half smile, the way you do when you recognise someone's face but can't remember where you met them. Pandora nodded demurely in return, hiding the imp of devilment in her eyes.

Shortly afterwards she saw James; he was talking to Lady Townley and an elderly couple near the entrance to the library, but as she got nearer he glanced up and let his eyes run over the dancers. His eyes fell on her and he stopped short in what he was saying, his eyes widening.

Pandora looked at him balefully. So he'd complained that she didn't smile at him enough, had he? Well, she'd soon remedy that! As she came opposite him, she opened her mouth and gave him her most dazzling smile, letting her whole face light up with it.

His left eyebrow rose and then he raised the glass in his

hand in a silent toast, bowing his head in acknowledgment.

And *he* probably didn't even recognise me either, Pandora thought as her partner turned and she was hidden from his view. But I'll make sure they both do before the evening's over.

When the music stopped she resolutely refused to dance with the young man again and walked through into the room where the drinks were being served. A waiter gave her a glass of champagne and she carried it back into the ballroom, standing near one of the stone pillars where she could watch the dancers. Cynthia was dancing again, with a different man this time, and gave Pandora a long, puzzled look as she passed. Her glass empty, Pandora placed it on the tray of a passing waiter and exchanged it for another full one. She found that she rather liked this champagne, the only time she had ever tried it before was at the twenty-first birthday celebrations of a fellow student, and then it hadn't seemed to taste much different from cider, but this was quite different, a much nicer taste; in fact she had a feeling that she could quite get to like champagne, after all.

'Pandora?' Her name was said on a questioning note and she turned to see Jon Thursby standing nearby.

She smiled. 'Don't look so worried; it really is me. How are you?'

'Oh, fine. I wish I'd known you'd be here; I'd have asked you to dance earlier.'

'I didn't know I was going to be here myself until a few minutes ago.' Across the floor she saw James excuse himself from the people he had been with and look around the room.

She drained her glass and looked round for somewhere to put it.

'I don't understand. How could you not know you were coming?' Jon asked with a frown. 'Didn't Sir James tell you until tonight, or something?'

'He didn't tell me at all,' Pandora replied baldly. 'I suppose you could say that I'm a gate-crasher.' She saw that James was making his way round the room, politely exchanging a word with people who claimed his attention, but purposefully heading in her direction. Rather unsteadily she held out her glass to Jon. 'Look, do you think you could get me another one of these?'

'Yes, of course.' He looked round for a waiter, but there wasn't one near. 'I'll have to go to the bar. Shan't be more than a minute.'

Someone had caught hold of James' arm and was insisting on taking a drink with him, then the dance ended and everyone crowded off the floor, getting in the way so that she couldn't see him any more. Pandora looked away and found herself looking straight into Cynthia Marsden's cold blue eyes as she came to stand beside her.

'I thought as much!' the older girl exclaimed. 'You're the maid! What are you doing here?' Her eyes widened. 'Sir James didn't give you permission to come, did he?' she asked sharply.

Pandora's chin came up. 'No, he didn't.'

'Of all the nerve!' Cynthia's voice had risen slightly and one or two heads turned towards them.

She opened her mouth to say something else, but James

suddenly appeared at her side and asked, 'Is something the matter, Cynthia?'

'Can't you see?' She indicated Pandora with a disdainful hand. 'Although I admit I had to look twice before I could believe my eyes. It's your new maid!'

'So it is,' James agreed softly, and Pandora raised reluctant eyes to meet his. The arrested expression she had seen once before – when she had run into the kitchen on that first morning with her arms full of flowers – was back on his face now, but there was also a bright flame in his eyes that sent sudden electric shock waves running through her. The atmosphere seemed to be charged with the current that ran between them, a current generated by two people who desperately want to make love but haven't been able to do anything about it.

The silence seemed to last for ever until Cynthia said fiercely, 'She's no right to be here. She's admitted that you didn't invite her.' And looked as if she would very much like to have ordered him to send Pandora away, if she had dared.

'No, but I did.'

With a physical effort Pandora tore her eyes from James and saw that Jon Thursby had come to stand beside her. He put a hand on her shoulder. 'Pandora is with me,' he said firmly.

James' head came up at that and his eyes narrowed.

Cynthia looked at Jon in amazement. 'With you? But you hardly know her, surely?'

'On the contrary. Pandora and I have met many times at the stables and we've dated before, so it was only natural that

I should invite her to be my partner. Not,' he added roundly, 'that I think it's any concern of yours, Cynthia.'

The blonde girl looked taken aback and opened her mouth to make an angry retort, but James intervened smoothly, 'No, indeed. And I'm sure, Jon, that you won't mind lending your partner to me for this dance.' And he took hold of Pandora's hand and led her firmly on to the dance floor.

The music had just started and there were only one or two other couples on the floor. For a few seconds he looked down at her enigmatically, waiting for her to come to him. Slowly she moved into his arms, her eyes never leaving his face. Gently but compellingly he pulled her close against him. Slowly they began to move around the floor in time to the music, although what the tune was Pandora had no idea. Every nerve end seemed to be on fire and her hand began to shake. James closed his over it tightly, his clasp warm and strong, and held it against his chest. People turned to stare at them as they danced, wondering who she was, asking their neighbours, but Pandora was quite impervious, lost to everything but the awareness of his body hard against her own, the warmth of his hand and the fire deep in his eyes.

More people moved on to the floor, filling it, but she didn't notice them; they seemed to be alone, encased in a glass bubble, like an ornament on a Christmas tree, with everything around them just distant sounds and shadows. Then James broke the spell by letting her go. For a moment she was bewildered, unsure where she was, but he tucked her hand under his arm and led her out through the long doors that lay open to the garden. He walked her down through the rose garden where other couples were strolling under the lanterns and on into the darker paths between the box hedges to a part where a stone balustrade overhung the lake. It was very quiet, the sounds from the house muted, the night heavy with the scent of honeysuckle.

James put his hands on her waist. 'You're trembling,' he said softly. 'Are you cold – or just afraid of me?'

She shook her head dumbly, knowing that it was neither.

'You minx! Why didn't you tell me your name was Pandora?'

She lifted her hands and rested them on his shoulders. 'I don't know. I felt that I – I had to hold something of myself back from you. That I couldn't just give you – everything.'

His hands tightened on her waist. 'But you told Jon Thursby. You were willing to confide in him,' he added on a harsher note.

'And what if I did?' Pandora retorted, immediately on the defensive. 'He was very kind to me.'

'Was he, by God!'

'Yes, he was. Which was more than you ever were,' she exclaimed hotly.

'No,' he agreed drily. 'That wasn't how you made me feel. I needed to arouse stronger emotions in you than kindness would ever have done.'

His words made her stop short, trying to discover his meaning, but it was too much to cope with and she pushed it aside. 'Why did you order me to stay in the kitchen tonight?' she demanded.

His mouth twisted a little, whether in mockery or amusement, she couldn't tell. He didn't answer her question, instead drawing her closer against him and saying, 'Did you know your eyes change colour when you're angry? Go from ice green to fiery emerald?'

'What's that got to do with it?' Pandora exclaimed indignantly.

'Everything,' he answered calmly. 'It was what first made me realise how much I loved you.' Then he smiled at her astonished face and bent his head to kiss her.

When James at last lifted his head, he held her trembling body close in his arms and said jerkily, 'Darling, earlier you said that you felt as if you had to hold back from me. Do you still feel like that?'

'No! Oh, no.' She reached up and touched his face wonderingly. 'I love you. I love you so much it hurts.'

'Sweetheart!' His hand covered hers as he buried his face in her palm. His voice muffled, he said, 'And you're happy now to give yourself to me?'

Her hand fluttered in his, but she replied unhesitatingly, 'Yes.'

'Oh, darling!' He pulled her roughly to him, holding her close. 'If you only knew how much I want you! It's like an ache deep inside me that's always there, and sometimes it gets so bad it almost drives me crazy. It was hell trying to ...' He broke off abruptly as the sound of voices, a man's cajoling, a girl giggling, reached their ears. They stood in silence for a while, hoping the intruders would go away, but it was evident that they, too, had slipped into the garden for a spot of lovemaking.

'We'd better go in,' James said softly. 'Lord, if only I wasn't the host and could just spirit you away tonight! There's so much I want to tell you, so many plans to make. But we'll have to wait until tomorrow, until we have Abbot's Arbory to ourselves again.'

He kissed her again and then put his arm possessively round her waist and led her back to the house.

CHAPTER EIGHT

THEY WENT back into the ballroom through the french doors and almost immediately James was buttonholed by one of the guests. Pandora hung back, but he kept a tight hold of her arm and motioned with his free hand to one of the waiters who brought them fresh glasses of champagne. For the second time that evening James raised his glass in a silent toast to her, but how different it was now from an hour ago. Then she had been angry and vengeful, but now she would have felt intoxicated even without the champagne. Her heart sang; she had committed herself to him and it was wonderful. She had told him she loved him, promised to give herself to him whenever he wanted, and she didn't give a damn! Her own moral scruples and her innate dislike of anything sordid or scandalous were lost beneath the overwhelming passion she felt for James. How could love ever be scandalous, how could the consummation of love ever be sordid?

His conversation over, James quickly led her on to the floor again before someone else could interrupt; but to be held by him, to touch him and to feel his hands on her was so tantalisingly exciting that Pandora could hardly bear it. Almost she was glad when the band swung into a faster number and he took her off the floor.

Jon was nowhere to be seen, but almost as if she had been

waiting for them, Cynthia came up immediately and said sharply, 'James, I'd like to speak to you. Alone,' she added when James showed no sign of letting go of Pandora's hand.

He frowned slightly, but turned to Pandora. 'Wait for me, I won't be long.'

But Pandora shook her head. 'No. I'd rather leave now and see you tomorrow.'

'Very well.' His hand tightened on hers for a moment and then he let her go, watching her as she went quickly out of the ballroom.

Many heads turned to look at her as she walked, tall and slender, her face radiantly happy, through the corridors towards the main hall, but Pandora was hardly aware of anyone else, she was still in a dazed, dreamlike state with her feet at least six inches off the ground. She paused in the hall, undecided whether to go out into the gardens again.

'Can I help you in any way, madam? A glass of champagne, perhaps?' asked a polished voice at her elbow.

Pandora turned and smiled. 'No, thank you, Uncle Charlie, I've a feeling I've had too many already.'

'Pandora!' He almost dropped his tray in surprise, then lowered his voice to a wailing hiss as he looked wildly around. 'Get back to the kitchens quickly! Oh, my God, I knew it was too good to be true!'

He shepherded her through the baize door to the kitchens and then turned to her angrily. 'Haven't you got any sense in your head? What on earth possessed you to do it? Did Sir James see you?' he asked anxiously.

Pandora smiled. 'Oh, yes, he saw me all right. In fact he danced with me.'

Her uncle groaned hollowly and sat down heavily in a chair. 'I knew if, I knew you'd get me the sack before you were through! I ought to have listened when you said you wanted to leave and let you go.'

Impulsively Pandora caught hold of his arms and pulled him to his feet, then swung him round. 'Forget about your silly old job, it's quite safe. Oh, Uncle Charlie, the most wonderful thing has happened! I've fallen in love! Really, really in love.'

He pulled himself free, his dignity seriously impaired, and looked at her with alarm. 'Who with?' he demanded apprehensively, then added more hopefully, 'Is it Jonathan Thursby?'

'No,' Pandora answered impatiently. 'With Sir James, of course.'

He made a strangled kind of noise and sat down again. 'But – but you can't be. It's impossible!' He tried to pull himself together. 'Pandora, you're just infatuated, that's all. You'll soon get over it.'

She went down on her knees and put her hands in his. 'No, Uncle Charlie,' she said softly. 'This is the real thing. I've fought against it almost since I first got here and I know I'm really serious.'

Something in her voice must have convinced him, because he didn't try to persuade her any more, but instead said, 'It's no good, child. You've got to leave here now and try and forget him. He'll never marry you – not someone who's been his maid.'

For a moment her eyes shadowed and she looked away. 'I know. I've always known that. But I'm not looking for marriage. I've never expected that.'

He stared at her. 'Do you mean to say that you're willing to – to live in sin with him?' he demanded, his face white with shock.

She nodded, and he exploded then, telling her not to throw her life away, that she'd always regret it, and much in the same vein, until Pandora cut sharply across his anger. 'It's no use arguing, Uncle Charlie. He's already asked me and I've agreed.'

He was silent, turning his back on her as he busied himself in the kitchen. The internal phone rang and he crossed to answer it. 'You're wanted in the library,' he told her, his face still set and angry.

It could only be James. Pandora's feet flew as she went by the back way, avoiding the guests. She pushed open the door of the library, her face lighting up with expectation, but there was only Cynthia Marsden waiting for her, a triumphant sneer on her face.

'Come in and shut the door,' she commanded peremptorily.

Slowly Pandora obeyed, eyeing the older girl suspiciously.

'Sir James has asked me to speak to you – no, perhaps it would be more honest to say that I insisted on telling you myself.' She waited, but when Pandora didn't speak, went on, 'To tell you that any understanding you think you had with

Sir James no longer stands. Let me explain,' she added when she saw the look of disbelief in Pandora's eyes. 'Sir James and I are very old – friends. He has asked me to marry him several times, but I have always refused because I value my independence and had no wish to be tied down by marriage. Sir James, however, became impatient and he decided to try to make me change my mind by making me jealous. Rather old-fashioned tactics, I must admit, but still effective. And he used you to do so.'

Pandora stared at her in horror. 'I don't believe you,' she burst out.

'No?' Cynthia smiled sneeringly. 'But you hardly thought he could be serious about a servant, surely? But his ruse did work; I did feel jealous, and I'll admit that tonight I really thought that he might be contemplating amusing himself by having an affair with you. Afterwards he assured me, of course, that he had only done it to provoke me, but one can never be completely sure where men are concerned, can one?'

'Afterwards?' Pandora asked in little more than a whisper.

'After I agreed to be his wife.'

Her brain almost paralysed with shock, Pandora said protestingly, 'But – but you can't be! He told me. He said he …'

'That he loved you? You surely didn't believe him?' The other girl crossed to the desk and took a cigarette from a silver box, lighting it with the desk lighter. She blew away the smoke and looked disdainfully at Pandora. 'You're really very naïve, aren't you? Exactly right for James' purpose. Surely you realised that he has a great deal of experience where women are concerned? In someone like you he can produce any reaction he wants. And telling you he loves you was guaranteed to lift you into this state of dewy-eyed idolatry so that I was bound to notice. Although I doubt if he could have borne to have you drooling over him and clinging to his hand like a lovesick puppy for very long.' She laughed mirthlessly. 'I shall have to remind him of what I've saved him from. But in the meantime,' she opened the top drawer in the desk and took out an envelope, 'he asked me to give you this. It's your wages, together with a bonus for the – er – services you unwittingly rendered. But now that you've served your purpose I want you out of the house at once. You can leave first thing tomorrow morning, and please don't try to see Sir James again, because you'll just be wasting your time.'

Pandora stared first at Cynthia and then at the envelope she held out to her. With a little sob she knocked it violently to the floor, then turned and ran out of the room.

Uncle Charlie was still in the kitchen and could only stare at her as she caught his arm and dragged him towards the door. 'She says she's going to marry him! You've got to go and find out for me. He'll tell you – he'll have to tell you. Oh, God, it can't be true, it can't! Please, Uncle Charlie, go and ask him. Make him tell you the truth!'

'Pandora, what is it? *Tell me!*'

Somehow she managed to speak coherently long enough to tell him of her interview with Cynthia Marsden. He listened with a growing frown.

'You'll go and ask him, won't you?' she demanded. 'You

don't have to say we're related. You can say it's your right to know if he's dismissed one of the staff. Oh, please, please go and ask him for me!'

'All right. Wait here.' He left with a grim look on his face while Pandora waited in an agony of torment. Within a quarter of an hour he was back.

Heavily, his face averted, he said, 'It's quite true. He's going to make the announcement shortly. And you're to leave tomorrow. He doesn't want to see you again.'

The powerful headlight cut through the swathes of mist that hung over the narrow road between the high stone walls. The night was cold, and the wind made her shiver even though Pandora was wearing her leather jacket and trousers. But perhaps it wasn't the wind, perhaps it was just the shock of having her love thrown back in her face in such a ruthless way. She had insisted on leaving immediately and her uncle had made no move to stop her, even helping her to carry her things to her motorbike and pressing some money on her for the journey, unable to hide the pity and worry in his eyes. Pandora smiled mirthlessly; did they all think that money could buy her off? But that wasn't fair; her uncle had only wanted to make sure that she would be all right until she found somewhere else to stay.

She had no real idea where she was going, had just got on the bike and turned it towards London, which had been an idiotic thing to do because she had been driving for nearly half an hour now and was low on petrol, and there weren't many petrol stations open in the early hours of the morning.

All the garages that she passed were closed and part of her mind was beginning to get worried, but mostly she didn't much care; what was one more problem on top of the blows she had already received that night? But when she turned on to the main London road she had only travelled a mile or so when she saw the lights of an all-night garage and pulled into the forecourt. Beside it was a transport café with several large container lorries parked outside, and she decided to go in to get a hot drink to stop herself shivering. And it would be somewhere to sit to pass some of the night away, the endless hours until daylight came and she could start looking for a job and somewhere to live.

Loud punk rock music from the jukebox hit her ears as she pushed open the door. The room was brightly lit and clean enough, with tubular steel tables and chairs, and as this was the only place open for a considerable distance, it was fairly crowded with lorry drivers. There was also a group of leather-clad motorcyclists sitting together at a long table, about eight of them, most of them with long greasy hair and earrings. Pandora hesitated when she saw them, but a quick glance showed her that there were one or two other women in the café, so she stepped inside and went to the counter for a coffee.

She carried her drink to a table as far away from the Hell's Angels as possible, over near the jukebox, and kept her helmet on, hoping they wouldn't notice she was a girl, but they seemed entirely concerned in something they were discussing and hardly gave her a glance. Pandora put her hands round the mug of coffee, trying to warm herself, but after that first, appalling shock and her instinctive reaction to get as far from Abbot's Arbory as possible, a kind of numbness had closed over her and she didn't feel any pain. She was just cold, so cold.

After about twenty minutes or so the music stopped and a couple of the Hell's Angels came over to select some more records. Pandora sat with her back to them, lost in her own unhappiness, oblivious to their conversation, but then the words 'a mile and a half after Arbory Magna' penetrated into her brain and she pricked up her ears.

'I still don't see why we can't go now,' one of the youths was saying. 'If they're having a party or ball, or whatever they call it, they won't notice us going down to the stables.'

'Jess says we've got to wait a bit longer, until they're all either drunk or asleep. Then there won't be anybody to stop us letting them out.' He chuckled coarsely. 'Then we'll chase his bloody horses till they all break their legs, and anybody who gets in the way, too! And serve that toffee-nosed git right for setting the law on to us last time!'

Pandora stared down at her now tepid mug of coffee in dismay. Obviously this was the same gang who had taken their bikes into Abbot's Arbory before and had been arrested for doing so. Pandora didn't know what sort of punishment they had been given, but it was evident that they intended to get their own back by striking at James through his horses. She thought of Greymist so near to giving birth to her first foal and her blood ran cold. She couldn't possibly let it happen. But what was the best way to prevent it? Her first thought was to phone the police, but was soon dismissed;

she had only hearsay evidence, no actual crime had been committed, and they could probably do no more than warn the gang off, which wouldn't prevent them returning as soon as the police had turned their backs. No, the best thing she could do was to phone the stables at Abbot's Arbory and warn them.

There was a public callbox in the entrance to the café, but the telephone directories were missing and she couldn't remember the number for Mr Langley's house. She would have to phone Directory Enquiries to give her the number, but as she waited for the operator to answer the gang of youths got up and filed past her on their way out, and she hastily put the receiver down in a panic. They must have decided not to wait any longer. Pandora realised that they would probably cover the ground to Abbot's Arbory much faster than she had, would probably take only twenty minutes at the most to get there. Frantically now she dialled the number for the house rather than wait for the operator again and then phone Mr Langley and wait for him to wake up and answer. She glanced at her watch. Three o'clock. The ball was due to end at two, but there must surely be someone up and around still.

Impatiently she waited as she heard the phone ring over and over again. Come on, somebody answer, she pleaded silently. Please, please answer! But after another few precious minutes she threw the receiver down in an agony of exasperation. *Now* what was she going to do? Then she remembered Jon Thursby and dialled his number with shaking hands, giving a gasp of relief when he answered almost at once.

'Jon, it's Pandora. Look, something's happened and there isn't much time. You must go back to Abbot's Arbory right away and warn them that a gang of Hell's Angels are on their way. They intend to let out the horses and panic them. No, I'm not at the house. It doesn't *matter* where I am or how I know. *Please,* Jon, just get over there as fast as you can. They're already on their way!' Then thankfully she slammed down the receiver as he agreed to go at once.

Pandora ran out to her bike and started it up, intending to follow the gang as fast as she could, but then remembered that she still needed petrol. Oh, hell! *Why* couldn't she have got it first? The garage attendant was inclined to be talkative and got offended when she impatiently snapped at him to hurry up, and deliberately went slower than ever. Tossing the money at him the moment he had filled her tank, Pandora tore away while the man shouted after her that she'd forgotten her change.

The mist was thicker now, but Pandora drove through it as fast as she dared, covering the road she had travelled such a short time ago but with very different emotions.

When she reached the house and let herself in through the tradesmen's gate all seemed quiet and peaceful and she almost began to breathe a sigh of relief as she coasted silently down the driveway, but then from the stables came a loud volley of sound, almost like continuous gunfire, then the high whinneys of frightened horses. Sick with fear, Pandora gunned the bike into life and tore furiously down the rest of the drive.

As she passed the corner of the house there were more

bangs, and flashes of coloured lights lit the sky inside the stableyard. With mounting fury she realised that the gang were using fireworks to further frighten the animals.

A couple of young colts suddenly galloped out of the entrance, almost cannoning into her, their nostrils flailed, their eyes rolling in terror, as they tried to escape from the fire-crackers tied to their tails. Loud whoops of laughter followed them and Pandora hastily drove her bike behind a bush as two youths ran out after the horses. They didn't see her and went back again. For a moment Pandora thought of trying to go after the colts, but Greymist was still inside and she was in an agony of fear for her. Leaving the bike where it was, she slid as unobtrusively as possible into the yard, hoping that if the gang did see her they would mistake her for one of themselves. They were still at the near end of the stables, opening the upper doors and sometimes throwing fireworks into the stalls, although one youth had tied a colt to his bike and was roaring round and round the yard in decreasing circles with the terrified animal running behind, trying to keep its footing. As she watched the colt fell and was dragged along for several yards, screaming and kicking, then it hit one of its legs against the wall and the screaming stopped as the poor creature lay still.

Pandora had started to run forward into the open, her heart filled with a rage so violent that she would have got hold of the youth and attacked him. Never in her life had she wanted to hurt anyone, but she could have killed – *wanted* to kill him. But from behind the red mists of fury the fear for Greymist held her back, and she turned and ran back into the shadows and down to the other end of the stables where the mare was stalled.

The already frightened horse plunged away from her as she opened the doors, but Pandora put up her visor to quieten the animal and held out her hand. The mare came immediately and Pandora led her out, holding her mane. There was no way out of the stableyard other than by the entrance that was blocked by the gang. They had another horse out now, James' black stallion, and were trying to tie a firework to its tail, but the horse reared and bucked, sending one youth flying with a kick from its hindlegs, then it broke free and headed for the entrance.

Good for you, Pandora thought exultantly, and took advantage of them chasing it to vault up on to Greymist's back. 'Come on now, my lovely,' she whispered as she bent low over the mare's neck. 'Don't be afraid. Just one short gallop and you'll be safe.'

Then she pressed her heels gently into the mare's flanks and the quivering animal shot forward as Pandora clung to her mane.

The youths began to shout at her, but they were howls of encouragement as they thought that she was one of the gang and then they jumped hastily out of the way as she rode straight at them, uncaring whether she hit them or not. Another firework went off and Greymist swerved wildly, but Pandora managed to hold on and to keep the mare's head towards the entrance arch. And then they were through and running from the hell the youths had made into the blessed darkness. As soon as they were safely out, Pandora slid off her back and ran alongside the horse down towards the lake. There were lights in the house now and she saw the headlights of a car coming fast down the drive, but she didn't stop until she reached the summerhouse and persuaded the mare inside.

'There now, my beauty, you'll be safe here until I can get someone to look after you. No, I haven't got any sugar-lumps. I'm sorry.' This last said almost on a sob as the mare nuzzled her pockets. 'It's not the night for sugar-lumps.'

Pandora pulled the heavy doors to and ran back as hard as she could towards the stables, aware of shouts as people ran from the house. But she was nearer and had to try and stop the gang before they hurt any more of the horses. Sobbing for breath, her chest heaving, she came to the entrance and looked in again. Her heart froze as she saw that one of the boxes was on fire, but even that shock was cancelled out as she heard a bellow of anger and saw some of the gang fighting a man who was trying to keep them out of the stalls, and recognised Mr Langley, his hair dishevelled, a pair of trousers thrown on over his pyjamas.

Without stopping to think, Pandora ran back to where she had hidden her bike and started it up, pulling down her visor: if the gang had mistaken her for one of themselves once, they might do so again. Accelerating into the centre of the yard, she sounded her horn and then braked sharply. In as gruff a voice as she could manage, she shouted, 'Rozzers! They've called the law. Get out, fast!'

It worked like magic; they let Mr Langley, who was by now on his knees, go, and ran to their bikes, afraid of being trapped in the yard. Pandora drove out first and they immediately followed her. She led them round the back of the house, away from the people who were rushing to the stables, past the garage block and up the back way towards the tradesmen's entrance, then she turned and headed across the park, an idea suddenly coming into her mind. Like a lot of sheep they followed her, close bunched together. Pandora accelerated, knowing exactly what she was going to do. There was a group of trees ahead of her and she suddenly switched off her lights as she neared them and swerved violently to one side. Turning off her engine, she coasted among the tree trunks. The Hell's Angels, not realising what had happened, roared by, the sound of their engines thundering through the night. A minute later there was a crash of metal and screams of terror as the ground disappeared beneath them and they dropped sickeningly down the drop of the ha-ha. They were packed so closely that there was no time for those at the rear to stop and they fell, bikes and men on top of one another. It wasn't a very deep drop and probably hadn't done them much harm, but it would at least delay them and possibly put some of their bikes out of action and make it easier for the police to catch them. And serve them damn well right! Pandora thought viciously, remembering the colt they'd dragged round the yard.

Turning the bike, she headed back fast towards the stables, terrified that the fire might have spread and Mr Langley and the rest of the horses be trapped inside. But as she neared it there was no glow of flames in the sky, and she prayed that someone had got there and put the fire out. From behind the stables a car appeared, roaring towards her, its headlights blazing. Realising that her lights were still off, Pandora hastily turned them on, but the car kept on coming, its headlights dazzling her. She put up a hand to shield her eyes and pulled as far over to the left as she could, but the car seemed to deliberately turn in the same direction and the next second Pandora's own scream of terror rent the night as she swerved again, hit something, and went hurtling over the handlebars.

She seemed to be flying through the air for a long time, but then she landed on her side on something fairly soft and rolled over and over until she banged her head and came to a stop with a cry of pain. She hurt, everything hurt, and there were mists of pain in front of her eyes. Sluggishly she tried to get up, but fell back again, biting her lip to stop the cry of agony that came to her lips.

Then she heard footsteps and the sound of someone scrambling towards her. A voice, furious with rage, said, 'You young lout! Where are the others? Where are they?' And she opened her eyes to see James towering over her, his face murderous.

He grabbed hold of her shoulders and hauled her to her feet, regardless of her gasp of pain.

'You'll tell me, do you hear?' he thundered. 'Where and who they are. Even if I have to break every bone in your body to find out!'

He was shaking her so hard that she couldn't have answered even if she'd been able to. His hand went to her neck and he almost tore the helmet off her head, throwing it violently to one side.

She heard him give a choking gasp and say her name, but then her legs gave way and she fell against him, trying to fight off black waves of giddiness.

'Pandora!' he gasped again. 'Oh, dear God, what have I done?'

He picked her up and seemed to be carrying her up some sort of bank, and then she felt herself being set down and he let go of her.

'James!' She opened her eyes in a panic, reaching out for him. 'Don't leave me. Please don't leave me.'

'It's all right, darling, I'm here.'

He was at her other side and she realised that he had put her in his car and gone round to the driver's seat. Fiercely she battled against another wave of faintness, clinging tightly to his hand. 'Greymist,' she gasped out. 'We have to get her.'

'We will, my darling, but first I have to get you to a doctor.'

'No, I'm all right. I just banged my head, that's all. Please, James!' She pulled anxiously at his lapel. 'We must go to Greymist. And those men – you must call the police and...'

James' hand came up to cover hers. 'They've already been sent for.' He looked at her anxiously, his arm going round her. 'Pandora, are you really all right? If only I'd known it was you – God, I'll never forgive myself for hurting you!'

Somehow she managed to smile at him, although her head felt as if Big Ben was being rung inside it. 'It's all right, I understand. I know you thought I was one of them. I just have a headache.'

'You're sure?'

'Yes. James, Greymist may be having her foal. She was so frightened. We must hurry. And Mr Langley, I know he was hurt.'

'No, he's all right,' he assured her as he started the car and began to turn it. 'He said one of the infernal louts came and shouted that the police were coming and they ran away before they'd done more than knocked him about a bit, thank goodness.' He frowned. 'Although the police haven't got here yet, so how ...' He broke off and shot her a quick glance. 'Good God, Pandora, was that you?'

'Yes.' She was sitting in the seat, her nails digging into the upholstery, biting her lip to stop herself from moaning as the car jolted over a dip in the driveway. Nausea rose in her throat, but there was no time to stop the car and be sick, she had to get to Greymist, so somehow she fought it down.

It was only a short distance to the stables, but it seemed to take forever before they pulled up near the entrance. Thankfully Pandora pushed open the door and got out, taking great gulps of the night air.

'Wait here,' James ordered. He turned to go into the stables, but just then Jon Thursby came out with a grim, bitter look on his face.

'I'm sorry, there was no hope of saving the colt. His leg was broken. I've had to put him down.'

'And the other horses?' James asked, his face white.

'There are two still in their stalls that weren't harmed at all. I think Mr Langley managed to stop the gang getting at them, and we've managed to catch three more, but the rest are scattered and probably frightened out of their wits. My

God, if I could get my hands on those thugs I'd ...'

'What about Greymist?' James demanded sharply, cutting through Jon's anger.

He shook his head. 'There's no sign of her.'

'Then we'd better start searching the ...'

'I know where she is. I took her to the summerhouse,' Pandora cut in impatiently.

James turned to her incredulously. 'You managed to get her out?' His eyes grew warm, and he reached out to touch her face. 'Oh, Pandora!' Then, rather unsteadily, 'Let's go and find her, shall we?'

The brilliant red rays of a summer dawn were lighting the sky when at last Pandora walked rather stiffly out of the summerhouse and down the steps towards the lake, pausing at its edge to listen to the bird song that filled the air and to look at the soft, hazy reflection of the house in the still waters. She felt cramped from sitting for so long with Greymist's head in her lap, continuously talking softly to the still trembling and frightened mare and encouraging it as Jon Thursby had acted as midwife. It had taken a long time for the foal to be born; James had been there with them at first, but the police officers had wanted him for something and he had only returned just before the foal, a colt, was born. Unsteadily the poor little thing had stood up on its impossibly thin, spindly legs, and there had been a wonderful moment of happiness and relief when Jon had pronounced both the colt and Greymist perfectly healthy. The sudden release from tension and worry had made Pandora realise just how tired she was.

Her head still ached, but it was nowhere near as painful as it had been when she first came off the bike, and her body wasn't too bad, just bruised and sore in places. But when Greymist had been got on to her feet and had turned her attention to her foal, Pandora had felt suddenly cold and lonely and had quietly slipped outside, leaving the two men talking together.

Behind her she heard the door of the summerhouse open and someone come out. Footsteps came towards her, but she didn't turn round, her body growing tense as James came to stand beside her. He was wearing an overcoat thrown over his dinner jacket and there was a black smudge on his cheek where he had helped to put out the fire in the stables.

He didn't speak at first, and to fill the silence Pandora said as lightly as she could, 'Have you decided on a name for the foal?'

'Not yet. Why don't you choose one for me?'

She looked up at the sky, shot through with the bright crimson rays of the morning, a morning so beautiful that it took your breath away and made you feel incredibly humble and grateful for being alive. Slowly she said, 'Why don't you call him Dawnlight?'

'Dawnlight out of Greymist. Yes, I like it.' She felt him turn to face her. 'Why don't we go up to the house and have a glass of champagne to celebrate his safe arrival?'

She turned away and began to walk towards the stables. 'Thanks, but I have to see how badly my bike's damaged.'

James caught her arm, stopping her. 'Why – so that you can run away from me again?' he demanded, his voice suddenly harsh.

Pandora didn't answer, her face averted.

'Look at me,' James ordered, impatiently pulling her round to face him. 'Why did you run away?'

Slowly Pandora lifted her head. He was staring down at her searchingly, his eyes intent, his brows drawn together in a frown, partly of anger, but there was anxiety behind it too. She gazed at him in growing enlightenment. Wonderingly she said, 'You're – you're *not* going to marry Cynthia Marsden, are you?'

He looked at her in amazement. 'Marry Cynthia? Of course I'm not. Who on earth put that idea in your head?'

Rather slowly Pandora replied, 'She did – and someone else.'

'*No*, I am *not* going to marry her,' James said forcefully. 'I'm not in love with her and never have been. There's only one woman I've ever wanted to be my wife.'

Putting aside that last statement, Pandora said, 'But she is your mistress, isn't she?'

A rather bleak look came into his face. 'She was, you mean. It was a relationship we drifted into; she made it plain that she was available and I accepted. But I made it clear right from the start that I had no intention of marrying her, it was purely an affair of mutual convenience.'

'Purely?' Pandora demanded on a derisive note.

'All right, impurely, if you like.' James took hold of her shoulders. 'No, don't turn away from me,' he ordered angrily. 'I'm thirty-five years old, Pandora. Did you really expect that I'd have lived like a monk while I waited for the right girl to come along?' Then, at the look on her face, he let her go and said abruptly, 'The affair between Cynthia and me lasted only a short while and ended over a year ago.'

Pandora's head came up quickly at that. 'A year ago? And yet her clothes are still kept in one of the bedrooms here.'

An exasperated look came into his grey eyes. 'Cynthia's parents often go away and she's afraid to stay in-the house alone since they had a burglary recently, so they asked me if I'd let her stay here on the nights they were away. Her people are old family friends and in the circumstances I was unable to refuse, but I always made sure that the housekeeper was around to act as chaperone. And last month – at the dinner party when you cooked for us – I made sure that my aunt came along so that Cynthia wouldn't get any ideas about staying the night. That – and because I wanted my aunt to meet you.'

Pandora's eyes widened. 'Why should you want your aunt to meet me?'

He smiled. 'What man doesn't want to show off the girl he loves to his relatives?'

She flushed and would have lowered her head, but James put his hand under her chin, forcing her to look at him. 'Darling, how could you have believed Cynthia when I'd already told you that I loved you?'

'It wasn't only Cynthia. And besides ...' she hesitated and then added with difficulty, 'that evening in your bedroom – do you remember?'

His eyes grew warm. 'How could I ever forget?'

'Well, the phone rang.'

'Mm.' His arm went round her waist and he drew her

closer. 'Just in time to stop me from losing control of myself completely.' Pandora put her hands against his chest, holding herself away from him, and his eyes grew serious again. 'Go on.'

The pain raw in her voice, Pandora said, 'You answered the phone and said you had to go out. Later that night I met your chauffeur. He – he said he'd taken you to Cynthia's house and that – and that you were staying the night.'

James swore, and she could feel his hands tighten on her waist as he said earnestly, 'It wasn't Cynthia who phoned; it was her father. We're both on the board of the local hospital and he asked me to go round there and discuss something before the next meeting. I sent the car back because I wanted to walk home – I wanted some time to be alone, to think about you and about the future. And,' he hesitated a moment and added slowly, 'and most of all to wonder if I'd made you aware enough of your own feelings to follow your heart and not your head, and accept my proposal when I asked you to marry me the next day.' His voice changed. 'Only you didn't come the next morning as you'd promised. Instead you went to Oxford and didn't come back until the early hours, while I went through hell wondering if I'd frightened you away.' Gently his hand came up to cup her chin. 'And all the time it was because you thought I'd been with Cynthia.' His eyes warmed. 'Well, at least it proves that I was right. You did love me then.'

Pandora smiled rather tremblingly. 'I only realised it that evening. And then – afterwards – I thought that you were just playing with me, amusing yourself by trying to seduce me. I couldn't understand why else you kept – kept kissing me and ...' Her voice trailed away and she blushed.

James smiled. 'I think the phrase you want is "making love to you".' Adding rather ruefully, 'Darling, what other choice did I have? After your outburst that day in Oxford you'd made it perfectly plain just what you thought of my position and way of life. If I'd tried to get closer to you by normal means – by asking you out and introducing you to my circle of friends – you'd have refused point blank. Also the fact that you'd put on that act to start with showed that you were on the defensive against me, and more than ready to rebuff me if I made the slightest approach towards you. So I reasoned that the only chance I had was to get under your guard and try to awaken your emotions enough to unsettle you thoroughly so that you didn't know your own mind any more.' He bent and gently began to explore her eyelids with his lips. 'I had an idea, you see, that you'd never been awakened before. You were like a rosebud waiting for the kiss of the sun before you opened your petals.'

He lifted his head to look at her and Pandora slowly opened her eyes. His voice changed, grew grim again. 'It came as quite a shock when you told me that you thought nothing of sleeping around.'

Pandora blushed. 'I don't – I mean it wasn't – I haven't ...' She came to a floundering stop, her cheeks crimson, and looked up quickly as James laughed.

'Do you think I didn't realise that when I'd had time to cool off and think about it? Oh, Pandora,' his arms went round her and he drew her close, moulding her body against his, 'do you know how long I've waited for a girl like you to come along? A girl with innocence in her eyes and who can find joy in simple things? Who can dance barefoot in the grass and fill her arms with flowers? Oh, darling!' he bent to kiss her gently. 'I've read of men who fell in love at first sight, but I never thought it would happen to me, and then I looked out of my window one morning and saw you.' He chuckled softly. 'At first I couldn't believe that you were real. I thought I'd fallen in love with a ghost.'

Pandora put up a tentative finger to trace the outline of his lips. 'But I'm very real.'

His arms tightened convulsively. 'I know *that*. Oh, God, Pandora, if you only knew how much I wanted you!' His mouth found hers, kissing her with a fierce hunger that was scarcely controlled and would not long be denied, and for the first time Pandora was able to respond with complete abandon, letting her emotions guide her and moving sensuously against him, longing to be a part of him.

Uncle Charlie, she thought bemusedly, when at last she could think more coherently. So that story of his about James not wanting to see her again had been as fictional as Cynthia Marsden's; her uncle had been so convinced that James had no serious intentions towards her, that he would only hurt her, that like Cynthia, he was prepared to stop at nothing to prevent his niece getting badly hurt. In any other circumstances Pandora would have been furiously angry – but now she could only try to see Uncle Charlie's point of view, and thank heaven he had done no lasting damage by his well-intentioned lie!

How long they stood in each other's arms, Pandora didn't know, but when she next became aware of her surroundings the sun had turned to gold and was quite high in the sky. The mist had disappeared, and summer lay across the house and park like a lover's embrace, warm and caressing. Pandora looked at it and caught her breath in wonder, still unable to believe that her future lay here. She turned a radiant, mischievous face up to the man she loved.

'You do realise that I'm only marrying you because I've fallen in love with Abbot's Arbory?'

'Of course,' James agreed gravely, as he stooped to pick her up in his arms and carry her back to the house, 'that's understood. And you know that I'm only marrying you because I can't stand Richardson's everlasting omelettes any longer, don't you?'

Pandora put her arms round his neck and gurgled with laughter. 'Oh, that reminds me,' she said happily, 'there's something I have to tell you. It's about my Uncle Charlie …'